Ravens' Brood

Edward Frederic Benson was born in 1867, at Wellington College, where his father, later Archbishop of Canterbury, was Headmaster. Brother of the equally prolific Arthur Christopher and Robert Hugh Benson, Fred, as he was always known to family and friends, was author of more than one hundred books – autobiography, biography, social satires (notably the famous Mapp and Lucia novels), thrillers, tales of the macabre and the supernatural and short stories. E F Benson died in 1940 and his rediscovery commenced in the 1960s. Millivres Books has also reissued *David of King's* and *The Inheritor*.

Geoffrey Palmer and Noel Lloyd are the authors of *E F Benson: As He Was* and, as Hermitage Books, publishers of an elegant series of limited edition booklets by E F Benson.

RAVENS' BROOD

E F BENSON

New Foreword by
Geoffrey Palmer and
Noel Lloyd

Millivres Books
Brighton

Published 1993 by Millivres Books
33 Bristol Gardens, Brighton BN2 5JR, East Sussex, England

Ravens' Brood first published by Arthur Barker, 1934
Copyright this edition, © Millivres Books, 1993
Copyright Foreword, © Geoffrey Palmer and Noel Lloyd, 1993

ISBN 1 873741 09 X

Typeset by Hailsham Typesetting Services, Hailsham,
East Sussex BN27 1AD
Printed and bound in Great Britain

Distributed in the British Isles and in Western Europe by
Turnaround Distribution Co-op Ltd, 27 Horsell Road,
London N5 1XL
Distributed in the United States of America by InBook,
140 Commerce Street, East Haven, Connecticut 06512, USA

Foreword

In the mid-1920s E F Benson, that prolific writer of best-sellers, took stock of his position and was not impressed by what he found. He had written dozens of sentimental novels, filled with chaste young girls and equally chaste young men, witless mothers who chattered like drunken parrots, society hostesses, scheming villainesses and effeminate middle-aged gentlemen skilled in embroidery. The plots were thin, melodramatic and predictable, with sacrifice heavily to the fore and death inevitable. *Dodo* had been the first, in 1893, and the rest had followed from one to even four a year, written with facility and without feeling. To be sure, there had been instances when his syrupy pen had been dipped into something more stringent, but usually his characters bustled about and talked with inconsequential sparkle. They lacked blood and guts, and they were plastered over with fake sentiment.

For his large and faithful following of readers, chiefly women, Benson could have gone on writing formula novels till the end of time and no one would have complained. They had made him a rich man and a welcome guest at society dinner tables. When he was not writing he was ski-ing, skating, playing tennis, golf, squash, shooting and fishing. His was an ideal existence – until his shocked realisation that all was not well. What, he thought, had happened to the young man who had dreamed of being a great writer, a stylist, a passionate advocate of fine feelings? What had happened to the emotions that had really touched his heart, and to the imagination that laziness and facility had stultified?

Of the fifty or so books he had written only a few still meant something to him because they had artistic integrity. Of the rest he could barely remember their titles. A few showed signs of what he could have accomplished if he had tried harder. He was proud of *David Blaize* (1916) and *David of King's* (1924); and *Mrs Ames* (1912), *The Oakleyites* (1915) and *An Autumn Sowing* (1917) dug beneath the shallow topsoil of the heart's troubles and uncovered genuine emotions. He now realised he must stop drifting or join the ranks of the great forgotten after his death.

His self-examiantion was honest and wholesome. He knew that he must observe more critically and feel more intensely, and that that would not be easy if he were to carry on writing novels. The solution would be a change of direction towards biography and memoirs, books which would demand intensive research, enhanced powers of observation and a retentive memory. He hoped that such serious application to his craft would revitalise his talent.

The stories of heroines struck down by tuberculosis and gallant soldiers killed in battle did not entirely disappear after Benson's momentous decision, but they became less frequent. The Mapp and Lucia novels of waspish comedy brought him to the notice of a new and enraptured public. *Paying Guests* (1924) and *Secret Lives* (1932) were models of their kind, the one a successful mixture of comedy and pathos in which he looked tolerantly at Lesbianism, the other sheer farce. *Travail of Gold* (1933) was the last throwback to his old style, in which stock figures re-appeared as preposterous and snobbish as ever. From 1927 onwards biographies and memoirs occupied the bulk of his time. *Drake*, *Alcibiades* and *Magellan* sold less well than his former works but gave him greater satisfaction; and *Charlotte Brontë* was particularly successful. *As We Were* (1930) and *As We Are* (1932), the former was a recapitulation of family history and a detailed treatment of the second half of the Victorian era to the end of the Edwardian; the latter a piece of fiction accompanied by a commentary on the chasm that had widened between the war generation and its successors. His last two books of ghost stories appeared in this period and enabled him to share the pedestal occupied by the great masters of the genre. From 1933 the lives of royalty obsessed him when he was not involved with Mapp and Lucia: *King Edward VII, Queen Victoria, The Kaiser and English Relations*, and *The Daughters of Queen Victoria*: all worthy of more hagiographies than investigative works.

Benson's life work was crowned by *Final Edition*, an autobiography published posthumously in 1940. It proved to be a testament to a charming, intelligent and civilised, yet in some ways unfulfilled, man who had watched life from the sidelines. It is rich in humour, anecdote and feeling, and a fitting monument to a writing career that had spanned nearly fifty years.

The bizarre *Ravens' Brood* was published by Arthur Barker in 1934, and was the last of Benson's serious novels. It was in such great contrast to the earlier novels that one must ask – why did he write it? *Ravens' Brood* stands out like a cromlech in a cornfield. None of his regular publishers, Hodder and Stoughton, Longmans, or Hutchinson, would touch it. It was left to Arthur Barker, a new arrival in publishing, to include it in their fledgling list; and it was his only book for them. Black magic, sexuality, blasphemy, violence and ecstasy surround and penetrate the plot and characters: none of them is among the usual ingredients of Benson's society novels or the tales of Tilling. Was Benson at last throwing off his mask and revealing his intense interest in the crude and earthy, the salacious and passionate, or was it an attempt to show the supernatural in a new light – one that had to shine through peasant characters as before it had shone through those of a higher class? Or was it the more mundane wish to keep up with the rising tide of stark realism that the library borrowers were demanding? Echoes of Mary Webb it might have, and the frankness of D H Lawrence; and some of the characters could have come from *Cold Comfort Farm*, but nevertheless it was written with genuine relish and sincerity. *Ravens' Brood* is a Benson 'sport' that throws a new light on a hitherto lightweight author.

As an early reviewer wrote: 'It is almost impossible to recognise the hand of the creator of *Dodo* in *Ravens' Brood*, though it has the same polished style, the same authenticity of character drawing, and something of the same sense of horror which he created in *The Luck of the Vails*.' But in addition to these qualities there are many more fingerprints: *leitmotifs*, even (a not inappropriate term to use of a besotted Wagnerite), which often reappear from earlier novels. One such fingerprint is a heightened and typically Bensonian homoerotic component which can first be seen in *David Blaize*: when Maddox surprised a naked David straight from his bath and was tempted to – what, we shall never know, but he managed to refrain from corrupting such white innocence. David, on his part, felt that he had escaped from some distant nightmare . . .

David of King's also had its moments of deep affection between young men, though not threatened by "filth'. "We've loved each other, thank God", said Maddox, putting his arm round David's neck. "I've been first in your life, and you in mine . . ."

In 1930 came *The Inheritor*, a compellingly weird pantheistic novel in which the beautiful Steven Gervase is adored by fellow undergraduate, Charles Merriman (the Child) and loved by Maurice Crofts, a young don. Steven and the Child go for a swim in the river late at night during which the Child heaves himself on Steven, who escapes by diving sideways and then vaults on to the Child as on to a horse's saddle and presses his knees close to his ribs, and down they go, locked together. "It was queer," Steven said later, "the night was full of spells . . ."

In *Ravens' Brood* the homoeroticism is altogether more explicit. The love that dares not speak its name almost succeeds in doing so when Dennis Pentreath, the clean handsome and happy hero and his friend, Willie Polhaven, the simple country boy, were fighting over an insulting remark that Willie had made about Dennis's mother. During the bloody battle, Dennis, who was winning, said to himself, "God, how I love that chap", and afterwards, as they lay on the sand, they were almost shy of each other, 'as if the fight had made lovers of them'. But Dennis was not for Willie and eventually turned to Nell for sexual love. Willie took comfort from the parson's sermon on the love between David and Jonathan, 'wonderful, passin' the love of women'. He never turned to women – "I reckon it's a kink in men, and not like to come out!"

Whatever problems arise from *Ravens' Brood* it is certainly a splendid read. It may sit awkwardly among Benson's other *oeuvres* but it is written with great verve and is almost neo-gothic in its intensity. Set in an isolated part of Cornwall, it tells the story of the lecherous and drunken John Pentreath, a man who, though rooted in a pagan tradition, has become a religious fanatic and an intolerant bully. His second wife Mollie, who he has virtually rejected, is from gipsy stock and well versed in their lore. She is obsessed with the desire to have a child and is preoccupied with devising ways of getting back into the bed from which her husband has banished her. John Pentreath lusts after his pneumatic widowed daughter-in-law, Nancy, but she is deeply involved with the artist, Harry Giles, who lives nearby and for whom she does nude modelling. Also in the household is Dennis, Nancy's son, a handsome, upstanding country boy who yearns for the servant girl Nell, Mollie's niece. John's hatred of Dennis is almost as obsessional as his fundamentalist religion, a feeling rooted in jealously of Dennis's virility and good looks. There are other, minor, characters to keep this simmering pot on the boil: mainly the devoted Willie Polhaven and Mr Willis, a silly mincing fop of a man who comes to lodge at the Pentreath Farm. He is a 'pretty, capering thing with a pink silk vest and pink silk pants, wrapping himself in a lovely blue dressing-gown', and the Pentreaths call him 'girlie'. He longs to ruffle Dennis's hair and paint him with his shirt wide open . . .

The story moves rapidly by way of witchcraft, fertility rituals, rampant sexuality, dramatic confrontations and an agonising death to a thrilling and inevitable climax. On the one hand the book is a celebration of true love winning against all the odds. On the other it is an eloquent denouncement of the barbarism that lies behind intolerant religiosity; while always in the background lurks the bleak malevolence of the secret rites of a pre-Christian religion.

Geoffrey Palmer
Noel Lloyd

There are two societies devoted to the life and work of E F Benson and anyone wishing for further information should write (enclosing an sae) to: The Secretary, The Tilling Society, Martello Bookshop, 26 High Street, Rye, East Sussex TN31 7JJ *and/or* The Secretary, The E F Benson Society, 88 Tollington Park, London N4 3RA.

INTRODUCTION

THE house and the adjacent buildings of the farmstead were not visible from the high-road that crossed the upland to St. Buryan and to Land's End, for a lane slanting rather steeply downwards led to them, and a copse of dwarfed and wind-combed trees intervened. The branches of these sloped almost horizontally away from the south-west, pressed there, like water-weeds in the current of a stream, by the flow of the prevalent wind. This lane was rough from want of repair, and channelled with the self-scooped drainage of winter storms; thick-built walls of shaly stone, in the interstices of which cushions of moss and polypody-ferns had established themselves, separated it from the fields that lay about it, and it ended in the spacious, straggling farmyard round which were set cowhouse and stablings and fowl-run.

The farm-house formed one side of this yard: two mullioned windows looked on to it, and between them, with a bundle of birch twigs to furnish a scraper for mud-laden boots, was the door into the kitchen, now the living-room of the family. Against the wall, below a broken-down shed, was piled a tumbled pyramid of mangel-wurzels nibbled and gnawed by sauntering livestock: cows took a bite at them as they passed to their milking, horses coming back from the plough crunched a mouthful, or a stray pig grunted and snouted among the roots, many of which were already sprouting again in the warmth of the spring weather. From the end of the farmhouse ran out the lichen-covered wall of the garden, in which was set a door covered with blistered and discoloured paint, and, on the side opposite, a gate sagging on its hinges led to the pasture; close beside this rose the supports and tarred roof of a haystack now nearly consumed. An untidy and ramshackle place, once solid and prosperous, but now mutely testifying to fallen fortunes.

Within, the house was a fine eighteenth-century homestead, two-storied and shingled with slabs of grey stone and pinnacled with heavy chimneys.   Out of the kitchen a second door communicated with the passage running the length of the building: a broad oak staircase led to the upper story, and from this passage opened two parlours, now never lived in.   Between these was the door, once the front door, into the garden: a big fanlight above it lit the passage and the stairs.

Outside, the square of flower garden lay sheltered and sequestered: the house screened it from the north, the rising upland from the west, a belt of trees from the east, and it lay open only to the softer airs from the south, where a plateau of pasture fields extended to the strip of down that fringed the low sea cliffs. This year the winter had been of singular mildness; no tweak of frost or flurry of snow had vexed the soft air, and now in this last week of February, doronicum and tulips, stock and wallflower were at the height of their blossoming, and a big square bed of daffodils danced and nodded in the light breeze.   Below the house-wall was a double row of polyanthuses: their stems, stiff and straight, were like the path of rockets that had shot up and burst into groups of many-coloured stars. Behind them, japonica and white jasmine threaded dilapidated trellises, and a great magnolia, thick of trunk, and with branches that climbed up to the eaves of the house, covered the greater part of the wall, framing the windows in its long varnished leaves. All this month it had been in flower, and the cream-coloured blossoms of thick leather-like petals dripped with heavy fragrance.

A short wing ran out from beyond the main oblong of the farmhouse and projected into the garden. Originally it had been a carriage-house with a couple of small rooms above it, but a few years ago, when money was not quite so scarce with him as it was to-day, John Pentreath, the present owner, had spent a hundred pounds in converting this wing into a separate apartment, turning the carriage-house into a big studio-like sitting-room. The two small rooms above had been knocked into one, a stairway had been constructed inside the house to give access to it, and now there were few weeks during the summer months when this lodging was not occupied by some tenant, artist or holiday-maker, who was in search of privacy and was content with plain and excellent fare, cooked and supplied for him from the kitchen of the farm. A door with panels of glass gave him access from his living-room into the garden and to the field path that led eastwards down over the brow of the hill to the village of St. Columb's below, and thus he could come and go without passing through the house. He had his own little fenced lawn and flower-beds unoverlooked from other windows, and from it he could see between the tree-trunks glimpses of the glittering bay and watch the sea-gulls circling in the sky or listen to the music of blackbirds in the bushes. Here, undisturbed, he could bask in the warm brooding quiet of the drowsy air, or, if his mood changed and he tired of these languors, he had but to leave the garden, cross the farmyard, and ascending the steep lane, find himself on the high empty uplands, which, treeless and austere, stretched away westwards to the Atlantic. Or if he was more gregariously inclined, he could take the path to St. Columb's, and ten minutes' walk would bring him to the grey-roofed village that lay huddled on the shore of the bay. A pier, solidly built against the battling of the great seas of winter gales, gave shelter to the fishing fleet, and he could sit there among the tawny nets hung out to dry, or bathe from the sandy beaches beyond. The narrow streets of the village, that were too steep for horse-traffic, were stepped for the convenience of foot passengers, and along them were set up the innumerable easels of the artists who all summer long flocked to the village and perennially and interminably reproduced in oil- or water-colour the picturesque corners, or recorded their impression of the bay in all aspects of storm and calm, or found models for their pictures among the sunburnt youth of the handsome fisherfolk. The Celtic blood had been crossed, it was supposed, with some antique Phœnician stock, that traded round these coasts before ever the Romans set foot in England, and the dark-haired black-eyed strain persisted still among the more northern type.

The natives regarded the yearly invasion of the English as an ingress of foreign folk: they put them up in their houses, they posed for their pictures, or took them out for the fishing when the pilchards had been sighted in the bay, and all night long the lights of the drifting boats moved with the tide, like a company of stars risen from the sea; but these Cornish were a race apart; their blood went to a different tune, and they knew secrets and hidden lore, of which they seldom spoke to strangers, however intimate. Should a farmer's cattle have been dying in some unaccountable fashion, there was not a native-born man who did not suspect that a witch had been at work, and perhaps a chance word would be dropped about it. But instantly it would be bitten off short, and the foreign-fellow, however much he might ask, would get no farther: he was not fit to know, being a foreigner, affairs that did not concern him. Again, the native population of the village would turn out in broadcloth and female finery to go to church or to chapel of a Sunday morning, and they might be instant in prayer, and loud in singing, and attentive to the long discourse of the minister, but it would be a mistake to suppose that their sense of religion, of the unseen and potent powers that guided or menaced the ways of their lives, was confined to the doctrines and dogmas that they recited there, or that their only prayers were addressed to the Persons of those doxologies. There were other powers besides these, not to be openly addressed, nor praised with loud mouth to the braying of a harmonium, nor talked of, even among themselves, except in whispers and mutterings and noddings. There was a copse, for instance, a mile away from the village, which no prudent man would enter after dark, preferring to skirt round it rather than risk the traverse of it by the direct path that led past a big slab of stone, altar-shaped, that stood in the heart of the wood. Old Sally Austell might have hobbled up there from the village, and it would never do to meet her there, when she was busy with her own concerns.

Out in the open, a couple of fields away from the garden of the Pentreath farmhouse and on land belonging to John Pentreath, was a strange circle of stones, monoliths of granite. Young Dennis Pentreath, his grandson, had ploughed the field, near the lower side of which they stood, only a week or two before, but of course he had not run his furrow through the circle, nor had approached within a couple of yards of it. Never had ploughshare trespassed on that precinct, but it lay virgin, and covered with the short down-grass, fragrant with thyme and bright with low-growing herbs, a green circle in the middle of the ruddy shining slices of fresh-turned soil. In all there were four and twenty stones, each set some few yards from its neighbour, at intervals as precise as those between the hours on a clock-dial. They were approximately uniform in height and of such stature that a man might conveniently lean his elbow on the top of any, as he stood musing about the origin of these roughly-hewn monoliths. At the eastern end of the circle, however, the interval between two of these stones was just double of that between all the rest, and these two stones were taller than the others: it was as if they might conceivably have formed a portal to the precinct within. Archæologists and antiquaries were mostly agreed that this was some Druidic or pre-Druidic temple: some held that the two tall stones at the east end were of phallic signification.

But if an English visitor to St. Columb's, however familiar to them, had asked any of the fisher-folk or the farm-folk of the neighbouring homesteads what local history was attached to it, he would certainly have been told only the childish Christian legend which was current about it. That circle of stones was once a company of lads and lasses, twenty-two of them, who had been light-minded enough to dance in the field there one Sunday morning, and those two tall pillars at the east had been the hapless fiddlers who had made music for them. There came by, as they were footing it merrily, the holy man, St. Columb himself, and they laughed at him and mocked him, when he rebuked them and bade them leave their Godless antics and follow him, as Christians should, to church on this morning of the Lord's Day. Since they would not hearken to him, he invoked the wrath of God on them for their wickedness, and behold, they were instantly turned into stone, where they stand now for a warning to all ungodly men. All that of course was nonsense: in no other spirit does a mother tell her inquisitive child that a neighbour's wife has found a little baby under the gooseberry bushes in the garden. It was a reply meant to stop further inquiries, and neither informant nor informed believed it for a moment. But the informant, it would have been plain, knew more than that, but did not choose to divulge it: he put you off with this foolish legend.

But if you had chanced to be at St. Columb's on some Midsummer Eve, then indeed you might have been sure that there was something behind the foolish legend, for on that night, unmindful of the doom that the saint called down on those who had frisked there, the circle that lay untrodden all the year round would be full of young couples, boys and girls, who had been lately married, dancing together, and there might be old couples, too, stiffly capering till their breath failed them. The rest of the folk, old and young, stood outside it watching, and half Penzance came up to see the dancing, and some to join in it, and all the farms for five miles round would be left that night in charge of sheep-dogs, while the families came in to St. Columb's. That night, too, in the field below there would be lit a great bonfire, and odd rites were practised there. As its flames died down and there was left only a bed of glowing ashes, a young couple, boy and girl, would run downhill towards it, hand in hand, and leap across it. That meant something surely: there would be whispered comments among the spectators, they pointed to the leapers, they laughed or they applauded. But it would be idle for the Englishman, the foreigner, to ask what it all meant, to inquire who leaped and why, and why some danced, and others equally young and agile refrained. There was something there, common knowledge to the natives, but not spoken of, some elemental creed passed on below the breath from generation to generation.

The wood where no God-fearing man would venture after dark, the circle within the twenty-four stones, inviolate all the year except on Midsummer Eve, when it was the dancing-floor of those who knew, these perhaps were the remnants of ancient sorceries, laughable and ridiculous to the educated, but firmly rooted in the instincts of the fisher-folk of St. Columb's and the farm-folk round sixty years ago. And it was sixty years ago, on one Sunday afternoon, that this narrative opens.

CHAPTER I

SUNDAY PRAYERS

JOHN PENTREATH came out of the porch that had once been the main entrance to the farmhouse, and now only led into the garden. It was a warm languorous Sunday afternoon, late in February, and a breeze spiced with the scent of wallflowers and of magnolia blossom came strong to his nostrils. There was something carnal and seductive in these spring odours, which penetrated through the austere atmosphere with which he habitually encompassed himself of a Sunday. As usual he was dressed in thick black broadcloth, for that was his habit on the Lord's Day; in his hand he held a well-thumbed Bible, and on his head was a silk hat dull with age. Round it ran a thick mourning band which had been sewn there for the funeral of his first wife, when the hat was newly purchased in Penzance for the occasion. A long tale of years had gone by since then, but this hat was for Sunday wear alone, and there was still a bit of nap left on it.

He stepped on to the weedy gravel path, and paced up and down it for a minute or two with firm, heavy steps. In height he was close on six feet, lean in flesh, but broad in build, and for all his three and sixty years there was scarcely a grey hair to be found in his black-thatched head. But the signs of age and the conduct of his life could be traced in the loose pouches that hung beneath his blue eyes, and in the sodden sallowness that underlay the sun-tan of his clean-shaven face. His

mouth was noticeably long, the upper lip thin and in-
sensitive, while the lower one sagged loose and sensual
in strange contradiction of the other.   A grim face,
hard and cruel and weak together.

There was a wooden bench, with the discoloured paint
blistered and peeling off it, in the angle where the
garden wall ran out from the house, and presently he
sat down there, opened his Bible at the Book of Revelation, and began reading to himself, forming the words
with his lips, as if dumbly speaking them:

" The same shall drink of the wine of the wrath of
God which is poured out without mixture into the
cup of his indignation. . . .   And the smoke of their
torment ascendeth up for ever and ever; and they
have no rest day nor night, who worship the beast
and his image, and whosoever receiveth the mark of his
name."

Yes, that was grand stuff, he thought.   Often and
often he read these chapters on Sunday afternoon, for
they never ceased to refresh him, and he rolled the
words round on his tongue like a greedy man relishing
a pleasant mouthful.   It was good to remember, as
often as Sunday came round, the inexorable Deity with
His vials of wrath, who promised to punish the light
and the careless who paid no heed to His ordinances,
unmindful of the hell-fire that surely awaited them,
in which they would burn conscious and unconsumed
through eternity.   He was the Master, and before Him
John Pentreath furiously abased himself on one day of
the week.   Every Sunday, whatever the weather, he
dressed himself in his hot black clothes, he attended
morning and evening service in the church at St.
Columb's (for the Pentreaths had always been church-
people, not chapel-people), and all afternoon, when

dinner was done and he had had a smoke and a snooze, until the church bells began again, he spent with his open Bible in front of him; and woe be to any who, in his presence, indulged in laughter or light conversation. Not a drop of liquor did he touch that day at his dinner, but Sunday terminated at supper-time, and then he was free to make up for his abstinence. Plentiful were those retarded potations, but even they were by way of being part of his service to the Lord, for when, after supper, the table was cleared, and the family gathered round it for evening prayers, his eloquence and power in extemporary oration was determined by the quantity of whisky he had drunk. His bawled devotions were chiefly concerned with the iniquities of those who formed his household, and his fulminations were most fiery when he had drunk most. Occasionally he must be helped up to bed, still loudly praying as he lurched and stumbled up the stairs, and his orisons resounded through the house till he snored off into a drunken slumber.

These hours of the afternoon, when on warm days like this he read his Bible in the garden, were the most irksome of all the week in spite of their spiritual uplift. On other days he would have had a couple of stiff drams at the midday dinner, and he went out to work on the farm till sunset and supper-time. But on Sunday there was no work doing, and he had to get through the hours uncheered except by the thought that his abstinence was his self-imposed penance, pleasing to the Most High and fully atoning for whatever had been his shortcomings in the previous week. His black and savage temper was made blacker yet by this sore business of saving his soul, and supper-time on Sunday was a long time coming.

2

As usually happened, his attention presently wandered
from the open book which he held, and though his eye
continued to follow the lines of the print, and his
mouth to form the words, his mind slid away from
it, and those pictures of years past and of present days,
which form the basis of a man's consciousness, began
to show themselves between the page and his eyes. . . .

The Pentreaths had come down in the world, and
for two generations now their land had been slipping
from them, sold slice by slice to thriftier and more
prosperous folk, till now there remained but fifty acres
of a property that a hundred years ago had been ten
times more extensive, and even this remnant was
sparsely stocked and badly cared for.   Lately this ill-
luck had been persistent: one year swine fever had
invaded the sties, there had been a cruel bad lambing-
season the next, a wet spring followed by a violent storm
in June had ruined the hay crop another year, but
whatever forms the ill-luck took, there was always the
bottle to mitigate it.   Then there had been the ill-luck
of his two marriages.   His first wife had been a comely
lass, God-fearing like himself, and of family as good as
his own, and while she was with him all had gone well;
never since had there been such harvests, and such
good fortune with the livestock.   But then in the third
year of their marriage she had died in child-bed, leaving
him while only twenty-five years of age with one son.

For fifteen years after that his mother had kept
house for him and looked after young Richard, and
not till her death did he take a second wife, satisfying
his needs with chance adventures with a woman or two
from the village.   But it was an ill hour for him when
Mollie Robson made a boiling in his blood: a lusty girl
she was, black-eyed and big, and indeed she had thrown

herself at him, making eyes at him, and waylaying him in the warm dusk till she had her way with him. He had really thought no more of her than of a blackberry picked by the wayside, a wild strawberry that offered itself for his casual eating, but before the summer was out her mother came up one day to the farm, telling him that he had got Mollie into trouble, and that his child was waxing within her. Such a scene there was: at first he had refused to marry her, but the old woman screamed and railed at him, and no prudent man would lightly cross Mother Robson when she was set on something. He had offered her money, but that was no good; nothing but his taking Mollie to wife would satisfy her. So married they were, and now he had been saddled with her for more than twenty years, while the baby which had been the cause of his taking her had been born dead, and never another had he got from her. Trollop she had been and a shrew she was, and she came of an evil stock, for none doubted but that Mother Robson had dealings with dark powers, and it soon seemed that her daughter was like her. John Pentreath had beaten her once, and sure enough next day the young bull he had just bought turned sick, and it was no good to put the cows to him. Once again he had locked her out of the house to teach her not to spend all the day down in St. Columb's instead of doing her work at the farm in the kitchen and the poultry-run, returning at an hour when decent women were in bed, and what had been the result of that? She went to her mother with the tale of his treatment of her, and the very next Sunday while they were in church there came a hailstorm that shredded every blossom from the apple-trees in the orchard. It was many years now since Mollie had been to church at all

or made any observance of the Lord's Day, and sometimes John Pentreath wondered whether it was she who
brought all the ill-luck on the house. Thank God,
Mother Robson had been taken at last: only a week
ago she had been found dead in her bed, and so now
perhaps better days might come, for she had always
hated him. But still he was mated with Mollie, and
there was a wife for a God-fearing man. Unfortun-
ately, he feared her but little less than he feared his
Creator, and the fear of her lasted all the week, whereas
God concerned him only on a Sunday.

The second member of his household was his daughter-
in-law Nancy, widow of his only son by his first wife,
and there was a daughter for a God-fearing man, she
with her tawdry finery, and her open-work stockings
on Sunday, and the red muck she put on her cheeks
and lips when she went to church, where there would
be men to look at her, and, by God, hadn't she got an
eye for them! There had been from time to time
rumours of her lightness with the artist-folk at St.
Columb's, and John Pentreath had seen her sitting on
the pier with her legs a-swing, talking and laughing to
four or five young fellows there, as no modest woman
would have done. She was handsomer now perhaps, in
the ripeness of her forty years, than she had ever been,
and in face and figure alike she took a man's eye.
For nearly twenty years now she had lived at the
farm, having come back there, still a mere girl, on
the death of her husband. The kitchen was her main
job, and she cooked plain savoury food: she and the
servant-girl did the housework between them, for
Mollie Pentreath took no hand in that. When Nancy's
work was done, she would stroll in the garden, singing
and humming to herself, and picking posies to bedizen

the house and particularly herself. Often she pinned some bright little nosegay in the hollow between her breasts, and then any man could see their firm and generous lines, as indeed he was meant to do, for Nancy would have shown off her points to anything that wore breeches, be he her own father-in-law or her own son. If there was marketing to be done in St. Columb's, she would spend half an hour first in her bedroom, among her trinkets and ribands, and when supper was cleared away of an evening, she sat in a rocking-chair and read some trashy story about dukes and duchesses and the ways of the light folk in London town.

She had married young Richard Pentreath up there in England, where he had gone, while still a boy, to seek his fortune with a hundred pounds which his mother had left him. Six months later he had been killed in a street accident, and the young widow, heavy with child, had come back to her husband's home. Well did John Pentreath remember her advent, with her Cockney speech, and her airs of a fine lady, and her elegant clothes of mourning. Richard, no doubt, had bragged of the estate to which he was heir, and apparently she thought that she was to be served and waited on, but she had soon found out that it was she who had to serve and wait in return for her keep. Three months after her arrival her boy Dennis had been born, and now he worked as a labourer on the farm that would one day be his. Dennis was a strapping young fellow, close on twenty years old, and as tall as his grandfather.

The breeze that had fallen asleep as John Pentreath read his Bible stirred and woke again, sprinkling the hot scent of the wallflowers over him, and rustling in the thin leaves of the book that lay open on his knee,

as if suggesting that these dark musings might as well
be shut up there, for they consorted ill with the seduc-
tion of the spring. His three and sixty years and his
habitual intemperance had as yet left his vigour unim-
paired, and his memory of his middle years, between his
first wife's death and his second marriage, were not
faded like photographs of old faces, but still stirred
lively in the fibre of his blood as he thought of them.
There had been that Bolitho woman, married to a
withered ape of a man, and he had done the pair of
them a good turn, for he had given that miserly old
pawnbroker in Penzance an heir to his business, and,
Lord, how the old man had strutted about when his
wife gave birth to a boy. He was as potent a man now
as he had been then, and here was he mated to this
barren woman whom he hated and feared, and with
whom he had had no commerce this many a year. But
to-day was Sunday, it was the hour for sacred reading
and penitential thought, and he shut eyes and ears to
the lure of memory, and tried to range himself on
the side of the wrathful God who had promised to make
sinners burn eternally for the sins they had so gleefully
committed. Yet the fruitful, fragrant penetration of
the spring continued subtly to invade him, making the
marrow in his bones to simmer in its warmth, and
the Bible slipped from his knees and lay unregarded at
his feet.

Somewhere in the house young Dennis was whistling
a jiggety tune, and though whistling on Sunday afternoon before now had been rewarded by a sound whip-
ping on Monday morning, that would be a hazardous
experiment now for the sake of godliness, so big and
strong had the boy grown. Moreover, John Pentreath
felt some unregenerate spirit within him secretly dancing

to the gaiety of the tune. Then a female voice joined in, singing the same refrain: no doubt Dennis and the servant-girl were sitting together at the open window of the kitchen, and perhaps their Bibles or those books of tales of Christian martyrs, which were the ordained reading for Sunday afternoon, had dropped from their knees, just as his had done, and they were looking at each other with the natural lasciviousness of a handsome boy and a pretty girl. Dennis as yet had taken little notice of girls; he was shy and awkward with them, and when, after supper of a summer evening, he went down to St. Columb's for an hour or two, it was not to make up to the girls or sit and spoon with them on the pier, but to seek out his great friend, young Willie Polhaven, and the two would stroll out from the village, bathe in one of the sandy coves, and lie there smoking, or on winter evenings go to the clubroom and be content with each other. But of late his natural manhood had begun to stir in him, and it was but seldom that he left the farm after supper, preferring to help Nell to wash up in the scullery, talking low to her there, with an occasional gust of smothered laughter, and the two had bright secret glances for each other. Not to be wondered at, for, by God, Dennis was a handsome boy, and any girl who refused to do his will must be a prude only fit for a meeting of Quakers. And the girl, Nell Robson, a niece of his wife's, was easily the prettiest lass in the place, dark in complexion, and with the black hair and black eyes of the southern strain. Dennis took after his mother: he was fair, with hair, thick as a rabbit's, that shone like ripe wheat in the sunshine; he was tanned brown on face and neck and up to the shoulders of his lusty arms, but beneath his shirt and breeches there

was the white skin of the Pentreaths. How the red
weals had leaped out across his bare shoulders when
his grandfather had flogged him. . . . He imagined the
two lying stretched on that bed of daffodils in front of
him, or in the shadow of the trees among the wreaths
of periwinkles. What a couple, black hair and gold,
blue eyes and black setting each other on fire, and
mouths a-thirst. There was a spring picture for you
in spite of Sunday! A month of Sundays and a thousand Bibles would not take the colour out of that.

The sharp click of the latch of the door leading
from the farmyard into the garden diverted his attention from this imagined picture, and his wife came
through, carrying the basket of eggs she had just gathered from the henhouse. The hens were her private
property, bought with her own money, and well she
looked after them. Two dozen eggs a week she allowed
the house, in return for their food, and when they were
not laying, or when eggs were scarce and fetched a
high price down in St. Columb's or Penzance, she
would contribute instead a cockerel or two for dinner.
Stringy and tough they were sometimes, for she kept
the capons for the market, but the worst of them
would make a hash or a tasty soup. She was his
junior by fifteen years or more, and her face, handsome still in feature, wore the hard and soured look
of thwarted fulfilment that often comes to childless
women. But so vivid had been to John Pentreath
his thoughts of youth, in this lure of the spell of spring,
that now he saw, not the lined and ageing face which
he had grown to fear and detest, but some wraith of
that provocative wench who had made his blood simmer
with her enticements all those years ago. She was still
upright in carriage and quick of movement, and the

gleams of sun dappling down through the thick woven boughs of the big ash tree that stood by the gate lit a brightness in her hair and tinged her faded face with warm colour: just for a moment that illusion lasted, queerly vivid, and then was gone again. She took him in from head to foot in a quick furtive glance, not missing the Bible, which had slipped from his knees and now lay on the path between his feet, and with unusual sociability she came and sat down beside him on the blistered garden-bench.

" A rare afternoon for to sit out and enjoy the sunshine," she said. " 'Tis a plum of a day picked out o' June. And have pleasant thoughts been with 'ee, John? "

The spell of spring was still spread over him, like gossamer webs on a dewy morning.

" Aye, indeed," he said. " I was being like a cat blinking and purring in the warmth. And when you came through the gate then, Mollie, I seemed to see you standing on the pier again as on some spring day, before we came together. The children whistling and singing in there and the wallflower scent took hold on me, I'm thinking. Queer is it how a scent can bring back old days."

Something in this gave her high pleasure. She smiled at him, and her upper teeth dazzling and regular shifted in her mouth.

" Well, and for Sunday afternoon that'll be a nice change for you," she said.

The day had gone clean out of his mind. Sunday? He looked, as if for confirmation of that, at his own black broadcloth sleeve, and the grimness came flooding back to his face.

" Why, so it is," he said, " and it had slipped me.

And young Dennis and Nell a-whistling and singing in there, all heathenish. Stop that noise there," he called out, " or you'll pay for it. . . . By God, to-morrow morning I'll give the boy a drumming that'll show him my arm has a bit of drive about it still! And you're no better with your gathering of eggs on the Lord's Day."

At the sound of his raised voice there came dead silence from within, but his wife laughed aloud.

" You'd best leave Dennis alone," she said, " or the lad'll give you a keepsake to remember him by, for 'tis a sappy young colt that he's grown and no mistake. And as for me gathering eggs on the Lord's Day, you give me a good laugh there, John Pentreath. Why don't 'ee go and wring the hens' necks for laying 'em on the Lord's Day? There's a bit o' sin an' wickedness for you! Surely a Godfearing hen would abide and hold herself in, though fit to burst, until the clock struck twelve on Sunday night, before she would do such a thing! "

" Now, none of your blasphemies, Mollie! " he said.

Her mocking voice rose shrill. Some squall of anger whistled in it.

" Blasphemy? " she cried. " 'Tis but a bit of good sense in answer to your rubbishy talk. Why, the man speaks as if there'd be a dollop of brimstone instead of a yolk inside of an egg gathered on Sunday! Eh! You're nought but a paltry hypocrite, John Pentreath. Would a God-fearing man, as you think yourself to be, get tipsy every day o' the week, and never do a kind deed nor a Christian one from year's end to year's end, but go cruel and black from Christmas to Christmas, and think he can make good by a couple of church-goings on Sunday, and sitting glowering till supper-time comes and he can take to the bottle again? You're no more than a child playing a fulish game."

He slapped his open hand on his thigh.

" I'll not hearken to you," he said. " Jabber on if you will, but I pay no heed. I'll mind my reading."

" Yes, pick up your Bible from where it lies on the path," she said, pointing to it, " and as you read I'll tell you how it got there. You heard the children singing, and Sunday slipped from you like the sheath off a flower, and you sniffed the spring and wished you were young and handsome again like Dennis, with a pretty girl beside you. That's what your mind's been brewing, and a sweet mouthful you found it."

He was afraid of her and of that awful power she had of exposing a man's mind, so that it was like a cupboard thrown open for all to see what was on the shelves.

" Well, Mollie, you're in the right of it there, I shouldn't wonder," he said in a conciliatory voice. " The spring gets into a fellow's bones, unless he's past feeling anything, like a bit of dried fish. I reckon it was God who made man that way. But have done with such talk."

" Ah, that's like you! " she said. " You say your mind about gathering eggs on the Lord's Day, and when I answer you with a bit of sense for that rubbish, you bid me have done with such talk! John, all Sunday long you're no more than a hypocrite, as I tell you, and what's more, you don't believe in all your prayings and Bible-readings. You're yourself from Monday to Saturday, and then you say your Sunday lesson like a child in school. A pack o' nonsense! If you believed in your hells and your damnations, would you be the man you are all the week? "

These clashing scolding moods of hers were something new. She used to be a silent, brooding woman, speaking hardly a word all day from sunrise to sundown, but in this last month or so she had broken out half a dozen times like this, and the outbreak had always preceded a certain topic. That was the way of women at her time of life. But at present it appeared that she had not done with what she had to say about this.

"You should listen to sense," she said. "You're a hard man and a cruel, John, and you act as if sitting glowering at your Bible for one day out of the seven will save your soul, and give you a harp and a pair of wings and a crown of gold and a sight of silly truck when you die, while all the rest of us'll be sizzling in hell. And in your heart you don't believe a word of it: it's nought but the task you've set yourself for Sundays. And what's the Lord God done for you in return for your psalm-singing and your thumbings 'pon your Bible? Isn't it plain that He sees through you? Sure, He's not such a flat as to be taken in by you. He's got your measure, and He knows what your kneelings and your Amens are worth, else He'd never be allowing you to get old without ever a spark of joy coming to you save what you get out of your whisky-bottle. Not a bit o' good luck has come out of it all, and the stock on the farm is dwindling, and you can scarce make two ends meet."

She drew a little closer to him till their knees touched.

"Belike He's paying you out for being such a hypocrite," she said. "The house is divided against itself. Have done with it, and see if a bit o' better luck doesn't come along, for, sure, you couldn't have worse. And then there's this. Dearly I'd like to give you a son for your old age——"

He broke in.

" Ah, I knew 'twas coming to that," he said, " and
yet you bid me listen to sense! Give me a bit of sense
to listen to! Why, you're an old woman: you're past
the power of bearing. 'Tis as if you tried to find a
harvest by lighting a fire in the stubble when the time
for reaping's long over."

" Nay, I'm not so old, John," she said. " There's
a power of life in me yet. Why, there was Sally
Austell down in St. Columb's who was fifty afore she
ceased, and I know all that Sally knows and maybe
a bit more. You'd soon be of the same mind as me, if
you'd give up your Sunday nonsense and let the spring
have its way with you. And as for that "—and she
pointed with forefinger and little finger at the Bible
that still lay on the path between his feet—" as for
that, what manner of blessings has that ever brought
you, John Pentreath? "

Borne on the soft breeze from the sea there came the
sound of church bells. He plucked himself from the
touch of her, and picked up the book. " Back at your
blasphemings again," he said.

She laid her hand on his arm. " I want a child by
you, John," she said. " Ye've got to give me one."

He shook himself free with an effort, for though her
fingers were but lightly laid on him, he felt as if they
gripped him.

" You and your Sally Austell! " he cried. " Be
wise, and put your black ways from you. And if there's
no luck about the house because it's divided, 'tis for
you to come over and save your soul while there's time.
And here's a godly conversation for the Lord's Day,
and may I be forgiven for the part I had in it. 'Tis
church time and I'm off."

Molly Pentreath had a gift of mimicry that was like an echo, and as she rose, tall and grim, facing him, and as she spoke, mocking him, it was as if he were confronted by some wraith of himself.

"Yes, 'tis church time and we'll be off," she said in his very voice, "and when church is done, 'twill be supper-time, and we'll get properly tipsy, and then we'll pray like a chosen vessel of the Lord, and we'll have no blasphemous talk on the Lord's Day, no, we won't."

"There, be done, Mollie," he said. "I didn't speak to anger you."

She picked up her basket of eggs.

"No, sure," she said. "We're a loving couple, John, and you'll hearken to me yet. Get gone, and thank the Lord for all His mercies to you."

Two hours later the household was gathered together over the silent business of Sunday supper. This took place in the kitchen, an ample whitewashed room with the door opening on to the farmyard, and curtained windows on each side of it. There was a big dresser against one wall, and a tall grandfather's clock; another door opened into the scullery, a third led into the main body of the house. The oven was cold this evening, for no cooking beyond the roasting of the joint for dinner was allowed on Sunday, and Mollie Pentreath, though the room was warm, had wrapped her shawl round her. She sat at the end of the table with her back to the stove, the door of which to-morrow and throughout the week would be thrown open, when cooking was done, so that she could enjoy to the full the heat that came from it. Facing her sat her husband. Dennis and Nell Robson, Mollie's niece, sat side by side on one length of the table, and Nancy Pentreath,

Dennis's mother, was opposite to them. A checked, much-darned cloth covered the board, and the sirloin of cold beef and a plate of lettuce were reinforced with the remains of an apple tart, a jar of Cornish cream, and a wedge of cheese with home-made bread and butter. Close by John Pentreath was his whisky bottle, and two mugs of wallflowers and a paraffin lamp stood up the centre of the table. No word from any of them broke the silence, till Dennis, passing up his plate for further supplies to Mollie Pentreath, who was carving the beef, let his fork clatter on the floor.

"You damned awkward lout," said his grandfather. "You go meatless for that. Not a bite more for you: take your plate back."

Mrs. Pentreath finished cutting the slice she had begun for Dennis, and tossed it on the blade of the carving-knife on to the boy's plate.

"Eat your victuals, lad," she said, "and don't mind him. Slish o' fat with it?"

"Do as I bid you, Dennis!" cried his grandfather. "Not a morsel more meat crosses your teeth to-night."

Mrs. Pentreath shot out her left hand at him with rigid pointing finger.

"And don't you mind Dennis, John," she cried. "You let him be, I tell you. He shall eat and you shall drink. That's the way: he'll grow tall and you'll grow tipsy."

John Pentreath's hand was raised towards Dennis, as if to clout the boy, or take his plate from him, and Dennis had half-risen from his place, his eyes alert, ready to duck his head, or snatch his plate away.

"Do as I bid you, John," cried his wife, not re-laxing the menace of that pointed finger, and muttering to himself he dropped his hand and finished his glass.

Nancy Pentreath thought to put in her word. She had been down to St. Columb's that afternoon and was dressed in the best of her finery. There was a touch of rouge on her cheeks; round her neck was a magenta riband that matched another in her hair; a fine, handsome woman she was, and no mistake. She made a little clicking noise with her tongue on her teeth, and spoke in her clipped Cockney speech.

" Such an awkward boy as you are, Dennis," she said. " No wonder you startled your grandfather with that clatter, and made him vexed with you. But there! It's all over now, so eat your good slice of beef, and we'll hear no more about it."

" Lord save us, and who's been seeking your advice? " said John.

Old Mrs. Pentreath gave a thin cackle of a laugh at Nancy's discomfiture, and again silence descended till supper was done. Then John pushed back his chair, and rising from the table, took his pipe and glass to the big arm-chair that stood handy, while the table was being cleared and the crockery washed. Nell saw to this to-night, with Dennis midway between a hindrance and a help; he sat on the edge of the scullery sink with a dish-cloth for drying the crocks, talking to Nell in whispers, while she threw the scraps into the, pig tub and did her best to scour the plates with the cold water of Sunday evening. Mollie Pentreath in the meantime remained in her chair at the head of the table, silent and furtive.

John Pentreath had drunk pretty well at supper, and while the room was being tidied up for prayers he smoked a pipe of his black shag tobacco and had a

couple more stiff glasses, and now the spirits began
to take hold of him. Walking to church that afternoon he had been ill at ease, for not only had his
ears been hearing blasphemous talk, but he knew that
in his heart he admitted that there might be some sense
in what his wife had said. What, after all, had he got
by all his dark pieties? What reward had the Lord
given His servant for all the prayers and Bible-readings
of those years, his church-goings, his black clothes, his
Sunday abstinence?—it looked as if all those pains had
gone for naught. Had he been on the wrong side?
Well he knew, and his wife knew better, that there
were other powers ready to befriend a man. That was
beyond question; he had seen their work too often to
have any doubt on that subject. If you crossed old
Sally Austell, for instance, of whom his wife had spoken,
you might know there'd be trouble ahead, and 'twas
wiser to make it up with the old woman with a flitch
of bacon or a basket of eggs before she got going.
And Mollie was just such another. He was always
crossing Mollie, and look at the way things were tum-
bling at the farm! . . . But then to reinforce his waver-
ing allegiance he had come in at the afternoon service
for a thumping strong sermon, forty minutes of the
best, from Parson Allingham on witchcraft, and the
certainty of eternal damnation for all who had traffic
with the powers of evil: God, you could smell the
singeing of the goats on the Day of Judgment! A
stout man was Parson, who spoke his mind and feared
nobody, for he was strong in faith, and what a glebe
was his, the fruitfullest meadows in all the place, and
half a dozen lusty children. Then at the end of his
sermon he had pointed to the red sunset that smouldered
in the west window. " See the fires of the wrath of

3

God," he cried. " You and I and all of us may still be
on earth, when they shall spread over the whole heaven,
and sea and sky and land shall vanish like a burning
scroll. And then shall He say to those on His left hand,
' Depart from Me, ye cursed, into everlasting fire prepared for the devil and his angels.' "

John Pentreath's waverings had been firmed up
again by so powerful a discourse, and as he came up
the hill home, he vowed to bear such testimony in his
prayer to-night as would atone for any vacillation
there might have been in his heart. Those of his
household present at his ministrations would know that
John Pentreath had made up his mind to side with the
Lord God; his words should be searching words, words
that should warn them to turn from their lightnesses
and their wicked ways, while there was yet time. So
to kindle his fervour of speech he filled his glass and
filled it again till his brain was inflamed with the
sacredness of his mission.

Soon all was ready for prayers: John shuffled over
from the window-seat to the end of the table where he
knelt opposite his wife, but Dennis took his place by
his mother's side, opposite Nell, so that he could make
chinks through his fingers to look at her. All but
Mollie Pentreath got to their knees; she continued sitting
where she was.

For a minute or two John knelt in silence, holding
himself in, so that his drunken eloquence might gather
itself up. Even in everyday life he was a man of
marrowy speech, and now the sonorous phrases of the
Bible chapters he had read that afternoon were fer-
menting in his head, and after a few mutterings and
mumblings his words broke out hot and smoking.

" Lord God of Abraham," he cried, " look upon us

poor sinners assembled here to bow before Thy just wrath and indignation at our wickedness. There are those of us who would fain turn their backs on Thee, and call on the power of darkness to befriend them, whereby they damn their souls and will suffer the eternal torments Thou hast ordained for them. They worship in the groves of idolatry, and they have made snares to entrap the godly. Smite them, O Lord, upon their lying mouths, set them in slippery places, and pour Thy plagues upon them, so that they may know and repent of their wickedness before Thy just judgment whelms them in the pit of Thy fury."

A faint crooked smile crossed Mollie's face: so that was a bit of his mind about her. He was praying fine to-night, the comic man, busy as a clown at the circus over nothing at all, just a mock to all who looked on him. Such a clatter of babbles: that wasn't the way to pray. She shrugged her shoulders, and let her shawl drop from them, for the lamp had warmed the room up.

Then the tipsy voice went on.

" Lord, there are those among us whose hearts are set on their lusts and passions, light women and harlots, who like Jezebel of old paint their faces and tire their hair, and entice the sons of men to serve their wantonness. Consume their beauty, O Lord, with heaviness, make their eyes to be dim, and disfigure their fairness, so that none shall desire them; purge them from their evil ways as with hyssop, and wash away their iniquities lest they be a snare to the righteous."

Mollie Pentreath watched him more closely: she had felt no more than an amused contempt for his allusions to herself, but now that he was directing them to Nancy, a new notion sprang up in her mind. Often lately

she had seen him looking at her with a kindled eye, as
she tripped about the room, and these mentions of the
snares that lewd women laid for the righteous chimed
in with that. That was like him; oh, that was very
like him to make her responsible for his own lecherous
thoughts, to pray that her beauty would consume and
her eyes grow dim, so that he should desire her no more.
She watched and listened to the bawling voice.

"Woe unto them, the whores and the harlots who
tempt a Godfearing man from the narrow way, and lure
him to the damnation of his soul, who bedizen themselves and make soft eyes to seduce the righteous. May
their children be fatherless and beg their bread, may
there be none to pity them nor have compassion when
their beauty consumes away like as a moth fretting
a garment; yea, let their sins be the garment that covers
them and the girdle below their breasts, until they turn
themselves to the Lord."

"That's what he's driving at," thought Mollie, "and
now Dennis and Nell will come in for a piece about
the fatherless children. He's primed, he is, and we're
having a rare praying to-night. . . ."

"And there are those, Lord, as well Thou knowest,
who in the spunk and insolence of their youth make
light of Thy ordinances and Thy holy days. They
wax fat, like Jeshurum, with their gluttonies and make
mock of Thy commandments. Behold, they were shapen
in wickedness, and in sin did their mothers conceive
them, so pluck not Thou the mercy of Thy chastise-
ments from them. Let Thy angel stand with drawn
sword at the entry of the pleasant road, and pierce their
hearts with fears and manifold tremblings, that they
may forsake the ways of wickedness and go in the
strait path of Thy commandments. Drive far from

them and from us all the powers of those who would ensnare us in spells of witchcraft, and shut not up Thy loving-kindness in displeasure. Defend this house, O Lord, from Satan's hosts, that compass us about to destroy us, and cast upon them the furiousness of Thy wrath, anger and displeasure——"

Mollie Pentreath had heard enough of this, and now she pushed back her chair and got up.

"Have done with it, John," she said. "You've spoken all that. Get you to bed."

Her voice rose suddenly and shrill, drowning his.

"It's struck ten," she cried, "and you go on like a mill-wheel, creaking round and round for ever and aye. Get up from your knees, and Nancy and Dennis shall take you to your room, for you're drunk, drunk, drunk, and I won't listen no more to your maunderings, and you can finish what the Lord has laid on you to say all alone with Him, for perhaps He's more patient than me. For all your cursings the seed potatoes must be got in to-morrow, and you've told about the witches."

John looked up with the ludicrous solemnity of a tipsy man at the sound of her voice.

"Wailing and weeping and the gnashing of teeth, hast Thou appointed for them——" he began.

"'Tis enough," cried his wife pointing at him. "Take him along, Dennis, and you, Nancy."

Dennis got on one side of him and his mother on the other, and they lifted him under the arms, and got him to his feet and supported his staggering steps. Gales of his sour-sweet breath blew on them as he continued to bawl out his petitions, tightly clasping his two supporters; a ludicrous sight indeed. "God, Thou knowest my down-sittings and my uprisings," he boomed out, "and my heart is open to Thee. A broken and a contrite heart Thou wilt not despise, and sore I repent me of my evil ways. Have mercy, too, on this poor Jezebel, and 'tis but a pure fatherly kiss—ah, you turn away your head, you slut, do you? . . . My God, Dennis, you've got the Pentreath muscles over your loins same as me. Twins, lad, get you twins when you take a wife for yourself, and show yourself a man. And have mercy on my loneliness, O Lord, and give me the comfort of Thy help again, and drive far from me all snares of the enemy——"

They laid him on his bed in the room adjoining his wife's, and Nancy unloosed his collar.

" Well, that's done," she said, " and there's a pretty Sunday evening! Put his basin by the side of his bed, Dennis, for he'll be sick soon, I shouldn't wonder, and that'll relieve his stomach, and he'll sleep and be as fit as a flea again in the morning. Leave the lamp with him, poor old dear, but out of his reach, or we'll have the house on fire. Why, if that isn't Mrs. Pentreath come to see him put away."

Mollie had followed the staggering procession upstairs, and had listened to all that was said.

" Thank you kindly, Nancy," she said, " for looking after the old man; I've seldom seen him as bad as this, and the more drink he has the more Lord God we've got to put up with. But he'll sleep it off now."

Nell had followed in the wake of this procession, and while Nancy locked herself into her room opposite, she went with Dennis up to the far end of the passage, where their rooms lay adjoining each other. Originally they had been one room with two windows, but a wooden partition had been put up when, as a boy, he had a room to himself, and Nell slept on the other side of it. The passage was dark, for the oil-lamp which lit it had been carried into John's room, and Dennis drew a matchbox from his pocket to light Nell to her candle.

"God, the grandfather was properly boozed to-night," he said, as he discreetly closed Nell's door, without latching it, and held the struck match between his hands. "That was a rare praying; witches and whores and wanton youths, which is you and me. He might have prayed for a drunken old devil while he was about it. Where's your candle?"

Nell looked about.

"I must have left it downstairs," she said. "You'll be burning yourself with that match all to no purpose."

The cave of his joined hands was rosy from the light within them.

"Why, that's pretty," she said. "Your fingers are sort of red and transparent. There! It's gone out!"

The room was not dark, for the blind was up, and a splash of moonlight lay on the floor. They moved towards the open window, tiptoeing across the room, and the magic of the clean springtime poured in on them. It was still outside, scarcely a breath of wind moved in the warm air, and the moon rode high and full. Neither spoke, but drew a little closer to each other. Then from somewhere near an owl hooted, and that broke the enchantment.

"That's a bit of ill-luck," said the girl.

"Don't you believe it," said he. "Grandfather was hot on witches to-night, though. What came over him?"

"Nigh on a bottle of whisky was the way of it," said Nell. "But down in St. Columb's they do say that they owls are the spirits of those as have been witches, and they fly around to see them as are like-minded on earth."

Dennis's mouth expanded with noiseless laughter. " There's a bit of foolishness," he whispered. " Do you think it's come to see my Granny? A pack of nonsense, Nell."

From down the passage came the sound of a turned door-handle, and the girl laid her finger on her lips.

" Hist!   Get you gone, Dennis," she whispered. " That's the handle of Aunt Mollie's door, for it needs a drop of oil and it slipped my mind.   Take off your shoes and go quick and quiet to your room.   The passage is dark and she won't see you."

Dennis's blue eyes looked black in the moonlight. " Why shouldn't I be staying and talking to you, Nell? " he asked.

" Nay, 'twould never do.   She mustn't find you here."

Dennis slipped out, and crept shadow-like to his room next door, and peering out stood there a moment looking down the passage.   He could see at the far end of it Mollie's figure outlined against the unblinded window over the stairs up which they had just hoisted John Pentreath.   She stood there listening, and then went down again as noiseless as himself.   From close at hand there was the creak of a drawn bolt and he knew that Nell had shut herself in.

It was not worth while lighting his candle, for he had but to throw off his clothes and get into bed, and jerking aside the curtain so that the light might wake him betimes in the morning, he pulled off his Sunday coat and his shirt, and standing by the open window sniffed the damp coolness of the night.   The air was clean and sweet on his skin after that reeking kitchen, and from next door he could hear the soft tread of Nell as she moved about.   Then with a quickening of his breath and his heart-beat he pictured her undressing too, till she stood white in the dusk of her room. He puckered up his lips and whistled the tune they had crooned together this afternoon, and paused listening for her echo. Often he made such a signal as he went to bed, and often he heard her take up the air next door. But to-night there was no reply.

He leant out of the window: the moon flooded the garden with light. Away to the right in the shadow was the seat where his grandfather had read his Bible this afternoon, and now, peering out, Dennis saw that it was tenanted again: Mollie Pentreath was sitting there. That was in no way surprising, for often, though all day she had hugged the fire, she strolled or sat there after dark. Then a shadow crossed the moon, and Dennis saw a great brown owl circling low over the garden and lower yet, till it flew right under the ash-tree by the door into the farmyard. Shy birds that they were, it was odd that it did not wheel off away from the figure that sat on the bench so close by. Perhaps it did not see her, for she sat very still.

CHAPTER II

NANCY

NANCY PENTREATH's room looked out, away from the garden, on to the pasture-land. It was a big room, sparsely furnished, but, like herself, highly and tawdrily decorated. The one good feature of its embellishment was that there were quantities of flowers there: wash-stand, dressing-table and chimney-piece were alike gay with them. A wicker rocking-chair had bows of magenta ribands on its arms; there was a pink bed-spread, and a dripping of dirty blue muslin over the sides of the dressing-table, and a china ornament of two cupids playing see-saw. What she prized most of all her furniture was a tall looking-glass, swinging on hinges, in which she could survey all her figure. By shifting this she could obtain a view of her back in the mirror on her dressing-table. The room smelt faintly of musk and she shut the window that had been left ajar, and drew the curtain over it.

Nancy had guessed very well to whom her father-in-law had alluded when at those drunken prayers he had spoken of harlots and whores, but she bore him no ill-will for that, for to her good-natured easy code it wasn't kind to hold a poor old tipsy-cake like him responsible for what he had said. Besides, though he had alluded to her as Jezebel on the way upstairs, he had wanted to kiss her. That was gratifying to her vanity, and vanity and good nature were the two really strong traits in her character. He had pinched her black and blue (an exaggeration) as he clung to her, and that was a much truer expression of his feelings towards her than the more uncompromising matter in his prayers. He was keen on her: and though, of course, it was shocking that a man should want to cuddle his own son's widow, Nancy was easily capable of getting over such shocks when there was a tribute to her charms behind them, and why shouldn't an " old feller " like that have a bit of a feeling for a woman still? She could look after herself, and knew where to draw the line. Lately he had taken to giving her a kiss at night, when she went up to bed, but she had always turned her head a bit, so that he got her cheek only. But she wondered how long it was that old Mrs. Pentreath had been wanted like that. She wouldn't have refused her mouth, if he had sought it. Poor old dear! There was a hungry look about her: any woman could tell what that meant. It was " a shime " that she should go wanting when she had a husband still fit and strong, though to be sure she would be a grim sort of bedfellow.

It was only just after ten when Mrs. Pentreath had broken up the prayer-meeting, and there was time for the rites which Nancy so often practised when she was alone. She had a private store of candles for this pur- pose, for had she used the household stock there would soon have been an inquiry as to where all the candles went, and now she lit a couple on her dressing-table and put two more short ends in the holders of the looking-glass. She touched up the rouge on her cheeks and refashioned the bow of her lips with a stick of red cosmetic. She put a puce-coloured velvet riband, rather lacking in nap, like her father-in-law's top-hat, in her hair, and enhanced the pretty effect by pinning to it a shell-cameo of a naked nymph in a pinchbeck setting.

There was violet powder for the tip of her nose, an adjusting of her gown in order to show a little more of her neck, and being thorough in her methods where the display of her own attractions was concerned, she put on a pair of faded satin shoes. A tattered fan that smelt of her favourite perfume, and two long white gloves that wanted cleaning completed her costume. The shoes, the fan and the gloves were ancient relics, brought out only for this ritual from the trunk under her bed, which had never made a journey since, twenty years ago, it had brought her belongings from London.

Not once as she made these embellishments had she surveyed herself in the big mirror, for it was her custom to let the splendid reflection burst on her when the toilet was finished. Then with a smile that showed the tips of her white teeth, she whisked round and revelled in the contemplation of her own image. Certainly it was alluring, for even the puce riband and the cameo could not mar her extremely comely face, and her figure still had the vigour of youth. Dennis had come rightly by his stature and his yellow hair and the turquoise-blue of his eyes, and indeed both in eyes and hair his mother's lustre rivalled that of his youth. A pity that there was no one here to share the pretty picture with her!

But now it was growing late, and, with the candle ends on each side of the mirror flaring and dipping into their sockets, Nancy began undressing for bed. She had got to make up her mind on a question of great importance to her, and as yet she really did not know what she was going to say to the proposal that Mr. Harry Giles had made to her this very afternoon. He was an artist who had lately joined the colony at St. Columb's, and Nancy thought she had never seen such a " perfect gentleman." They had first met a month ago, quite by accident, as she recited to herself, on the narrow path that led through the fields between St. Columb's and the farm, and, most politely, he had stepped aside into the wet grass to give her the path. It was only natural that she should lift her eyes to him with a glance of acknowledgment, and in turn he raised his hat with such an admiring smile. It followed that, after walking on ten yards or so, she bent down to do up a shoe-lace, and there he was still looking after her. So they went on their ways, and no lady and gentleman, thought Nancy, could have behaved more properly.

Then came developments, and, since they led up to the decision she had to make, she reviewed them with verbal distinctness in her mind, telling herself the exciting story. "So it was no surprise to me," ran her thoughts, " that if it wasn't the next day, it was the day after, that there he was again on the path, sitting on an artist's stool, doing a sketch. So interested he was in his painting that I got quite close before he saw me at all, so I got a good look at him. He had his hat off, nice greyish hair, quite a mop of it, and I took to him instanter. Forty-five or so, I guessed, p'raps a bit more, but give me a man with some experience, one as wants more than an apple-faced girl, and for my part I never really liked boys, for they're hot stuff to-day, and just how-der-do to-morrow if they've seen something else as takes their fancy. But there was Mr. Giles, a fine figure of a man, and something steady about him. He was quite taken up with his picture, him and it blocking up the whole of the path and him not seeing me yet. But when he did, lor', how quick and brisk he was, begging my pardon for having set there like that, and me saying pray don't mention it.

After that, I couldn't do less than look at his sketch; beautiful it was, with the path just true to life, puddles and all, so that you could have fancied yourself a-walking on it, and the blackthorn in bloom already and the roof of the farm behind. Didn't I think, he asked me, that it wanted a figure standing by the blackthorn? I saw what he was after, and so of course I agreed, and said I'd stand there for a few minutes, if that would be any use to him.

"That was just what he wanted: very kind of me," he said, and he sat himself down again, after excusing himself, so polite, for sitting in the presence of a lady. And in ten minutes there I was in the picture, standing under the blackthorn, with my arm akimbo, and I'm sure, for all that it was so little, anyone could have seen it was me. And then, as we were both going down to St. Columb's, nothing would serve him but that we must walk down together, him carrying my basket, and me telling him that as often as not I went down to the village round about three of the afternoon, and so it all commenced."

The sequel was up to the same fine standard of felicity as the commencement Mr. Giles had taken the house at the corner of the Kenrith lane, which was on the direct route from the farm into St. Columb's, and naturally, next day, he was sitting in his garden after lunch. Rain threatened, but Nancy set off from the farm before it had begun to fall. Nothing could have been luckier than her timing, for just as she came opposite his house the first heavy drops of a downpour hissed on the path, and so he had begged her to take shelter in his studio, for she had no umbrella, until the rain stopped. In she went, and he asked her her opinion of the unfinished sketches there, and since the

rain continued, he was ever so keen to make a charcoal
sketch of her head. A sitting, of course, to be paid
for, he said: he would not dream of it otherwise, and
on her consenting, he had brought out a half-bottle
of champagne for her refreshment. Pop went the cork,
and the bubbly stuff went creaming into her glass.
Nancy had " heard tell " of champagne; it came in the
novels she read beside the kitchen fire at the farm,
and a very tasty drink it was, she thought, and him
making no more of opening it for her than if it had
been a bottle of beer.

That had been a pleasant half-hour, for he had such
agreeable conversation, and positively refused to believe
that Dennis, that big handsome boy whom he had seen
ploughing in the field where the circle of stones stood,
was her son. Impossible, he said, and all the time as
he drew, he was casting those quick, admiring glances
at her; it was evident that he thought a lot of her
looks. And the champagne and all, and his hopes that
he was not boring her (he need not have been afraid
of that), and his good luck at having been out in the
garden just as she passed, and just as the rain began. . . .

Harry Giles was equally pleased with his sitter: she
struck him as being an admirable example of a type
which he had been on the look-out for, but which it
was not easy to find. A whore, no doubt, he said to
himself, at heart: voluptuously good-looking, superla-
tively common, but one who had arrived at middle-age
without having become completely coarsened. Perhaps
she had not had the opportunity for unlimited in-
dulgence, or perhaps there was in her some sort of
fastidiousness that had kept her from degenerating
into a mere animal who will do anything to assuage her
unsatiated femininity. He fancied he read that into

her face, and it was just what he wanted for a picture that had long been simmering in his mind. As was the fashion of the day, it was to be a picture that told a story: " Leicester Square, 11 p.m." would be the approximate title of it. The audience was emerging from a music-hall, light drizzle was falling, and in the foreground on the wet pavement, where the street lights were reflected, was standing a woman, just of this type, gaudily dressed in the manner of her kind. A man in evening clothes and top-hat was accosting her, and though it was clear enough why she had taken up her place there, she drew back from him: her face was not of one who was willing to go off with anyone who beckoned. She was not yet promiscuous nor wholly ravenous. . . . There was the idea, and, thought Giles, you can put anything into a picture if you know how, but what had stood in his way was to find a model whose face conveyed that mixture of welcome and withholding.

But when he saw Nancy first on the path from the farm, he guessed that he had found the face which he wanted, and now, when for half an hour he had studied her as she sat for the charcoal sketch, sipping her champagne, and purring at his admiration, he felt certain of it. She had a beautiful figure, too, mature and vigorous, deep-breasted, with flowing curves of firm flesh. He imagined that she would be a splendid model for the nude, but as yet he was not concerned with that, nor with any personal relation that might develop between them; his picture was the immediate objective.

Nancy, ignorant of these undercurrents, pursued her review of the events which led up to the qustion which she had to decide, as she undressed before the

guttering candles in her looking-glass. . . . The charcoal sketch was far from satisfying Mr. Giles: he said
he must use his paints on her. So for a couple of weeks
now she had been sitting to him on occasional afternoons for a study of her head and shoulders in oils.
She had put on that straw hat trimmed with the red
bow and artificial cherries, with which she had been
making effects just now, and he was delighted with it.
It just suited her face, he said, and indeed he could not
have devised a more characteristic headgear. Very particular he was, too, about the light: she stood in the
darkest corner of his studio, and he lit two big oil-
lamps just over her head, and these had to be adjusted
so that her face was brilliantly lit up, while the brim
of her hat, with a couple of cherries lolling over it, threw
a fantastic shadow on her left cheek. He put up his
easel twelve feet or more from her, so that while he
painted by daylight she stood in a flood of artificial
illumination. She had thought that a great waste of
paraffin: paraffin, she told him, must be cheap where
he came from. . . . There was always a glass of champagne for her when she got tired of standing to freshen
her up: this gave her that added touch of natural
colour that made the rouge, which she always put on
for these sittings, betray itself. In all ways—champagne, compliments and the payments he made her
which she knew to be in excess of the usual tariff for
artists' models—he showed himself the perfect gentleman which she had instantly recognised him to be.

But long before his picture was done, Nancy had
begun to feel a little piqued that he made no direct personal tribute to her charms, for she had taken an im-
mense fancy to him, and not even a hint at a kiss or
anything innocent like that! He was glib with his

4

compliments, it is true, in order to make her smile, but he seemed not to want the smile for himself, but only for his paint-brush. " There, that is exquisite, you look perfectly entrancing now," he would say. " Stop like that just one moment! " Then he would look eagerly at her, with no answering smile, but a frown as like as not, biting the end of his brush: then he would give a couple of minute touches, and stand back from his canvas, seeming to forget all about her, looking backwards and forwards from her to the picture, just as if his picture meant more to him than she did, as was indeed the case.

To-day she had sat for him an hour or more while John Pentreath was reading his Bible in the garden, and he had scarcely noticed her at all, so absorbed he was in his work, and Nancy, rather piqued, had said to herself that he wanted nothing of her except to get her likeness and then ta-ta. But suddenly, what a change!

" It's done," he cried. " Come and look at yourself, and tell me what you think! "

Nancy walked across the studio to where he stood. Now at last she would know whether he had any thought of her for herself, or whether it was going to be " ta-ta." She might give him a hint, in case he was one of those shy ones. . . .

" Well, I must say you've caught my expression something beautiful! " she said. " What a thing to be able to paint like that! That's just how I look, I'm sure, when I'm talking to someone who's taken my fancy."

With that last biting of his brush-handle, his last frown in answer to her smile, his last touch of bright red where the light shone through the rim of her ear, he put the artist from him for the present. He had got exactly what he wanted, captured it, recorded

it, so that it was his.   But that was done, and now he
knew that all the while he had been looking at her, there
had been storing up, drop by sensual drop, his desire for
her.   She was an exceedingly good-looking woman, and
he did not mind her commonness.   Indeed, common
women were more fun: they demanded no effort: they
just enjoyed, and enjoyment was the whole object of
the business.

" That's good hearing," he said, " because, as you've
been talking to me, I flatter myself that I take your
fancy.   Is that it? "

So she had kindled his spark: he did not frown
on her now when she smiled at him, his paint-brushes
were laid aside, and the eagerness of his eyes was for
her and not for his picture.   All the joylessness of her
wasted years of maturity clamoured to her and sharpened
her sexual hunger.   In spite of her rumoured looseness
with men at St. Columb's, Harry Giles was right about
the legend he had read in her face: she was not a
woman who had sought or given herself promiscuously.
A few years ago she had had a week's intrigue with a
young artist hardly more than a boy, with the dew
of youth still on him, and the first down on his lip.
That had been a good bit of fun certainly: such laughter
and violence, such a frolic of the flesh, but signifying
nothing.   Then again, last summer, coming up late to
the farm in dusk that was almost darkness, she had
met a stranger on the path by the Circle.   Scarce a
word had passed between them, a bit of madness that
was, and she had never set eyes on him again.   But
this was not a mere rampant boy who flamed into brief
lust for her, nor one who had met her casually under
the soft lascivious spell of the night, and went his
way whistling half an hour afterwards.   Harry Giles

had looked at her and studied her: they had got to know each other a bit first, and now if he wanted her it was no momentary whim.   She felt herself "all of a tremble," as she answered.

"Why, Mr. Giles," she said, "you don't suppose I should have spent all these hours here, and drunk your champagne and all, unless I'd had a fancy for you? But with you just looking at me and frowning and turning to your picture again and forgetting all about it, I began to think I was no more to you than the blackthorn where I stood for you first.   I wasn't one to thrust myself forward, I hope."

Giles had been here a month: he wanted a woman, and this one attracted him far more than any he had seen yet.   She was handsome and she was common and she was keen, and if you weren't content with that, you were hard to please.

"Darling Nancy," he said.   "You're delicious.   I want you.   Give me a kiss."

It was their mouths that met, and that was no wonder, for each sought each, and that close animal clinging of man to woman was wine to Nancy.   That was a nice kiss, she thought: not just a peck, and then get on to something else, but it had a sweetness in itself.   She withdrew her mouth, and her breath came in quick pants through her open lips, betraying her.

"Lor', Mr. Giles," she said, "I never would have sat to you at all, if I'd thought it would come to this."

"Then I'm glad you didn't think," said he, "and so are you.   Where's the harm?   If you want and I want, what does it concern anybody else?   Or shall I say, 'Good afternoon, Mrs. Pentreath.   So good of you to have looked in.'   Perhaps that would be best.   So good afternoon, Mrs. Pentreath——"

" Lor', I do like you," she said, still pressed close, bosom to chest, in his encircling arm. " You've got such nice ways. I shouldn't be here if I didn't like you, should I? "

He drew her with him on to the big sofa under the large window to the north.

" Oh, this won't never do," she whispered, without the faintest show of resistance. " And you're crumpling my hat."

" Take it off then."

" But Sunday afternoon and all," she said, as she unpinned it. " Besides, some of your friends might be coming in to see you, and then what a to-do? "

" My dear, don't go on like that! The old woman who looks after me is out, and she won't be back till supper-time. I'll go and lock the front door, if that will content you."

An hour later, she was pinning on her hat in front of the big mirror in the studio, for it was time to get back to the farm to make supper ready before John Pentreath came back from church. This way and that she moved it, half an inch at a time: it was most important that it should be just right. And now it was she who put her arms round him.

" Well, it has been nice," she said. " And you do like me a little bit, don't you? "

" No: a big bit. When shall I see you again? "

" Well, we must be careful," she said. " There's lots of sharp eyes in St. Columb's, and sharper yet up at the farm."

" Can't I come up there? " he asked, " when they've all gone to bed? "

" Save us, no! " cried Nancy. " Too much of a risk:

we could never be comfortable.   But I've got a notion.
'Twould be easy for me, every now and then, when
supper's over, to say I was fair dropping with sleep,
and go up to bed, and then nip down the stairs by my
room, and out through the door in the studio, for
there's no lodger there now, and no one would know
whether I came or went."

" Capital.   And now there's another thing, Nancy,"
said he.   " You must come down by daylight too, and
stand for me again, not your head only, but all of
you.   You've got a lovely skin, I know that now, and
my word, what a figure, fit for a goddess.   And I'm
badly wanting a nude model for another picture, and
you're the one for me."

" Eh, Mr. Giles; I shouldn't like that at all," said
she.

" But I should: I should like it immensely.   If you
won't, I shall have to get another girl——"

" Girl!   Get along with you! " cried Nancy.

" Well, woman if you like, and a fine one, too.   Do
come in and stand for me to-morrow afternoon.   Else
I must get another fine woman instead."

It was that she was thinking over as she undressed
to-night.   In the queer way of a woman of her type,
some sense of respectability, of delicacy, made her
hesitate.   It was one thing to lie in a man's arms in
the dark: that was quite proper and natural; but it was
another to stand naked in front of him and have
him staring at you in broad daylight.   Then there
was another consideration: was she fit to bear that
scrutiny now?   And she stood stripped in front of the
big looking-glass with a candle from the dressing-table
in her hand, examining herself.   It would never do if

she wasn't fit to look at. As yet he had only had a glimpse of her in the darkened room.

She raised and lowered the candle, so that by its direct light she could judge of herself. There were hints of sagging skin, of slackness in what should have been firm. That soft luminous marble, faintly rosy, of girlhood was hers no longer, and she stood frowning and undecided. An awful thing would it be, if, when he looked at her, his eyes grew stale and indifferent. But then he had said that if she would not serve him he must get someone else, and instantly her jealousy stirred at the thought of being supplanted in other ways as well by some woman who was willing. He might get one of those girls from St. Columb's in the first vigour of young womanhood, and who knew whether she might not take her place altogether? And then what would be left for poor Nancy Pentreath but to go back, after this brief flame of fulfilment, to the dreary routine at the farm and the joyless existence of work? All over again would start the succession of drab days, the early rising to light the kitchen fire, the cooking of meals, the sweeping of rooms, right on to the grey end, with perhaps a carnal adventure or two which only made her hungry for more. She had got a man now who had given her an hour of joy, and she had satisfied him well, too; he wanted her again, and he wanted her badly, and she was risking a lot if she let another woman have a chance with him. Very soon no man would desire her at all, not even her tipsy old father-in-law, who called her Jezebel, and yet gave her such a squeeze, and but a few years yet remained in which she could hope to light the spark of longing in a man's eye, and warm herself in its blaze. She mustn't imagine, too, that she was irreplaceable to Mr. Giles:

it had only just "commenced," and what chance would
she have if every day some girl stood white-flowering
before him?   Indeed, she had had wonderful luck
already in taking his fancy, and it would be pure madness not to let him have his way in this.

"I'll chance it," she said to herself with a final look
at her reflection in the glass.   "I'm not so bad, after
all."

The house had long been silent, but at the very
moment that she slipped on her nightgown, she heard a
stealthy step in the passage that betrayed itself by a
creaking board, and then came a tap at her door.   She
went close to it, but did not unlock it.

"Who is it?" she said.

Then came her father-in-law's voice.   "Open the
door, Nancy," he said.   "I want but a word with you."

She hesitated.   His voice sounded quiet and sober
enough, and a fair wonder he was, for an hour ago
he had been as drunk as ever she had seen him, and
now he could walk quietly and steadily and control his
voice.   She put her ulster over her nightdress, and
opened the door a couple of inches.

"What is it, then?" she said.

"I was hard on you to-night, Nancy," he said; "I
called you a lot o' sour names at my praying.   You
don't bear me any ill-will?"

"Sure, is that all?" she said.   "Why, of course I
don't.   You were properly boozed to-night, and didn't
know what you were saying.   Get you to bed, Mr. Pentreath, and sleep it off, and we'll be all cosy and bright
again come morning."

He pushed the door a little wider open with his
shoulder.

" God! Richard was in luck when he set eyes on you, Nancy," he said. " And you're still just as you were when you came back to us before Dennis was born. It's little pleasure that has come your way all these years."

Outside in the passage or on the dark stairs at the end some board creaked again, and he looked round. The light of the oil-lamp from the open door of his room threw an oblong ray of illumination across the passage, and that beam cut off all that the darkness behind it might hold.

" Hush, go to bed," said Nancy. " 'Tis someone moving."

" No one there," he said. " You never gave me a good-night kiss to-night, Nancy. Give me one now to show you forgive me."

Up the stairs came Mrs. Pentreath from the garden. She had heard the sound of voices, and now stood looking through the stair-banisters, ready to pop her head down. Her husband's figure was visible to her half inside Nancy's door.

" There then," she said. " And now go quiet to bed."

" Ah, there's a good girl," he hiccupped. " You're a morsel fit for a king, you are, Nancy. King David, he liked a pretty woman to the end of his days, and mayn't a poor sinner, like old John Pentreath, do the same? "

She giggled, and pushed him from the room, waiting to hear him shuffle away down the passage. Then locking her door again, she got into bed. What a day it had been! First of all there was that hour with Mr. Giles, and now there was her own father-in-law coming tapping at her door at this time of the night, and she his son's widow!   What an old man, to be sure!

"I declare I shall have to lock my door every night," said Nancy delightedly to herself, "if he's beginning to feel like that about me.   Why, I believe he's really gone on me.   And two men after me on one day, and me turned forty!"

CHAPTER III

DENNIS

ONE window in Dennis's room looked eastwards, and he knew very well by the quality of the light that came in there in the morning whether it was time for him to be getting up and going out to his work: it told him, as if he looked on the face of a clock that had only the short pointer, what sort of hour it was. Now the spring days were lengthening, and dawn was coming earlier, and when next morning he drowsily stirred and stretched himself in bed, a glance at the window was enough to show him that he could lie awhile, if he chose, lightly dozing before he need leave his bed. In midwinter, when he had to be at work in cowhouse and stables with a lantern, before the darkness of the night was dispersed, he would drag himself yawning from his blankets, and feel for his clothes with sleep-laden eyes, knowing that for him day had begun, while in midsummer the sun would be hot on his yellow head, and he could still sleep again.

This morning, however, he roused himself before he need, for it was not yet day. The birds in the bushes were chirruping with faint tentative flutings and whistlings, but presently they would cease, to break into fuller song at dawn, when the activity of bird-life began in earnest. But now he did not doze again with the cessation of their tuning-up; instead he pulled himself up in his bed, with hands clasped behind his head, and his chest raised above the clothes. He never slept in any sort of nightdress, but rolled himself tight in his blankets, like a moth full-formed in its cocoon. Sometimes his mother would put a couple of sheets on his bed, and he lay in fine linen much darned, marked with some old Pentreath monogram, and dating from the more opulent days, but oftener there were no sheets, and he lay curled and warm in the good rough wool. In winter it was hard to break that outstretched comfort beneath the blankets which his body had heated and go out into the rain-soaked darkness, but on these mild mornings there was no struggle. To-day life was bubbling within him; it was not enough to lie there in lazy quiescence.

It was the thought of Nell that claimed his vigour, and reaching out a bare arm and turning over in bed, he took a gimlet that he had brought upstairs in his pocket last night, and began boring into the partition wall above his head. This was in execution of a plan that he and Nell had made yesterday, when their singing and whistling had been stopped. Nell was an adept at oversleeping herself in the morning: so deep did she lie in slumber when it was time for her to get up and help Nancy in the kitchen that the noise of his thumping on the wall did not permanently arouse her. She but groaned at the interruption, and as soon as it ceased went to sleep again. So through this hole which Dennis was now boring was to be passed a string, the end of which she faithfully promised to tie to thumb or to wrist before she went to sleep, while the other end of it dangled in his room. Thus, when he got up, he would continue pulling on the string, until, as by the strugglings of a hooked fish, she would show that she was really awake. However fine a sleeper, she would find it impossible to compose herself again when her arm was being drawn and jerked towards the hole. She would tap when she had had enough.

It was not long before the point of the gimlet encountered no further resistance from the thin partition, and after withdrawing it, Dennis put his eye to the hole to see that it was all clear for the passage of the string. The hole was far out of the straight: it inclined steeply downwards, and, putting his eye close to it, Dennis had a glimpse of her lying there in bed, and a loose plait of her black hair on the pillow. The plan had been a mere bit of ingenious foolery, but now there was a sort of spice to it, as he squinted on her and pictured her struggling up, tied to him, to tap the wall. They must begin it to-morrow morning.

The sun rose above the hills across St. Columb's bay as Dennis sponged face and neck, tugged with a comb at his thatch of hair, and got into his farm clothes, corduroy breeches and a dark-blue fisherman's jersey. It was full early yet, and he leant out of his window looking at the brightness of the garden. Not till then had he thought again of that rather strange thing he had seen last night, when the brown owl circled without alarm so close to where his grandmother sat, and now he remembered that as he dropped off to sleep he thought he had heard talking out there, or was it only the dry patter of the magnolia leaves outside his window, stirring in the wind? Certainly the last sound he heard was the low fluting of the owl as it quested over the garden. A pack of rubbish had Nell talked last night when she said that women who in life had been witches took the form of owls when they were dead, and visited the like-minded. Not a word of that did he believe, any more than he believed the yarn of Jonah being three days and nights in the belly of a whale. A rare funny yarn was that, and he had burst out laughing when Parson Allingham had read it aloud at the Sunday school which he used to attend, and had got a clout over the head in consequence that made a singing in his ears for an hour afterwards. Jonah and witches, not a pin to choose between them, he thought.

But below that breezy ridicule, there lurked some consciousness which dwelt in his very blood, that there were hidden powers best to be treated with respect and not provoked. He always had a salutation for that old hag Sally Austell, and he could not help knowing that the folk at St. Columb's were very polite to his grandmother if they met her in the ways; women would stand off the pavement to let her pass without messing her foot in the gutter, while, if they saw her coming some distance off, it was likely that they would nip round the corner till she had passed. Old wives' tales, however, was his general conclusion about Jonah and witches alike, and they concerned a lusty boy very little. Farm work all day, a great appetite for supper, and then perhaps on the long summer evenings a bathe with Willie Polhaven, and a lie-out with him on the beach, just they two alone, with talk or laughter or silence, or they would make a cock-shy of a bottle and see who could smash it first, or take off shoes and coats and wrestle together. The day's work and the dreamless night that followed were enough for him before this new tangle about Nell had started.

Till now the friendship with Willie had been far the strongest emotional tie in Dennis's life, and strange to say, it had sprung out of a quarrel and a fight: the two boys had been just good friends before, even then preferring each other's company to the gatherings of the village on the pier or a shadowy corner with a girl. Then, three years ago now, Dennis's mother had had that affair with the young artist, and there had been a bit of a scandal over it. Dennis had been sitting on the pier one day when his mother passed, and two fellows near him had nudged each other and pointed at her. "There's a whore and no mistake," said one, and the other laughed. Dennis didn't properly know, in the innocence of his sixteen years, just what that meant, but it was something queer, for one of the fellows turned and saw him and gave the other a warning touch. A hot summer evening it was, and presently Willie Polhaven came up, and the two went off for a bathe as appointed. Willie was in a foul temper: his father had beaten him, and he snapped off Dennis's head whatever he said. Presently they sat half-stripped on the beach, with the low sun warm on their shoulders, and says Dennis:

"Willie, what's a whore?"

"Well, you should know that," said Willie. "It's just a dirty woman who makes bed with any man she picks up."

"One of those fellows said my mother was a whore," said Dennis.

"And who's denying it?" said Willie. "Shouldn't wonder if you're a bastard."

That was a more familiar word, and up Dennis jumped. "Come on," he said, "I'll knock that down your throat for you, Willie Polhaven," and he spat in his face.

At that they set to, for there was no other way for it. They were fine strong boys, without an ounce of science between them, Willie more stocky and a bit the heavier, Dennis lighter of build but with longer reach. The sand made a good foothold for their naked feet, and it was grim earnest. Sometimes they came into a clinch with locked arms and panting chests pressed close, but one flung the other off him, and they were at it again, keen as two fighting cocks, seeing red, both of them, with blue eyes and black steadily glaring at each other and arms flying out like piston rods, and teeth clenched. They had some sort of guard for their heads, or were quick enough to duck, but soon Willie got home on Dennis's cheekbone, staggering him for a moment, and his left eye began to swell. Dennis in turn landed a jab on Willie's mouth, and he saw him spit out a broken tooth, and the blood streamed over his chin. Then the oddest thought came into Dennis's mind. " God, how I love that chap," he said to himself. " Let me get another smack in like that, and he won't call me a bastard again." And as if to answer him, Willie's eye lit up with the friendliest gleam, as he gave Dennis a couple over the heart that shook him badly.

They were fairly winded now, the drive of those random blows was losing steam, and Dennis felt his knees growing weak. They were both of them growing a bit wary also, looking for an opportunity to get in some punch that would finish the business. Willie was forcing the other back to where the sand at the edge of the sea was softer and Dennis was aware of that; his feet were slow in this slushy stuff, and he stepped sideways to get on to the firmer sand. Willie thought he saw his chance, and let out with his right, just missing, and before he could recover Dennis had landed him one full on the chin, and over he went with as clean a knockout as anyone could desire. " Got him, by God, with a beauty," shouted Dennis, for there Willie lay, spread like a star-fish, with his bleeding mouth hanging wide, and slack as a bit of chewed string.

As he looked at him, still with that crow of triumph on his lips, all the fight went out of Dennis. Right and proper it was that they should have fought, and Willie had paid for calling him a bastard; and now that was over, and there was Willie, whom he loved better than anyone in the world, laid out flat. But that did not last long: presently his eyes opened, and he stared vaguely about.

" Hullo, Willie," said Dennis. " You've come round? "

" Reckon so. What's happened? "

" Just a knock-out," said Dennis.

" You don't say! And I thought I'd got you." He sat up, and half struggled to his feet. But his joints were slack as a kitten's; and he would have fallen had not Dennis got hold of him round the waist.

" Sling your arm round my neck," he said, " and so we'll get to the head of the beach. There's a pool of fresh water there, and 'twill be useful."

It was a limp process, for Dennis was not in much better case, and Willie was a dragging, shuffling weight on his shoulders, but soon they got to the shingle-bank above which lay a pool of fresh water from the spring in the cliff above. Puffy of face were they both, Dennis's cheek had swelled up so that his eye was but a slit between it and his eyebrow, and there was a bit of a lump coming on his forehead, and the bruise-flowers of Willie's knuckles on his chest were beginning to open. Willie had an upper lip already as big as a thrush's egg, and his teeth had cut it deep within, but the last punch of Dennis's that knocked him out had not revealed itself, and he was the less marked of the two. Presently he sat up from his bathings of his

5

mouth, and for the first time had a good view of Dennis's bunged-up eye.

" God, I got you fair there, Dennis," he said.

" That you did, but you was nearer finishing me here," and he pointed to his chest.

" Aye, I remember that, and then you had me clean and square."

Dennis's only available eye sparkled.

" And I liked you terrible, Willie, when I smashed you," he said.

" Same here. Lord, two bashings in one day, and I feel fine in my innards."

They had their postponed bathe, but that was no prosperous affair, for the salt water smarted sore on cuts and bruises, and then they lay out on the sand till the sun dipped behind the hills, almost shy of each other, as if their fight had made lovers of them. Then it was time for Dennis to get home for supper, and more than time, for it was half over, and his grandfather in the quarrelsome stage of his evening's tippling.

" Late again," he said as Dennis entered, " and I warned you, so you'll go supperless. Why, your eye's bunged up. What have you been up to? "

" Fighting," said Dennis.

" Who with? And did you smash him? "

" Yes, knocked him out," said Dennis. " 'Twas Willie Polhaven."

John Pentreath's grim face relaxed.

" Well done, by God," he cried. " Get him a bit o' raw meat for his eye, Nancy, and a good plateful for his stomach. That'll show them the Pentreaths aren't done for yet."

So out of that fight had come one of those strong boyish friendships, utterly void of sentimentality, but of the quality of passion. It was in vain that the girls made eyes at the two handsome young fellows, who had no more than a smile and a shrug for them, and they wandered off out of the lights and the jabberings for a contented solitude of their own. There were half a dozen Willies in the village, but Polhaven got to be known as Dennis's Willie, and the folk looked with kindly eyes on this male attachment, for it was no rare thing that two boys or two young fishermen out at sea from dusk to dawn at the night-fishing should pair off together like this, independent for awhile of female attractions. For a year or two they would be allied, and then the natural call of sex would come to one or the other, and the idyll would be over. That had come to Dennis now, just like a change of wind, and soon, no doubt, Willie would get a girl, too.

Dennis put on his thick farm-boots, which he had cleaned the evening before (the cleaning consisted of scraping off the heavier lumps of mud with an old dinner-knife) and clumped down the passage. He was up first this morning, for there was no one stirring in the house, and all the doors of the bedrooms were still shut. Nell should have been up by now, or his mother, to get the kettle boiling and give him a cup of tea and a hunk of bread and cold bacon to take out with him to last him till the one o'clock dinner, for he would have been six hours at work by then. But this morning he had to kindle the fire himself, stuffing it with paper and sticks and a sprinkle of small lumps of coal on the top, for he had no intention of going out till he had got something inside him. There were his grandfather's big Bible and empty glass and nearly empty whisky-bottle still on the table, and on the ragged floor-rug below it, beside his arm-chair, lay his pipe. This rug was covered with numerous burnt holes, where he had knocked out the smouldering end of his tobacco. Some day, as Mrs. Pentreath told him when the singe-ing smell was strong after supper, he would spill a drop of whisky there too and be burned to death as he slept and snored in his chair.

The windows of the kitchen had been shut all night, and it reeked of stuffiness and stale smoke, and while the fire was taking hold, Dennis threw doors and win-dows wide to let the fresh air sweeten it. A grim and cruel old blackguard was his grandfather: how Dennis had feared and hated him when he was smaller, with his heavy hand and the dogwhip that hung by the kitchen-door. But physically he feared him no longer now, only the hate remained, and it would be a fine day when John Pentreath lay white and still in his coffin, and the lid was put on him: the sooner that day came the better, else surely more acres of the farm would go hissing down his throat. He himself would be marrying Nell before long, if she had a mind for him, whether the old folk dropped off or lingered like rotting pears on the tree, and when they were shovelled into the earth, there would be rare good times at the farm. His mother should live with them if she liked, for both Nell and he were fond of the foolish, good-natured woman, with her ribands and her tawdry finery, and her warm heart and her eye ever roaming round to see if a man wasn't looking at her. It was not unlikely, he thought, that the fellow on the pier, one summer night three years ago, had been pretty right in what he said of her, and these last few weeks she had been down to St. Columb's a sight of afternoons with her Sunday hat on bobbing with cherries, so maybe

she had gotten another man. Though he despised her
for her gadding, chattering ways, and knew that she
came of common stock compared to the Pentreaths,
he had affectionate feelings for her, and he cared little
for her way of life: it was her business, not his. But
it was a different matter if another fellow called her so,
and then there would be a couple of fists at his service,
and a swinging kick on the bottom when he had had
enough.

Dennis scratched together a breakfast for himself,
beating up one of the Sunday eggs into a cup of tea,
as the milk had turned, and then he went across the
farmyard to the stable. He had to put the heavy
harrow over the field which he and another farm-hand
had ploughed a couple of days before, where stood
the circle of stones, to break up the big clods left by
the plough, before putting in the grain. The harrow
was already there, and he put the gear on the two
horses and he called "Kep-kep" to them and they
followed him across the farmyard to the gate that led
through the pasture to the arable land. The kitchen
windows which he had left open were closed again,
and he saw his grandmother inside, who nodded and
smiled to him, and he wondered what had put her in
so cordial a temper. He grinned to himself as he
thought it was her conversation, maybe, with the old
brown owl last night. A rare pack of nonsense was that,
and yet Nell had been as grave as a judge about it.

The sun had not yet risen long enough to have dried
up the heavy night dews, and when Dennis came to the
field to be harrowed, the furrows lay richly red and
shining with moisture under a net of gossamer webs:
it was as if some pearly silk coverlet were spread over
them. The morning was quite windless, and there hung

in the air the odour of damp earth. This early hour was still chilly enough to condense the breath of the horses, and soon the steam rose from their backs and shining flanks, for this harrow was a ponderous machine with its curved iron tines biting deep into the heavy soil, and there was mingled with the smell of wet earth the sharp horse-odour. Dennis walked by the side of the beasts, with a rein in his hand and a backward eye to see that the harrow kept a straight course, for the cross-grained bitch liked to go askew if she wasn't watched, and close behind it there hopped a robin, the bold thing, with beady eye alert for a breakfast from the broken clods. Primroses were a-bloom in the banks and wild violets, and at the far corner, where he must turn his harrow, was a gorse bush in full flower, and now the sun was warm enough to spread the honey-sweetness of it on the air. Somewhere behind it, in the crevices of the shaly wall, a pair of oxeyes were building; Dennis had seen the smart little birds popping in and out as he came up from St. Columb's yesterday, and now, while he gave his horses a breathing-space, he looked about for the nest, and saw the head of the hen-bird as she sat on her eggs. Not an atom frightened was she, but just scolded at him to scare him away. That set Dennis smiling: there was a rare bowldacious bit !

At this end of the field the ground began to decline sharply to the village, over the roofs of which, unseen below the hill, hung the smoke of early fires undispersed in the still air. Penzance lay sunning itself on the shore of the gleaming bay beyond, and a feather of steam shot up from the engine of a train that was crawling into the station: that would be the night train from London. Then the feather vanished, and soon there came to his ears the sound of the whistle that had caused it. Never yet, except when he came from London in his mother's womb, had Dennis been in a train: they said that one of those puffing, snorting engines could pull a load of folk along at the rate of a mile in a minute. Old wives' tales were such talk as that: 'twas a wonder that a man should not be ashamed to repeat them.

As the harrow moved up and down the field it got nearer to the unploughed circle of stones that stood there and to the short grass path that led to it from the gate in the hedge. To plough close up to it was a tiresome business; and now there was continual turning of the harrow to be made on these curved lines, and he and the horses alike were in a muck of sweat before the angle was finished. He took a bit of a rest when this was done, munching his bread and bacon, wondering when the time would come for him and Nell to dance on Midsummer Eve in the circle. Anyhow, this year they would leap the bonfire that was lit that night in the field beyond, for those who leaped the fire together would surely be wed before the year was out, and it was only after marriage that they danced in the ring of stones. . . . It would be a fine day when he and Nell danced together, for that caused a woman's womb to be fruitful, even if she had long been childless. Often and often to Dennis's knowledge had that spell proved its potency: it was no use, though you laughed at poor old Jonah spewed up by his whale and that owl-nonsense of Nell's, to mock at the bonfire on St. John's Eve and what it could work for a boy and girl who leapt it, and what the dancing in the circle could do for them afterwards.

He finished his bacon, but there were still some crusts of bread, and these he gave to his horses, the

soft-muzzled giants, and listened to the chumping
rumble of their broad grinders. And then he saw
something that made him stare, for perched on one of
those tall erect stones at the eastern end of the circle
he spied a magnolia blossom with a sprig of wallflower
tied to it. Who should have put that nosegay there
and for why, he wondered? He plucked it from its
place and examined it. The dew was on the flowers, so
they must have been placed here last evening or during
the night. They were stuck in a twig of elder, out
of which the pith had been scooped, and the whole
was loosely bound together by a scarlet woollen thread.
As he handled this odd contraption, the leather-like
petals of the magnolia fell off, and the elder-twig slipped
from his hand. The damaged remains of the nosegay
he put back on the stone where he had found it, and
thought no more of it.

By now the sun was high and hot, and, as Dennis
continued his harrowing, the spell of the spring, of
the everlasting fertility of the earth, bubbled and
seethed about him, while he and his horses and his harrow
were helping it to fulfil itself, for the harrow was
penetrating the womb of the shining soil, making it
ready for the seed. Even as he who treads the vintage
in autumn is enveloped in the vapour of the sun-ripe
grapes, so now, when all the potency of renewed life
surged round the boy, there grew an intoxication in
his blood which made the fertile strength of his young
manhood stir in him. That clean and lusty tide was
on the flow all round him, the gorse was a-flower, and
the brave little oxeyes were nesting, young colts were
scampering round the field beyond, a wind-hover was
poised high above his head, and the sea was a-glitter
between the blossoming branches of the blackthorn.

He could not have given any sort of definition to his thoughts, far less have put them into words, but as he went sweating and striding up and down the field with the robin scouting behind the harrow, he became just an opened sluice, through which the stream of life poured foaming. His legs and arms, his dripping chest and back and smooth strong neck were tugging at him with their appropriate virile desires: they wanted to run and to fight, to cling close, to wrestle and to love. Meantime, his conscious self was directing their immediate offices. His eye was alert on the straightness of his course, and his arm to haul on the harrow when it went awry, and his hand was on the rein; and his lungs drew in the warm air and his pursed lips whistled the tune that had weaned him and Nell from their Bibles yesterday afternoon, and made a brightness in the kitchen which later in the evening his grandfather had blackened again with his prayers and his cursings and his whisky. Some night soon he must go out for one of those solitary runnings in the dark, the need for which came over him irresistibly now and again in the springtime: he had not told even his Willie of them, though there was little else of his that was not Willie's. Childish nonsense it was, but it was of the stuff of his heart, and it would never do for Willie to laugh at it, or indeed to want to share in it.

It was like entering some airless vault to go back out of the spring noon-day into the kitchen. Nell was in charge of the cooking to-day, and the cabbage she was boiling made a mucky smell, though the stew of meat promised agreeably. His mother, with her hair still in curl-papers and her print dress hitched up, had not yet finished cleaning the room, and the beams of the

sun blazing in from the window to the south were
thick and dusty with the work of her broom. Mollie
Pentreath was in her usual place alongside the oven,
her hands occupied with her knitting, but her eyes
busy with all that went on round her: she sat with her
head bent forward and looked upwards from under her
black eyebrows this way and that. She had smiled and
nodded to him this morning as he went out to his work,
and that rare good-humour must have lasted with her,
for instead of silently observing him, she again had a
smile and a word for him.

" We're all a bit late this morning," she said. " Ready
for your dinner, dear? "

" That I am, Grannie. Powerful hungry."

" And where have you been working? " said she.

" Putting the harrow over the plough beyond the
garden. Heavy going it was, and there's a good bit
more to do."

Mrs. Pentreath's needles clicked together for a minute
before she answered.

" Ah, where the circle is," she said. " You don't
meddle with that? "

Instantly Dennis connected the magnolia flower and
the elder-stick with his grandmother.

" Lord, no, Grannie! " he said. " That's never
ploughed, as you know."

Mrs. Pentreath gave him a sharp glance, and Dennis
moved away to get a breath of fresh air by the open
door, on the threshold of which was his mother shaking
out into the yard the rug on which John Pentreath's
pipe-ash had fallen last night. He had but exchanged
a glance with Nell, who, flushed and heated, was doing
the cooking to-day and busy with the dishing-up of
the stew. He must remember, when dinner was over,

to see to the fixing up of the string between her room and his, and then she would be tied to him all night, with one end of it noosed round her wrist, and the other round his. . . .

" And just shette that door, Dennis," added Mrs. Pentreath, " 'tis a plaguy draught it makes."

Dennis pulled the door to and stood with his mother outside.

" Something's happened to please your grandmother this morning," she said. " Quite affable she's been, you may say, and offered to lay the table for dinner herself."

" And what may it 'a been that's pleasured her? " asked Dennis.

" Just some notion that's come to her what tickles her fancy," said she, beating the rug with her broom handle. " She don't let on about that, though I daresay we'll know when she gets it complete. She's been knitting and smiling to herself, Nell says, since she came downstairs, with a bit of a laugh sometimes all to herself about what's in her head."

There was something about his mother, too, thought Dennis, that betokened a happy mind, and in spite of the screws of curling-papers over her forehead, and her slovenly attire, she looked gay and handsome beyond her wont.

" And you look fine and content yourself, Mother," he said. " Something gone right in your inside, too? You're all of a bloom this morning."

Nancy always found any tribute to her looks acceptable, and reached up to pat Dennis's cheek.

" Well, where's the good of 'aving the 'ump? " she said, reverting to the Cockney talk which twenty years of the soft Cornish speech had not purged from her.

" Sit up and be cheerful, I say, and encourage a good time to come along for you. I declare if I didn't make a bit of brightness for myself, there's little I should pick up from others. There, I must go and have a clean before dinner, for I was late this morning. Took an extra snooze, I did, after last night. Lor', your grandfather was properly boozed. I call it a disgrace."

To hear Nancy criticising the manners and customs of the Pentreaths, however justly, made Dennis range himself with them.

" So that's the way of it, is it? " he said. " But I reckon he's a right to do as he wills in his own house. Who be you to say him nay? "

" Well indeed! " said Nancy, still in high good-humour. " Aren't you getting a bit big for your boots, Dennis, and I'm sure they're big enough, talking to your mother like that? But there it is: we all take our pleasures our own way, and I'm sure your grandfather holds his drink something wonderful. And I'm looking forward, ever so, to a nice hour's reading after me and Nell's cleared up after dinner. It's a beautiful story, as I got from the lending library in Penzance: all about a pore girl, such a lady, too, married to an earl. What a time he gave her to be sure; earls must be a wicked lot. Crowned heads, I say, but cold hearts."

Dennis followed his mother back into the kitchen, not quite believing that it was an interest in the poor young lady's tribulations that accounted for her gusto, and Nancy went upstairs to tidy herself up. Dinner was ready now, and just as the big clock in the corner of the kitchen pointed to the hour, his grandfather came in from the yard, and they sat down to the solid, silent business of dinner. Nothing that he had drunk the night before made much difference to his appetite next day, and his piled plate of boiled cabbage and stewed meat had half vanished before Nancy came down ever so elegant with her curled fringe and a clean print dress. He spat out on to his plate a mouthful that was not to his liking, and then came a slog of cheese with a relish of radishes, and he went to his armchair with his pipe and his glass of whisky.

" How's the lambing, Dennis? " he asked.

" Not been down there. I've been harrowing all morning," said Dennis, with his mouth full.

" Off with you, then," said his grandfather. " You've stuffed yourself enough."

Dennis glanced at the clock: he wasn't going to be put upon like this. " Not for a while yet, Grandfather," he said. " I'll take my dinner-hour like anyone else, and 'tis long short of that."

Mrs. Pentreath had removed her upper row of teeth while she ate, and had laid them by her plate, for they got muddled up with her food and were a hindrance. But she had finished now and replaced them, and she smiled and nodded to Dennis.

" Are you going to do as I tell you, you lout? " roared John.

" Not till I've had my hour off," said Dennis, " and more'n the half of it's to come yet. Then I'll go after the lambs, if you bid me, but there's a good stretch yet of the harrowing to be put over. P'r'aps you'll be seeing to that."

The injudicious Nancy again put in her word, siding with her father-in-law, for he had apologised for his rudeness at prayers last night, and asked for a kiss, and then gone quietly to bed: that was how a gentleman should behave.

" Lor', Dennis," she said. " What a way to speak to
Mr. Pentreath! "

Instantly the whole lot of them turned on her. What
the hell had she got to do with it?

" Just hold your mouth, Mother," said Dennis.

" Yes, 'tis a good thing to mind your own business,
Nancy," said Mrs. Pentreath, speaking for the first
time since dinner began.

" God! and thank you kindly for your good word,"
said John Pentreath. " Here's a proud day for me! "

" Well, I'm sure," said Nancy, putting her little
finger separate from the others in a very polite manner,
as she buttered her bread. No radish for her: radishes
got into your breath almost as bad as an onion.

Silence: and Dennis caught Nell's eye in a momentary
glance. It met his with a tribute of encouragement and
admiration. Time and again of late he had showed his
grandfather that he wasn't to be put upon, and Nell approved; so, like some stiff young turkey-cock, he was
" strutting " before the girl, and she was pleased with his
taut feathers. Indeed, it was a disappointment when his
grandfather did not turn on him again, and provoke a
further display. He just growled to himself, filled his
glass again, and stuffed the burning tobacco closer in
his pipe without more speech. Presently, without looking at Dennis, he stalked off into the garden.

Mrs. Pentreath nodded to the boy.

" You were in the right of it there," she said, " and
'tis proper you should stick up for yourself. But you
bear in mind, too, that he'll be adding it all up against
you."

" Well, I thought you spoke very rude to your grandfather," said Nancy, " whatever others may say."

" And who'll be caring one damn for what you

think?" said Mrs. Pentreath shrilly. "A popinjay like you to be judging between Pentreaths!"

Dennis would not have been loth to go back to his harrowing at once, rather than sit for another half-hour in the kitchen, but he was determined not to do that till his full hour of leisure, and maybe a bit more, was over. He helped the two younger women to clear away, and sat and whistled in the window seat overlooking the garden, so that his grandfather might know he had not yet gone back to work, while Mrs. Pentreath drew her chair closer yet to the oven, and Nell went off to finish with the Monday morning's washing, and Nancy to her bedroom to fetch her book for an hour's reading about earls, till it was time to go down to St. Columb's, and tell Mr. Giles that she would serve him for a model. Pleased he would be to hear that, and Nancy wondered what sort of a pose he would give her. Something to show off the best of her, she hoped.

The clock whirred in its works and was silent again, for the striking gear had long been out of order, and soon Dennis went out into the garden where his grandfather was snoozing in the sun.

" Shall I be going after the lambs," he asked, " or get finished with the harrowing?"

John Pentreath yawned and stretched himself. A rare afternoon it was for February, the sun warmed up his marrow, and he would sit and browse here a bit longer.

" Get finished with that," he said, " to be ready for the sowing, and then we'll go down to the pastures."

" Right. 'Twill be a couple of hours more."

Dennis went back to his work in high good-humour. He had stood up to his grandfather as a man should,

and had had his way: what was more, he had done it
in front of Nell. But where was the use of the sodden
old fellow in the world on a clean spring day? He'd
be better employed in making the grass grow on his
grave.

The house was empty and quiet when he returned,
and after stabling his horses he went to look for his
grandfather. But he was nowhere about, and it was
likely he had gone down to the pasture where the lambing ewes were. As he set out to join him, he caught
sight of Nell hanging up the wash on the poles by the
kitchen garden, and went across for a word with
her.

"And where's all?" he asked. "Are you alone
about the house, Nell?"

"Mr. Pentreath's gone down to the sheep pasture,"
she said. "He bade me tell you follow him."

"And Granny?" he said.

Nell nodded in the direction of the path down to St.
Columb's. She could not answer for the moment, for
she had taken a clothes-peg in her mouth, while she
stretched out an arm of Dennis's blue jersey, to pin it
to the line; the movement caused her dress to lie taut
over her bosom. Then with her peg she clipped the
sleeve in place.

"Aunt Mollie set off but five minutes ago down the
path, with a posy of wallflowers," she said, "and your
mother's been gone to St. Columb's this last hour. She
had a read in her book after dinner, and fair burst out
crying. 'Tis a queer thing to read a book for the
pleasure o' blubbing over it."

Dennis wanted to see her again with arms stretched
out, and head thrown back.

"That'll be grandfather's Sunday shirt," he said.

" Hold the wrist-bands to the line, and I'll clip the pegs for you."

" You for a laundry maid! " said Nell. " You'd better be gwain after your grandfather."

" I'd sooner have a chat with you. Nell, I bored a hole through the wall betwixt our rooms, and we'll rig the string through it come night. You play fair, mind; you've got to tie it round something of you."

She laughed.

" Well, of all the babbies! " she said with a swift quiver of a glance.

" And you've got to be another. God! how the spring took hold on me to-day! I shall go for a running some night soon."

" What's that? " she asked. " Something atween you and your Willie? "

" No, Willie knows naught of it."

" Tell me," she said.

Dennis hesitated: none knew of his runnings, but maybe Nell would understand.

" Don't you go mocking of me then," he said. " 'Tis a fit that takes once and again in the springtime, and I must go out and tramp and run along in the dark night."

Her glance brightened on him.

" Oh, Dennis, should I mock you, indeed! " she said. " Don't I know what would be just the feel of it. A hot spring night and dark, and you alone with it. Cloudy, would it be, with spits of rain showers to make the earth smell good. Shouldn't I love it! "

" Come then," said he. " I'll pull on the string some night when it's hot and dark, and we'll go together. Do'ee."

She laughed again.

6

" You're just a creature from the woods," she said,
" and how could I keep up with your going, me in skirt
and all and a girl? "

" But we'd go steady and slow, Nell," he said.
" Some night, to be sure, you'll come with me."

" That I will not. What sort of a name should I get
for myself if I ran by night with Dennis Pentreath?
Besides, I should want no one with me, not you nor
another, if the spring drove me out of doors of a night.
There should be a wind and gusts of rain, and the earth
drinking deep of it, and not a soul abroad but me."

" Eh, you understand it, Nell," said he. " That's one
sort of night, but there's another sort when it's moonshine and stillness. 'Tis then you want someone with
you who'll understand."

They stood close to each other now, with the magic
of youth flashing forth and back between their eager
eyes, and desire grew. Then Nell's gaze faltered before
the battery of his, and she turned to her clothes-basket.

" I must get through with these," she said, " or the
dew'll be falling before they're dry, and your grandfather's gone to the lambing this half-hour. Go you
after him, and don't rile him too sore, for he's a crafty
one."

Dennis sniffed the air.

" Lord, there was a stink in the kitchen at dinner
to-day," he said. " Whisky and grandfather's foul
pipe. I'd sooner take my grub in the trees like a
squirrel."

" And have three or four nuts for your dinner in
place of the good stew I made you," said she.

" Oh, I've got naught against the stew," said Dennis.
" And you'd put a sprig of burgmott in it, which made
it tasty. 'Twas that which made Grandfather spit in

his plate, for he can't abide it."

" It's hard to please all," said Nell.

Off went Dennis, and when he came to the gate
between field and garden he put his hand on the top
and vaulted over it. That was a bit of showing-off
before Nell, and to make it the more effective he never
glanced back to see if she was looking after him; it was
just his habit to vault over a five-barred gate to save
the trouble of opening it. In front of him now on the
left was the field which he had harrowed to-day, and
approaching it he crouched down behind the bush of
blackthorn, and peered through the branches, for there
in the circle was standing a woman, whom now he saw
to be his grandmother. She was by the tall stone where
he had found that strange nosegay this morning, and
her hands were busy with something. Whatever it was,
it did not long detain her, and in a minute she walked
off down the path to St. Columb's, and disappeared
below the brow of the hill.

Curiosity was too strong for the boy, and he ran
across the plough to see what she had been after. There
was another bunch of flowers now on the stone, freshly
gathered, tied to an elder-twig.

" Well, there's a strange bit of work," thought
Dennis. " Whatever'll she be after now? . . ." Then
he trotted off to the field on the other side of the path,
where the ewes were lambing.

CHAPTER IV

WEAVING THREADS

Throughout the week early hours were kept of a night at the farm, and it was only on Sunday that John Pentreath's prayers made a longer evening. The time for supper varied: it would be at eight or after in the summer when the days were at full stretch, and as early as six in the winter. Just now in March they supped about seven, and John Pentreath, the last to return, would generally have drunk his fill by ten, and reeled upstairs.

As the lambing progressed, the old man struck a streak of rare good humour, and there was no wonder at that, for nigh on half the ewes had dropped a double, and with the exception of one weakling, which now lay beside the kitchen fire in a box of hay, with long slack legs extended, they were all sturdy little beggars and doing well. This warm still weather, too, was ideal for the hazards of their first days of life. His supper was pleasant to John Pentreath, and his drink extra welcome, and Dennis's late revolt from authority seemed to have gone clean out of his mind. To-night he had told the boy he was a good worker, and had offered him a glass of whisky.

" Time you began to take your liquor, lad," he said. " No Pentreath I ever heard of didn't thrive on it."

" I'd sooner not, Grandfather," he said. " But I'll have another glass of milk."

" God! beeant the boy weaned yet? " asked John.

84

" Pass me my bottle back again."

Mrs. Pentreath had eaten her supper, a mouthful or two and no more, without word of speech. Now she picked up her knitting again from her lap.

" Dennis is in the right there," she said. " There's enough drunk here without his meddling with it."

She looked up at him under those black brows, and Dennis thought he knew just what was coming.

" He can learn something, though, about meddling with other things that aren't his concern," she said. " There's no such ill-luck as what comes to those who put their fingers in other pies."

John Pentreath laughed.

" What's the boy been meddling in then? " he asked. " He's got a couple of rows of teeth in his head, hasn't he? Not been trying on your mouth jewellery, Mollie? And doesn't his hair curl natural, or has he been pinchin' his mother's curling tongs and a bit of rouge to give him a colour? "

Nancy tittered.

" Lor'! Get along with you, Mr. Pentreath," she said. " You're in rare good spirits to-night. Curling tongs, indeed! I never used such a thing: just a screw of paper."

Mrs. Pentreath pushed her chair back nearer the open door of the range, and bending down stroked the lamb for a couple of minutes along back and stomach this way and that with gentle pressure, and then put the feeding bottle, which it had refused before, between its lips. But now the little beggar sucked greedily at it, and wanted more when it was empty.

" Dennis knows what I mean," she said, " and if he's got a spunk of sense in his head he'll hold his tongue and not be nosy and meddlesome again. There! I've run

my hand over the lamb, and 'twill do well now, for it
needed but a touch.   Take it back to the field, Nell:
it'll be keen for the teat now."

Nell looked inquiringly at John Pentreath for his
assent.   The lamb had got on its legs with little treble
bleatings and tail-twitchings.

"What's the girl staring at me for?" said John.   "If
your aunt says that's the way of it, what more do you
want?   Eh, Mollie, it's a magic touch you've got.   I
reckon God Almighty couldn't have done it quicker."

"And I reckon God Almighty 'ud have let it die
before morning instead," remarked Mrs. Pentreath.
"Off to the meadow with it, Nell, and see it finds its
dam.   The moon's up: you won't need a lantern."

While Nell was gone Dennis and Nancy cleared the
table and washed up.   Mrs. Pentreath turned many
furtive observant glances at her as she went to and
fro, humming some gay tune of the London streets
twenty years ago.   She had on a shabby bodice and her
old cotton skirt with a dirty hem, but she also had on
a pair of smart buttoned walking shoes, and below the
skirt were a pair of openwork stockings, such as she
only wore on a Sunday.   Her hands, too, were unusually
clean, with nails shining and polished, and there was a
touch of rouge on her face.   What could be the purpose of these embellishments?   Surely not just to read
her crazy book for an hour, and then go to bed?

Nancy finished her washing-up, glanced at the clock,
and sat down in the rocking chair with her book.   But
her eyes kept wandering to the clock, and presently
she gave a great yawn and got up.

"Pardon for such a gape," she said politely, "but
I'm a rare sleepy-head to-night.   I reckon I'll be off
to bed, and pray don't come clumping down the pas-

sage in your great boots, Dennis, waking me up just as I'm dropping off. Why, my eyes are that heavy I can scarce keep them open, try as I will. Good night all and pleasant dreams."

Clip-clop she went to the door in her smart shoes, and they heard her cross the flagged hall and so upstairs. Then from the chair by the fire where Mrs. Pentreath sat came the very echo of Nancy's singing voice and clipped speech.

" I can scarce keep them open," it said, " try as I will. Good night all and pleasant dreams."

Dennis looked round, thinking his mother must have come back. Then he realised that it was Mrs. Pentreath who spoke, and gave a great guffaw of laughter.

" Eh, Grannie, you hit her off fine," he said. " I'd 'a sworn 'twas Mother speaking."

" 'Iss sure, and I did, too," said John, getting up and tapping the tall barometer that hung by the window.

" Steady and fair," he said, " though I trust you, Mollie, more nor all the instruments that were ever made. I was wrong when I thought I smelled the rain in the air this afternoon."

Mrs. Pentreath went to the door into the farmyard, and looked out, sniffing the warm dusk.

" Never a drop of rain did you smell, John," she said, as she closed it again. " More like 'twas a drop of Highland dew in your nostril."

Silence descended again, broken only by Nell's entrance with the news that the lamb had found its mother and was at the teat. Dennis was more alert now that she had come back: an occasional glance or a word or two passed between them as the girl sat darning a pair of his socks. John Pentreath refilled his pipe and glass; his pipe dropped from his mouth as his head nodded, and he refreshed himself with a swig at his glass. But Mollie sat bright-eyed and wide-awake, busy at her knitting, and looking into the door of the range, where the embers were beginning to burn low. She smiled to herself sometimes, or she sat frowning, as if puzzling something out. Then when the clock whirred for the hour of nine she got up.

" I'll be off to bed, too," she said, " for I'm as sleepy as Nancy to-night. Don't be setting alight to yourself, John."

She lit a small oil-lamp and carrying it upstairs with her, went along the passage past her own room, and paused opposite Nancy's. She tapped softly at the door and then louder, but there came no response, and (just in case Nancy was asleep there) she turned the handle noiselessly and entered. There was one cause for her smiling to herself this evening, for, as she had suspected, the room was empty. On a chair lay Nancy's shabby skirt and bodice, and a candle on the dressing-table was still soft from recent burning. Then looking into the wardrobe she saw that Nancy's Sunday frock and the hat with the cherries on it were missing. The window was shut, the blind down, and the room smelled of her favourite musk.

Mrs. Pentreath did not linger here, for her lamp was burning smokily, and perhaps Nancy on her return might catch the whiff of it, and suspect that her room had been entered in her absence. Like most suspicious people, she thought others as wary as herself, and Nancy must not know that she had been here. She tiptoed back along the passage to her own room, quenched her lamp, and set the door an inch ajar so that she could hear any sound of movement in the house. Then, as if drawing out of a box in the dark the thoughts that had been occupying her, she began fitting them together, hardly yet knowing herself what lurked there.

The two first fitted flush and square. Nancy had feigned a powerful sleepiness, and on the plea of seeking her bed had gone out on a quest of her own, which called for the top of all her finery and for rouge and polished nails. Mrs. Pentreath had no doubt as to what kind of errand this might be: had she gone out for a casual airing or for a chat with some woman in the village, she would surely have said so, instead of feigning this eager drowsiness, and, above all, she would not have dreamed of bedizening herself for such a purpose. Of course she was gone to see a man. Well, there it was, and after all, Nancy was a handsome, good-natured sort of slut with a taking sort of way. Mrs. Pentreath had not a particle of moral objection to her having her pleasure, and something might come of it for herself, if she thought it all out.

Her mind diverted itself to a side-track. Nancy had managed her exit very cleverly, for she had certainly not gone out by the kitchen door, nor yet by the door into the garden, for Mrs. Pentreath, passing it on her way upstairs, had seen that it was locked and bolted from the inside. She must therefore have gone out by the door in the studio of the flat that was let to lodgers, for there was no other exit. To make sure of this she lit her oil-lamp again and went along the passage to the supplementary staircase that led down to the studio. As she had expected, the door into the garden was unlocked, and she left it like that, for she wanted to put no hindrance in the way of Nancy's excursions. Back she went to her room and resumed her watching.

There was a stir from below, and the shutting of

the door from the kitchen that led into the hall: there
was whispered talk, and the tread of feet on the stairs.
That would be Nell and Dennis going up to bed: the
boy had remembered to take his boots off, according
to his mother's request (there was a pretty piece of
cunning for you!), and only a creaking board and a
quiet word or two betrayed their going along the passage past Nancy's room. Then came the sound of the
discreet shutting of their doors, and now John alone
was in the kitchen. She drew out another piece of her
thoughts which must fit in here. John might be coming
up soon, and there was something that must be done
before that. She tiptoed from her room, and withdrawing the key from the inside of Nancy's door, she
locked it on the outside. By and by she would replace
it, but not just yet. Should Nancy return now, and
find her door locked against her, there would be a to-do,
but that was not likely. A woman didn't get herself
up in her Sunday togs to return as soon as that. John
would surely come up long before she was back. Ten
o'clock, when supper was at seven, was enough to make
him ripe for his bed. For a week or two now she had
been marking him, and keen thoughts about Nancy had
often been in his head: he looked at her as a man looks
when desire lights his eyes. On that Sunday night when
he was so far gone, he had fair hugged her on his tipsy
journey upstairs, and had shuffled to her room to get
a good-night kiss. Perhaps he would be after another
kiss to-night, and it would upset everything if he
tapped, and getting no reply, tried the handle of her
door and found her room empty. He must reckon that
Nancy was asleep within.

    Mollie had not long to wait, for presently the kitchen
door opened and shut, and his slippered feet shuffled

on the stairs and the banisters creaked to his weight.
Cautious and careful of step he was to-night; there
was no blundering at that awkward corner on the stairs,
and she would scarce have known he had passed her
door but for the shifting of that thin line of light from
his candle, through the chink where she had set it ajar.
When he had gone by, she opened it a little wider, and
saw that he had passed his room as well as her own,
and had paused opposite Nancy's. He tapped at it,
and tried the handle, but found it locked. He called
to her in a thick whisper once or twice, and then, muttering to himself, returned to his own room and banged
the door. Nancy was with her man by now, thought
Mollie, and she herself was the only clean one among
the three of them, for one was gone a-whoring down
to St. Columb's, John was lusting after his son's widow,
while her own desire was for her husband, just as the
law of man and of John's Sunday-book ordained. And
she would get him yet, when she'd thought things out
a bit more.

There was a door between her room and his, never
bolted nor locked on her side, but it was years now since
he had come through it to her. To-night she had no
hunger for him, for her thoughts were busy thinking
out how she would entrap him into the ardent approach
which made fruitfulness. A deal of thinking out it
would require to attain this godly end, but a clue was
in her hand now, and she would follow it, ever so
patient. . . . Then through the door she heard her
husband snoring, and once more she went back, on
tiptoe, to Nancy's room, unlocked it and left the key
on the inside. The woman had been gone a full hour
and a half, for Mollie could hear the kitchen clock
whirring again for eleven o'clock, and she could come

now when she pleased, and find her room just as she had left it.

When Mrs. Pentreath came down next morning there was an uncommon air of brightness and comfort in the kitchen. The housework of dusting and cleaning was over, the oven was hot, the kettle was boiling, and a rasher of bacon frying, and there was Nancy arranging a bunch of dewy flowers for the table: as she bestowed them in their mugs she was humming that favourite old music-hall song of hers which she had heard twenty years ago. Young and buxom and gay she looked, as if the world were treating her handsomely.

" And good morning to you, Mrs. Pentreath," she said with voluble cordiality. " I was down bright and early after my long night. I've given Dennis his breakfast, and he's gone to work this half-hour ago. There's a rasher just ready for you, if you'd fancy it, for scarce a bite of supper did you take last night, and these spring days, they say, always make a call on a body's strength."

Mrs. Pentreath expanded to these genialities. She had followed the clue a little further now, and winding was the path it traced for her.

" Well, I could relish a bit of bacon," she said. " And thank you kindly, Nancy: you're a good girl to me."

" Girl, indeed! " cried Nancy, feeling like one, " and me turned forty. You're making fun of me, Mrs. Pentreath."

" Not I, indeed! And John's of the same mind as me. Why, 'twas only last night, after you'd gone up to bed, that he was saying that you'd not aged a day since you came here twenty years ago, before ever that big Dennis came forth from you. John thinks a deal of you, Nancy, and I was wanting to have a word with you about that when we were alone together, if you'd excuse me."

"Why, I'm sure there's no call for you to excuse yourself, Mrs. Pentreath," she said. . . . Had the poor old woman only just discovered that?

"Well, I'll make so bold then. When John's got a drop or two inside of him, his eye keeps playing on you like a beam of fire, and it's right you should be warned. Why, last night, would you believe it, when he went to bed, I heard him go to your door and knock and call you."

"Well now, I thought I heard someone at my door last night," said Nancy.

"The silly liar," thought Mrs. Pentreath. "She'd knocked on another man's door before that, and was inside it." Then aloud: "Did you, indeed? Sure, you behaved very properly in not answering him, for presently I heard him go mumbling and muttering back to his room. 'Twould be wise of you, Nancy, always to lock your door when you go to bed, for you don't want him making a rumpus there, I know."

"Lor'! I should think not!" said Nancy. "I'd make a pretty to-do if he did."

"To be sure you would, for you're a proper-minded woman, and 'tis a shocking thought indeed that he'd come tapping at your door o' nights to see if you'd let him in. So just be a bit cool and stand-off with him to show you're not wanting any of his visitings. And you'd be wise, as I say, to keep your door locked, for it's between his drink and his sleep that he's so set on you. Ah, dear me, I wish I'd kept my youth half as well as you, but my time's past to kindle a man's eye, so it's no use for me to think o' such things."

Nancy's vanity was of that simple and childish sort

that never looks for ulterior motives in those who
gratify it: only wanting to be fed, it heeds not what
hand it is that proffers agreeable morsels. To be sure
Mrs. Pentreath was so flattering that there was no
understanding it, but Nancy was not concerned to look
for a cause when the effect was so much to her mind.
Little as she intended to give her father-in-law any
return for his admiration of her beyond silence and a
locked door, if he came to try his chance again, it was
vastly pleasant to her to know on so sound an authority
that he was set on her. And it was a comfort to know
that Mrs. Pentreath was taking so friendly a view: she
might have flared up with jealousy, as if it were Nancy's
fault, but instead the poor old thing was quite " touch-
in' " in her lament that her days of lighting up a man's
eyes were over. Above all, she congratulated herself
on the clever way she had managed her affairs last night.
Not a soul in the house had any suspicion that her
drowsiness was feigned and that she had not gone to
bed so particularly early; not a soul imagined that she
had tiptoed back to her room long after they had all
been asleep. But certainly fortune had favoured her
as well, and now, when Mrs. Pentreath went out to the
kitchen garden to pick the outside cabbage leaves for
her hens, she broke into one of her habitual internal
soliloquies, turning her thoughts into words, and finding
them thus easier to deal with, much as a child shapes
his mouth to the print he reads in order to grasp its
meaning.

" The old man must have been fair boozed," she
communed with herself, " not to have found my door
was unlocked, for if he'd tried the handle, lor', what a
kettle of fish there'd have been when he found my room
empty. That was an escape, to be sure! Next time I

must lock my door from outside, and put the key somewhere handy for when I get back. Then he may knock and call till Mrs. Pentreath comes and finds him there and gives him what for, poor old lady, and she just wanting him as never was, for I can see it in her face that there's that hungry look, that's been in mine, I daresay, before now. . . . Well, what a thing it is to keep your looks while you get your experience."

Nancy disposed the mugs of wallflowers on the darned tablecloth, and buried her face in them for a moment. That sensuous fragrance of spring mounted to her head like wine, and she laughed to herself as she sniffed it in.

" Such a perfect gentleman," she remarked to herself, " as I knew the moment I first set eyes on him. There he was with the studio door ajar, waiting for me last night, and there was a tasty bit of supper spread out, and when I'd taken off my hat and sat down with him 'twas as if I was at home, and him and me man and wife. ' Take a bit of that chicken pasty, Mrs. Pentreath,' he says to me, and I caught what he was after and said, ' Thank you kindly, Mr. Giles,' and after that it was Harry and Nancy again. And there was his beginning of the picture of me, sitting in front of his looking-glass with nothing on, and doing up my hair, so as my face could be seen in the glass though my back was turned, but he wasn't thinking of his picture now, nor I neither. Then when we'd done our supper we had a bit of a chat, ever so cosy and pleasant, and to think that but a year ago I was wanting it so badly that I made up with a chance man in the dark, whom I wouldn't know again nor he me! Fair ashamed I was to think of it, specially when Harry asked me if I had any other friend but him, for that he would not permit

for a moment, and quite right. 'No, not one,' says I,
' if you'll let what's been bygones for a year be bygones
now, and even then it was nothing to me.'   And he
said I was a good girl as had wiped her mouth properly,
and he could kiss it and call it his.   That's the sort of
man for me, a bit of romance about him.   So that was
that, and then he asked me if I didn't want to know
anything about his doings, but I said, ' Garn!   I know
all about you.   You've always had a fancy for a pretty
face, and if I've had one predecessor I've had fifty,' I
said, ' for that's the sort of man you are, and that's the
proper nature for a man, so I ask no questions and
you'll not have to tell me any lies.'   How we laughed! "

Nancy was doing Nell's work this morning in laying
the table for dinner.   She had no inclination to-day
to sit and read her book, for her own adventures were
more enticing to run over in her mind than to pursue
the hapless fortunes of the poor girl married to the
wicked earl, and employment seemed to suit her better
than sitting idle.   There was a vegetable soup for
dinner to-day, and that had been simmering for an
hour already; cold beef followed, with potatoes in their
jackets, and she put these into the oven for a long bake,
for Mr. Pentreath liked them black with burning outside, and crumbled to powder within.   Everyone should
have his way and enjoy themselves, as far as she could
aid to make the day as much to their minds as last
night had been to hers.

" And then our chat was over," she thought, " and
I nipped upstairs, and gracious me, how surprised we
both were when he lit a match and found it was close
on one o'clock of the morning.   The time had gone
quick.   And to think of his dressing himself again and
walking with me right up to the garden gate.   So un-

usual, I call it, for mostly a man wants to get rid of
his girl as soon as he's had his fill. I declare it's like
a honeymoon again, and there's a bit more money in
the honey this go, though I don't take any account o'
that. And then he must needs know which was the
window of my room, but 'twas best to be honest, and
I told him it was the other side of the house. A rare
bother it is that he'll be off so soon for a visit to London,
for then there'll be no more evening performance till
he's back. . . Eh, it's sweet to be loved! "

All morning this exuberant good humour possessed
her: it was sweet to be loved, and her appreciation of
that overflowed into kindliness. Happiness and pleasure
had always an unlocking effect on her warm elementary
heart: when good luck came her way she was always
eager that other people should profit by it. She took
the cabbage leaves from Mrs. Pentreath to spare her
another excursion to the hen house, she bade Nell take
her ease, and saw to the dinner herself; she was at the
cupboard to give Mr. Pentreath his morning drink
before he could so much as ask for it, mixing it so
strong in her beneficent exuberance that he had to add
a drop of water to it himself. Then Dennis came in
half an hour before dinner was ready, and she split an
egg for him and fried it with a sprig of bergamot in
the butter to give it the flavour he liked.

All the time there was an unusual sum of money hot
in her pocket. Nancy loved money, not for the sake
of hoarding it, a feat of which she was entirely incap-
able, but of spending it. When she " 'ad the 'ump "
herself, nothing cheered her so effectively as the spending of a shilling or two on a riband or a bit of finery
for herself, but when she was happy her first thought
was to make a fairing for others. Lewd and common

7

she might be, but she bubbled with good will towards everyone round her, in the contentment of her unreflecting animalism, and she wanted to share her good fortune with them. Here she must walk with caution, for she must not seem to have suddenly become a millionaire, else there might be some curiosity as to the origin of her capital: there was five pounds of it now, and that called for disposal. Assuredly a little present for Mrs. Pentreath, poor old thing, would be a wise investment and a pleasant one, for Nancy was genuinely sorry for the barrenness of her days, and at the same time she was the likeliest of them all to get thinking how she was so flush of money, and something nice for her would stop her mouth, if she wanted to make trouble. So Mrs. Pentreath should have a new Shetland shawl, for her own was wearing sadly thin, and there should be a leather belt for Dennis, who had but a hank of string to keep his trousers on his haunches, and a new tobacco pouch for Mr. Pentreath, instead of that old leaky thing . . . but, no, perhaps it would be better not to give him anything. For herself she really desired nothing, for she had more than all the milliners in Penzance could provide: just a bottle of scent, Flowers of Musk, would be enough for her.

She bought the Shetland shawl for Mrs. Pentreath that afternoon: it had long languished in a shop at St. Columb's, and often before now Mollie had referred to it, as a thing she had her eye on, but, poor soul, she couldn't bring herself to spend the money on it, for close she was with the cash her hens brought her in, putting every penny of it away in the bank. It wasn't often, thought Nancy, that something pleasant came the old lady's way: she couldn't have a night out and be all the better for it in the morning, and it was with a mixture of compassion and her own genuine joy in giving that she untied the parcel that evening before supper, and made her presentation.

"It's a reel pleasure, Mrs. Pentreath," she said, "to give you something that'll lie a bit warmer over your shoulders than that old rag you've worn so long, and it'll be a better protection against your poor rheumatics, come winter again. There! Let me spread it for you."

Mollie bristled with silent resentment at the flavour of patronage in this speech. Nancy did not intend it, any more than she intended her triumphant benevolence: it just oozed from her. And the mention of the "poor rheumatics" was not less clumsy and complacent: the speaker was so clearly conscious that *she* hadn't got rheumatism yet. On the other hand, Mrs. Pentreath had long coveted the shawl.

"Well, I'm sure that's most handsome of you, Nancy," she said, "and I'm much obliged and thank you kindly, though indeed I feel loth to let you spend your little savings on me. And don't you trouble: I'll fix it myself as it suits me."

Instinctively, with the shrinking of hatred, she withdrew herself from Nancy's touch, as she smoothed the shawl over her, and tweaked it straight. In that shrinking was all the envy of an undesired woman in whom desire burns, towards one, so few years younger than herself, who was giving her some fraction of the money that must have come to her from the joys that Mollie longed for more than a shopful of Shetland shawls: those were Nancy's "savings." There was this bitterness, too, that the man who was rightfully hers had an eager eye on Nancy: only this morning she had counselled her to lock her door against an entry for which her own was ever unbolted. Mollie had not a particle of love for her husband, but her want was as decent as thirst or hunger.

On went Nancy's genial insolence.

"Lor'! Don't talk of my little savings like that, Mrs. Pentreath," she said. "Where's the use of savings except to spend them, and I'm sure I couldn't do nothing better with mine, than to give you a bit of comfort for your aches and pains. Nice and warm, isn't it? I threw it over my shoulders in the shop, and I'm sure I had to take it off in a jiffy, else it would have brought the sweat out on me, so snug it is. But you're a one for keeping warm, you are."

"Well, it's kind of you, my dear," said Mollie, "and a kindness never goes astray. Warm and comfortable your shawl is, and I'll sit in it often, I hope, and think of you."

"My! Don't trouble your head about me!" cried Nancy. "I'm up to a bit of enjoyment yet, and, lor', what does anything matter if you can only enjoy yourself?"

She gave her silly giggle of a laugh and tripped upstairs singing, to clean herself for supper. How Mollie hated her! She would gladly have smothered her in the folds of the Shetland shawl, but Nancy alive, she made no doubt, was to serve her purpose better than Nancy dead could ever do. But there was a lot to be thought out still.

It was soon evident that Nancy was not intending to be tired and go to bed early that night, for there was no sign of smartness about her, and, when supper was cleared away, she sat down close to the lamp with her book. Nell was washing-up in the scullery next door, with Dennis to help her, drying the plates and dishes after she had scoured them. The door from the kitchen was open, and they spoke low, but every now and then some suppressed ripple of laughter emerged, hovering, like a sunbeam above dark water, over the black silence in the kitchen. There they sat, the three of them, and it was as if they watched each other moving round in the eddies of some bubbling cauldron. John Pentreath was in his chair beside the singed rug, with his bottle and glass beside him for occupation; Mollie sat beside the range, the door of which she had opened, so as to get the glow from the embers within. Her new shawl was on her shoulders, her knitting busied her hands though not her eyes, and she had drawn her chair sideways, so that she could look either at her husband or at Nancy without moving her head. Nancy was in her rocking-chair, with her book held up in front of her, but it remained long to-night with leaf unturned, for there were more vivid images in her mind than those that the printed page conveyed. From time to time, quick as a winked eyelid, she glanced up, and as often as she did that she saw with a glow of self-approbation that Mrs. Pentreath looked cosy in her Shetland. And when she looked at John Pentreath she saw that often he was shooting sidelong glances at her with a smouldering eagerness. That was pleasant, for she piqued herself on looking what she felt like, ever so attractive and alluring. But it was a bit disconcerting seeing that Mrs. Pentreath was on the watch, and remembering their pleasant talk of this morning she folded her lips tight, as if she were being photographed, and kept her eyes on her book. It was clear that John was " thinking a deal of her " that evening, and not a look of appreciation nor a smile should he have from her. But, though she met them no longer, those glances were like a whiff of incense,

sweet to the nostrils, which she breathed in. Nobody
could find fault with her for breathing, she supposed:
even Mrs. Pentreath would allow her to breathe!

Not one atom of all that concerned her husband and
Nancy escaped Mollie. It was serving her purpose,
she was studying it, she was winding up a ball of it,
like yarn from the skein, to be knitted into the fabric
that was being fashioned in her mind. The fire was
prospering, and the black iron top of the range was
beginning to grow dusky red, for Nell had heaped the
coal on, finishing the scuttle, when she made it up at
supper time. Mollie stretched out her hands to the
heat, then wrapped them again in her shawl, and fingering the fringe of it she felt, adhering to it, the shop
ticket which Nancy had forgotten to take off. Or
perhaps, more likely, Nancy had purposely left it on,
so that the recipient of her gift might discover how
much it had cost. She quietly detached it, taking care
not to tear it, and holding it concealed in her hand as
she read the figure by the firelight. Thirty-five shillings was what Nancy had paid for it.

Bitter as bile rose an intolerable jealousy. How much
had that common slut received for the pleasures of
last night? She could only have spent a portion of
that on the shawl, for there was Dennis's leather belt
as well. And more than all that, there had been a
man loving her, a man, a man . . . and here in the
kitchen to-night was another man desiring her, and
he the man who was her own. Out of all that treasure
Nancy had chucked these shillings at her, as a woman
with a pocketful of gold might compassionately throw
some silver change to a beggar in the street.

She stood up, plucking the shawl off her shoulders,

and dropped it on to the red-hot plate of the range. Nancy looked up as she rose, and saw.

" Gracious me, Mrs. Pentreath," she said. " What have you done? "

Mollie sniffed in the smell of the burning wool. Sweet it was to her.

" Why, there's an unfortunate thing now! " she said. " If I haven't dropped my new shawl on to the oven top. What a bit of carelessness! "

Nancy ran, tongs in hand, to pick it off.

" Nay, let it bide," said Mrs. Pentreath. " It's burned through, and 'tis no use to fill the kitchen with that nasty smell. Stuff it into the fire, and the smell'll go up the chimney."

The price ticket had dropped from her hand, and she bent down, supple and alert, to pick it up.

" Aw, my dear," she said, " and to think of your having spent that sight of money on me, and all gone now but for the damnèd stink of it! There's an unfortunate thing! I must go upstairs and make do with my old rag again."

" Well, there's a pretty return for Nancy's kindness," said John with a hiccup. " I'd value it more, if she sent a bit of it my way."

Instantly Mollie made up her mind not to leave them alone together. He was just in that hot tipsiness when he might tell Nancy he wanted her, and then Nancy might make it plain that she was disgusted with his filth, and that would make an end of her own plans.

" Be a kind woman," said Mollie, " and fetch it for me, for I've got stiff with sitting so long. It'll be on the foot of my bed, and hadn't I been looking forward to having two shawls over me to-night! "

"That I will, Mrs. Pentreath," said Nancy good-humouredly, and she lit a candle and went upstairs. Grim and cheerless was that bedroom, not a flower nor a bit of chintz anywhere to brighten it up, and that square four-poster bed, long barren of joy, was the dreariest thing of all. The sight of it enlightened her with compassion, and suddenly the meaning of that burning of the shawl came to her. Till now she thought that by some inconceivable awkwardness Mrs. Pentreath had accidentally dropped it on the stove: now it flashed on her that it had been thrown there: there had been purpose behind it.

"Poor old lady," she thought with pity and hardly a touch of resentment. "I reckon she was all wrought up with watching Mr. Pentreath sitting there and making eyes at me all evening, for she wants him bad, she does, and it must be fair poison to her to know that he came knocking at my door last night, with her only wanting him to come in to her without any knocking at all. And then she'd be looking at me, sitting so cheerful and happy, without any fancy for what I could get so easy and she couldn't get at all, and it made her mad to think of taking a kindness from me, and that was how thirty-five shillings went up the chimney. I wonder if she guessed that somebody else had been wanting me too: that would have added to it. It was a deal of money, for sure, to spend on her, and it'd be like her to be puzzled at where I got it and want to light upon the way of it . . . and, lor', what a crash! That'll be a dish gone. Well, if it isn't a night of misfortunes."

She hurried downstairs again with Mrs. Pentreath's old shawl, to find storm raging in the kitchen. Dennis had dropped a vegetable dish in his washing-up, and there he stood in the door of the scullery, and John Pentreath bawling at him.

"That's why there's never a bob in the house," he shouted. "You're for ever breaking things, you damned geck, while you chatter and laugh with that girl. I'll give you a couple of sound clouts on the head for that. Come out here and get them."

Dennis took a couple of quick steps towards him, his eyes dancing and his white teeth showing in his mouth. His arms hung by his side, loose and ready with a clenched fist at the end of each, tingling to let fly.

"Here I be, then," he said. "Now just hand over the first of those clouts, Grandfather, and you'll see what you get."

"Lor', that's my son, and he's a beauty!" thought Nancy. But she ran and threw the shawl on the table, and clutched John's raised arm.

"Now you leave Dennis alone, Mr. Pentreath," she said. "You come and sit down and I'll fill your glass for you. He's an awkward boy, but there! Mrs. Pentreath's been awkward too this evening. It's just a day of misfortunes, it is."

"You let him be, Mother," bawled Dennis. "Let him try an' clout me, if that's his wish, and then I'll have mine."

Out shot Mrs. Pentreath's forefinger at Dennis.

"Enough of that, Dennis," she cried. "Finish up in there, and hold your tongue."

John turned savagely on Nancy as she still grasped his arm. She had no business to interfere, but she was a tasty wench for all her commonness.

"Have your way, then," he said, "but that boy of yours is adding up a long score against himself. Pour me out a glass, and you can take a sip yourself: that won't spoil the taste of it."

" Eh, I wouldn't touch the fiery stuff," said Nancy. " But there you are, and now let's all sit down and have a bit of peace before bedtime. Why, there's my book face down on the floor."

Silence descended again: Dennis and Nell came in from the scullery, and she took up her darning, and the boy went to fill the coal scuttle and bring in a handful of firing for the morning. But below that silence there were perilous things stirring unseen: there was a tenseness, as if a whispered word or the flick of an eyelash might have been like the striking of a match in a room charged with inflammable gas. But no such word was spoken, nor yet any other, and when next the chimeless clock whirred for the hour, first one and then the other went up to bed. Mrs. Pentreath, the first to go, sat waiting by the half-opened door of her bedroom, till she heard the click of Nancy's lock.

CHAPTER V

DENNIS GOES RUNNING

FOR a week more the warm bright weather of March continued. Now and again there would be a drift of rain for an hour, but no more than to refresh the grass, and make a softness in the ploughed land where the wheat was germinating, and then the clouds melted away, lightened of their moisture, and the sun gleamed again on the wet pasture, and the new foliage of the spring. On other days it would blow strong from the south-west, and then the shadows of clouds bowled darkling across the fields, one succeeding another in swift-moving patches, and out they went across the bay, and the sea lay striped with purplish darknesses as they passed, and kindled again into depths of translucent green. A morning of wind raised caps of foam on the shining shield, but before nightfall the wind dropped, and the clouds built themselves into snowy towers, the tops of which shone rosy bright long after the sun had slid below the horizon. Then till dawn the sea twinkled with the lights of the fishing fleet sliding seawards on the ebb, and morning brought the heavy-laden boats to the pier of St. Columb's, and they discharged their shining booty into the handcarts that carried it to the rail-head. By now the lambing was over: the pasture was dotted with young lusty beasts with tails twitching as they tugged at their dams' teats, and there was scarcely a half-dozen of barren ewes in the flock.

To-night supper was late, for neither Dennis nor his grandfather got home till close on eight, and John sat down at the table without going to clean himself in rare good spirits.

" There's not been such a lambing season since I was a lad," he said, " praise His Holy Name. Aw, dear, if the women down to St. Columb's behaved them like the ewes are doing this spring it 'ud soon be as big as Lunnon town. Scarce a barren one, and I never knew them throw so many doubles. Hullo, Nancy! You're looking as frisky as a lamb yourself, and there's something smelling damned good. Be brisk with supper."

For the last half-hour Nancy had been restless, wondering what kept the men out so long, and making suggestions that Mrs. Pentreath and she and Nell should begin their meal without waiting for them. Even her book could not keep her mind busy, for she was for ever jumping up to look now out of the door, and now from the window to see if they were coming: such a good mutton hash she had made them, so she grieved, and now it was spoiling. Mrs. Pentreath could have laughed at that lamentation, for sitting furtively observant she saw that Nancy never once took the earthenware pot off the fire to prevent the meat from over-cooking, as any woman would have done who was thinking of her stew: all she wanted was to get supper over. The lamp was burning ill to-night, and she could not see whether she had her smart stockings on, but she'd have made a bet she had.

" Well, I'm sure I thought you'd never come in," said Nancy in answer to her father-in-law, " and as for being brisk with the supper, it's been waiting this nigh an hour for you. What's been keeping you? "

John Pentreath poured himself out a rinse of spirits.

" Bit of midwifery," he said. " There's not been much call for that in this house for a many years, nor won't be again, I daresay."

Nancy tossed her head in the most approved manner.

" You speak very coarse, Mr. Pentreath," she said. " I began to be afeared that you and Dennis had fallen out, and I knew who'd have had a broken head then."

She glanced at the clock, as she brought the stew from the oven.

" Set the potatoes, Nell," she said, " and be quick. I never saw such a slow-coach. Well, there we are, and you can fall to. No such sauce as appetite, they say."

It was not so late after all, thought Nancy, as she calculated the time before her tryst down at St. Columb's. She had begun ladling out the stew, when John rapped on the table and stood up to say grace. This was usually a Sabbatarian observance.

" Well, if Sunday hasn't come round quick again," she said, " and me thinking it was only Friday. But I'm not one to object, for I'm sure we've got plenty to be thankful for. Pass up your plate, Dennis."

Mr. Pentreath had got through his first glass at a gulp, and set it down on the table.

" That's done me good," he said, " and the sight of those lambs did me good, too. I'll take another go of your stew, Nancy."

Nancy glanced round.

" Why, but Mrs. Pentreath hasn't had her first go yet," she said. " I declare I forgot about you, Mrs. Pentreath. Pardon, I'm sure. Now, aren't we all happy and pleasant to-night instead of those accidents! "

" Nay, we won't have any accidents to-night," said John. " That we do, we'll do on purpose, and enjoy ourselves, and thank the Lord for all His benefits."

Mrs. Pentreath had taken no more than a mouthful of Nancy's savoury mess, and now she pushed back her chair and had done with her supper. The plan that had occupied her mind so much these last days was pretty well matured now, but there were some bits of things to be learned yet before she could proceed with it. She made no doubt, when she saw how impatient Nancy was about supper, that the woman would soon be gone from the kitchen with a sleepy fit or what-not, and presently would be out of the house, hot-foot to her man. But what of the key to Nancy's door, which she herself would need? Nancy always locked it of nights now, since their conversation, but to-night she would have locked it from the outside. It was unlikely that she would take the heavy thing with her; 'twas more probable that she would hide the key somewhere handy, and that cache must be found first. Then there was John to reckon with. A godly mood he was in to-night: he was thinking of nothing but his lambs, and how gracious the Lord was to him for causing his ewes to throw so many doubles, and send him such a spell of seasonable weather for their infant days. To listen at him you'd have thought the Lord had naught to do but to attend to His servant John Pentreath. He was paying no heed to Nancy at all: not a look did he give her as she helped him to a second go of stew, and changed his plate for him. Moreover, he wasn't drinking according to his wont, and he must be chockful of his whisky before that propitious night came, when Nancy would have gone off to her man, and then she would have a bit of a talk to him, telling him that Nancy was fair mad with desire for him. . . . But this evening all was awry:

there was no certainty as to the whereabouts of Nancy's key, and the lambs had turned John into one of themselves. She must give up all thought of her design to-night.

Supper was over now, and pulling her old shawl round her she went to the door of the kitchen and looked out.

"A bit of rain coming up," she said, "'twill fall heavy and steady before an hour's out, and be passed before day. A bit of a blow, too, I shouldn't wonder, but nought to harm."

She could have laughed aloud at the effect of her words on Nancy, and she could read plain as print what was in the woman's mind. She was all bustle and hurry again to get the table cleared and be gone, in order to get down to St. Columb's before the rain began and made mischief with her smart clothes. In five minutes the cloth was off and folded away, Nell and Dennis took the plates and dishes to the scullery for washing-up, and Nancy picked up her book.

"Well, with supper so late and all," she said, "I reckon I'll go up to bed now. Good night all."

She tripped upstairs and changed her dress in a rare hurry, for Mrs. Pentreath was never wrong about the weather, and there! there came a puff of wind and a gust of rain pattered on to the panes. It would never do to take the hat with the cherries on it out into a wet night, and instead she tied a red woollen scarf round her head, glancing into the glass to see how it suited her. Her umbrella, bad luck to it, for all its pretty handle with the blue glass knob on the top, was little use in the rain, for half its seams were agape, and Nancy only used it, tightly furled, for ornamental purpose. As for her dress, she could keep that dry with her

mackintosh. There was nothing ornamental about that,
but she would strip it off in a jiffy when she got to Mr.
Giles's house. Then she came cautiously forth, locked
her door on the outside, and considered where to put
the key, for it was an awkward, heavy thing to carry.
But the top of the broad door-lintel was just the place
for it, and having deposited it there she went down the
narrow stairs to the studio and let herself out. It had
been an ingenious thought to use this means of exit
and entrance, but before long she might have to think
of some other way, for Mrs. Pentreath had received an
inquiry only to-day as to whether she had this lodging
to let in May for a month or perhaps the whole summer.
The gentleman wrote from London, Mr. Willis was his
name, and he had heard from a previous tenant how
comfortable he had been made there. A sad pity it
was that she and Harry had not met before he took
that house in Kenrith Lane, for then he could have
come to lodge at the farm. That would have been a
cosy, comfortable plan, the way things had turned out!

As she came opposite his house she saw that the
garden-door into the studio was not shut, but ajar, and
a long thin pencil of light came from it. That was a
signal: by ill-chance there might be some friend of
Harry's in the studio at the hour appointed. If so, the
door would be shut, and she was to wait in the summer-
house in the garden till all was clear. But to-night the
door was ajar and she pushed it open and entered.

II

Mrs. Pentreath sat knitting by the open door of the
range for a quarter of an hour after Nancy had gone.

Then she lit her candle and went upstairs and along the passage till she came to Nancy's door. Locked, of course, and peeping through the keyhole she saw that there was no key there, as anyone could have guessed. She reached up to the lintel, and there it was. What would happen, she wondered, if for the sheer devilry of it, she just took it away? Nancy would find herself in a fine pickle when she returned after her pleasuring and could not get into her own room. A rare bit of fun it would be to get her caught like that, to hear the slut explaining that she had gone for a saunter this wet night in her Sunday clothes after she'd said she was off to bed, and had locked her room and then lost the key! But Nancy with her locked room was to give her more than a rare bit of fun, and she replaced the key, and went quickly back to her own room, for there was the kitchen door opening again, and young Dennis and Nell coming up together. It wouldn't be a surprise if they made a match of it soon, for the bright ferment of the spring, as anyone could see, was bubbling in them both. Dennis clumped along the passage in his heavy boots, the inconsiderate boy, not thinking that his mother might be just falling asleep. " But you may dance a jig outside her door," thought Mollie, " and there'll be no complaint from her in the morning! "

Click, click went the latches of their two doors, and then once more the kitchen door opened, and up came John, steady and sober. There was no stumbling nor creaking of the banisters, and he went straight to his room without making any excursion to Nancy's door. " 'Twould turn the Lord against him, he'll be thinking," grinned Mollie to herself, " and with all his lambing ewes that would never do."

8

III

The lure and enchantment of the spring was potent
indeed. Dennis and Nell had gone to their rooms as
Mrs. Pentreath had conjectured, and there each stood
for a moment listening for some sound from the other.
But something else had taken hold of Dennis to-night,
and presently he went across to the window, and threw
it wide and looked into the darkness. The rain was
falling now, steady and soft, hissing on the shrubs in
the garden and tapping on the magnolia leaves. The
air was still, but then there came a stir from the open
fields beyond, and the trees in the garden bowed as
the wind threshed through them and drove the rain
before it. It smelt of the sea and of the wet trees and
of the fruitful earth, and as if it had been a fire pouring
in instead of a wet wind, it set him burning to be out
in it. The gust passed, and again the rain fell straight
and thick through the warm starless night.

Dennis leant out farther. " Nell! " he called, not
raising his voice, for her window was but a few feet
from his, and maybe she was looking out, too.

" Yes," she answered from close by.

" I'm going out for a running, Nell," he said. " Will
you come 'long? "

He heard her laugh softly.

" Not I," she said. " 'Tis the wet windy night, for
wind's coming, Aunt Mollie said. 'Tis the night when
you want to do your running alone."

" Maybe I do," he said, for the urge of spring was
pulling strong at him from the darkness, and he knew
he didn't want Nell with him to-night. But for a
moment yet they leaned out, their heads sundered only
by a few dripping magnolia leaves and one great

fragrant leather-petalled blossom, two clean flames of youth in that house which reeked of dying wicks and furtive smoulderings.

" You'd better wait a bit yet," she said, " others'll be awake still."

" No, I'll don my beach-shoes, and none'll hear, and I'll nip down the stairs to the lodging and out at the studio door. Sure you won't come too? "

" Sure," she said.

" I'm off, then. Mind to put our string on ye for morning."

" More like I'll be rousing you," she said.

Dennis drew in his head and made ready. He pulled off his boots, and stripped, putting on a pair of canvas trousers that were waiting for Nell's washing on Monday, a jersey and his rope-soled shoes, and felt his way down the staircase and into the studio. The glass door into the garden was unlocked, and that was a surprising thing, for Mollie usually fastened all doors at nightfall, but he left it like that and put the key in his pocket, so that none could lock it while he was gone; then out into the warm throbbing darkness of the spring night.

It mattered not where he went so long as he was alone under the spell of it, and he crossed the garden below the trees that now stood motionless again, whispering with the rain, and out into the open fields beyond. Somewhere behind the low pall of the clouds there must be a moon, for there was light enough to see the outlines of trees against the sky and to keep his feet from stumbling. The rain was but a drizzle now and the air was thick with the scent of herbs and grasses unperceived by day; some were sweet, some acrid, and all were stirred up, like savourings, in the smell of the wet earth. And now the heady intoxica-

tion of the spring began to bubble in his brain, and he
laughed and drew a long breath into his lungs, or
stretched his arms upwards and outwards, filled with
the wine of his own youth. Then from walking he
broke into a run and leapt as he ran, unconscious of
himself as any loose-limbed colt in the meadow. Field
after field he traversed: in one there was a flock of
sheep, a huddle of dim grey blots on the grass, and
Dennis ran in among these, scattering them to right
and left, save a valorous ram, who stamped at him and
stood his ground. He vaulted the gates if he happed
on them; if not, he scrambled up and over the shale-
built walls, till, near ahead, he saw the black lump of
Kenrith copse. He swung out to the right, giving it a
wide berth, for there were endless dark legends con-
cerning it: that there were to be heard coming at night
from the heart of it weird cries and chantings, and that
lights could be seen moving about between the stems of
the wind-slanted firs. Old wives' tales, he thought to
himself again, but it was an ill-omened place for prudent
folk, and he had no desire to hear sounds where all
should be still, and see lights where all should be
dark, for he was not come out into the night to seek
out sorceries, but to be flooded within and without by
the rain and wholesome wind and the white magic
of the spring. Not one atom of this formed a conscious
thought in his mind, but body and mind alike were
harnessed to the primeval instinct that drove them.

The rain had begun to fall thick again, and still the
uncomprehended rapture grew, and he must shout as
he ran. His skin dripped with the sweat of his swift
going, and he paused to strip off the encumbering
jersey which clung close to him, and gasped to feel
the cool wet pricking on his back and chest and

shoulders. The wind had risen now and was blowing steady and fresh from the sea, and it brought with it the sound of the thump of the surf on the beaches below, and he could taste the saltness through the sweet water of the driving rain, that seemed to soak into him and renew his very bones and inward parts. He had left the fields, and there lay in front of him a long stretch of downland: half an hour's running brought him to the head of a wide valley that sloped seawards. A stream ran down a pebbly bed in the centre of it, and passed into the shelter of a wood that stretched from one side to the other of the combe. Here the wind sounded loud in the tree-tops, but below, the thick growing trunks broke the force of it, and now the instinct that had driven him forth took entire possession of him. He threw himself face-downward, bare-chested, on a bed of sprouting bracken, and lay there panting, while the arteries throbbed in his throat and temples. He flung wide his arms and legs, as if to wrestle with the earth his mother, or hold her in strong embrace, and with his spread fingers he dug into the soft soil, and with his teeth he bit the sappy fern stems. Then, as the ecstasy subsided into content and quietness, he lay there with eyes shut. God! what a good running it had been, what a spell, what a magic of springtime and night!

He gave a long sigh, and sat up, brushing the earth off his chest, and squeezing the water from his hair. Close by the stream broadened into a good-sized pool, and he stripped off his trousers, which were thick with mud, and washed them and wrung them out. Then he stepped into the pool himself, and lay there full length, head under, and tingled with the shock and glow of

the cool water on his hot body. That was good: that
gave a finish to it all, and he stroked the water off him
with his hands, and struggling back into his clinging
trousers set off on his homeward journey.

The veiled moon had set by now, and when he neared
the farm again it was so dark that he had to feel his
way through the trees into the garden, and move
cautiously across it to the door of the studio, with
shuffling feet to avoid stepping on to some bed of wallflowers. He could smell them in the darkness, but that
tamer scent was less to his mind than that of the acrid
bracken shoots, and the wild thyme of the downland.
Then as he groped for the door handle in the black
wall of the studio, he saw a light moving along up
the path from St. Columb's. For one disconcerting
second he bethought him of the rumoured lights in the
Kenrith copse, but then came the click of the garden
gate, and an audible footstep on the gravel path, and
misgiving gave place to curiosity: who could it be
coming to the farm where all but himself had been in
bed this long while? He slipped behind a shrub of bay
and waited, watching the gleam through the sheltering
leaves and unable in the gross darkness to see anything
of the bearer of it. Next moment it came flashing in
his eyes, and he heard a little cry of startled surprise
in a voice that he recognised.

" Lor'! Why, if it isn't Dennis! " whispered Nancy.
" Why, wherever have you been? "

" Turn the light on the door, and let's find the
handle," said he.

She directed the lantern towards it, and he opened it.
Nancy stepped inside and went on talking in a high ner-
vous whisper, as he extricated the key from his soaked
pocket, and locked the door.

"And what a time for you to be out," she said, "with nothing on but a pair of bags and them soaking wet! What would anyone think to see you going about half-naked like that, a fair mad thing! There's a bit of candle on the table. Light it, and I'll put out the lantern. Where've you been?"

Dennis's radiance still transfigured him. It was no use to struggle back into his jersey, and he just tied the arms of it round his neck.

"Over the hills for a run," he said. "And you?"

"Why, just seeing a lady friend down in St. Columb's," she said. "I stayed a bit longer than I meant, thinking that the rain would stop, but it got worse nor ever. I slipped out after supper instead of going to bed, for I wanted a breath of fresh air, so stifle hot was it in the kitchen to-night!"

Insensibly the black secrecies of the house were stealing round them like wisps of fog. She looked closely at Dennis as he held the candle: radiant he was still and flushed with running and dripping with rain, and the thought that this beautiful wild boy with his young manhood bubbling within him was bone of her bone and had been nurtured at her breast roused in her a sort of shallow shame for herself, such a clean white thing he was. Steadily his clear eyes regarded her, and an unspoken amusement uncurled his lips. Obviously he did not believe a word she said.

"Dennis, you won't tell on me?" she said.

"Along of your going to see your lady friend in St. Columb's?" he asked. "What's there worth the telling? Late hours she keeps, don't she, and eh, that's a lovely little lantern she gave you to light your steps. That'll have come from London town. I'll be taking that back to her in the morning. What's her house and her name? "

" It's true," said the silly woman, " I'll swear——"

" Don't you trouble to do that, you might get visited for it! " Suddenly he bubbled with silent laughter. " And there's a funny thing to think on," he said, " that I gave Willie the knock-out for calling you a whore and me a bastard. Happen I am a bastard."

Nancy began to whimper. It was no use wasting any more perjuries over her lady friend.

" And there's pretty names to use to your mother," she sobbed, " and asking her if you're a bastard, you the spit and moral of what your dad was. I never thought to hear such things from you."

" Well, lebbe then," said Dennis. " You riled me 'cause of your silly lies, and I spoke rough. What you do is no job of mine, and why should I let on about it? Stop blubbing, Mother; there's no sense in that, and let's get up quick and quiet to bed."

Dennis stood in the passage, while his mother reached up for her door-key and vanished within, then let himself into his room. The blind was flapping in the wind, and he pulled it up and looked out once more into the night that had given him those sexless and almost discarnate hours. But now the spell was broken, he was back in the black house where everyone had secret businesses. A damned ill-chance to have met his mother just now, though it was lucky for her that she was no later, for surely he would have locked the studio door, and she would have had a night in the garden. But it was scarcely news to him that she had a man down to St. Columb's, it did not come anyhow with any shock of surprise: he felt now that it had been somewhere hidden in his consciousness that she was like that, and to-night the knowledge had popped out. Well, 'twas her business; a rotten poor time she must have had at the farm all these years, and why shouldn't a woman take a bit of pleasure as well as a man?

He slipped off his dripping trousers and mud-smothered shoes, and rubbed himself down with a blanket from his bed: then his eye fell on the string that communicated with Nell next door. Perhaps she was awake, and he pulled it very gently to tell her he was back: if she was asleep it would not disturb that admirable slumberer. From the other side of the partition came a jerk in answer, and he waited, with heart suddenly leaping in his throat, to see if there would be more. But evidently she had just acknowledged the news of his return.

He slid into bed. Some other night, when there was moonshine and the serenity of the stars, perhaps she would come with him, but that would be a different kind of running.

He rolled himself round in his blanket and fell asleep, hearkening to the drip of the rain on the magnolia leaves outside.

CHAPTER VI

THE STORM

THE rain had ceased during the night, and morning came warm and windless. Somewhere high up in the air were floes of greyish-yellow vapour veiling the sun, and below tattered fleeces of cloud forming and dispersing again. It was a stale, sticky day, with no refreshment in the air, and Dennis, when he went out to his work in the kitchen-garden of the farm felt slack in body and grumpy in mind. Weeding took him a couple of hours, and after that he set up a line for the drill where he would sow the peas. When that row was finished, he must shift his line three feet for the next: peddling, wearisome work it was, for ever bending down, then moving a yard on and bending down again. What the hell was wrong with him this morning? Reaction perhaps after his running last night, and a smouldering resentment against his mother. She had truckled to him when he slouched down to breakfast, and kept an appealing eye on him, as if she were afraid that he would go back on his promise and talk about bastards and lanterns and lady friends. And Nell was riled with him. For, as she had predicted, it was she who had had to wake him to-day, and he had damned her for jerking his hand against the bars of his bed. Plaguy things were women: he was better off before she began to trouble him, for he and Willie had understood each other better than he and Nell. Not a word had she to say to him this morning: she was tight of

mouth as a dog-fish when he had asked her for a slog
of bread, and she had given it him without a glance or
a smile, and gone off to the scullery waggling her behind
as she walked. He had followed her there, but there
was nothing but sulks and dignity: a sound spank
would have done her good. He and Willie would have
had that right in no time: they'd have called each
other damned fools, and sat stubborn for a minute or
two, and then one would just have grinned at the
other, and that would have been finished. Or another
mode of reconciliation would have been that they'd
have met on the pier when the day's work was over,
and the young fellows sat about on the parapet, and
there would have been no need for words at all, but
they'd have strolled off together with shoulders
touching to clubhouse or hillside.

Willie was ever so pleased with himself just now, for
that artist fellow, Giles, who had the house at the entrance
of Kenrith Lane, had taken him on as house-servant.
He served Giles's meals, and cleaned up his studio and
brushed his clothes and called him in the morning.
Dennis had congratulated him on his enlarged prospects,
which included fifteen shillings a week and all found,
but he wondered how one man could make himself
servant to another. For himself he could plough the
land which would one day be his, and feed the horses,
and midwife the ewes, and mate the itinerant bull to
the cows, and slice the throats of the pigs when their
time came. But he couldn't think of himself as folding
a fellow's suit of clothes, or picking up his snotty handkerchief. " You'll be chewing his food for him next,
Willie! " he had said, " and 'twas a pity I broke that
front tooth of yours. . . ." Willie, for some reason,
hadn't answered him back proper, but had just said

that his master was a decent chap, and could chew his
food for himself. He was doing a picture that was
always turned to the wall, except when he was at it,
and he had bidden him not touch it. "Backside of
some wench, I reckon," Dennis had said, and that was
a pretty good guess, for Willie, as was only natural,
had looked at the picture and knew who it was, for
the face in the looking-glass was admirably like the
original.

Nancy was bustling about the kitchen when Dennis
got back for the midday dinner, obsequiously anxious
to please everybody, and earning contempt rather than
gratitude for this amiability. John Pentreath's thank-
fulness to the Lord for causing his ewes to throw so
many doubles was less acute than it had been the night
before: he was making up, in fact, for his abstinences,
for his eye was pretty often on Nancy, and his hand on
his bottle. But Nell seemed in the sulks still, and Mrs.
Pentreath had not a word for any of them nor yet a
mouthful of dinner for herself. She had not even
troubled to move her chair up to the table, but sat
close to the oven, for all the hot languor of the day,
clicking her teeth in her mouth, as if she were tasting
something, though assuredly no morsel had passed her
lips, and her eyes moved this way and that, furtively
observant. There was an air of tension and unease
which Nancy's amiabilities only emphasised.

Suddenly Mollie put her knitting down, and opening
the kitchen door stood there a minute sniffing like a
dog puzzling out a scent.

"There's a sluice o' rain coming," she said, "and a
gale—a gale of the Lord's anger maybe, John Pentreath. A wild night there'll be before dawn, and a
day of trouble to follow. Get your lambs safe in fold

unless you want to lose them. Give them hurdles round, and a shelter above them, else they'll be drowned sure as fate, and blown away like fleeces."

"Lor', and I do hate the wind," said Nancy incautiously. "'Twas that which made me such a sleepy-head last night, I shouldn't wonder."

Dennis bent over his plate to hide an irrepressible grin, and neither he nor Nancy saw the spasm of mirth had popped out of Mollie's face and back again quick as a lizard. John pushed back his chair with a scrape and tapped the antique barometer.

"'Tisn't anything," he said. "Just gone down a bit. Are you certain sure, Mollie?"

The very echo of his voice answered him.

"Just gone down a bit and that's all," said she. "But she's certain sure, is Mollie."

"Damn you, don't go mocking me," he said with a sudden flame of anger.

"And don't you go blaming me," she said, "after I've warned you. Get a couple of men and Dennis, and build you shelters for your lambs and ewes, or you'll be thanking the Lord t'other side of your mouth. That's my word to you, John Pentreath, for all your damnings. I've said my say, and 'tis all you get from me. And make up the fire, Nell, for there'll be a spice of cold for a seasoning I shouldn't be surprised."

Despite the comparative steadiness of the barometer, John Pentreath preferred to trust to his wife's warning, and though it was Saturday afternoon, and the farm-hands had knocked off work, he sent down to St. Columb's for a couple of them to return, and they loaded a cart with hurdles, and went down to the meadow where this good company of mothers and lambs was feeding, to make shelter for them. Already there were signs that some change of weather was on the way; sharp puffs of wind blew intermittently from the south-west, which was the storm quarter; and round the sun, visible only like a white plate through the floor of vapour which now had spread over the whole sky, was a pearly halo at the distance of about ten diameters from it. Below, the air was notably clear, the cliffs of the promontory across the bay were as distinct as if seen through a telescope, and the sea lay waveless without a ripple breaking at its rims.

It was easy to find a suitable place for the fold, for right out in the centre of the field stood three sizable elms at a distance of some twelve yards from each other, and these would make fine buttresses for a row of hurdles lashed strongly together, with stakes driven in to support them. Another row of stakes was hammered in to leeward of this line, and more hurdles laid across them and firmly tied, made a roof for protection overhead. From the north and the east there was little to fear: besides, on those two sides of the field were shale-built walls affording good shelter should the wind, by some unusual chance, shift round and blow from those quarters.

They were wise old dames, these ewes, when the care of their young was on them. Some had been standing sniffing the air in their intervals of cropping; they seemed to agree with Mollie that there was something threatening in the day, and before the roofing of their shelter was complete, many of them had moved up near the hurdles or into the lee of the elm trunks, seeking cover from a wind that as yet blew only in puffs of no great violence. Before long there was a good company of them there, some lying down with their lambs by them, others still cropping at the grass with widespread legs, to let the young tug at their teats, but they too were gravitating towards shelter. Strong sturdy little beggars the lambs were: never had there been so promising a lot. And now a mist was drawing in from the sea; thick it was, and the moistness of it formed like a heavy dew on Dennis's jersey and his hair: it was queer that it should come up now, when there was wind about.

John Pentreath was determined to run no risks about his flock. Each hurdle had a couple of stakes on the leeward to support it, and they were stout timbers, driven in deep, so that no violence of gale could uproot them, and the roofing hurdles were corded together and stayed to the ground. There were three hours' hard work to get it all to his mind, and before they went home they rounded up the few sheep that still strayed about the field, barren ewes for the most part, and drove them into the protected area.

"Come wind or rain they're out of harm now," he said to Dennis as they walked back together to the farm. "I doubt I've been over-careful, but when your granny talks like that, 'tis wise to heed her. God, I want a drink after all that hammering of stakes."

"Reckon she's right," said Dennis. "See, the mist's all dispersed again, and not a breath of wind: that's queer. But there's wind up above: look at the clouds torn to tatters, and it's banking up thick in the sou'west."

Already the curtain of greyish-yellow vapour that had hung all day across the heavens was breaking up: rents appeared in it, showing the remote blue beyond, but in the south-west, as Dennis had said, a great indigo stretch of cloud, hard and coppery-red at the edges, was beginning to spread upwards. But the flock had

been made safe from all assaults of wind and rain, and
on arriving at the farm, Dennis found that Nell had got
over her fit of sulks, for she looked at him with shy
appealing glances.   He had meant to go down to St.
Columb's to seek out Willie, and spend till supper time
with him, in that less complicated masculine com-
panionship, and let Nell see that her airs and poutings
didn't worry him, but now, when she asked him to
hold her skein of wool for her as she wound it up into
a ball, he was wax to her, and he sat down opposite
her with spread arms, and her winding hands travelled
along the span between them, turned the corner where
the skein lay between his thumb and his fingers, and
went back along the lines again.   By degrees his open
knees closed on hers, and there they sat silent and aware.
Never yet had he had even a kiss from her, nor yet
from any other girl, save one who came up behind
him in the dark as he sat with his Willie on the pier
at St. Columb's a long while back, and put an arm
round his neck and kissed him before he knew what
she was after.   He could remember the pressure of her
breast on his shoulder, and how it had roused in him
then no sort of desire, but a vague repulsion: puffy
bumpy bodies girls seemed to have.   But it was not
like that with him now.

The skein-winding got done; and Nell lit the lamp,
for it had grown very dark in the kitchen, and then,
while she and Nancy busied themselves with the preparations for supper, Dennis went out again to see that
the ewes and lambs had settled down in their shelters.
That indigo bank of cloud in the west had spread up
half-way across the sky, and the last rays of the setting
sun piercing through a rent in it, turned the edge to
a dusky glow, as if a red-hot wire had been laid along

it. There was still not a breath of wind, but the air
had grown very much colder, and the ewes and the
lambs were huddled together in a compact company
behind the hurdles. That was as it should be, and he
turned back, going round by the field where stood
the circle of stones. Some Midsummer Eve, surely, he
and Nell would be dancing there together, for that was
a spell that no couple in St. Columb's, desirous of children, would neglect. But first must come that leaping
across the embers of the bonfire that made it sure that
they would be wed before the year was out. He walked
across the blackened cobbled pavement where it had
been laid year by year, far back beyond all reckoning;
from there he could see the roofs of St. Columb's and
the pier. Usually by this time the harbour would be
empty and the lights of the fishing fleet be twinkling
in the bay, but to-night they were all at anchor behind
the pier, not a boat had gone forth: perhaps the fisher
folk knew that this would be no night to be at sea.
Utterly still it was, and now he noticed that there was
not a sound of bird-song, and this was just the hour
when it should have been at its fullest: thrush and
blackbird and robin and willow-wren should all have
been at it. And throughout the afternoon the gulls
had been winging inland: a great flock passed overhead
as he stood there, and he watched them join a company on the ploughed fields below. To the east across
the bay another bank of dark cloud had risen high
behind the promontory: the birds looked like specks
of flake-white against it as they hovered before settling.

Supper was close on ready when he got back to the
farm, and he looked at the barometer by the kitchen
door. His grandfather had set it at dinner time, but the
machine must surely be crazy, for it had gone down a

9

full inch, and as he tapped, it jerked downwards again. Then there came out of the dead calm a sudden wail of wind that set the trees in the garden tossing, and a tattoo of rain beat against the panes, loud and startling as if somebody outside was tapping at the window. It lasted only for a couple of minutes and it and the blast that drove it ceased.

John Pentreath had had a drink or two since he came in, and he laughed.

"There's your storm, Mollie!" he said, "not so terrible bad, and the ewes might have got through it without my paying extra time to the fellows and putting up a palace of hurdles for them. What's the barometer at, Dennis?"

"An inch and more down since you set it at dinner," said he.

Pentreath looked at it.

"God! and I set it when I came in," he said. "Maybe we haven't wasted our labour."

"Maybe you haven't," said Mollie. "Maybe you'll go to church to-morrow morning thankful that you hearkened to me. Give me a cut of that mutton, Nancy, for I'd like a piece of meat to-night: rare and hungry I am when there's a storm coming up, and such a one as none of us'll forget."

It was a silent supper, and silent the hour that followed. Nancy had her book, Mollie her knitting, John his pipe and glass, and Nell her eternal darning with the wool she had wound, and Dennis a pack of greasy playing-cards. Nell was the Queen of Hearts, he thought to himself, and he the King. He shuffled and dealt them out in four lines: should those two cards be touching each other, that was a good omen. Then he added grannie as a black queen, and twice she got between them, and so he must deal again, and not leave it like that. . . . The clock whirred out the hour of nine, and though he was sleepy from his run last night, he'd wait to go upstairs with Nell and tell her of it, for not a word had he had with her all day, since she had sulked at him all morning, and he had been hard at work all afternoon. To be sure they had sat over skein-winding, but they couldn't talk then, and after supper Nancy had helped with the washing-up, and there was no room for three in that cupboard of a scullery. Sleepy though he was, too, there was something alert within, listening and expectant.

That same unease seemed to possess the others, for there was Nancy with her book unregarded on her lap, and Mollie had put her knitting aside, and Nell had thrust her darning into her work-basket. All were waiting for this tempest to arise, which should justify three hours' work on Saturday afternoon. He went across to the barometer again, but it had not fallen farther. Inside and out, dead silence. As he stood there, something whispered outside: rain had begun to fall, straight and rather thick in the dead calm of the air, for not a drop specked the windows. Then came a more sonorous noise: here was the wind at last, and again the rain splashed the panes. It was a strong breeze out of the west, and it continued steady, though not violent, just such a night as last night, with nothing to fear for the flock. A bit of wind was but usual this month and a dash of rain with it, and there seemed no more to it than that after all this to-do with the hurdling.

Nancy was the first to go upstairs, and Nell and Dennis followed, with John Pentreath hiccupping on their heels. Nell went into her room without a glance at Dennis, but surely she couldn't be in the sulks again, and he opened his window and called softly to her. She answered with a whistle through the magnolia leaves.

" 'Tis all right again, Nell? " he said.

" Surely: I was just a crosspatch."

" Mayn't I come in and talk a bit, and tell you of my running? " he asked.

" No, best not," she said.

" And what if I did? " he asked.

" You'd find my door bolted. Good night," and she shut her window.

Well: there it was, and they were puzzling creatures. Why shouldn't he have gone in, and sat on her bed for a talk, and told her about his running? What hurt could come of it? But she must have her way, and, had he known it, she was still standing by the window with trembling fingers that yearned to unlatch it again, and call to him.

Dennis slept sound and late that night, and when he woke it was broad day, and the boughs of the trees in the garden were clashing together as the wind, now risen to half a gale with occasional violent gusts, streamed through them. But there was no need to get up yet, for he could lie a-bed on Sunday morning as long as he pleased, with no further penalty than finding breakfast cleared away when he got down, and having to pick something from the larder that would last him till dinner. But before dinner came the church-going in his cloth clothes and a linen collar and con-strained, uncomfortable boots which he must black before he set out on the grim walk to worship with his grandfather and Nancy and Nell, leaving Mrs. Pen-treath to mind the house and have an eye to the dinner.

The wind had done sore havoc in the night with the garden: flowers were shredded from their stalks, and the grass was strewn with broken branches from the trees, and the paths were deeply channelled by the rain. That had ceased, and perhaps was over altogether, for rifts, showing spaces of watery blue, appeared in the tatter of scudding clouds overhead. In the south-west, out of which the wind was coming, there was an arch of clear sky, like a funnel from which it was blown, and watery sunshine gleamed. As he went downstairs a violent gust swept by with a screech as from a living thing, and he thought he heard some crash outside in the garden.

John Pentreath had already been down to the field where the sheep lay; the hurdles had withstood the force of the wind, and the ewes with their young were snugly cuddled up in the shelter, while a few barren ones with no maternal cares to worry them were at feed again. He was in his Sunday humour of grim piety, with a day's abstinence in front of him to blacken his temper.

"The Lord's been a-riding on the wings of the wind and no mistake," he said, "and it's blowing as strong as ever. The sheep and lambs are safe though, praise His Holy Name for putting it into my head to see to them yesterday, else they'd have had a sore rough night of it. But the Lord is my shepherd, that's a true word of King David's."

Mollie gave a little thin high laugh.

"I'm thinking it was I who put a notion of shepherding into your head, John Pentreath," she said, "whatever your King David said about it."

John did not argue that point, and he pushed back his chair.

" A fine time of day to come down to breakfast,
Dennis," he said. " But you mind you're ready to start
to church with your mother and Nell and me. I won't
have you coming in when it's sermon-time. I'll just
take a look round the yard, and then we'll be off.
Where's my hat? "

Nancy, still obliging, jumped up.

" It's in the cupboard, Mr. Pentreath," she said,
" I'll give it a bit of a shine against you're ready for
it."

" Thank you, Nancy," he said, " that's a good girl."

He went round to the kitchen door, glancing at the
barometer as he passed.

" God save us! " he said. " The bitch has gone down
another full inch since I set her last night. Very
stormy, and low at that. What do you say to it,
Mollie? "

" Just what me and the Lord said to you yesterday,
a wild night and a day of trouble to follow. Step out
quick, man, if you're going, and shut the door after
you."

It was not a couple of minutes before he was back
again.

" Mollie, there'll be the deuce to pay out in the yard,"
he said, " for the ash at the corner has fallen across the
wall, and the wall's bulging full dangerous with the
weight of it. If it goes, it'll fall smash on to your
poultry. And you can't get at them, for a heavy
bough lies right over the door."

Dennis ran out and came hurrying back.

" I'll fetch the two-handled saw," he said, " and
we'll get the top branches off the tree. That'll ease
the weight, Grandfather, and you and I'll have them
off in a jiffy."

John Pentreath hesitated, then brought his hand down thump on the table.

"That will I not," he said, "till church is done."

"And till all my poultry are buried flat underneath the wall," cried Mollie.

Again he hesitated, and came across to her, speaking low, as if for fear that the Lord was listening.

"Mollie, can't you find a word that'll keep them safe, till I'm back?" he said, "and then sure as sure I'll help, though 'tis the Lord's Day."

She shook her hands in his face.

"Yes, I know something that'll keep them safe, and that's that you go out with the boy, and saw the branches off. Go and take your Sunday blacks off, while he's fetching the saw, and do your praying when my hens are safe."

He spat into the fire.

"So that's all the word you know, is it?" he said, "and hearken to mine. Them's the church bells going and it's time to start. Come on, Nancy and Nell and you, too, Dennis; off we go."

Dennis turned his back on his grandfather.

"Nell, run 'ee down quick, quick, to St. Columb's and tell Willie I want him here hot-foot. He's at the first house in Kenrith Lane, with the garden in front. Mr. Giles, it is, an artist-fellow."

"I bid you come to church, Dennis," roared John, "and you too, Nell."

Dennis faced round, as Nell scuttled off.

"Sure you do, and you may bellow at me ten times and I'll not hear you."

Mollie nipped in between them, with finger pointing at her husband.

"Enough said," she yelled. "Leave the lad alone,

and go off to your holy pow-wows. Do you think I'm
going to have all my fowls killed along of it being
Sunday? Get you gone, if you haven't the spunk to
help the boy. I'll make you tremble, John Pentreath,
worse nor God ever did, if you cross me, and if once
I give you the tremblings they'll last you a prayerbook
full of Sundays. Get your saw, Dennis, against young
Polhaven's coming. You're a good lad."

The wills of the two came to grips, and wrestled together, but his was ludicrously the weaker for such a
tussle, for he was backed only by his bogy-fear of God,
which was all that his religion amounted to, and half
of him was already on her side, for had he not asked
her for a " word " that would keep her hens safe
against disaster, until he had made his obeisances, and
could lend a more material aid? The silent fight lasted
but a few seconds, and he took up his hat, and went
off with Nancy. And a fine score was adding up, he
thought to himself, against young Dennis, for it was
he who had engineered this impious business in place
of church-going, and he who had bade Nell run off
to St. Columb's and fetch his Willie. The boy would
rue this morning's work, sure enough.

Dennis had scarcely got into his working clothes,
when Willie came trotting up from St. Columb's, and
the two went out with the saw and consulted how to
tackle their work. The trunk of the tree that had
stood on a high knoll behind the wall had fallen across
it, and lay there almost horizontal, and the wall bulged
ominously with its weight, threatening to collapse. It
was necessary therefore to sever the trunk close to where
it rested on the wall, and thus relieve it of the weight of
the heavy branches that now hung over the henhouse.
But it would not do just to cut the trunk in half,

for the top part of the tree would then simply fall on to the coops and crush all beneath it. So first they propped up the branches with stiff strong stakes thrust below them so that when the trunk was severed they would be supported. After that they could lop off the smaller branches, and get access to the imprisoned animals without fear of the wall collapsing.

Half an hour's furious work in hammering the stakes against the underside of the branches rendered them pretty secure against their crashing when the trunk was severed, and now they climbed up on to the wall and got the big saw to work on the trunk. The quicker this was done the better, for every moment was dangerous, and swiftly the saw buzzed to and fro: luckily the sap flowed late into the ash in springtime, and the wood was not yet toughened and moist with it. Out came Mrs. Pentreath to watch them, her hair blown across her face by the wind, and heedless of the flaws of cold rain that dashed against her, and screamed encouragement.

"Good lads, good lads," she cried, "you're more nor half through already. You'll save my hens yet, and good fortune will light on your house, Willie, like the swallows returning year by year, and the desire of your heart shall be yours. Well done, Dennis, you made the sawdust fly with that strong stroke, and for you there'll be a lass so fair to hold in your arms that you'll wish the morning would never dawn, and the farm shall prosper in your hands when you come into your own, and the blight shall spare your corn——"

She paused in this spate of benedictions: the trunk was all but cut through and the danger over, when she saw the wall quiver, and mortar crumble out from

between the bulging bricks. She waved her arms
in the air, then grew rigid as the stones of the circle,
with eyes shut and mouth working furiously. When
she looked again, the wall still stood and with two
more pulls of the saw the trunk was severed. The
top part creaked as it subsided on to the stakes and
struts the boys had put there to support it; the
other piece, relieved of the weight of the upper branches,
was now harmless.

They scrambled down from their perch; there was
Mollie fairly dancing on the threshold, and she threw
an arm round each.

" The best morning's work you ever did, lads," she
cried. " Come you both quick into the kitchen and
have your dinner, whether my old psalm-singer is back
from church or not: I'll dish it up for you. And
there'll be a bit of gold for each of you that I'll cross
your palms with, and 'twill bring you days of pleasure
and nights of joy. And when you've fed, off you go
again to loose the boughs off my henhouse, and I'll give
them their victuals."

She took them into the kitchen just as the church
party returned, and now that her hens were safe all
her fury against her husband was gone, and genially
she gabbled.

" Eh, John Pentreath," she said, " a rare morning's
work have the lads done, 'twas good to watch the hefty
fellows. And you with your church-going! Well, I'll
not rile you more over that: one thinks one way, and
one another; you're for the Lord, but give me a pair
of lusty young men like them if I'm in a fix. But
I'll meet you half-way: I'll say 'twas the Lord that
heard your prayers, if so be you minded to mention
my hens, and He put the vigour into their arms. Eh,

they made the sawdust fly like spurts of water, beautiful
to see. But let's have dinner: there's a roast cockerel,
and I was feared that my broody hens 'ud soon be as
dead as he. Say grace, John, and whatever you say, I'll
give Amen to you."

A pleasant old lady, thought Willie, for she had
clasped a ten-shilling piece in his hand, and bade him
sit next her, but, God, how her pretty speeches frightened him! She was friends, as he knew, with old Sally
Austell, who kept house for his master, and there was
trouble for those who crossed them. It was just as well
that he had earned Mrs. Pentreath's good-will, for those
two old hags between them knew a terrible lot. She
put her teeth on the table, and sucked and swallowed
at bits of that bird that must surely have been a fighting
cock in the days of his youth. Would it be polite to
say, " What beautiful teeth, ma'am! " or were they
just a bit of absentmindedness, sitting grinning at him
by his elbow? But he thought but little of her, for it
was Dennis who mattered most, and not a look did he
get from him: Dennis's eyes were all on Nell. So
that was the way of it. Dennis was turning to the
girls, as he had suspected this long time past, and that
was why he so seldom came down to St. Columb's now
when his work was done.

Next Dennis sat his mother: Willie thought she
seemed a bit shy of him, and little wonder, for she had
brought back the lantern yesterday, meaning no doubt
to go into the studio through the garden door and pop
it down, but, as ill-luck would have it, Willie had been
cleaning up there at the time, so now she knew he must
have guessed who had come in the night before and
stayed so late. And at the end of the board was
Dennis's grandfather, black and silent. As soon as

dinner was over he had moved from the table, and gotten a great Bible, and sat smoking his pipe in a chair by the window.

Then Dennis and Willie went out to make sure of the security of what they had done, and to cut away the boughs that still sprawled over the hen-run. They were as clever as two mechanics over it, working just by common sense. The thick sections of the trunk and boughs must first be sawn off and removed, and so surely had they strutted them up that they could work on them as if they stood on the solid ground. After they had been taken off the lighter boughs were easy to handle, and in an hour the whole was clear, and Mrs. Pentreath could get at her hens again, and bring them their provender. There were a rare lot of eggs to be gathered, and she heaped her basket.

The two boys took the saw to the woodshed when they had finished, and sat for a while on the bench outside, for neither wanted to go back into the kitchen. For the first time since their friendship had blossomed out of their fight, there was an embarrassment between them, and perhaps it was better to speak of the cause of it now, thought Willie, for the longer the delay the harder it would be to bring it out.

" That Nell Robson's a rare pretty piece, Dennis," he said.

Dennis had been troubled just like his friend. He laid his hand on Willie's shoulder.

" Iss sure," he said. " And it's come to me, Willie. I'm fair top-heavy wi' the thought of her. It happens to all, don't it? "

" Pretty nigh. I thought there was something when evening by evening now you've never come down to St. Columb's for a talk and a saunter."

" Savage with me, Willie? " asked Dennis.

" Nay, not savage, for 'tisn't your fault. Might have happened to me instead. But there 'tis, and I reckon all's past and done with now."

" And what'll you be meaning by past and done with? " asked Dennis.

" This last three years. You and me, not wanting aught else but us."

" Well, there's a silly thing to mean! " said Dennis. " You're the lad of my heart, same as ever, but 'tis no use talking, if you haven't got that in your marrows after all this long while. There you are, Willie, and there you'll bide, and none can come betwixt you and me, not Nell nor another."

" And you'll give your hand on that? "

" Iss, fey, and a thump with it afterwards for making such rubbishy talk about the love of us two being past and done with."

They sat there a while yet in a silence as intimate as any talk could be. The wind of the night had subsided into an absolutely dead calm, and the rain had ceased, but it was dark for so early in the afternoon, not yet much after two o'clock, for the whole sky was overlaid with that yellowish curtain of cloud thicker now and completely concealing the sun, and the light that came through it was wan, like the breaking of a stormy morning.

" A rum day," said Dennis at length, " with the barometer-glass in its boots, and yet not a breath of wind. Eh, what's that? "

On the still air there rose a noise like the roar of a furnace, when the doors are thrown open. It grew rapidly louder, until the sky boomed with the bellowing of it, and it came from above, for now, though still no wind reached them here, the vapours overhead were torn asunder like the rending of a woven fabric: then down the hurricane plunged like a stooping hawk on to the earth. Crash went another tree in the garden, and the blast struck the house with a solid blow that made it shudder. Yet this was but the fringe of the central fury that yelled its way across the fields a few hundred yards off, and Dennis, with a sudden apprehension, ran round into the garden, from the wall of which he could see the field where the sheep were folded. The wind nearly blew him back again as he leapt up, but he steadied himself and beheld. Of the three trees between which the shelter of hurdles had been erected two had fallen across it. A few sheep only could be seen cantering distractedly about.

Dennis jumped down again.

" God, the ewes and the little ones! " he cried to Willie. " The trees have fallen right across the fold we made for 'm. I'll go tell Grandfather, and then we'll be off with an axe and a saw and a crowbar: maybe there's some buried there unhurt."

He ran into the kitchen. John Pentreath had put his Bible from him at the sound of that huge wind, and turned round as Dennis entered, as if knowing he had news.

" Well, out with it," he cried.

" Two trees have fallen across the fold, Grandfather," he said. " We're off there, Willie and I, to see what can be saved."

" I'll be following you," he said.

Straight along the line of the hurdles had the trees fallen, and there was shambles beneath. What lay directly under the trunks needed no guessing, and there was havoc enough without that. Here a heavy branch

had been snapped off by the fall, and lay across the
buttocks of an ewe, pinning her under it.   She turned
dying eyes on them, with little bleating moans as they
levered the branch away.   She was all smashed up,
and her dead lamb lay flattened out beside her.
Another was caught by a hind leg, but was quite unhurt, scrambling to her feet when they released her
with no more than a limp: another's head was crushed
in, and her two lambs were tugging at her teats, and
others were burst asunder, a pool of blood, and a pool
of milk.   John Pentreath had soon joined them, and
he had brought his gun with him: those injured beyond hope of recovery he shot.

The wind still blew half a gale, though the hurricane
was past, and now the rain began to fall heavily again
on the lambless ewes and the motherless.   Not a word
did he give either of the boys, and when about sunset the work was over he counted up the number that
remained, and shouldering his gun, went home.

All supper time there had been silence but for the
wind and thick falling rain outside.   There was
nothing to be said about so dire a disaster.   John Pentreath had eaten nothing, but he had drunk more than
his wont, and now he sat with an empty pipe in his
mouth waiting for the clearing of the table to be done.
Then, as was usual of a Sunday evening, Nell and Nancy
and Dennis ranged themselves by the table for prayers,
and Mollie pushed back her chair.   John stared at
them all a moment, seeing nothing of them, as if he had
wakened in a strange room, and did not know where
he was.   Then he made his bearings and got up.

" Aye, it'll be prayers you're waiting for," he said,
and went to the head of the table.   But instead of

kneeling there he stood.

"I've been meditating on the Lord God," he said, "and do you all hearken to the voice of my prayer. What I tell you is that I, John Pentreath, curse the Lord God, and spit on His damned name. He's been playing the dirty on me, while I've been busy worshipping Him, and while I've been calling on Him as a present help in trouble it's He who's been sending the trouble on me, and I'm not going to slobber on Him no more. Black ways He has to his friends."

Mollie gave a great cackle of laughter.

"Well done, John Pentreath," she cried. "I like your prayings to-night. Talkin' a bit o' sense at last."

The bawling voice went on.

"Never a Lord's Day for twenty years have I missed His service, and to reward that, where's the comfort of His help? Answer me that, any of you. You, Nancy, what do you say to that?"

"Lor'! Mr. Pentreath, do have done," said Nancy. "You'll be sorry for what you've said."

"Is that so? I'll be sorry when the Lord gives me back my ewes and my lambs. Iss, indeed, there's a fine loving Shepherd for you! That's what He's done for me, and cursed be His Name and His works for ever and ever, Amen. Now get you all to bed, and that's the last prayer you ever hear from John Pentreath. Amen and Amen, say I, if none of you has the spunk to say it, too. God, I'm going to have a proper drink to-night. Off with you!"

II

When John was left to himself, he soon finished his bottle and went to the cupboard to get another. To-

night the drink seemed to take no hold on him: that
muddled content and sense of comfort that should have
been his by this time wouldn't come near him, and his
step was as steady, when now he walked up and down
the room trying to blur that ruinous tragedy of the
afternoon, as when he set off in his Sunday blacks to
church that morning. There it still was, ghastly and
distinct as ever, that stricken field, the dead beasts
and the maimed which he had shot, and up above the
windy sky that terrible Lord God laughing at him.
And perhaps He hadn't done with His jokes yet, for
the wind still roared round the house, and rain, with a
volley or two of hail, beat on the windows, and that
would be fine for the young springing corn, and for
the ewes and lambs that had survived. More jokes yet,
perhaps; for the old house, solid though it was, was
full of strange groaning creaks as the wind punched it.
Likely the cow-house would fall in, and there'd be a
rare pasty of blood and milk again; strawberries and
cream no doubt for the Lord God! He'd be fair
blown out with blood-sacrifice! Well: he had said
what he thought of Him. . . .

There was no abatement in the fury of the wind, and
as John sat and shuddered at it, wondering what new
disaster the morning might reveal, his mind began to
misgive him as to what he had said, calling his family
to witness that he had done with the Lord. But had
the Lord done with him yet? What if He had sent
this disaster just to test him as He had tested Abraham,
to see if He submitted to His will, with the purpose of
rewarding him a hundredfold for what he had lost,
if he took his chastisement as from a loving Father?
Now perhaps he had made God his foe indeed. Perhaps
God had said to Himself, " So be it then, John Pen-

10

treath!"; had taken up his challenge, had lifted a
finger and nodded to the terrors and the pestilences
that lay couched beside His throne, bidding them go
forth and get on the trail of John Pentreath. Eh, it
was an awful thing to make an enemy of Him; He
could open the vials of His wrath, and pour them out
upon you, and at the end topple you over into the pit
of eternal damnation. Sure, He had always the last
word!

The terror gained on him as he glowered and drank,
and hearkened to the thump and squeal of the wind
and the rattle of the rain. He rose from his seat,
dropping his pipe on to the floor, and slid on to his
knees by the table, clasping his hands together. Perhaps
it was not too late yet, and he was eloquent with all
he had drunk.

"Lord God!" he hiccupped, "have mercy upon
me, a miserable sinner. I have erred and strayed from
Thy ways, and there is no health in me. Thou didst
send on me to-day a sore chastisement, and instead of
receiving it as from a loving hand, I started aside
like a broken bow, and in the stubborn wickedness of
my heart, I cursed Thee and blasphemed. Lord, forgive the iniquity of my transgressions against Thee. I
spoke in the anguish of my soul, and I knew not what
I said. Justly Thou visitedst me for all my backslid-
ings, wherewith I have provoked Thine anger and
indignation against me. I will make atonement for all
my wickedness, and conduct myself uprightly in
humble fear of Thee and Thy judgments. I will
follow a godly and sober life, and I will lead those
whom Thou hast committed to me in Thy way. . . ."

He paused: what had happened? Even as he prayed
the wind had dropped and the rain beat no longer on

the panes. A sign, for sure, that his prayers were heard.

"Praise the Lord, praise ye the Lord," he gabbled. "He spake the word, and the wind was still, and there came a great calm. He heard the voice of my humble petition: He sent down from on high, and took me out of the deep waters. Amen and Amen."

He scrambled to his feet, and opened the kitchen door: a night of stars was there and of full moon near to its setting over the west. The Lord was good: what should he do to reward Him?

He tipped some more spirits into his glass: the water jug was empty, but he could make shift without it. He had made some promises to the Lord just now in his praying, and he'd keep them too, for John Pentreath was a man of honour. There was something about leading those of his household in the Lord's way: he must set about that. Not so easy though, for there was Mollie in the forefront of them, and a terrible lot of leading there would have to be before she got into the Lord's way. She must go after her own devices, for he was just downright afraid of crossing her.

He listened for a while after his conclusion that Mollie had best be left alone. But there was no disapproving sound of the wind rising again: the Lord God seemed to agree that this was reasonable. Perhaps He had a thought of dealing with Mollie himself.

Then there was Nancy: and his mind began slipping back into old grooves before he knew it. A good-looking buxom wench she was, with her firm breasts and her shapeliness and that clump of golden hair, and the full ripe mouth and the whorish eyes. She'd make a lusty armful in bed one night. . . . Eh, but

there was a sinful thought, an adulterous and an incestuous thought, likely to call down His wrath again.
. . . Nancy had light ways, he was afraid (that was better): there had been that artist-boy in St. Columb's a year or two ago, and it was rumoured she used to bed with him, the lucky fellow. What was he to do about Nancy, to help her turn to the Lord? He must have a tussle with himself first, and then when he'd trampled his thoughts underfoot, he must try to tackle Nancy's lightness, and bid her remember she was a woman with a grown son. Too many ribands and rouges about her. . . .

Then there was Dennis, and at the thought of Dennis he ranged himself heart and soul with the Lord. He had a long personal score against Dennis, and a drop more whisky made it stand out as clear as the print in his Bible. Again and again lately the boy had defied him: he had refused to go back to his work when ordered, he had smashed one of the old Pentreath vegetable dishes, and when John had told him to stand out and take a couple of clouts for his carelessness, he had just given that hitch to his shoulder to show his arm was loose and ready. Then, by God, this very morning he had refused to come to church, and had sent Nell down to St. Columb's to fetch up his lad, and they had made the wife's poultry safe, and gotten each of them a ten-shilling piece for their wickedness. . . . That extra dram of whisky had cleared his brain wonderful, and he began to see it all rightly. The Lord had looked down on this godless household, and seen how they made a mock of His holy day. "Two can play at that game," thought the Lord; "they've saved their chickens, but I've got a bit of a wind somewhere that'll make Me quits with their ewes and their lambs." 'Twas

Dennis's fault all along. It was all clear now, and the
Lord had sent that hurricane to mark His displeasure.
John had been a bit slack with Dennis, noting his big
fists and lithe arms, but he had promised the Lord to
lead his household in His way, and there was a long
score against the boy, anyhow.

His eye fell on the dog-whip that hung near the
kitchen door. It was a tight-plaited thong of leather,
with a bone handle to it: a dog didn't need more than
a few cuts of it, however thick its coat. Often when
Dennis was younger he had had his hands tied to the
bed-post, and had writhed under it with no coat to pro-
tect him. But now there should come to him the
chastisement of the Lord, and bitter should that chastisement be. The fear of the Lord should be put into
him, so that he'd turn from his godless ways, and learn
to fear his grandfather as well.

He took the whip down, and thought over just what
he would do. Dennis would be asleep by now, and by a
few quick movements, if John got quietly into his room
without waking him, he would awake powerless against
those slashing blows. That was what God laid on His
servant, John Pentreath, to do. Once pinioned in bed,
he would admonish him: it was the Lord who struck,
and the Lord would strike heavy and often, till he'd
learn to keep holy the Sabbath Day. John's will and
inclination alike were in the Lord's service here: there
was no tussle with himself, for desire and duty were at
one.

He had it all clear now in his mind, and he took off
his boots, and with candle in hand went noiselessly upstairs and along the passage to Dennis's room. The
handle of his door turned without a sound, and he
entered. The boy was lying fast asleep with legs out-

stretched, and turned over almost on to his face. His head lay on one arm crooked on his low pillow, the other was tucked below his chest.

John put the candle down on the washstand, tiptoed over to the bed, and planted a knee across the back of Dennis's calves, clipping them both beneath it. He stripped the blanket off him down to his hips, and with his left hand he grasped the back of the boy's neck between thumb and fingers, pressing his head down on to his arm. Then with all the savage drunken force that was in him, he slashed his back from shoulder to loin with the whip, and raised his arm again for the second cut, that was to be but one out of many more to follow.

Dennis woke out of deep sleep mad with burning pain. He saw above him grim, and tight-jawed, his grandfather's face, and knew that his legs were powerless. But before the second blow fell, he twisted his head round, lithe as a cat, and bit with all his force into the hand that gripped his neck, above and below the big thumb-joint. He felt his teeth crunch through the gristle and sinews, and grate on the bone.

At that the red lust of murder came over John Pentreath, and dropping his whip on the bed he seized Dennis's throat in both hands with a hold that was meant to strangle. And in some fanatic fashion, his drink-sodden brain encouraged him, telling him that he was fighting an enemy of God.

His movement enabled Dennis to get one arm free, and while still he held on like a bulldog to his grandfather's thumb, he picked up the whip that lay by his side, and slashed with the bone handle of it at his face. The first blow fell wide, and already his ears sang and his eyes were growing misty with this strangling clutch.   Knowing that in a few seconds he must be choked into unconsciousness, he aimed his second blow more carefully, and got home with it. Right across that savage face it fell from forehead to chin, cutting an eyelid open and biting deep into lip and cheek.   At that the pressure on his neck and throat relaxed, and he released that gnawed thumb and wrenched himself free.

He spat the blood with which his mouth was full on the boards by the bedside; his legs were still imprisoned, and there was strength in the tough old drunkard yet.   Out shot his hand, and with open palm he hit him with all his force on the cheek, and at that the pressure on his legs became a mere inert weight, and he easily shuffled free of it, and struggled out of bed.   He took hold of his grandfather's shoulders, and shook him till his head nodded to and fro like a marionette's.

" That's what you get from me," he cried, blind with fury.   " And do you give in now, or I'll shake the head off your lousy shoulders.   Answer me, you old scruffy-head! "

Dennis waited a moment, standing over him ready to bash him again if need be.   But no answer came, for John Pentreath collapsed across the bed.   Then, without more ado, Dennis picked up the limp burden, slinging it over his shoulder like a sack, and with John's candle in his hand carried it down the passage.   He rapped hard on Nancy's door as he passed, and before he had come to his grandfather's room, she had opened it, and followed him.

" Lor'!   What's up, Dennis? " she said.   " What have you done to your grandfather?   And you without a stitch on, why, 'tis shameful."

He dropped the burden on the bed.

"Hush!" he said. "No need to wake Grannie. You look after him. Bleeding like a pig, he is."

He turned round, showing his back to her.

"That's what he gave me while I was asleep," he said; "aye and near scragged me. Go and tend him, Mother, and see what I gave him when I woke. His face is a wisht sight, ain't it, and look to his hand: same as if someone had bitten it, and I shouldn't wonder if it had happened so. God, how my back burns, and my throat's squeezed in half. So that's what he got for it, the bloody old drunkard, and I'll give him twice as bad next time. I'll get my coat and bags on and come back."

Dennis broke into silent laughter.

"Looks as if he made a bit of a mistake in his manner of praying to-night," he said. "Cursing God doesn't seem to do much for a man. What the hell for did he want to go for me, who'd saved Grannie's hens and worked like a nigger to do summat for his sheep? And me asleep, too, the swine!"

CHAPTER VII

KENRITH COPSE

ONE afternoon, some three weeks later, John Pentreath strolled into the kitchen from the farmyard to sit and have a pipe in his arm-chair. The kitchen was empty, for Nancy had gone down into St. Columb's for her shopping, Nell was weeding in the garden, Dennis out at work, and his wife packing a crate of eggs for the market. Never had the poultry been so fruitful: the hens seemed to be made of eggs, though on the farms round they were still scarce and the market prices high. Mollie was in luck and no mistake, but that didn't profit John, for all her money went into her own pocket. But she had been decent about letting him have plenty of chicken broth during the days when he had been on slops.

For the first time since that Sunday evening, he was feeling himself again. Till to-day all his life-force had been absorbed in the work of physical repair, just doing the mending, but to-day it was flowing back into its accustomed channels. His eyelid had had a couple of stitches put in it, but it had done finely, and the stitches had been taken out that morning. His hand had given the most trouble: there had been a lot of suppuration, but now it had healed from the bottom of the wound upwards and the new skin was healthy. There had been some very bad days, and what made them worse was that his drink had been cut off altogether, and the craving for it had been harder to bear than all the pain. But the doctor from St. Columb's, the first to cross the threshold of the farm for the last ten years, had told him pretty roundly that he might as well take a pint of weed-killer as get to his whisky again: the weed-killer would do for him a bit quicker, but the other was just as sure. So, for all these days, he had had to bear the fever and the weakness and the fierce stabbings of his hand without other alleviation than ointments and dressings.

Another kind of fortitude not less stubborn was required to face the profound physical humiliation that Dennis had heaped upon him, and that which he had suffered at the hands of some infinitely more potent agency, though, God knew, Dennis had been potent enough! What that was, or how it had all happened, his appalling theology, based on the existence of a jealous God swift to avenge Himself on sinners, was unable to determine. Had he offended by not preventing any rescue of the poultry during church-time on that Sunday morning? It looked as if that might be so, for the disaster to his sheep had followed close on its heels. That surely had driven him mad, and he had cursed God and blasphemed against His Name. But swift again on the heels of his blasphemy had followed his repentance, and God had surely sent a sign to show He accepted that by causing the storm to cease. Then to demonstrate that his repentance was real, he had gone upstairs to flog Dennis for not keeping holy the Sabbath morning and pay off other scores against him, with untoward results. There was no unravelling it at all: Mollie, who had not said a prayer nor been to church these twenty years, was jingling with coin from the hens. Was it possible to wonder, silently so that no one should hear, whether she wasn't the wiser of them? Often she had mocked at him for his church-goings and his Sunday abstinences, telling him that God must be a mighty flat if He didn't see through him, and that his observances were a mere bit of hypocrisy, a spell for Sundays in which he did not really believe. All these reflections, running round and round in his head, made a pleasant accompaniment indeed to the long sleepless nights, and puzzle as he might he could not get things straight.

Then why had he not been more careful how he had gripped Dennis's neck, instead of letting him wriggle his head round and get his teeth into him? He'd have taught him a lesson that would have marked him for a lifetime if he had gripped him more securely, and held him down till he had flogged him into utter surrender of body and spirit, though it had taken all night to do it. He'd have broken him down, so that a glance at the whip by the kitchen door would have made him go white. Not a day or an hour would have passed, when the boy was fit to move again, in which he would not have rubbed in his abject humiliation. He would have gelded him of all courage and spirit. He would have made a shambling shame-faced coward of him, he would have told all St. Columb's what he'd done to him; he'd have taken him down to the pier and cuffed and kicked him before the fisher-boys and women, so that all should see how John Pentreath brought up his family in the fear of the Lord. . . . But things had turned out otherwise, and when two days before he had come down for the first time for midday dinner, it was he who had dreaded Dennis's entrance. If Dennis had taken the dog-whip off its nail, and said, " Now, sit you there, Grandfather, and I'll give you a bit more of what I owe you," John knew

that he'd no more fight left in him, and would just
have cowered in his chair. But Dennis hadn't even
given him a glance, and since then he had spoken only
half-a-dozen words to him, just ordinary, about the
farm, asking him whether he wanted the cows turned
into the far pasture, or put in the field where the sheep
had been. But John had been aware, in the very
marrow of his bones, how the boy despised him, and
if he did not rub in his contempt with insults and
jeerings, it was merely because he did not consider
him worth it.

And all the women in the house knew what had
happened, and had the same contemptuous commisera-
tion for him. . . . There had been a fight to-day between two fisher-fellows in St. Columb's, and Nell had
brought news of it. " And then Jim Carlyon gave the
other fellow a fine clout and split his eyelid for him,
much the same as Mr. Pentreath's," she had said. And
Mollie had been equally explicit. " Glad to see you
down again, John, after all your misfortunes. Well,
we've all got to learn not to loose hand or tongue
against them that's stronger nor us. There's a couple
of eggs for you: better that than meat just yet."

That grim saying gave him something to ponder.
Did Mollie allude to Dennis only, or to his own blasphemies that Sunday night?

All these days when he had been in bed, Nancy had
looked after him entirely. She knew a bit about nursing, she was far more active and quick-handed than
Mollie, who bungled with the bottles, and once poured
out a dose of liniment into his medicine glass, and
would have given it him to take, had not Nancy intervened. It was much better that one woman should be
in charge, and it was at Mollie's suggestion, made to

Nancy and sanctioned by the doctor, that the two had changed rooms so that Nancy could be near him at night, with an open door between them, and often she had come in, just in her nightgown, to give him a sedative draught, if the pain was bad, with the sexless indifference of a nurse, whose only thought is for the patient, be he man or woman. But as he regained his strength, there was more in it than that for him: pretty feet she had with slim ankles, and by the light of the candle she carried he could conjecture the outline of her breasts and the full haunches of her, and he would call her without reason, in order to have a look at her. But in the morning when she came to see to him and bring his breakfast, and do the dressings, God, how tactless she was in her encouragements, letting her pride in Dennis involuntarily betray itself.

" Why, your thumb's healing finely," she said, " and at last there's the good skin coming over it as soft as a child's! Lor', what a bite the lad gave you: lucky he always keeps his teeth clean, else he'd have poisoned you. And now for your poor cheek: that's doing well, too. My word, he let out at you then! Something cruel, wasn't it, with that nasty dog-whip, and him pinned down under you! But such arms the boy's got, they're more like the limbs of a young horse. I *was* surprised when he tapped at my door, for all naked he'd carried you along to your room, just as if you was a baby, six feet high, slung over his shoulder. Now you hold your head still, Mr. Pentreath, while I attend to your poor eye, and don't you move if I hurt you. I'll go as gentle as a woman can. You men don't know what it is to bear a bit of pain without wincing, though I'm sure Dennis was steady enough with a great weal across his back, and his throat, why, it's swollen still where you tried to strangle him. He won't let you off so easy next time you think to go for him. There! Now I'll run and fetch you a bit of toast for your breakfast and a cup of tea."

But wonderful kind and attentive, he allowed, Nancy had been. She had been in and out of his room all day, bringing him his food or his bedpan, and cleaning and dressing his wounds, according to orders, deft and cheerful and nimble with her fingers. She brought him any bits of news there might be, telling him how the hay was getting on, trimming her new hat as she sat by his bed, or reading to him aloud out of her trashy book. She seemed to like to be with him, to wash and tidy him, to brush his hair for him. The woman, so he began to figure it to himself, enjoyed ministering to him. All this kindled his sex-feeling towards her, and most of all those visits to him at night. But now, worse luck, there would be no more of them, for Nancy was moving back to her room, and Mollie would be sleeping again next door. Dr. Symes had been this morning, and congratulated Nancy on her success with the patient, but there was now no longer any need for her to be within call at night. Nor would he pay him any more visits, and by way of rubbing the smart in, told him that a hard-drinking fellow like him positively had no right to have recovered so quickly.

" And if you take my advice, Pentreath," he said, " you'll cut down your drink, say, to a quarter of your usual dose. I'd tell you to stop it altogether, if I thought there was the slightest chance of your doing so. But if you don't cut it down, you'll have an attack of delirium tremens that'll carry you off without your having the trouble of getting bashed about first. I advise you to respect your constitution, because it's a most respectable one."

" Aye, that's the way of my family," said John.

" And that Dennis of yours inherits it. He's the strongest and finest boy in these parts, so you'd better respect him as well. I've given him a good talking to, I may tell you, and told him he was a bloody young ruffian, and he'll be quiet and civil with you, and do his work."

All this John thought over as he smoked his pipe in the empty kitchen. Then Mollie came in, after sending off her crate of eggs, and Nancy began busying herself with boiling the fowl that Mollie had granted out of her superabundance, for supper. There was more to think over yet, the clatter disturbed him, and he strolled out into the garden as the sun began to redden in the west, conscious, after these days of bed and low vitality, of the lure of the matured spring, even more keenly than when on that Sunday afternoon in February it had danced and dangled between his eyes and his Bible-reading. But to-day was not Sunday, so he could indulge any sort of fancy without fear of offence to the Inexplicable Ones. And there was a thrill, a keen edge to his perceptions, the like of which he had not known for years, and he sat there in acute, not stupefied, content. Every sense seemed bright and shining, like polished channels through which the stream of his consciousness passed: it was with delight that his nostrils drank in the scents of the garden, stewing in the warm air, after those stale smells of oint-ment and lotions, and with delight that his eyes, after the days of staring at the discoloured walls of his bed-room, looked across the fields to the quivering azure of the bay. His food at dinner had not been mere material to be hungrily bolted, but a sweet savour with the conscious sense of nourishment to follow. There had been Nancy, too, at dinner to be looked at greedily in swift glances. She had always been an attractive wench, but doubly so she was now, when he had seen her night after night coming into his room with just her shift to cover her. He knew now how seductive she was when she smiled at him with eyes suffused with sleep, and the fibre of his blood stiffened at the thought of seeing her thus again, though she would no longer come to him of a night. . . .

Perception and desire alike, after these days of apathy, were beginning to flow again like a stream restored by rains, and among desires came that of drink. If food tasted so good to-day, what unimaginable nectar would be his first glass of whisky! But he must go carefully, after what that outspoken doctor had told him, and certainly he must drop that habit of sitting soaking every night. A glass or two after supper could not hurt anybody, and perhaps his abstinence had something to do with these quickened perceptions and sense of heightened enjoyment. Just once a week or so, he might let himself go, and have a proper drink again; and if you came to look at it, these twenty years and more of getting at least half tipsy every night hadn't hurt him yet, for the doctor had been amazed at the speed and completeness with which his hurts had healed. Bitten down to the bone he had been, and there was little power in his thumb, for some of the sinews had been severed, and the joint was very stiff still. But power would come back in time, he was assured, and externally now there was only visible the slightly curved scar of pink new skin on each side of his thumb where that damned boy's teeth had bitten.

Among all these quickened perceptions there was none more acute than his hatred for Dennis and the surety that he would get even with him some day. There was no flogging that he could give him, even if he was capable of administering it (and he'd had the best chance that man ever had) which could make up for all he had received at his hands, but the account had got to be squared with a bit of balance in his favour too. There surged into his mind again the memory of that distinct and definite desire, when Dennis's teeth were bulldogged into his hand, to strangle him. He had been drunk then, he had been in the clutch of that hellish pain that shot up his arm like a redhot iron, but now when sober and sitting browsing in the sun, he could visualise that murderous fog that had turned everything scarlet.

The click of the garden gate sounded, and there was the boy himself coming back from his work. He wore a sleeveless shirt, open at the neck, his hair gleamed gold in the sun, his bare arms swung loosely as he walked. His neck, round and muscular, rose like a pillar from his low square shoulders, and there was still the mark of a bruise on the left side of it. He was whistling, and he passed close to his grandfather, just nodding to him, without a word and without ceasing his shrill tune, and went through the gate into the farmyard.

So that was what the boy thought of him, was it, going by as if he were an old mangy dog, crawled out to warm himself in the sun. He would think different some day, when he found himself looking down the barrels of John Pentreath's gun. Dennis mustn't be asleep then, he must see what was coming, and at whose hands he faced death: just to kill him while he slept would rob revenge of half its honey. And then perhaps his ruddy brown face would go white beneath its tan, his eyes would be raised in hopeless appeal, and he'd stop his whistling. But it must all be carefully planned, and nothing could be done for a long while yet: he must wait till Dennis's mauling of him had been forgotten, or no one would believe it to be an accident.

To-night for the first time he sat up for supper: rare and tender was the chicken, and Nancy had cooked it to a turn. She was in the best of spirits, for she had received a most welcome letter from Harry Giles. He had been away up in London for the last fortnight, but now he wrote saying that he would be back at St. Columb's on Friday, so that if by chance she had another sleepy fit that night, she would be very welcome if she cared to come and take a nap at the corner house in Kenrith Lane. Arrangements about the studio door as usual. . . . So like him and his fun! It had gone to her heart to burn his note, but the fire was the best place for it. You couldn't tell who mightn't be prying and watching in this house, which seemed to be all eyes and ears. So into the fire it went as she served up the chicken in high good-humour.

"You'll be cutting up your meat for yourself to-morrow, Mr. Pentreath," she said. "I believe you could do it to-night, but you like to be waited on. I saw Parson down to St. Columb's this afternoon, who asked after you, and I told him as like as not you'd be in your place in church again come Sunday. You're a wonder you are for healing after such a chaw-up; I'm sure I never thought we'd see you about again for a long while yet. There's a nice piece of wing I've cut up for you, and there'll be another bit cold to-mor-row. And won't you have a glass of your usual to-night? You'll 'most have forgotten the taste of it."

"Aye, that I will," he said. "Fetch me the bottle from the cupboard, there's a good girl."

"Yes, that'll do you good," said Mollie.

Nectar indeed it was, and he sipped it, smacking his lips for the fuller appreciation of it. "That's what I wanted," he said. "Seems to me you always know what I want, Nancy. You've done a lot for me, early and late, since I was last down for supper. I'll take just a drain more, and then you can put the bottle back in the cupboard, for that's my ration for to-night."

Supper over, he had his pipe, and his eyes kept fol-lowing Nancy as she helped in clearing the table. She took off the cloth, holding the edge with arms out-stretched, then brought them together as she folded it, just as if she were casting them round something that lay against her breast. Then she got her book, but to-night she had little diligence; it was as if her thoughts made a more attractive picture, and her eyes wandered from the page, and catching his, she would smile at him and bend to her reading again. Nothing of this was lost on Mollie, and what she saw seemed to please her. All was going just as she wished: John was coming alive again, and, though he could spare an ugly look at Dennis, it was on Nancy that his thoughts were fixed, and well Mollie could read them. He was getting afire for her, just as Mollie would have him do: it had been a rare thought of hers that Nancy should take the room next him while he was ill, and attend to him night and day, a rare thought indeed, and well it had worked: it might be useful, too, to have been tenant of Nancy's room during these days, for she could find her way

about it in the dark, if need be. But now Nancy's nursing was done, and one night before long she would be
getting sleepy again after supper, and nip off, after
she'd locked her door and put the key above the lintel,
to see her fancy-man down to St. Columb's. That was
the night for which Mollie was waiting: a long wait it
had been, and a fair puzzle it had been to work her plan
out, but she had been patient and contriving, and it
was ready now. And John would be ready too, she
surmised, when she had chatted with him a bit after
Nancy had felt herself a sleepy-head, some night soon.

The speechless clock whirred, indicating nine, and
John went to the cupboard and took a stiff dram for
a nightcap.

"I'll be off to bed," he said.

"Get a good sleep," said Nancy, "and, come morning, you'll be frisking like a two-year-old."

Mollie bent her head over her knitting, in some
noiseless spasm of mirth.

"And I'm next door again to you," she said; "if
you want aught before morning give me a call. Nancy's
had some broken nights, I warrant."

Dennis had occasion on the afternoon of this Friday,
so eagerly expected by his mother, to go on some farm-
ing errand over to Penerth, which lay in the combe
below the pool beside which the ecstasy of his running
had come to its climax on that spring night of wind
and rain some weeks before. He was detained there
longer than he had anticipated, and before he set out
on his return the sun was setting, and a crescent moon
low in the sky was beginning to gild itself. His

directest way home lay through a strip of the ill-famed
Kenrith copse, to which that night he had given a good
wide berth with a prudence he half despised, which yet
sprang from some inbred instinct. But to-day it was
only early evening: at the worst he could but meet
some old dame like Sally Austell, muttering to herself
as she gathered a bundle of fallen sticks, or whatever
her business there might be; if he did, he would be
very polite to her, help her for a few minutes, and
maybe he'd get a blessing from her instead of a cursing
and a twitching of her lips. So wanting to get home
as quick as might be, he struck into the footpath that
led through the wood.

Strangely dark it was under the trees, when he had
got a bit of a way in. The red-grey fir-trunks stood
close, like pillars supporting the sombre roof of their
branches, and the air was dead still, as if in a shut room.
The ground was strewn with lichen-covered boulders:
they gleamed whitely on this side and that as he
threaded his way along, with foot noiseless on the fallen
needles. But ahead it was lighter, for not far off now
was the clearing in the centre of the wood, where stood
that old stone table, which had been there, it was said,
as long as the circle in the midst of the ploughed field.
There were legends about it, similar to those attached
to the circle. It had been an altar according to tradition, and blood-sacrifices were made on it, and magic
dances done round it, and women who performed such
rites got their heart's desire if it was a child they
wanted: all knew that not many years ago old Sally
Austell used to be seen capering there, and sure enough
a child she had, though she was gone fifty, and none
knew who the father might be. But these things were
not much spoken of, for Kenrith copse was an evil

place, and such spells were black, not the white magic
of the circle, where every Midsummer Eve lads and
lasses newly wed danced together, and Parson, being
Cornish bred, himself looked on.

Dennis had come close to the clearing; glimpses of
it appeared between the tree-trunks. Then suddenly,
on the still air there shrilled up the cry of an animal,
as of a creature caught in a trap. Two long yowls it
gave, and there was silence again. Moving a step on
he caught sight of the stone table. There was a woman
standing beside it, her hands busy at something that
lay on it with a kneading movement, and he saw who
it was. At that, sheer curiosity, with horror pricking
through it, as to what she was doing here, overscored
all other feelings, and he peered out, bending low, from
behind a tree and watched her.

Mollie picked up that which was lying on the altar,
and Dennis saw that it was a cat. The fur was soaked
in blood, and she squeezed the twitching body with
both hands, as if squeezing a sponge to wring the water
from it. She dipped her fingers in the blood that lay
in a pool on the stone, and opening her dress smeared
her breasts with it. She was muttering to herself the
while, and he could see her mouth working, milling out
the words silently, as if at some private devotion, but
presently, when she had anointed herself, her voice grew
audible and rose to a shrill gabbling sort of chant, and
then she curtsied three times, swift and low, so that
her skirts billowed up round her.

Still chanting she began some uncouth kind of dance
round the stone table. Her hair fell on her shoulders
as she whisked about in those frenzied antics, all alone
in the black circle of pines beneath the moon. Had
Dennis imagined for himself such a spectacle as this

lone woman presented, the thought of it would have made him laugh, but now, when he was witness of it, the very spring and source of merriment froze within him and the antique creeds and superstitions of his race stirred in his blood. Some ritual, secret and reverend, ordained the extravagant gestures, the prancings, the jerky wooden pirouettings; glee and the spirit of worship inspired them, and the sight made his skin to prickle and his hair to stir. Then suddenly her chants and her dancings ceased, and she threw herself on her back on the ground spent and panting for breath after these awesome antics.

Dennis crept stealthily away back along the path he had come, with glances behind him to see if he was being followed, and once clear of the wood, he ran like a hare.

Supper at the farm was nearly over when Mollie came in. Nancy had been in a fine fuss over her lateness, for in these lengthening days the hour had been moved to eight, and it was gone half-past before she came into the kitchen. Nancy bounced up to give her the plate of meat which had been kept hot for her.

" Well, and what a time of night, to be sure, to come in at, Mrs. Pentreath! " she said sharply. " Where can you have been all this long while? "

Dennis glanced up at Mollie, and she sat down at the head of the table. She'd got a bit of colour in her face to-night; no wonder, he thought, after all that dancing. And now, away from that sombre ill-omened copse, the ludicrous side of what he had so fearfully witnessed overcame him. To think that an hour ago that black silent woman had been capering and cantering around, blood-bedaubed, and chanting like a mad thing. He bent over his plate, silently shaking.

" Where've I been? " she answered Nancy. " Why, just out for a saunter."

Suddenly she flared up, as any inquisitiveness was apt to make her do. " And so I've got to give an account of myself to you, have I? " she cried. " That'll be a new thing, I reckon. Mayn't I leave the house without your seeking to poke and pry into what I've been doing? Faith, there'd be some queer things known if we all told what we'd been up to."

" La! Mrs. Pentreath," said the startled Nancy. " What a taking on, to be sure! I but asked you friendly-like, no offence meant."

She passed round by the head of the table to draw the dumplings from the oven, and Mollie saw that she had on her smart Sunday shoes and a pair of new stockings. Instantly all her ill-humour vanished.

" I spoke a bit hasty, Nancy," she said. " You spoke kind and friendly like you always are, and there's no offence taken."

Silence descended again. Nancy cut up the scraps she collected from various plates, and set down a platter for the cat.

" Pussie's not been in all this evening," she said, " and him usually so keen for his supper."

" Out mousing, maybe," said Mollie.

CHAPTER VIII

VOWS RENEWED

JOHN had gone back to his usual allowance at supper, and now while the table was being cleared he filled his glass again, and set the bottle by him. That doctor had only been trying to frighten him: he had a bee in his bonnet about drink, and always told his patients that they'd be ever so much better if they never touched the muck. Little did the man know about it, and how should he, seeing he never took a glass himself? John had never felt fitter than he did to-night: he was all alert again; food was good, tobacco was good, and never had Nancy looked so alluring. He had been a fool, he thought, not to have tried his luck when she had been coming so often at any hour of the night into his room, just in her nightgown. Likely she had been inviting him all the time, or surely she'd have thrown a cloak over her: she'd been wanting to show herself to him, to see how he liked her, and, by God, he'd never liked the look of a woman more. But then all those nights he had been in pain and fever, and had done no more than take note of her without desire. What a waste, what a bit of ill-fortune that when he had such opportunities he hadn't been man enough to grab them! Once, it is true, he had determined to put such thoughts from him, but that was when the Lord had been so gracious to him over the fruitfulness of his ewes, but then the Lord had turned against him, and, after all, perhaps Mollie was right, and God wasn't much more

to him than a superstition. Besides, what of King
David and his Bathsheba and his concubines? God
favoured him, and it was Bathsheba's son that sat on
the throne of his father. As for concubines, King David
went to them just as often as he felt a lech, and here
was John Pentreath, who'd not been near a woman for
ever so long. And as for Nancy being his son's widow,
why, the boy had been in his grave for twenty years,
and the very thought of him never entered his head
now, nor that of Nancy either, he'd warrant.

Dennis and Nell had gone up to bed, and Nancy was
at her book, a bit restless, with glances at the clock,
or maybe at him. If only Mollie would go to bed,
thought John, he would get a word with Nancy now,
and see how the land lay. But Mollie still sat on by
the fire, and presently it was Nancy who got up.

" I'm rare sleepy to-night," she said, " and I'll be off
to bed, too. It must be those nights when I was sleeping with one eye open, Mr. Pentreath, in case you
wanted something, that need to be made up."

Mrs. Pentreath could have kissed Nancy for that
word.

" It was kindly indeed that you tended him," she
said, " and many a long night do you deserve. Sleep
you well."

" And not a good-night kiss for your dad? " asked
John.

" Well, there you are, Mr. Pentreath," said Nancy,
bending to kiss his cheek. But he slipped his head round
and met her lips with his.

As soon as she had gone Mollie left her fireside chair,
and sat herself near her husband. His glass was empty,
and she refilled it for him, keeping the bottle near to
hand.

" There's a word or two I want with you, John,"
she said, " if you'll give me your ear."

" Take your choice between the pair of 'em," said
he, in high good humour.

She paused a moment, looking to see that Nancy
had shut the door, and began talking shrilly and rapidly
like a woman who had some crying grievance.

" 'Tis about Nancy," she said, " and I tell you flat
that Nancy's making up to you, and it's a thing not
to be borne, the shameless wench. Perhaps you've not
taken note of it, but I have, and you can trust a
woman's eye for that. She's fair beside herself when
you're within eyeshot. When Dennis chawed you up
she would give me no peace till I let her take my room.
I didn't think at first what she was up to, or I'd never
have let it be. She wanted to be washing you and
meddling with you all day, and having the door between you open at night, and coming in when all was
still and seeing to you. She's set on you, that's what
she is, and you must make it plain to her that you'll
have nothing to do with such ungodliness, she, your
own son's wife, and me under the same roof. Giving
airs to herself, too, and asking what I'd been doing to
be so late for supper, as if she was mistress here, and
I the widowed woman."

From under her brows she saw him grow alert and
eager, straightening himself up from his sprawling
attitude in his chair.

" A pack of nonsense, Mollie," he said. " What's
put such flightiness into your head? Me and Nancy's
good friends, as is but fitting, but you've no cause to
think that such a notion's ever come to her."

He spoke with an excitement he could not suppress,
and as he turned to fill his glass again she could hear

the bottle's lip ticking against the rim of it. She broke in again.

"But it's the truth I tell you," she cried, "that you may be on your guard, else some day you'll find her arms round your neck, and her comely face against yours, and after all, man, you're but flesh and blood, as I'd good cause to know once on a time, and you've lost none of your fire yet, I'll be bound. What'll you do then, John, when you feel her hugging you? Will you say to her, 'Get out with you, you shameless wench'? Maybe you might of a Sunday night, when you'd been hot in prayer against lascivious women, but there's more nights to the week than Sunday. I saw her kiss you to-night and press her lips to yours, and that was a pretty thing for your own wife to look on at. I tell you she's after you, and if she can get you she will."

Was it Nancy, he began to wonder, who had sought his lips just now? It had appeared so to Mollie, and perhaps she was right, though that was news to John. Little did she know, poor old soul, that every word she said was kindling him, and inflaming him with un-looked-for hope. Never had he found his wife's shrill tirades so much to his mind.

"You've got no call to say that," he said. "When has Nancy ever behaved herself other than modest and respectable toward me? Flighty she may be with her fineries, and that eye of hers that she turns on all men alike, inviting them to admire her."

"Aye, for she's a whore at heart," said Mollie; "but I'll tell you the name of the man she's set on, and that's John Pentreath. She's lying awake in her bed now thinking of you, that's the sort she is, and thirsty for you to come to her. Some night she won't contain herself any more, and once she thinks I'm in bed and asleep she'll come to you, and happen she'll get you. And then she'll go flaunting her pleasure in my face: that'll be my portion in it, and bitter herbs 'twill be."

He had had enough of her now; why wouldn't the old woman be off to bed?

" I'll hear no more of it," he said. " I'll tell Nancy what you've been saying of her, if you don't have done."

" Shouldn't wonder if you do," she said, " some night when you and she's together, and you'll laugh fine over it."

She saw his eye kindle again at that; heavily gone in drink as he was, and filling up his glass again, there was something he wanted more than the spirits. But she had set him on fire with her talk, and that was enough for Mollie.

" Well, that's all I've got to tell," she said rising, " just to set you on your guard, for you're decent-minded, and do 'ee take care of that woman, or she'll catch you one night when you're a-fire with drink and not rightly minding what you do. Eh, it's little but sorrow and bitterness that waits a woman when she comes to my age, and her man has no more use for her, while there's you, nigh fifteen years older, and two women under this roof still wanting you. I'll wish you good night."

She could have laughed to see him shrink from her kiss, and she shuffled from the room, the picture of soured womanhood. But thereafter her step became quick and light, and swiftly she ascended the stairs and softly went along the passage to Nancy's door and tried the handle. As she had expected, the door was locked, and there perched on the lintel was the key. She turned the lock and just peeped into the room, now familiar to her, which of course was empty. Nancy would be down in St. Columb's by this time, and it was no short visit that she made there, when she had gone early upstairs with a sleepy head. There'd be a clear hour and more before she was back.

But there was no time to lose, for she must be ready before John came up, and that, if she had read him aright, he'd be sure to do as soon as he thought she was gone to bed, and replacing the key on the lintel she slipped back to her own room, and undressed. She threw her wasp-striped bed-gown round her, closed her door, and went back to Nancy's room, shading her candle with her hand. On Nancy's dressing-table stood her bottle of musk-scent, and she smeared it plentifully over her mouth and neck, and blowing out the candle crept into the bed: the pillow smelt of musk, and she need hardly have troubled to daub herself with it.

Downstairs alone, but not to be alone for long, sat John Pentreath. His fuddled brain was dancing with the phantoms of desire, and he could have laughed aloud at the remembrance of that screechy voice of Mollie's counselling him to be careful about Nancy and telling him just precisely what he wanted to know. Yes: damned careful he would be, and that was why he sat here, giving the old woman time to get to bed: for a quarter of an hour by the clock would he remain before he followed her upstairs. Then he would go audibly shuffling and stumbling along, as was his wont, making the banisters creak, and so to his room, noisily opening and shutting the door but not entering. After that, no more stumblings: cat-footed he'd steal to Nancy's room. She wanted him, did she? It would never do to disappoint a handsome woman, and, by God, she'd get him.

Again he had to stifle his laughter at the thought that
Mollie for all her furtive observation had never given
an eye to him. Too busy watching Nancy: that was
a rare joke!

The voiceless clock whirred to indicate the hour of
ten, and the period of waiting which he had set himself was over. He was full up with drink to-night, and
there was no need to feign stumbling steps and make
the banisters creak. But once he had come to his door
and made pretence to close it behind him, the need for
silent going took charge of his random staggering, and
lighted by the moonshine from the passage window, he
moved ghost-like to Nancy's door, tried the handle,
and opened it.

The merest glimmer of light came through a chink
of the drawn curtains, but the odour of musk told him
that Nancy was there. Then there came some little
stir of movement from the bed to the left, and a
whisper, thrilled with expectancy.

" Lor', who's that? " said the voice, which he never
doubted was hers.

He closed the door very quietly, with the handle still
in his hand.

" Nancy! " he said.

" Why, if it isn't Mr. Pentreath," said the answering
whisper.

He felt his way across to the bed.

" Yes, 'tis me," he said. " You're not gwain to turn
me out, are you? "

" But are you sure it's safe? " came the answer. " Has
she gone to bed? "

" Yes, a quarter of an hour ago. Nothing's stirring.

" Lor'! How I've been wanting you! " said the
voice from the darkness.

Just about the time that John and Mollie were having their talk in the kitchen, Nancy was on her brisk walk down to St. Columb's. The London train got into Penzance at eight: Mr. Giles would have had his dinner, and be expecting her, "And if he's as keen for me as I'm for him," thought Nancy, "I'll be borrowing his lantern again, for the moon'll have set." Soon she saw below her the roofs of St. Columb's, silver-grey and glimmering, and the lights of the fishing fleet far out on the bay. Her step slowed down as she came opposite the house in Kenrith Lane, and she looked to see whether the thin line of light showed that the door of the studio was ajar for her entry. But it was shut, and now she must wait in the summer-house till it was opened. It seemed as if the studio itself was dark also, for no ray escaped from the window: usually a glimmer came through the chinks between the drawn curtains. But perhaps the train had been late, and he had not yet finished his dinner.

Then suddenly the light leaped up within, and she heard a footfall there. A key grated in the door, and then, instead of its being put discreetly ajar, it was thrown wide, and Dennis's Willie stood there. The light shone into the summer-house, where she had risen to her feet: to move, in the attempt to escape, would certainly betray her. If she stopped quite still he might not notice her. But even that was not to be: some slight movement of hers perhaps caught his attention.

"Hullo! Who be there?" he called out, advancing into the garden. "Why, 'tis Mrs. Pentreath, surely."

There was nothing for it, and she stepped out of shelter.

"Yes, it's me, Willie," she said. "I chanced to be down in St. Columb's seeing a lady friend. . . .   I thought I'd rest here a minute, before going up the hill again."

Willie's voice trembled with suppressed laughter.

" Was it Mr. Giles you wanted to see, ma'am? " asked he. " He's not back yet. There's been a rail accident by the Saltash Bridge, and he sent a telegram to me an hour ago that he'd not be back to-night."

" He's not hurt? Nothing wrong? " asked she.

" Not a word o' that, only that the line's blocked, and he's sleeping at Plymouth to-night, and'll be down here first train in the morning. Was there any message I could give him? "

" No, 'tis nothing. But I'd be rare obliged, Willie, if you'd say nothing of having seen me. Seems so hard to explain exactly—I'll be getting back to the farm again."

" Shall you be liking to take Mr. Giles's lantern again, ma'am? " asked Willie. " I'll have it ready for you in a jiffy."

" No, thank you, Willie: there's the moon not set yet. And you'll be sure not to speak to Dennis."

Nancy went back up the hill near as quick as she had come down it, and soon came opposite the circle of stones. An awkward thing to have happened, indeed, not to mention the cruel disappointment. " He should have telegraphed to me," she thought, " and yet that might have been awkward, too, with all those spying eyes round me. And another awkward thing would be if Mr. Pentreath hasn't gone to bed yet, and he found me stealing in, for he looked like making a boozy night of it. And him kissing me on the mouth like that, reeking he was, and it's lucky if Mrs. Pentreath didn't notice it. It was another set of lips I was wanting to-night, and, my, didn't it give me a turn when Willie said there'd been a railway accident. Nasty things

12

those trains are, and I've not set foot in one since
I came here twenty years ago. Aggravating it's all
been, but he'll be here to-morrow. I'll stop and get
my breath again a while, else I'll be blowing like a
grampus when I get to the farm. . . . Queer the stones
look in the moonshine with their long shadows: 'tis
said that there's a powerful spell in them. Yet look at
poor old Mrs. Pentreath: she visits them constant with
her bits o' bunches o' flowers, and what good luck have
they brought her? Why, nothing at all, save to eat
her own heart out with wanting. Poor thing, I'm
sure! "

She got her breath and her coolness back, and once
in the garden went very quietly, moving on the grass
instead of the crackling gravel, for who could tell who
might be watching and listening? There was an owl
scouting about, one of those big brown owls, flying
low and noiseless as a bat, and she hurried her steps to
the house. She closed the door of the studio, and felt
about for the candle-end and box of matches she
always left there. Somehow, she was ill at ease; was
there to be another awkward moment? But all the
house was silent, and she tiptoed along the passage to
her room, and found the key on the lintel. But, lor',
the door wasn't locked: that was a bit of carelessness
on her part, for in her absence anyone might have
turned the handle, and found her room empty. Very
quietly she slipped inside.

The flame of the candle she carried, still not burning
firmly, was almost blown off its wick by the draught
from the door, and before she actually saw anybody
she knew, by some animal sense, that she was not alone.
Then the flame, shaded by her hand, got a grip of the
wick. Beside her bed was standing John Pentreath,

just slipping his braces over his shoulders, and while yet her eyes had hardly taken in what they saw, she heard a rustle from the bed just behind him, and there was Mollie, sitting up, and wrapping her black and yellow bedgown round her. The faces of both, gleaming in the close candle-light, were a-fire with physical exaltation. Man and wife, to be sure, they were, indeed. But why were they in her room? Then for a moment Nancy was spectator only: neither of the others seemed to be aware of her at all, she but held the candle.

Nimbly did Mollie jerk herself out of bed, and she came close to her husband. He was fumbling with his coat, and thrust his arms into the sleeves. Dazed and drunk he was, but the fire still licked round him.

" So I'm none so amiss, John," said she. " We've sampled each other again, we've had a loving darkness together after all these years."

He moistened his lips with his tongue: his tipsiness was clearing fast.

" You? " he said. " God Almighty, you? "

She reached her arms about his neck, pulled his head down to hers and kissed him, lip to lip.

" Yes, sure, 'tis your Mollie," she cried, " and you should go down on your knees and thank your God that I've delivered you from the sin you was so keen on. I've saved you spite o' yourself. 'Twas Nancy's voice you thought spoke to you from the darkness, and Nancy's arms you thought were round you, and, 'twas I, your own wife, and we've served each other well."

Her voice rose to some chanted pitch of triumph.

" Am I so sparkless yet, John? " she cried. " Look upon my breasts and see if they're not fit to suckle a

child, and, by God, they will. Look upon my loins and
see if they're not lusty to bear their burden for nine
months. Old and withered did you think me? Sure
you've learned your error. Aren't I a harp for man's
fingering, and a well of wine for his thirst? 'Twas a
bridal night, sure enough. And now we'll be off, you
and me, and leave Nancy her room."

Up till that moment she had been dominant in the
triumph of her fulfilled desire, and he bewildered, trying to realise the actuality of what had happened. She
laid her hand on his arm, and now at that touch, which
had so lately been flame to him, fury at having been
cheated, blind resentment at the monstrous trick, which
had beguiled his senses, flared up in him, and for answer
he struck at her in the pit of the stomach with all his
force.

She gave one little thin cry, and fell like a thing
broken. Sober indeed he was now; memory of the last
half-hour, mixed with some wild fear, chased the fumes
of drink from him as the east wind drives the clouds.
He dropped on his knees beside her.

"God, what have I done?" he cried. "Mollie, I
never meant to do it. Sure I've not hurt you, have I?
Here, you bitch," he called to Nancy. "Run and get
a drop of whisky from below."

He took Mollie round the shoulders, propping her
in his arms, and pressing her to him, and before Nancy
could come back she had opened her eyes, while her
mouth writhed in pain.

"No, 'twas nothing," she said. "You was angered
a moment, and I'll bear you no ill-will, John, now I've
got you back again. I want none of your drinks, nor
Nancy to help me either. Pick me up yourself, and
just lay me on my bed. I'm a bit queer yet."

He carried her to her room, and drew the bedclothes over her.

"I'll do well now," she said. "Just fill me a glass of water for my teeth, for 'twill never do if I go choking myself with them, on my bridal night. And set the window open, a breath of fresh air'll do me good after that smelly chamber."

All was silent in Mollie's room when John awoke next morning, and thinking she might be still asleep he went downstairs without looking in. Dennis had already gone out to his work, and Nancy was alone in the kitchen.

"Been to see her yet?" he asked.

"Lor', yes," said Nancy. "I took her a cup of tea half an hour ago. Such a bruise as she's got. That was a cruel thing to do, Mr. Pentreath. But she seems pretty fair; she'll be down presently, she said. You might have killed her, hitting out savage like that. 'Twas lucky you haven't got Dennis's strength."

Nancy was still completely in the dark as to the history of the amazing situation she had returned to last night, and was bursting with curiosity. Not a word had she been able to get out of Mollie, who just gave her no answer at all to her questions, as if they had never been asked.

"Well, Mr. Pentreath," she said, as she brought him his breakfast. "I think you've got to let me know what's been going on. A pretty thing for me to come to my own room and find you there, to say nothing of Mrs. Pentreath in my bed."

"Aye, and a pretty thing for you to come back, all dressed up at that time of night," said he, "when you told us all you were so sleepy that you must get to bed

as soon as supper was over. Been walking in your
sleep, maybe."

"Never you mind where I was walking," said Nancy.
"It's where you were walking is what I want to know
about. I found you in my room, and that's where I
never invited you to come."

Suddenly Nancy put down the teapot she was carrying, and burst out laughing as a notion struck her.

"Lor'! If I don't begin to see daylight," she cried,
"and more shame for you, Mr. Pentreath. 'Twas me
you came looking for, and she guessed you would, and
gave you something to satisfy you. Well, I'm sure!
Real sporting I call it of her. Look me in the face,
and tell me that wasn't the way of it. But what must
you take me for, to think I'd 'a let you into my room?"

"Shouldn't wonder if I took you for what you are,
my girl," said he. "What does a handsome wench
like you dress up for cruel fine when all's dark, save to
go and see a man? Or was you thinking of showing
off to Mollie's hens? So do ha' done with them airs,
Nancy, and your wondering what I take you for. 'Tisn't
the first time, I guess, that, when you've been sleepy
after supper, you woke up wonderful a bit later. Look
me in the face, if it comes to that, and tell me that
you haven't been trapesing down to see some feller in
St. Columb's. There's a godly trick."

"And I'll find you another to match it, Mr. Pentreath," said she, annoyed that her sleepy-head formula
was solved, "and that's when you came creeping to
my room and thinking that 'twas I giving you welcome.
That's a bit o' godliness! Talk of airs, too, with you
setting yourself up to pray for light women, hoping
as they'd lose their looks and be turned from their
wantonness. A pack of hypocrisy, I call it. . . . Why,

if there isn't Mrs. Pentreath come down already! Fresh as a daisy, I declare, after all that's been said and done."

Stiffly and a little bent she moved across the kitchen to where he sat, and kissed him, no kiss of forgiveness, but rather of ownership. Stooping like that gave her a stab of pain, but it was nothing. Then she turned to Nancy. "I'm a bit late," she said, "so you'll look to my hens this morning, I'm sure. You might be getting about it now: no time like the present, they say."

Dearly would Nancy have liked to stop and hear what the two had to say to each other.

"I'll be glad to, Mrs. Pentreath," she said. "I'll be clearing up here first, and then——"

"You'll be getting along now," said Mollie, without raising her voice or even looking at her.

When Nancy had gone, she sat down by her husband. She took a bit of bread from his plate, dipped it in his tea, and ate it.

"Well, you've learned to love me once more, John," she said. "See you don't forget it again."

The same hard wrinkled face, which he had long hated, was close to his, but fresh was the memory of an hour last night. Ice-cold and bubbling hot the two were, not mixing, but each standing separate.

"Eh! to think that all these years I've known nought of you," he said. "You old wife with your wrinkled face, and your hot heart! I doubt you've bewitched me, Mollie, with your spells, but such a bowerly body I never yet came nigh to, and there's a long tale of wenches to my account, just riotous dolls."

"They're past and done with," she said. "And Nancy, too, by my reckoning. What's left is you and

me, John, so don't make any mistake about that. I,
your wife, was your desire last night, and sweet you
found me. So don't forget that again, or maybe I'll
remember that cruel dab you gave me."

There was menace here.

"Nay, don't 'ee do that, Mollie," he said.

"Not so long as your manhood's mine," she said.

The grim eager face smiled at him, and even while
his flesh revolted, it stiffened with desire.

"You darned old conjurer!" he said. "And me
never doubting that 'twas Nancy's voice what called
to me."

Mollie laughed.

"Yes, 'tis easy to make her voice, the silly slut," she
observed. "I'll make it again for you in the dark,
John, before long, and you can think you're tucked
up with her, if you will."

During the next week the new values and relations
of the three elder folk at the farmhouse readjusted and
confirmed themselves. John's theology easily adapted
itself to them; right-pleasing, he was sure in the sight
of the Lord was the casting out of his mind his adulterous desires, and his turning again to his wife. That
disaster to his sheep he now felt sure was a judgment;
he had learned his lesson, and already the Lord was
rewarding him, for the hay promised a bumper yield,
and that would put things a bit more square. He
drank as freely as ever, and the ascetic warnings of Dr.
Symes were all forgotten, or remembered only for
mockery, for never had he been in better trim. Even
the score against Dennis sank below the conscious surface of his mind, instead of remaining a vivid pre-
occupation; it was there, but for the present stowed

away and ripening perhaps in secret, till something
came to bring it under notice again. His fear of his
wife was in similar abeyance; she, like the Lord, was
well pleased with him, and there was nothing to be
afraid of while that lasted.

There she sat now, evening by evening, close by the
open-doored oven, busy with the knitted bedspread
she was fashioning to keep her warm on winter nights.
A rare lot of wool it required, but her hens continued
laying bountifully, and week by week she was putting
money away in the savings-bank at Penzance, and there
was enough over for her to be setting up a fine new
henhouse in the yard, and wiring in a further space for
their run. Equal luck was she having with her bees. Two
swarms already had she had in this first week of May,
and a May swarm was worth two of a later month, for
then the bees established themselves earlier, and yielded
during the summer double the weight of honey. A
sight it was to see her gathering them: she went out
without veil or gloves, for never a bee would sting
her. One swarm had settled in the magnolia on the
south front of the house, just beside Dennis's window;
there was no getting the skep smeared with bergamot
above it nor yet below it, so as to shake them into it,
and Mollie had leant out of his window, and taken
handful after handful of the bees, and dropped them
into it, as if she were handling nuts or raisins. All the
time she chanted a little crooning song, just the song of
the bees, so she said, but the words she would tell to
none but to Nell, for she was of the Robsons, and the
bee song was known to none else. She walked stiffly
still, and now and then she had stabs of pain where
John's fist had felled her, but there were none of those
shrill tirades, nor did she look round, furtive and obser-

vant, when they sat in the kitchen after supper, to see what was passing.

As for Nancy, since the significance of her sleepy fits was known to John and Mollie and indeed to Dennis, she had no return of them, and came and went as she chose. She would soon have to use some fresh exit and entrance, for Mr. Willis, the lodger who had taken the rooms in the wing of the house, was coming next week, and the studio door would be no longer available. But the other door into the garden would do: not quite so discreet and retired, " but where's the use o' making a mystery," thought Nancy, " when they all know about it? " Anyhow, the old folk heeded her no more.

CHAPTER IX

THE LODGER

SUNDAY prayers were going on. The young moon which Dennis had seen in the sky above the Kenrith copse was now approaching the full, and he wondered if Nell would ever come out for a moonlight running with him; she had half said she would do so, before the spring was over. For the last night or two he had leaned out of his window and called or whistled to her, but she had given him no answer, and during the day she had kept a bit aloof. She wasn't vexed with him, for he had asked her, and he had done nothing amiss. Just a mood, he supposed, such as girls had. . . . On went the praying, of much milder sort than it used to be, though Grandfather had got a lot of liquor on board that night. There was a bit about being defended from all dangers ghostly and bodily, but not a word about spells and sorceries or the wiles of lascivious women. The pride and wantonness of youth came in again (and Dennis winked at Nell), and after that just petitions for the welfare of the stock and the growing corn, and the praying was soon done.

Almost directly afterwards Nancy was off to bed, as all might have guessed from her new smart clothes, and Dennis and Nell washed-up together. When that was finished, Dennis went with a lantern into the cowhouse, for one of the beasts had but lately calved. All was well: the calf was on its feet, as sturdy as anyone could wish, and old Buttercup knew him and

welcomed him with a puff of sweet breath through her
wet nostrils, and soft watchful eyes on him as he
handled the calf. It was a young bull-calf, and it
lowered its head with a baby menace as he rubbed its
neck. Then emerging, he heard the bell of a bicycle
at the sharp corner from the highroad into the lane,
and saw the jiggling of the lantern as it came jolting
over the uneven surface. It was a wonder how a fellow
could keep upright perched on that high wheel. He
brought a telegram, addressed " Pentreath," and Dennis
took it into the house, and gave it his grandfather. He
had been questioning with himself whether his prayers
had been sufficiently fervid to please the Lord to-night;
and here was a chance to make up for his tepidity, and
he thumped the table when Dennis held it out to him.

" Nay, 'twas written in sin," he called out, " and
'twas sin of the lad to bring it up to-night. Let it
bide till morning."

" Open it and see what it is," said Mollie to Dennis,
" and don't mind him."

Dennis tore it open.

" Mr. Willis," he said. " Coming down from London this night, and'll be here at eight to-morrow morning. His rooms aren't ready yet, Grannie; Mother
and Nell were meaning to do them to-morrow."

" Heh, there'll be no train that runs safe through
o' Sunday night," said John. " The Lord shows me
that He'll bust it up, and all in it'll go down quick
into hell."

Out shot Mollie's forefinger.

" Now not a word more, John Pentreath," she said,
" or the Lord'll show you something you won't relish.
You've had your fill: get you to bed."

" Eh, what's that? " he said.

" Just what your ears tell you. Finish your drink,
and light your candle and go. I'll come and talk to
you presently."

" But the Lord——"

" Ha' done with the Lord! " she cried. " An' don't
let me have to bid you twice."

He shifted to his feet.

" Well, Mollie, I didn't go for to anger you," he said.

" Take care you don't. Be off."

She waited in silence, not looking at him again till
he had lurched out of the kitchen door.

" You and Nell 'll have to get the room ready,
Dennis," she said, " for 'twould never do if Mr. Willis
came and found everything mucky. I'd help you myself, but I'm terribly uneasy to-night in my innards,
and your mother—well, there, 'twill be no good to knock
at her door. Be brisk, you two, and make all fresh and
clean for him."

Dennis and Nell got to their work. There was the
bedroom above the studio to be made ready, and first
of all Dennis threw open the window, for it was stuffy
and unventilated, and the night air drifting in would
freshen it up before morning; then the room must be
swept and set in order, and the bed must be made, for
after that night of travel, Mr. Willis would be like to
want a sleep. That was Nell's business, and she took
blankets and spread them, and brought sheets from the
linen cupboard at the top of the stairs, and slips for
his pillows. Water must be fetched for his jug and
bottle, the drawers and cupboards be dusted out, paper
be spread on the wooden shelves, the drugget be
unrolled for the floor, and the sponging tin bath be
dragged from under the bed.

Dennis had bolted the baize door at the end of the passage which shut off the lodging and its staircase from the rest of the house, lest the grandfather should get some further sabbatarian scruples, and the sense grew on them both that they were there alone and together in the night of full moon. They had little to say to each other, for both were busy, working mostly apart at their jobs, but now Dennis had to heave up the end of the bed, while Nell pulled the drugget under the castors, and her shoulder was pressed against his knee. Soon all was finished here, and Nell stood holding a candle high, moving it this way and that to see that they had forgotten nothing. Their eyes met, blue and black, gleaming to each other.

" That's all done then," she said.

" Aye, and what next? "

" Put the baize strip down on the stairs. It's in the cupboard there with the rods. Pull it out."

Dennis tugged at the roll of baize, and all the rods fell down on the uncarpeted landing with a huge clatter, and they stood regarding each other with silent laughter.

" Lord! 'Twas fit to waken the dead," said she.

They waited a moment.

" I reckon there bain't no dead about, then, for none's awoke to all seeming," said Dennis.   " Come along."

He set the candle on the floor at the top of the stairs and, standing on the end of the drugget, tipped the roll over, so that it went bumping softly down the steps, unwinding itself. He fixed it against the wall with carpet pins, and then they went down step by step, pushing the rods into the eyelets, and moving the candle as they progressed. Their fingers touched sometimes over this, as one smoothed the carpet for

the other to press the rod into place, or Nell's loosely
bound black hair brushed against his cheek. Not a
word did they speak now, but the face of each was
bright from the candle perched on the step above them.

They finished with the stairs, and now there only
remained the studio to set in order. There was the
parqueted floor to be gone over with a damp cloth
and the grate to be blacked; then the rugs must be
unrolled, the dust sheets taken off the furniture, the
chairs and table moved out from the walls, and the
window flung wide to air the place. Now they lingered over each item of their work, for it was nearly
done, and then all that remained was to go quietly back
to their rooms and sleep or lie awake till morning, in
the annihilation of solitude. Though they had said no
word to each other yet, save about their occupation,
their very silence was breeding fire, and every moment
that passed piled fuel on to it. Yet for all their
lingering the time came when all was done. Already
the candle was nearly consumed, and even as Nell once
more raised it over her head to look round, the wick
drooped sideways in the socket, flared up, and then
fell into the liquid tallow and was quenched.

They stood there together close to the glass-panelled
double door that led into the garden: each side of it
had its separate curtain drawn across it. Nancy had
not latched it when she went out that way after supper,
and just then a breeze woke outside, and the two sides
of the door began noiselessly to open. Nell, startled,
came close to Dennis, and laid her hand on his arm.

"Dennis, who is it?" she whispered. "Who is
there?"

A stronger current of air swept into the room from
the open window and the doors swung wide. For a

moment Dennis raged in his heart to think that this
might be his mother returning, but there was no one
there: the garden lay quiet and empty under the spell
of the full moon and the night. It was that season of
the year when the tide of life flows strongest, when
the sap riots in the trees, and the accomplished springtime is merged in summer. For weeks that tide had
been advancing on them: now with a moonlit foam-
crested billow it poured over them.

"Who is it?" he whispered. "Why, it's just us,
Nell, and the night."

For a little while they stood there in the grip of
the absolute moment.

"Shall we go out, then?" he said. "You were to
come with me some night, you as good as promised,
when there was moonshine and stillness. What say you,
Nell?"

The breath came quick through her parted lips, as if
she had been running.

"Yes; let's be gone," she said.

II

Dennis had gone out to his work on the farm
and Nell was busy with the Monday's wash, when Mr.
Willis arrived next day: neither of the two old folk
was down yet, so Nancy saw to him. He would have
a hot bath, please, to refresh himself first after his
night journey, and when she knocked at his door to
bring him his can, a funny little scream answered her.

"Come in if you won't be shocked," he called out,
and she was quite prepared to see the little man in shirt
or trousers only, and would not have been shocked
at all. Instead, there was a pretty capering thing

with a pink silk vest, and pink silk pants, wrapping himself in a lovely blue dressing-gown. His feet were bare, and he tried the temperature of the water with his toe as she poured it out.

"Delicious, delicious," he said, "and now for my bath-salts, and I'll soap and soap to wash off that horrid train, and you won't know me again."

He had begun his unpacking, and already on his dressing-table gleamed studs and tie-pins and innumerable bottles.

"And perhaps one more canful, Mrs. Pentreath," he said, "if you'd be so good. But this time will you leave it outside the door for me? Don't come in, whatever you do. And my breakfast down in the studio in half an hour. How I shall enjoy it!"

"Silk, 'twas all silk, vest and pants and dressing-gown," said Nancy to Nell, as she drew another canful of hot water from the copper. "And putting sweet-smelling crystals into his bath. Such a sight of luggage, too, I never beheld. Bags and portmanteaux and hat-boxes and a bullfinch in a cage to twitter to him, and hop about much as he does himself. Well, we have got a sample!"

Nancy's opinion was confirmed by the impressions of the family generally when Mr. Willis came and tapped at the house door of the kitchen, as dinner-time was approaching, and was bidden enter.

"Just a little formal call," he said, bowing right and left. "How-de-do, I think this must be Mr. Pentreath: how-de-do, I'm sure I'm speaking to the other Mrs. Pentreath—one I've met already. Just to say how charming and comfortable I find it all. Such a good breakfast: how I gobbled it up."

13

John Pentreath looked him slowly down from head to foot, his white hairless face, his silk shirt and tie with a pearl pinning it, his yellow flannel suit and high-heeled brown shoes.

" Glad you're finding yourself pleased," he said. " You'll take a glass of whisky with me? "

" So kind, but I never touch it," said Willis. " Can't bear the smell of it; can't bear the taste of it. But may I be allowed to smoke a cigarette? Will the ladies let me? Is smoking permitted? Ah, I see it is. I see Mr. Pentreath has a pipe."

" And you've come here for a bit of a rest? " asked Mollie, for so important a person as a lodger must be politely treated; otherwise she would have shooed such a doll from the kitchen.

" No, I've come to work. Can't paint in London, always too busy. Little runnings about, little lunches, little dinners. Isn't it so, Mrs. Pentreath? "

" Sure it is, if you tell me so," said she. " I never went to London myself."

Mr. Willis clapped his hands. " Charming! Too charming," he said. " You've never been in London. How refreshing! "

Nell came in from her washing for a fresh kettleful of water from the boiler, and this singular young man rose to his feet and bowed.

" And Miss Pentreath? " he asked.

" Nay, you're out there," said John. " 'Tis Miss Robson."

" Just as fair by any other name," said Willis neatly.

" Beggin' your pardon? " said Mollie.

" Nothing, nothing. I must be going now. Lots of jobs and tidyings to do before dinner-time. Dinner now, isn't it, and supper in the evening. Such kind hosts! Can I get round into the garden from the farm-yard?"

John got up to show him the way, but at that moment in came Dennis, and collided with Willis at the door.

"I beg your pardon; I beg your pardon," said Willis.

"No need; you haven't hurt him," said John with a grin. "It's my little grandson Dennis."

"So pleased," said Willis. "So will Dennis—it is Dennis, I think you said—will Dennis just show me the way through?"

"Take him along, Dennis," said John.

Willis made a final bow.

"So glad to be here, so very glad," he said.

Dennis took him across the yard, and through the gate into the garden. Willis was transported with the deliciousness of the lilies of the valley that grew in the shade by the ash tree.

"Mustn't steal, mustn't steal," he said, "but if you picked me one or two for my buttonhole, that wouldn't be stealing, would it, Dennis?"

"Sure, no," said Dennis, amazed at this funny prattling little man, dressed up like the dude at the fair, who was married to the fat lady.

"And put them in my buttonhole for me, will you?"

"Aye, but they soon die when plucked," said Dennis.

"And will it be you who looks after me, and calls me in the morning, and brings me my meals?" asked Willis.

"No," said the boy. "That'll be my mother or Nell."

"And is Nell Miss Robson, that very pretty girl who came in with a kettle?"

"Shouldn't wonder a bit if 'twas," said Dennis.

"And I'm sure you walk out with Nell," said Willis.

"I dessay I do sometimes, but not to mention."

Willis gave a little skip.

"Trust me: I won't mention it," he said. "But I guessed, didn't I?"

"Couldn't say what you'd been guessing," said Dennis.

"Ha, ha. Mum's the word. Aren't I a chatterbox, and me having seen you only two minutes ago? Here we are: that's the door of my studio, isn't it? Nell or your mother will be bringing me my dinner presently, I hope, and the sooner the better, for what a hungry place! Till then I shall be finishing my unpacking, and getting my paints and canvas ready to begin work."

"So you're a painter chap, are you?" said Dennis. "We've got a sight of them down to St. Columb's."

"Yes, and I'm longing to begin. And there's something to begin on if you let me."

"You'll be wanting to do a picture of Nell?" asked Dennis intelligently.

"I'd like to do one of you, with your hair all untidy and your shirt open."

"Sakes alive!" said the astonished Dennis.

Mr. Willis came in for a little searching comment presently as the family sat at dinner. Nancy had just returned from taking him his meal.

"Well, I do call him a polite little gent," she said. "Up he jumped when I came in, and hoped the tray wasn't heavy. But, lor', his jools and his silks! I never see such a missie!"

"A pretty young fellow," said Dennis, broadly grinning. "I gave him a sprig of lily for a nosegay in his coat. Aw, he was polite, and he wants to make a picture of me."

" If I'd caught yon fellow when I was gwain fishing," said John; " I'd ha' put him back. I warrant his mammy didn't know if she'd dropped a boy or a girl when she was brought to bed of him."

" An' 'twould puzzle her to-day wi' such a pin-tail," remarked Mollie. " Mighty finickin'."

" Well, pin-tail or no, he pays well, and maybe he'll stay the summer through, so see that you all make him content and comfortable; mark that, Dennis."

" 'Iss sure: that's business," said Dennis. " Wonder what he'll pay me for limning my putty face."

" Three bob an hour's the regular thing," said Nancy, rather incautiously. " Not but what some pays far handsomer than that."

" You may reckon your mother knows," said Mrs. Pentreath cordially. " Happen you'll be making a fortune from your face, too, Dennis."

This pleasantry was not quite to Nancy's taste: private affairs shouldn't be talked about in public. But if personalities were floating about, she could take a grab at them as well as anybody.

" Well, 'tis true enough that if some folk want a fortune, there's no use for them to seek it in their looking-glass," she observed.

Mollie only laughed: she was in wonderful good-humour these days.

" I reckon then I'll go and seek my fortune in my chicken-house," she said.

She got up, and as she rose her face suddenly twisted with pain.

" Touch of that stomach-trouble," she said.

CHAPTER X

MIDSUMMER EVE

THE growth of the hay was fulfilling its earlier promise: the barometer kept high, and Mollie was certain sure that the fine hot weather would last till it was safely in. It was a treat to skirt along the edge of the meadows and feast the eye on the richness of it. Highest in that exuberant growth rose the feathery heads of the long oat-like grasses, already yellow-brown, for their tallness was baked all day by the sun, and nearly up to them in stature were the ox-eye daisies and the meadow-sweet, with spirals of bindweed climbing up the stems of them: these were the pinnacles in the temple of the fields. A little shorter than these were vetches and sorrel, ragged robin and pink and white campions, hard-headed knapweed and branching buttercups. But thickest and juiciest was the undergrowth: it was the very fur of the fruitful earth, and would need a sharp scythe and a close swinging stroke when the cutting came, for not an inch of that luxuriance must be lost. The shorter, sappier grasses would scarce allow the more lowly herbs to prick a way through them, but the frenzy of blossoming life had conquered, and the meadows were a diaper of flowers. There were purple clovers and pink centaury and stitchwort and starwort; and, lowlier yet, tawny-yellow trefoils and white clover, shepherd's purse, blue and red pimpernels, and hawksweed and daisy were thick among the grasses. All effervesced together in bubble and foam of flower-

ing, struggling upwards to bask in the sun by day, and
share the drench of the dew and the soft nourishing
darkness at night. Before the month was out, the
fields were ripe for the scythe, and soon they lay prone
and drying, and were gathered into haycocks. Then
to and fro creaked the laden wains, and high rose
the new stacks standing on trestles outside the farmyard. Lucky indeed was it that John, earlier in the
year, had refused to sell the crop forward and have no
risk about it, but he had taken the risk, and now the
yield would exceed by 25 per cent. the price that had
been offered him.

All this looked as if the luck were turning again
after that disaster to the sheep, and there was another
item to add to it, for the " girlie," as Willis was now
called, had engaged his lodging till the end of September, and that meant a profit of two pounds a week
clear, for it was not much he ate, and there was
no need to get a hired girl in to help: Nell and Nancy
between them could cook and see to him easily. Never,
at all the watering-places where he usually went for
August and September, had he found a place which
suited him so well. Nature no doubt had made a careless mistake when at his birth she had stamped him male,
but in point of fact he was not so strongly of either
sex as to be worth stamping at all: if anything, the
female quality predominated. In addition to this error,
she had given him no deeper vitality than that of gnats
that dance over still water on summer evenings; just
like theirs were his capers and his excited shrillnesses.
Nothing could create robustness for him in himself, but
vicinity to it, so that he could dabble and bask in
it, was stimulus, and never had he come into touch
with folk who so glowed and throbbed with force as

those at this solitary farmhouse.

Of the elders it was Mollie who possessed it most
abundantly: silent and observant, she had little to say
to him, but something secret and intense, running like
a torrent below black rocks in tumult of deep eddies,
surged about her, and most mornings he would pay her
a little visit very polite and chatty, as she sat knitting
by the oven in the kitchen, in order to feel that force
flowing round him. Lined and seamed was her face,
grey her hair, and she walked stiffly and bent as she
gathered her eggs and came back with a full basket
to the fire, but in her black eyes, bent mostly on
her knitting, there was something tingling and electric
that braced him. At the same time a little of Mollie
was enough, there was something sinister about her,
" not quite comfortable," so he phrased it to himself.
But Nell and Dennis were not like that: they were
just two fountains of life, flashing in the sun and
spilling refreshment all round them. Like a thirsty
little lapdog Willis licked it up.

Here his essential feminity asserted itself, and of the
two it was Dennis in particular who gave him the sense
of being bathed in life. While the crop was being
cut and gathered, he would spend an hour at a time
watching the boy swing his scythe or pitch those great
lumps of hay into the waggon, and he made countless
little drawings of him in his sketch-book. The sight of
that unconscious vigour and exuberant youth nourished
him, and when Dennis came back from the field he
would be sitting at the open door of his studio like
an eager little spider, to lure him in with the bait of a
cigarette, in order to get a taste of his quality. In
some perfectly sexless manner he loved the boy, much as
an elderly spinster loves her yapping dog; he would

have liked to stroke his smooth neck, to pat his big
shoulders, to tweak his yellow hair, just for the touch
of his youth and sappy elasticity. He wanted Dennis
to be close to him, smelling of the stable or the hay-
field, with tousled hair and chest dripping with the
sweat of his toil. Once, in this greed for the contact
of his rough vigour, he had thrown his arms round
the boy's chest, bold yet terrified, like a maiden aunt,
of his boldness in giving such expression to his need.

"You do like me a little, Dennis, don't you?" he
chattered at him.

Dennis looked down on him with his white teeth
lining his lips in sheer amusement, not pushing him
away, nor feeling the slightest embarrassment.

"Aw dear, if you beeant a fair little curiositee," he
said. "Best lemme go, Mr. Willis."

"But it's so nice to hold you," said the girlie. "I
like to feel how strong you are."

"Just a little curiositee, that's what you are," Dennis
repeated, untwining his arms, as if undoing a loosish
knot in a hank of string. "I'll be off to my dinner
now, Mr. Willis."

"You shall. And then, when you've finished your
work this evening, you'll come in, won't you, and let
me get on with my picture?"

He drew out a dainty little leather purse with his
monogram on it in gold, and picked a ten-shilling piece
from it.

"That's what I owe you already," he said, "for our
two sittings."

"Well, I'm sure, 'tis very handsome of you," said
Dennis.

In this lengthening splendour of the June evenings

Dennis and Nell would often be out in the garden when supper was done, and John had got to his bottle, and Willis would call to them from his studio-door to come and chat to him. There were chocolates for the girl and cigarettes for Dennis, but Nell would only stop a minute, for fear she would burst out laughing at his little bows and chatterings and compliments. Willis never attempted to detain her: he was more at ease with Dennis alone, and Dennis himself was more natural when Nell was not there. Glances passed between the two, there were signallings and silent comments which rather disconcerted Willis. So to-night when he called to them he was not displeased that Nell said she had some jobs to attend to before she went to bed, and Dennis came in alone. There was a chill in the evening air to-night, thought Willis, and he closed one side of the studio doors.

"That's more cosy," he said. "Now come and sit down for ten minutes. What a pretty girl Nell is! I believe you kiss her when there's no one by."

"Powerful odd notions some folk have," observed Dennis.

"Aha! Discreet! I shall call you discreet Dennis, and I'm your little curiositee. Have a drink? Just a glass of port to finish your supper with. I shall come and sit by you on the sofa and pour it out for you. Now tell me of all you've been doing and thinking about. Tell me all about yourself."

Dennis was no more shy of the curiositee than he was of Willis's piping bullfinch that hung in the window and whistled its broken little tunes or made its little bows. He was queer enough, but he was kind, and it was a pity to see his loneliness and his eagerness to talk to any of them. Mollie had given him a good snub this morning: she had told him that she couldn't get on with her knitting while he was hopping about. So though Dennis could not indulge him with any details about Nell, he was quite ready to talk about anything else if the girlie wanted company.

" Well, the hay's finished with now," he said, " and a lovely load it was. The carrying of it's the best job of the year. Sweet it smells as you yoick it on to the growing stack, sweeter nor the cows' breath at milking time. But that's done with now, and to-day I've been chopping up wood, and cut wood's not a bad smell: I judge a lot by smells. We lost two big elms in a gale of March; Grandfather sold the trunks at a fine price, and the branches will serve us for firewood the winter through. A bad business that was: they fell across the sheepfold and killed a sight of ewes and lambs."

Dennis took a good mouthful of the port which Willis had placed by him in a tumbler. Never had he tasted it before: a sweet agreeable beverage, that made a kind of purring within. He was pleased to see his glass filled up again.

" And what other good smells are there? " asked Willis.

" Well, there's the October morning that smells of a sheer cleanness, and, good Lord, there's the best of them all to say yet, and that's the smell of a wet night in springtime. 'Tis that which takes hold of me strongest."

" Tell me about that," said Willis.

The wine certainly was loosening Dennis's tongue. If the girlie wanted to know about it, why not?

" I've told none of it but to Nell," he said, " and you'll be sure, won't 'ee, not to let on. But it's a craziness that gets into my blood some nights of spring, and

I must let myself out of the house and go running in the dark and the wind and the wet. Lord, such a running as I had one day in March, half-stripped and dripping with rain and sweat. I ran the best of four miles to the wood above Penerth, and clung to the ground and bit the bracken-stems, and bathed in the brook. Just a craziness that comes to me."

Willis wriggled with pleasure. He was getting at something now; it was as if his ear were pressed to a tree trunk, and he could hear the sap boiling up within it at springtime.

" Go on, dear fellow, go on! " he cried. " I love to hear about your craziness: I love to picture you running in the dark all alone, because you had to. Not a word will I say to anyone about it. What did you do next? "

" Why, the craziness was sweated out of me by then, I reckon," said Dennis, " and I plodded home. 'Twas over for that time."

Willis got up for a box of cigarettes, and pirouetted across to the table.

" It makes me gay to think of it," he said, " it makes me want to dance. And talking of that, your mother said something to me when she served my dinner about the dancing to-morrow night in that circle of stones in the ploughed field below the garden, and about the bonfire. I must go and see it, she told me. Do you dance there that night, Dennis? Take a drop more port."

" Nay, I've never danced there yet, though maybe I shall some day," said Dennis, filling his glass.

" But you must dance with me," cried the girlie. " You and Nell must both dance with me."

Dennis suddenly choked over his wine, and exploded with laughter and strangled coughing.

" Eh, bless and save us all! " he said. " You'll never beat that, Mr. Willis, not in a month o' Midsummer Nights."

" But what have I said? Why shouldn't I dance with you and Nell? What have I said that makes you laugh? "

Dennis recovered himself, and when there was nothing left of his explosion but a hiccup and a hoarse voice, he explained.

" Why, of course you couldn't know," he said, " and 'twas rude of me to guffaw. 'Tisn't a thing we talk of, for all we know of it, and you mustn't go saying I told you. You see, 'tis only them as want to get a baby that dance on Midsummer's Eve. You'll see the young folk just married as'll be dancing there till they drop from weariness, and lie panting there, and you'll see old folk too, maybe, as wants another child. To be sure, it was that made me laugh, when you asked if Nell or me 'ud dance with you. A queer thing surely that would be."

Dennis began to laugh again, but pulled himself together.

" Eh, there's lots we know in this land which we don't speak of, because we know it," he said. " It'll sound strange, I reckon, to you foreigners, but you come and go, and the circle remains and the spring nights and the spells of them. Foreigners know naught, begging your pardon. And that's a clean white spell, in the circle. Pass'n Allingham, he'll come down and watch the dancing."

Dennis was sprawling along the sofa, talking of things he knew he had best be silent about, but the wine had loosened his tongue.

" And then the bonfire? " asked Willis.

Dennis laughed again.

" That's another spell;" he said. " You come down to-morrow night, and when the flames burn low, you'll see dozens o' couples leaping over it."

" But what does that mean? " asked Willis. " Everything seems to mean something."

" Why, that means that the two's got a fancy for each other, and if she says she'll leap with you, and you both jump clear, you'll be married 'afore All Souls' Eve. Sure it was time you married, Mr. Willis, for you'll be thirty or forty years old, I dessay: about that, wouldn't it be? "

" Never mind me. Go on about the leaping."

" Aye, there'll be a lot of leaping over the fire to-morrow," said Dennis. " A sight of fellers and lassies from Penzance and the villages round 'ull be taking the fire, as they call it, if they're thinking of marrying and making bed together. 'Tis an old custom before ever the Romans came here, and sometimes it comes wonderful true. And then next year there'll be those who have taken the fire, dancing together like mad in the circle, if so be they're barren yet. Sometimes my grandmother, though she's no real grannie of mine, tells powerful curious things of them as had meant naught but a foolishness by dancing together within the stones, and sure enough the child came, just a still-born as they say, that never lived, though a child it was. She fair scares me sometimes when she gets on the gabble, thought 'tis oftener she's no word from dawn till evening. Secret ways she has, God Almighty knows, but she beeant afeared of Him."

Sleepy sweet stuff was this port, thought Dennis, but it purred in the head, and was mighty pleasant in the stomach. He didn't mind what he said now.

" So she won't be dancing on Midsummer Eve, any more than I shall," said Willis.

" She dance? " said Dennis. " No, I reckon her dancing days are over, though who can tell with such as she? There's summat in her innards as makes her brisk and blithesome, and never's she been like that not by what I remember. Something's pleasing to her: there's summat as tastes good in her mouth, and gives her joy. Surprising it is. She's been walking a bit short and slow, like th'ould mare, of late, but then there's times when she steps out brisk and frisky. But as for dancing, why, she knows what that means, and she's past dancing surely."

Dennis sat up from his sprawling posture, and put a hand on Willis's shoulder.

" Yet not so many weeks ago," he said, " there she was in Kenrith copse skipping and dancing like a young mare on heat. I was coming home that way, and it fair scared me, and I skedaddled off quick as I might, for I don't want to meddle with any doings there. Lord in Paradise, what's that? "

There sounded from close outside the half-closed door of the studio the call of an owl, and the great tawny bird hovered in the doorway.

" There's one ever about the house this year," he said, " so bold, as if 'twas its own. Best shut the door, Mr. Willis, else they'll mess you up fine with their belchings and their dumpings, if one happened to take a fancy to roost here. And for me it's bedtime."

Willis went to the door, shut and bolted it, and drew the curtains over the glass pane. He felt he was getting drippings from some hidden secret spring which perhaps gave this amazing force to these silent, aloof folk. All of them, except Nancy, the most talkative of them all, had it: in her its place was taken by a mere Cockney vitality, the like of which you could see any evening in London, seething about the pavements and in the promenades of music-halls. But it lay, deep and hot, below the surface-life of the others: the tipsy old grandfather, the bright-eyed, withered Mollie, Dennis with his spring-runnings, and Nell with her quiet ways had all some hidden life of their own, and now Dennis, off his guard with wine, was giving him hints about it.

"Now, go on, dear fellow," he said, "I've shut the owls out."

But the thread was broken: Dennis, who had been talking so heedlessly, stiffened into silence. Perhaps that sudden appearance of the owl had reminded him not to speak to foreigners about things that belonged to blood and birthright. If his reticence had not been melted out of him by so many glasses of port, guilefully supplied, he would not have said so much. He might even have just shooed the owl away, in the same contemptuous spirit in which he had derided Nell's conjecture about the night-bird. As it was, the appearance of it just then served to close his lips, for there were many things in the magic of night and day which, though you did not believe them, had best be left untalked of. So when Willis, having shut the doors, bade him "go on," Dennis gave him a shake of his head and a low whistle through pursed lips.

"Best not," he said. "I doubt I've been talking too free, so do 'ee forget it all, Mr. Willis. But that liquor o' yours seems to make a feller's tongue go clacking like a hen as has laid an egg. Enough said!"

He got up from the sofa, swaying a little on his feet.

"God! I'm taking after Grandfather a'ready," he

said. " My head's a-swim, and I'm damned if I can trust my legs. Where they'll be gwain to I don't know."

He tried to fix his eyes on the door, to which he wanted to get himself, but the walls jerked round him, as he attempted to hold it in focus.

" Have a nap on my sofa, Dennis," said the girlie. " You'll soon sleep it off."

Dennis looked at him with sleep-shining eyes. " Well, that would be a fine plan, if I bain't putting you out," he said. " Don't you mind me, Mr. Willis: you get to bed."

He dropped back on the sofa, and was almost instantly asleep. Once or twice his eyelids fluttered, but presently they closed themselves smooth and firm over his eyes, and his limbs lay soft and relaxed, but some aura of his superb youth seemed to spread round him like a tonic tide, and Willis basked in it. But before five minutes were past, there came the flapping of wings against the studio door, and the sound of claws against the glass. Dennis sprang up.

" There's that damned bird again," he said. " I'll be off to bed," and he shuffled across the room and went stumbling upstairs in the dark.

II

Though no word was said between the members of the family on the subject of the bonfire, they all took a hand next day in the building of it: John Pentreath fetched a truss of straw from the stable, and carried it down into the field, just beyond where the stones stood from which the unploughed path between the rising corn led up to the circle. The lower field had already

14

borne its hay crop, and in the middle of it was a strip
of rough stone paving, black with the fire of im-
memorial years, and on this he dumped his straw.
Mollie was already there: she had brought down a tin
of paraffin, which would be poured on the fuel before
the fire was lit, and she helped to spread the straw while
he went back for a second load. On his way he passed
Nell wheeling a barrowful of the dry tindery hay of
last year: no need was there to ask what she was about.
Half the village of St. Columb's came up during the
morning, and took part in this silent co-operation; some
of the fishermen brought coils of old tarry rope, or
broken thwarts and oar-blades; others dry garden refuse
and faggots of wood and paraffin, and none made question or comment any more than they would have asked
a man what he was at if they saw him smoking his
pipe or eating his dinner. By midday there were a
dozen men there with pitchforks for the spreading of
the lighter stuff, while others handled the wood and
small boughs of trees, laying them criss-cross. Their
hands were busy, for now there were stacks of such
material piled beside the pavement: it was fifty feet
long and ten or twelve across, and the whole had to be
piled high before it was ready for the firing. Parson
Allingham paid a visit there: he tossed down a couple
of fine bundles of brushwood, and had a word with
Dennis for not being in church last Sunday.

Before long there was a scare about the weather: a
heavy bank of cloud was piling up in the south, moving
against the light north wind, and that was the way
that a thunderstorm approached. It would be a disaster
indeed if the bonfire got soaked, and half a dozen men
went down to the village to fetch some coverings, and
Dennis up to the farm for the big tarpaulin that Mollie

put on top of her hen-run in stormy weather. He was
bent double under the weight of it, and in a bath of
sweat, which would be the port wine coming out.
Willie Polhaven helped him drag it into place, and up
came Mr. Willis with his Malacca cane and his fawn-
coloured London clothes, ever so anxious to be pleasant
and useful.

"So this is where the bonfire's to be, Dennis," he
said. "What time shall I come down?"

Dennis was not feeling very kindly towards the girlie
this morning. That port had given him a prize head-
ache when he woke: the girlie ought to have warned
him instead of plying him with it. Besides, no foreigner
might have a hand in the bonfire. He took not the
least notice of him.

"Hitch that corner a bit more towards you, Willie,"
he said.

"But let me help: let me help," said the girlie, putting his stick down. Willie was another specimen of
the dark native type: a great big black-eyed boy, not
quite so tall as Dennis, but limbed like a young horse.

"I can manage, sir, thank you," said Willie. He
had picked up the " sir " from domestic service: Dennis
never called anyone " sir."

"Oh, but let me help," said Willie. " Please let me
help. May I get some sticks and put them on the bonfire? "

Dennis frowned, and gave a great tug to another
corner of the tarpaulin.

"We'll do nicely, Mr. Willis," he said. " Happen
you'd best not meddle."

"How cross you are to me, Dennis," said the girlie.

Willie bent down to hide a broad grin. He had
already been chaffing Dennis about his little curiositee,

who paid him five shillings an hour for looking at his pretty face.

" 'Tis best you sit down and let be," said Dennis. " We'll be done presently."

Willis picked up his stick with a little titter of laughter: it gave him an old-maidenly thrill to be ordered about like this.

" Everybody spoils Dennis," he said, sitting down on a pile of faggots. " Don't they, Willie? "

" I'm sure I couldn't say as to that, sir," said Willie with another grin. " Maybe you'll know best."

" I could say who spoiled your face for you, Willie, once on a time," observed Dennis.

" What, did you two great fellows have a fight? " asked Willis. " What was it all about? "

" Just some of our own affairs," said Dennis.

The tarpaulins were duly spread, and the bonfire safe from any rain that might come before night, and then all trusted that St. John would see to it, for never yet within memory had there been a wetting when, after sundown, it was kindled. The two boys walked off together for a dip in the sea to the cove where a fight had been the beginning of their friendship. That was in the heads of both of them as they stripped, sitting side by side on the sand, and Dennis, leaning shoulder to shoulder against Willie, stretched out his longer but slimmer arm along his.

" 'Tis a power of brawn you've got there," he said. " I doubt you'd give me a walloping if happen we fought again."

" I'd do my best, but you've got more reach nor me. I reckon we'd hurt each other now, Dennis. Eh, that's a 'quisitive little gent of yours, sniffing after you like a little lap-dog."

" He wants to know too much," said Dennis, " and damn me if he didn't fill me up with some sweet liquor of his last night. Potent it was, though you'd think it was more like a syrup, and my tongue went crazy, and I told him bits of things that I never oughter. God, such a tipsy head I had this morning."

" What did you tell him? "

" Just about taking the fire and the dancing. But it don't signify. He'll not let on."

Willie was silent a moment as he peeled off his socks.

" Gwaineter take the fire to-night with Nell? " he asked.

" I reckon so. And ain't you got a girl yet you fancy a bit? "

" Never a bit, neither to kiss nor to cuddle nor to be chums with," said Willie. " I reckon it's a kink in me, and not like to come out."

" You make me feel bad when you talk like that, Willie," said the other.

" Whatever for? 'Tisn't your fault, nor mine either."

" Maybe, but I wish it were different with you."

" Don't you bother your head with it. Happen I'll change some time and be like other fellers. An' don't you ever think I'm sore for that you've got your girl. Passon Allingham he read summat about David and Jonathan in church Sunday last, and the love of one for t'other, he telled, was wonderful, passin' the love of women. That made me think of us, and I looked round to see if I could catch your eye, but you wasn't there."

" You bet you'd 'a caught it fast enough, if I had been, and I'd 'a understood fast enough," said Dennis.

" That's all I ask, then. Now let's have done and take the sea."

Dennis jumped up.

" And have a bit of a sweat first," he said. " I won't fight you, but I'll have a wrestle with you to a fall, both shoulders on the ground."

They circled round each other, arm on arm, to find a grip, and then Dennis bored in, getting him round the chest, while Willie took a hold with one arm half round his neck over the shoulder, the other round his ribs. The sand made good foothold, and Willie crooked his right knee outside Dennis's left, and brought his whole weight to bear, but the other stepped out of that and freed himself. They closed again, and this way and that they swayed, chin pressing into shoulder, and chests glued together, till with a sudden sideways jerk Willie twisted him off his feet, and got him under on the sand. But Dennis, wriggling like an eel, escaped before his shoulders were pinned, and with the purchase of his bent leg turned him off. Their breath was coming short now, ribs were heaving, and the sweat made their holds slippery, and they tumbled and rolled over together, cheek to cheek, a tangle of intertwined arms and legs, till at last Willie had the other fairly under again, and pressing on his shoulders with all his weight got him flat.

" Yes, 'tis your fall, ye hulking Jonathan," panted Dennis.

They lay there a moment, all slack and relaxed after the tussle, Dennis with arms spread out, and the other lying across him. Then Willie rolled off and got up.

" Eh, that was rare! " he said. " The body of a feller is better than the tongue at talking."

" Sure. Pull me up, and off to the sea."

The threatening storm had passed away eastwards,

and when they got back to the bonfire it was safe to pull the tarpaulin off, and finish the building of it. It must be piled high to make a fine flare, for its light had to carry across the bay to where, on the ridge above St. Orde's, the next pyre would be lit after sundown. There were half a dozen of these bonfires that would blaze that night in the country round the bay, signalling to each other in symbolic flame, as they had done for a score of centuries, that the fires of life were aglow, but it was at St. Columb's alone that the leaping was done, as Dennis had said. When the flames died down into glowing embers, boys and girls, who had chosen each other to wed and bed, would run hand in hand together and leap with closed eyes and held breath: if they jumped clear, for certain they would be wed before All Hallows Eve, but if a foot came down in the embers, there would be a cry of " Hot Ankles," and then they must jump again if they wanted to make sure of their wedding. As well there would be dancing in the circle of stones, and that brought fertility. About these rites there was nothing of black and secret magic, it was a clean spell that both the fire and the dancing wove: these were customs and beliefs, the heritage of the race, an heirloom of the spirit handed down almost without word of speech to all inheritors of native blood. Neither Nell nor Dennis could have told how they had come to know of these things: the germs of them were there, and they had developed with their growth. But none except the natives had any part in them: aliens, foreigners from England, might come and look on and gratify a tourist-curiosity. They might leap across the embers or dance with each other, but they had no true part in the rite: it was as if a heathen man received the sacrament, and for him no spell would be wrought, since he was blind in unbelief and ignorance, and whether such leaped or danced none heeded them any more than if they had been moths that singed themselves in the blaze, or the insects of the earth beneath the feet of the dancers.

No word was spoken at supper that night at the farm of what was coming, and when it was over John sat him down as usual with his pipe and his glass, while Nancy and Nell cleared the table. But instead of drawing the cloth and folding it away, they brought out mounds of saffron-buns, which had been baking these last days, and put plates of them along the table with jugs of beer and glasses, so that any who willed might come in and take their refreshment. But when the clock whirred at the hour of ten, Mollie got up, and wrapped her shawl round her, and John, pretty full of whisky, finished his glass and was off with her. Nancy followed them, and Dennis and Nell were left alone in the kitchen. He caught her to him, and kissed her on the mouth.

" Nell, will 'ee leap with me this night? " he asked.

" Sure I will," she said.

She looked him in the face, expectant, waiting for what he should ask next.

" Nell, will 'ee dance with me this night? " he said.

She did not answer for the moment.

" Dennis, I've summat to tell you," she said.   " I reckon there's no need for us to dance."

" No need?   D'you mean——"

" Aye.   I must make sure, though; I must go and see Dr. Symes to-morrow."

" God, then to make it sure we'll dance," he said.

" And if Dr. Symes says 'tis so, then we'll not wait,

Nell, but be wed straight away."

"But what'll your grandfather say?"

"Just exactly what he wills."

She hid her face on his shoulder.

"Eh, how I love you!" she said. "Fair shocking!"

"Shocking, is it? Then there've been two shocking folk in the world for everyone as is here now. Make haste and let's go down."

She looked up at him, still clinging.

"Dennis, was it in sin I conceived?" she said.

"Aw, that's nought but grandfather's tipsy talk on Sunday," he said. "'Twas in love you conceived, and 'twas in love I begot, and that's enough. Come on down."

Already when they got out the sky in front of them was dusky red, for the bonfire was blazing high, and there hung above it, drifting slowly away southward, the thick smoke of its burning, while the moon, a little past its full, and travelling through a cloud-flecked sky, was blanched to an unbelievable whiteness in contrast with the red flaring of the bonfire. The shadows of the circle of stones cast by that light stretched far across the field of corn that encompassed them, and the high moon, as it shone out between the clouds, cast shorter separate shadows of its own. Mingled with these, crossing and recrossing them, were other shadows that moved this way and that: these were thrown by the couples already dancing there. Dennis and Nell went down by the footpath at the edge of the corn to where in the field below the bonfire blazed. High and lustily it roared greedy of the piled fuel, and there would be no leaping yet awhile, for it burned too fervently for any to approach it, far less to think of leaping through those high-flung sheets and snake-tongues of flame. But it was held to be of good omen if the bonfire blazed well, and there would be plenty of leaping in an hour's time, for the field was dotted with couples from Penzance and St. Columb's, and a dozen villages round who wandered about with linked arms or waists. This saunter of those intending to take the fire was equivalent to a declaration of betrothal, and glances and salutations passed between them. The faces of those turned towards the bonfire glowed red with its illumination, as if they had been lit within, those coming away from it were black silhouettes. The young trollop who had kissed Dennis one night on the quay was there, but seeing him with Nell, gave up her pursuit as a bad business, and made after Tim Trehern, rather a lout, but better than nothing, who was still not paired off. The folk were streaming up now in hundreds from Penzance, and flitting about in the crowd was Mr. Willis, very smartly decorated, drinking in the tonic suggestions of this soft, amorous night. But there were no signs of John and Mollie, nor yet of Nancy; perhaps she had gone to see her fancy man in St. Columb's.

" Come, Nell," whispered Dennis. " There'll be no leaping this hour yet. Come up to the stones. You and I've got to dance."

" But the blaze is bright still," she said, " and there's the moon, too. All the folk'll see us, and 'tis only the married ones as dance."

" Dance with you, I will," said Dennis. " Put your shawl over your head, so as none will spot you, and I'll walk small and low, with a hump and a limp, and they'll think we're just strangers. Besides, it's a queer flickering light; none'll know."

Nell wanted but little persuasion, for her heart was set that way, and she threw her shawl over her head, and Dennis crouched and hobbled beside her, and up they went along the grass path that led to the stones.

They squatted down by one of the stones, outside the circle, to see who was there, but, as Dennis had said, the light was strange and flickering: now a burst of flame came from the bonfire, now a cloud obscured the moon. No sort of music accompanied the dance, and in silence the dim couples footed it as their instinct drove them. Some whisked madly round, holding each other by the hands at arm-stretch, leaning outwards with feet planted close: others made queer cantering steps; others loosely clasped, pirouetted together; others slid gravely this way and that to some slow rhythm of their own, but all were worshippers in this rite of desire. Sound there was none save the soft thud of feet on the turf, and the quick panting breath of the more active dancers. Leaning against the stones inside the circle were a few couples exhausted by their exertions, and getting their wind again. Just now the moon was passing behind a thick belt of cloud and the light dim, when suddenly a fresh blaze of flame shot up from the bonfire.

" God, there's Grandfather and her at it," Dennis whispered.

So indeed it was: that was none other than John Pentreath, who followed rather than directed the antics of his partner, staggering and stumbling after her. She whisked him about, with great leaps and high steppings that sent her skirt flying about her knees; of all the women, young and old, there was none who capered and circled with such frenzy. Her face, red in that blaze from the bonfire, was alight with some wild exaltation: she was a Mænad driven by the urge of her longing. Yet the primeval force of her womanhood redeemed her from all grotesqueness. To her this dancing was an act of passionate worship, her faith must needs work the miracle of fruitfulness within her; and now Nell, who had hung back before, was swept into that dynamic vortex, and fairly pulled Dennis into the ring.

"Dance, dance," she whispered. "I care naught who sees, and let them make of it what they will."

The flare from the bonfire died down, and they jumped into the ring, adding their contribution to the force that these couples, all moved with one desire, were generating, just as the whirling, humming dynamos generate electricity. Yearly for centuries that power had boiled and seethed here, and the stones that formed the circle, and the grass and the trodden thyme were soaked in it. Here was an eddy in the river of life, circling and piercing down into the very heart of the stream. Borne round and round at first on the rim of it, Dennis and Nell were sucked inwards deep into that revolving funnel, and soon they were scarcely conscious of the presence of any but themselves, and their very individualities were merged in the power which their dancing set at work. The gleaming eyes of other couples, faces illuminated by the glow of the bonfire, or white with the moon, came within their ken and whisked out again, but these, too, had no individuality: they were but wavings of the wand of magic.

At last they rose to the rim of the eddy again, and slipped out of it: spent and exhausted and inspired they dropped, outside the circle, in the shadow of one of the stones, and lay there, individual again, panting for breath. The flames of the bonfire had died down now, and presently they went along the short grass path, to where it smouldered, flaring no longer, but glowing only. Feathery white ash of wood floated away from it, and round it were strewn half-consumed fragments of the fuel: Dennis and the other young fellows who meant to leap, swept these back on to the red-hot embers, till the edges of it were straight and defined, a canal of incandescence a full ten feet from bank to bank.

Then Dennis ran to seek Nell, who was waiting for him at the entrance of the field.

" Quick, quick," he cried. " 'Tis all ready for the leaping now, and we'll be the first over it, for that's the best luck of all."

Nell drew back.

" Eh, Dennis, I can never leap that! " she said. " We shall come plump in the midst of it."

" That we shall not," he cried, " you trust me; give me your hand, Nell, and keep step with me, and we'll fly it like a pair of birds."

They went back some yards more to get up speed for their run: on each side, forming a lane up to the bonfire, the crowd was gathered to watch the leaping.

" We're off," shouted Dennis, and he grasped one of Nell's hands in his, while with the other she held up her skirt and they began running.

" Lift your feet," he called to her, " left, right, left, right, that's the way, and when I say leap, leap for all your worth and leap high."

They went down the slight slope towards the fire with ever-increasing speed, Dennis adapting his longer stride to the girl's steps, and they moved as if they were one. The boy ran a foot or two in advance of her, lending his strength to aid her swiftness, and she was but a light weight on his arm so active and fleet she was. The wind of their movement blew her skirts close to her legs, defining her strong round thighs, and her arm raised towards Dennis's hand moulded the supple muscles of her shoulder beneath her gown. Willie had been standing close to where they started, and she had given him her shawl to hold, and now her hair slipped from its comb and streamed out thick and long behind her; and the glow of the fire, brighter and brighter as they raced down to it, turned her white gown to crimson. Then Dennis increased his pace to the full power of her going, and she but skimmed the ground, feeling weightless as a flying bird in his grasp. Three more steps now would take them to the edge of the embers, and he drew in a long breath.

"Leap, Nell, and leap high," he yelled.

They soared together, and Nell, through her half-closed eyelids, peeped at the fierce red glow beneath them. Next moment they alighted with a yard to spare on the singed grass beyond the fire, and a bellow of shouting hailed the first leap.

Other couples followed: this leaping was not so deadly serious an affair as the dancing in the circle of stones which set the mysterious spell of fertility at work: it was more the intimation that a boy and a girl intended to get wed, and a successful leap would make their mating sure; comedy was mingled with it, as when Tim Trehern's girl took fright as they neared the fire, and, pulling her hand out of his, left him to do his leaping alone. Shouts of congratulation went up when Jim Paget, veteran bachelor of near forty years, was towed down the course by Janet Graeme, that great buxom wench, who had been in hot pursuit of him

these last five years. " Pull 'im 'long, Janet," cried her
delighted mother. " Don't 'ee leave hold of him now
ye've got him." Then as the fire burned lower Tim
Trehern's girl plucked up her courage, for, after all,
she wanted Tim more than she feared the fire, and
leaped with him: shy youths made up their minds to it,
and said, " Will 'ee leap? " to girls who had long determined to get them, or shy girls rewarded constancy
with a consent to take the fire. But below the chaff
and laughter on the surface ran the stream of belief
that sprang from the heart of the granite hills, and was
as steadfast as they.

The moon had set, and the sky to the east was tinged
with the approach of day before all the dancing and
the leaping were over. One by one the stars, flowers
of the night, folded up their petals, as the dawn drew
on, and soon the heavens were empty, but for the planet
of love which still burned there. Birds chirruped in
the bushes, larks rose from the tussocks of grass and
hovered singing, the cattle got up and cropped a mouthful or two of the dewy herbage, and a flight of gulls
high overhead were rosy with dawn. The breeze of
morning awoke, scattering the ashes of the burnt-out
bonfire, and night hid itself away with the spells in its
keeping.

CHAPTER XI

EXPECTATIONS

A GUST of violent wind plucked the door-handle from John Pentreath's grasp as he entered the kitchen from the farmyard one afternoon in mid-September, and the door was flung wide, letting in a sharp spatter of driving rain. He swore angrily as he forced it shut again, and stood dripping on the mat as he stripped off his mackintosh, which was streaming with water. He unlaced and kicked off his soaking boots, and came across the room to where his wife sat by the oven, with his footsteps printing themselves in wet on the tiled floor.

" 'Tis black ruin for the harvest," he said. " There's not a blade of corn left standing, and the wreck of it's sprouting as it lies there."

Mollie's hands were always busy now: to-day she was employed in knitting a pair of tiny woollen socks, and the needles flashed swiftly in her fingers. She paused before answering, counting her stitches. " That's a bad business, John," she said indifferently.

" Bad business it is. I reckon I'm with you there," he said.

He thrust his feet into the slippers that stood by the hearth, and shuffled across to the cupboard where his bottle stood.

" Never did the corn look fairer nor fuller in the ear than a few weeks ago," he said, " and me thanking the Lord for it punctual every Sunday, as you well know. But this last fortnight's done for it: rain, rain, rain, day and night. Can't you give me a bit of help, Mollie? Your hens and your bees have made you a fat purse this year."

"Nay, not a penny," said she. "I don't spend from it on myself, 'tis all put by for the child that's coming to me."

"I guessed so. Then there's nought for it but to sell them two meadows above St. Columb's. And I can get a good price for them. That lawyer chap over to Penzance has been wanting to buy them this last six months. I met him this afternoon, and I told him I'd sell."

"And does Dennis say aye to it? That's needful, you told me."

"Damn the boy!" said John, filling his glass again. "He gave me a surly answer, when I said something of it to him before, but I'll make him see sense. Leave Dennis to me!"

She gave a little thin cackle of laughter. "Eh, John, 'twas a pretty hash Dennis made o' you last time you went for to tackle him," said she. "I thought you'd never be the same man again. But indeed you recovered wonderful, for 'twas scarce a fortnight after that that you was as lusty as ever, and you and I came together again after all these years."

"Never mind that," said he. "Dennis has just got to sign as he's bid, agreeing to the sale."

"Maybe he will, and maybe he won't. The boy's just as obstinate as any Pentreath can be; and now 'tis not he only, but Nell 'll be backing him up, and she's of a stock that equals yours, for it's my own. They're wedded folk now, and there's a child coming. That'll stiffen her against selling what'll one day be

her son's, and she'll stiffen Dennis against it. It wants
a bit o' planning, if you're to get your way with him."

Her voice rose as she began to speak fast with that
shrill gabble he knew so well. But now there was no
scolding or rating in it.

" 'Tis strange how things turn out," she said. " Just
round about the time that you and me came together
again after twenty years, there was your own grandson and Nell burning for each other, and now us two
women are expecting. Eh, he and Nell were quiet and
secret about it; I couldn't 'a been more secret myself,
and never shall I forget the evening, two nights or three
it must 'a been after the bonfire, when he came sauntering in, as if the place was his a'ready. ' Nell and
me's gwaineter get married as soon as Passon can put
us through the banns,' he says. She was with child
by him then, and 'twas on Midsummer Eve that she
told him she was fruitful by him. They danced in
the circle that night, same as you and I, skipping wild
they were, and 'twas strange that a grandfather and his
grandson should be there together. Wild they skipped,
but Mollie Pentreath's heels were as high as theirs,
I reckon, spite of the generations as severs us. 'Twas
that night, I'll be bound, that I conceived, though
she got the start of me, and now in the spring days
there'll be born to you a child of your grandson, while
your own's just coming to ripeness. Lord! that'll be
something to think about for Passon, as is so bent on
hell-fire. The fire of earth ain't burned itself out yet,
and maybe t'other'll cool down first."

She rose to her feet, waving the little half-knitted
sock.

" Eh, there was fire abroad that night," she cried,
" the old great fire of the world, as kindles women

twice as hot as Passon's hell, or as man either. Man takes his pleasure, as did you of me, and Dennis of Nell, but where's your joy to mine, or Dennis's to hers, for when your bit of pleasure is over 'tis we women that day and night grow great with the fruit of it. Indeed, yes, there were powerful good friends o' mine about on St. John's Eve, there in the circle, and in Kenrith copse too, I shouldn't wonder."

She pushed him down into the chair from which she had risen, and came and sat on his knee, nestling to his shoulder. Whatever had been the trick whereby she had brought him back to her, renewing their marriage rites by the harlotry of his desire, even as by harlotry she had married him, he was hers again now, as if newly wed.

"But be you sure that you're waxing with child?" he asked. "Isn't it, maybe, some fancy of yours, because you long for it? Women have strange notions, they say, when they come to your time of life, and they go crazy with wanting. Shan't I get Dr. Symes to come and have a look over you?"

She laughed in his face.

"Tush for your doctors!" she said. "Do I want a doctor to tell me I've a head on my neck or a womb within me? No more do I want one to tell me what's waxing there. And the sickness and all: why, man, I glory in it. There's Nell, not yet born when I was first wed to you, and I'm fruitful still, no withered branch to be lopped off and thrust into the oven. The tender leaf's sprouting from it yet, for all my years, and I need no 'pothecary to tell me that. 'Twas of your begetting, John: the stroke of your manhood met my desire, and tush for your doctors."

"Yet I'm not at ease, Mollie," he said. "You look

thin and worn, you do, when a woman should be
stout and buxom, and your face is yellow when it
should be growing roses for your baby to pluck, and
slack and fallen are your breasts that should be growing
firm for your child to suck. 'Tis little good your
food does you, and you're light as a fleshed bone on
my knee, when 'tis heavy you should be.   Look at
Nell."

She laughed again.

" Aye, and look at Dennis, if it comes to that,"
she said, " and then behold yourself, John Pentreath.
Dennis is all spring and sap and fire, while you're old
and heavy-footed, and if I'm different from Nell, you're
different from Dennis, though you made yourselves
fathers together.   'Tis in nature that you haven't his
fibre and his lustiness, and why should I be buxom and
firm of breast like Nell?   But I'll not be paying a
doctor for telling me what I know already.   Time for
him to come when we send for the midwife."

" Well, you're a wonder," he said.

He held her close to him, astonished at the ardour
he felt towards the woman whom for years he had
regarded as a blackened, weather-worn hull stranded on
the shore.   Though at the first moment when, maddened by her trick, he had dealt her that savage blow,
there was no deceit about the joy she had already given
him, for there was fire and challenge in her, fit to
match any riotous young poll of half her years.   Then
too she had proved for him his manhood's efficiency,
and that flattered his pride, for it was not everyone
who could reel tipsy to bed on most nights for a solid
thirty years or more, and at the end be capable of
begetting a child.   It was a proud thing to be a Pentreath who could play hell with every rule of whole-

some living, and yet prove himself as good a man as any of the sober and stiff-lipped.

A flap of rain beating on the window recalled to him the thought of his ruined harvest and of Dennis's possible obstinacy about the sale of the fields.

" The boy's got to come round to my way of think-ing," he said, " and I'll have no nonsense. I'll speak him fair about it, but he's got to give way. Damn that father of mine, who made th' entail, so they name it, after he'd sold more nor thirty acres himself."

" Father or no father, 'tis wiser not to go damning the dead," said she, " for happen they can heed you yet."

" Nay, Mollie, d'you think that? " he asked.

" Reckon I do. But talking of the acres, those acres went down the old man's throat, same as these'll go down yours if you manage to sell. John, can't you give up your drink, with a child coming to you from me and a great-grandchild to Dennis? Nigh on a pound a week goes in your bottles. Strong and lusty you were when you went without it after Dennis's mishandling of you. He and Nell know where the price of the land will go, for she spoke to me of it when you tried Dennis before. ' What'll Dennis or our children see o' that money? ' she said. ' 'Twill all have gone down a red lane I know of, first."

" I might offer him half the purchase price," said John. " That'll be a hundred and fifty pounds in his pocket."

" And for why should he take that, when one day t'other half will be his, too? " she asked.

" That's so. God, how I hate that feller! It makes me writhe to think he'll be strutting here when I'm no more than mould. All flesh is grass, well I know it, but I reckon there's some grass as is tough and wiry yet, and I'm o' that breed."

Mollie knitted awhile in silence.

" The lad won't sign if he knows what he's signing," she said at length. " Nell's behind him in that, and I'll back their will against yours. But can't you get his scrawl out of him without his knowing? Can't you get the deed wrapped up in lawyer's language, so that he don't rightly understand it? "

He turned a pleased but fuddled face to her.

" Faith, and I believe you've hit it," he said. " 'Tis worth trying, anyhow, and if it comes off, he'll look pretty when he finds that I've condiddled him. That'd put things a bit more even between us, and mark you, I shan't be satisfied till I've paid him back. Dearly should I like to look at his dead face, and give it a clout and say, ' Aye, you thought to step into my shoes, did 'ee? But a winding sheet's all you need, for the dead go barefoot.' "

"Aye, you hate him sure 'nough," said she, " for I've seen your eyes glint when they light on him or on Nell either. And I'm with you in that, for if 'twasn't for him, and her brat that's coming, 'twould be my child as would have and hold the farm when you're gone. But, there, I can't think o' that for long, for my mind goes back to what's coming to me, and then 'tis not in me to think ill for any."

She put her lips to the tiny sock she was knitting, and kissed it.

" 'Tis the fruits of autumn, maybe, as are the sweetest," she said.

All that week the boisterous, pouring weather continued, completing the ruin of the harvest in those parts, and then too late for the saving of it, windless days and the clear shining of summer suns returned. But already the corn was flat on the mire of the fields, and as if in mockery and derision, the ripened grain was sprouting everywhere, and the poppies were ablaze. In the field where stood the circle of stones, not a blade was left upright, and grey and indifferent the monoliths regarded the ruin, for what mattered it to them and their centuries of stability? For this year they had done their work for those who had danced within the circle of their spell: there were two couples, it was said, down in St. Columb's, each with five years of barren wedlock behind them, and their dancing had done it for them now. Dr. Symes would bear witness that both of these wives were pregnant, and what could have brought that about but their dancing? And then it was said that Mollie Pentreath up at the farm was expecting, but Dr. Symes hadn't been asked for his opinion there, and so he couldn't say as to her.

Nell and Dennis, on the evening of one of these hot days after the return of the sun, were coming up from St. Columb's. Nell was a bit out of breath with the ascent when they came opposite the circle of stones.

" We'll sit awhile, Dennis," she said. " 'Tis only a cold supper to-night, and your mother and I made all ready before I came out. Eh, that Midsummer Night! Gracious it was to us, for we leaped and now we're married, and there's a child coming. And there the stones stand, so heedless and quiet. Do you mind you of Aunt Mollie that night? 'Twas a strange thing to see her capering there."

" And 'twas a stranger thing that came of it," said Dennis.

" Yes, if so be there's something coming of it. Yet

there's Betty Poltalloch and Susan Burton down to
St. Columb's, who are in the way, and both danced
that night."

" Lord, there was power abroad," said he, " and who
can doubt it?   Not you and me, Nell, for we danced
as frantic as any, and leaped too.   Maybe 'tis we who
believe as make the power, same as faith, that Passon
talks about in church, makes you lusty enough to move
mountains."

" Happen that's it.   There's Aunt Mollie, who
wouldn't see the young moon through glass for a pocketful of guineas, and perhaps it would do her a mischief
if she did.   But I'd stare at the moon through glass all
night before it would hurt me."

Dennis laughed.

" I like that," he said, " for what about that silver
piece you wear round your neck to keep your blood
pure.   A rare taking you were in that night when I
filched it, and hung it round myself for a change, and
'twasn't till you saw it there that you'd be comforted."

" Well, that's a match for the moon, I allow," she
said, " and there's a sight of things I don't know
whether I believe or not.   But there's one thing I
don't believe for sure, and that's that Aunt Mollie
has a child coming."

" Why, how's that? " he asked.   " What makes her
believe so then?   She's been having the morning sickness, hasn't she, same as you? "

She shook her head.

" Nay, there's plenty o' things which can make a
women spew beside that," she said.   " And then to
look at her!   She's thin as a lath, and yellow-brown
for colour, and there's not an ounce of juice in her
body, and she grows more davvered every day.   She

can't nourish herself, and you don't tell me that there's nourishment for another as well. And for all that, she goes smiling and eager with her knitting o' baby clothes. She's got queer pains, too; and I've seen her clutch at herself and turn white, and what's she doing with pain yet? And the sweat breaks out on her; many a time have I seen her sitting close to the fire, but 'tis not the fire that gives her the sweat. It lathers on her, and there's a corruption in it, soapy, I'd call it."

"Well, I know a lass who was in a lather just now, coming up from St. Columb's," said Dennis.

"Yes, and 'twas me," she said, "and you might give me a wipe of your handkerchief, for I came out wanting one."

Dennis drew a big square of coarse stuff from his trouser-pocket.

"Reckon it's not very dainty," he said, "and there's a streak o' blood on it, too, for I cut myself pruning the hedges, and it's soiled."

She took it from him.

"Sweaty and bloody it may be," she said, "but there's a wholesomeness."

She passed it over her forehead, and held it, crumpling and kneading it in her hands.

"Don't I know the whiffs you get in soiled linen," she said, "me that spends a day every week of my life over the wash-tubs? There's a sourness that's wholesome, and a sweetness that's rank, thin-like and acid. I couldn't make out an account of it, but there it is. And, Lord, there's your mother's musk. That's just a silly stink. Makes me laugh sometimes."

She leaned back, fitting her shoulder between his arm and his chest.

" Dennis, I can't get Aunt Mollie out o' my head,"
she said. " She may knit her baby-socks, but who'll
be wearing them? She and I sit together, often, after
supper at our knittings, but what does she think of as
she knits? Just her desire for a child as she wants to
make true. She's full of spells still: she sits in the
garden, when the owls are flighting, and she goes sauntering across the pasture to Kenrith copse, for I've seen
her popping in, and what for? It's barren she is, like
the sour earth, where you may plant year in and year
out, and nothing will grow. Maybe, she's come to believe that she's fruitful, who knows with one as secret
as that? "

She stuffed his handkerchief back into his pocket.

" And often, as she knits," she said, " Aunt Mollie's
thinking of your grandfather and naught else. Do I
do that? Don't you believe it, for when I knit a baby-
piece I think o' nothing but what'll be wearing it.
And when it's forth from me it will desire nothing of
you, but just my breast only. There 'twill suck and
grow strong, and it and me will be the whole world
to each other, and I reckon poor old Daddy may go
rot in hell when it's pulling at me."

" Thank ye for that, I'm sure," said Dennis. " Very
handsomely spoken."

Nell looked up at him a moment, but there was
his face all full of sunshine.

" It takes a woman to understand a woman when
the child waxes within her," she said, " so give it up,
Dennis, and listen to what I tell you. It isn't with
Aunt Mollie as it is with me. She may kiss the little
bits o' things she's knitting, but it's her desire for a
child as has crazed her wits into the belief she'll have
one, while I could go and sing Magnificat by the hour

with Passon, for I know. Sometimes I doubt whether she's not a bit queer in the head with her spells and her copses and her secret ways. She lives in a world as is different from ours, and she's treading dark paths. Women often go a bit queer when the child's coming, but hers ain't a queerness like that. Withered she is and barren. Maybe, it's ill-luck for me to talk of it, so we'll have done."

She drew his head down to hers.

"Dennis, sometimes I feel there's something stirring in me, and, Lord, the rapture of it, though I doubt it's only my fancy, but a pretty fancy it is, and I like to think on it. 'Tis as if a little teeny hand tapped as if to say it lived, and I must laugh for the joy of it. But soon it'll be stirring indeed, and when my time comes, every pain will be a joy, for 'tis you and I as'll be born then. Remember that, and don't let them give me any sleepy stuff, for I'll not miss a pang of it. And don't you come hanging round, or sit sweating on the stairs, and making a botheration for everyone. You get hold of your Willie, to take your mind off me. Lord, how you two fellers love each other: it's fine to think on. Pull me up, for it's time we went home."

They stood there looking out a moment over the tops of the house roofs in St. Columb's and the shining bay beyond, molten with the sky-fires of the reflected sunset and shadowed here and there by dark wind-breaks. Then they saw coming up the path from the village the figure of John Pentreath and a couple of men following him. They halted some distance off, and stood talking, pointing out over the fields below.

"And what be they up to?" said Dennis.

One of them stood still on the path, while the other

with John walked forward, holding the end of a long tape-measure. A hundred yards brought it to its full stretch, and then the third man on the path rejoined them, reeling it in, and off they set again.

"Measuring," said Nell, "and what'll that be for?"

"That's one of the fields Grandfather was wanting to sell," said Dennis. "Something's afoot again about it."

"Well, you be wary," said she.

A couple of evenings later the two young folk and John Pentreath were whiling away a silent hour after supper. Nancy had hurried them through the meal, and had set off to St. Columb's in a brand-new hat that quite eclipsed the cherry-bower, leaving Nell to wait on Willis, and clear away. Mollie had already gone to her bed, taking her knitting with her. Dennis had been helping Nell with the serving of the lodger's supper, and when the washing-up was done, took out the old dog-eared pack of cards, and instructed her in the principles of "Beggar-my-neighbour." John watched them a while, smoking and sipping in his arm-chair, and then, as if he had made up his mind, got up pretty briskly and pulled a long folded paper from his pocket.

"Just come you here, my lad," he said, "and bring a pen and th' inkpot along with you, while I go ask Mr. Willis to step in. It's some tax collector's botheration about the farm, and it needs your signature and mine and a feller to witness them."

Nell was paying out four cards to an ace Dennis turned up, but she stopped.

"Be sure you know what you're signing," she whispered. Then aloud, "Two, three and four, and there's your ace paid."

John had half unfolded a long sheet of foolscap, so that little more than the place for signatories and witness was visible.

"I scarce understand it myself," he said, "but at the office they tell me 'tis all in order."

The moment he had left the room to ask Willis in, Nell got up in a fine hurry.

"What's it about?" she said. "Quick: open it and let's look."

She bent over it with Dennis in frowning silence. There were two paragraphs written in large round hand.

"'Tis gibberish," she said. "There's no head nor tail to it. 'The two fields abutting and adjoining the road known as St. Columb's Lane, with all the hedges and walls appertaining to and bounding the same, excepting only the wall abutting and adjoining to the field of corn-land, where are situated the circle of stones or cromlechs——' Help us; I see what they're talking of: 'tis the fields next where the circle lies, where we saw him and the two fellers measuring——"

Then came the sound of Willis's amiable cackle from the passage leading to the studio, and Nell slid back to her place by the cards.

"Don't 'ee sign nothing till ye understand, mind," she whispered. "Maybe it's to do with the sale of land he was talking of a while ago."

The other two entered.

"'Tis just to witness Dennis's signature and mine," said John, "if ye'll be so good, Mr. Willis. It won't keep you a moment. I'm sure I'm sorry to have disturbed you."

He picked up the pen and scrawled his name.

"There: sign just below me, Dennis," he said, "and don't keep Mr. Willis waiting."

"I'll know what it is I'm signing afore I put my name to it," said Dennis.

"Well, haven't I told you? It's some matter of tax: just a formality. That's where your name goes."

"Nay: I'll know more nor that first," said Dennis, not taking the pen John held out to him. "Will you be so good as to cast your eye over it, Mr. Willis, since my grandfather says he can scarce understand it himself."

"Just sign, and don't bother Mr. Willis with affairs as don't concern him," he said. "Mr. Willis is naught but the witness."

"He'll know first what he's witnessing, and so'll I," said Dennis.

"Dear me, that's not unreasonable, Mr. Pentreath," said Willis. "Let me have a look at it."

John put out his hand as if to get hold of the paper again, but Dennis nipped it from under his fingers before they closed on it.

"Now, Mr. Willis, take a squint at it," he said. "I sign nothing till I know what 'tis."

Nell had been sitting at the far end of the table while they talked, turning cards face upwards, as if not heeding them. But she was closely following what went on.

"You stick to that, Dennis," she said.

John Pentreath turned savagely on her.

"And who, maybe, was asking for your advice?" he said. "You mind your own affairs."

She jumped up.

"Happen they are my affairs," she said. "We'll know more o' that soon. You mark and learn all that you're putting your name to, Dennis."

" Hell, and am I to be sent right and left in my own house by the slavey as let herself be seduced? " cried John furiously.

Dennis stuffed the paper in his pocket, leaving his hands free.

" Now you take back that word, Grandfather," he said, " before you add another one to it, or I'll make a sorrier plight o' you than ever I did before. Quick: take it back. 'Tis you are keeping Mr. Willis waiting now. There's the dog whip all handy, and you know the taste o' that."

For a moment it looked as if John was going to hurl himself on the boy, as he turned to unhook the whip from the wall, but he distrusted that cat-like swiftness.

" My temper got the better of me," he said, " and whatever I said, I unsay it. But mark, I'll have no interference from any. God! here's a pleasant family party to ask Mr. Willis to assist at! "

" Iss sure, that it is," said Dennis. " Mr. Willis won't often go to such a brisk, lively little party, I reckon, when he's in Lunnon town. And now we'll all sit down, cool and comfortable as is our way, and perhaps Mr. Willis'll be kind enough to tell us what's all this bother-ation from the tax-collector, as I've got to put my name to."

He spread the document open before Willis, with an eye on his grandfather, lest he should try his snatching again. In John's half-tipsy brain there was still the vague hope that the girlie would be able to make nothing of it, for who could understand that entangle-ment of words?

Willis put on his gold pince-nez and began reading. Leaving out hedges and walls and so forth, the general purport was clear enough.

" I don't see anything about the tax-collector," he
said to Dennis. " Ah, there it is! The purchaser pays
all taxes on the land as from the date of signature."

" Didn't I tell 'ee that? " said John.

" Certainly you did, Mr. Pentreath," said Willis,
" but I can't agree with you that it's just a tax-collector's botheration. It's a deed for the sale of the two
fields above the road to St. Columb's. The purchaser
agrees to pay three hundred pounds for them."

" Aye, and Dennis gets a half o' that, paid down in
good money," said John.

" Happen you'll make sure that's written there, Mr.
Willis," said Dennis.

Willis glanced through it again.

" That isn't stated here, Mr. Pentreath."

" What? Have they left that out? " said John. " That
was my intention."

" And was it, indeed? " said Dennis, looking across
at Nell. " That comes as a bit o' news. And I'll give
you another bit o' news to match yours. 'Twas a fool
ye thought me to be as would sign blindfold, and not
a word o' your intention writ there. And I'll tell you
what it is, Grandfather: 'tis a rank cheat you meant.
I was to sign away the land, not knowing what I did,
and every penny o' that would have gone into your
pocket. Ain't that so, Mr. Willis? "

" I can only tell you that there's nothing said about
your share, Dennis," he said.

" So that's where we be," said Dennis. " Just a
swindle. That's your tax-collector's formality."

" Eh, that's well said," cried Nell, sweeping up the
silly cards from the table.

John Pentreath sat gnawing at his pipe-stem, silent
under this monstrous humiliation. Here was he, under

his own roof, where his word was law, made a mere mockery by these two young devils who were dependent for their broth and their bootleather on the wage he paid them. Dearly would he have liked to give Nell just such a punch as he had dealt to his wife a few months ago, but between him and her was that great young tiger-cat, not asleep now, but quivering and taut. And then on his other side was this little girlie-fellow, tapping the deed with his gold pince-nez. It was he who as much as any was responsible for this mocking of him, for he had been brought in just to witness a couple of signatures, and there he was being lord-judge of it all, the little puny creature with his mincing steps and his simpering ways. John didn't dare quarrel with him, for he was a paying proposition, worth two pounds a week, and he was thinking of stopping on now till the end of October, so well was he suited. Had John been properly drunk he'd have done something, and damned whatever might come of it, but he was no more than half afloat and his keel grated on actualities. There lay the deed still unsigned, and there round the table were three witnesses to this promise to give Dennis half the purchase money. And they all despised him as an exposed swindler: Dennis had stated the case for them all, that son of a woman who was gone whoring in St. Columb's. A sanctified lot, weren't they?

Dennis broke the silence.

"Well, 'tis time to settle all this," he said, "for we're keeping Mr. Willis. You told me false about what you asked me to sign, Grandfather, and Mr. Willis to witness, and maybe I'd best tear the tomfool deed up and stuff it in the oven, and there'll be the end of that. Give it me, Mr. Willis."

16

John saw the entire three hundred pounds slipping from him.

"Wait a bit," he said. "I've promised you half of the purchase money, and I'll give it you and draw out my promise regular, if you'll sign. 'Tis a fine price for the land, and I reckon I'm good for a sight of years yet."

Nell was listening with all her ears. There was her child coming before many months were out, and she would be laid up, not earning her wages, and there'd be lack of money, sure enough, before the winter was out. Better, she thought, to get that big sum banked away than take a risk. She nudged Dennis.

"Take it," she whispered.

"D'you mean that?" he asked.

"Yes, for sure. 'Twill make us safe."

He turned to Willis.

"Perhaps you'd be so kind then as to write out something for my grandfather to sign, and we shan't lack for witnesses. I'll consent to the sale of the fields, and I'll sign his deed, and he's got to give me half the price of what he gets: a hundred and fifty pounds that'll be, and the same for him. That's the way 'twill run, and you be sure to fix it down secure, so that there's no wriggling out of it."

Instantly John tried to get better terms for himself.

"Take a hundred pounds, Dennis," he said, "and have done with it: a hundred pounds is a lot of money, and I'll sign and promise to give it you the day the price is paid. That's fair."

"I'm thinking a hundred and fifty'll be fairer. Same as had been your intention all along, as you told us yourself," he said.

John thumped the table.

"A hundred it shall be," he shouted, "and damned generous o' me, too.   Write it out, if you please, Mr. Willis, and let's have an end o' this haggling."

Dennis took up the deed of purchase.

"May as well stuff it into the grate," he said, "for you'll get no signature from me."

"Well, take a hundred and ten," said John.

"Nay, let's make an end o' this haggling," said Dennis.

John looked from one to the other.   Still and quiet they sat, just despising him.

"God, then have it your own way," he said at length.   "'Tis a sucking blood-leech I've gotten for a grandson."

"Thank you kindly," said Dennis.   "Draw it up, Mr. Willis, and we'll all sign and witness, first one and then t'other."

The business was now soon concluded.   First, the promise to Dennis of half the purchase price of the land was signed and witnessed, and, when he had secured that, came the purchase deed itself.   John snapped it up when it was executed, and off he went to his bed, without a word to any of them.   A sore defeat it had been, and a heavy score there was to be chalked up to Dennis's account.

CHAPTER XII

THE LUMP

THE influx of ready money had relieved John Pentreath's mind of any fear that he would find a difficulty
in procuring as much drink as he would be likely to
want during the coming winter months, when it was
but natural that a man took a drop more than in
summer-time to while away the lengthening evenings,
and in the early closing in of the November days he
would often pull his chair up to the oven by four of an
afternoon with his bottle handy, watching his boots
steam till they were dry. Mollie would be there, too,
doing her sewing or knitting, and when his boots began
to smell of scorching leather, she would bid him get
them off and put his slippers on. Evening after evening they sat there, mostly silent, he dropping off to sleep
from time to time, till Nancy or Nell came to do
the cooking for supper, and then they must push back
their chairs to give access to the oven.

Between these dozings there were three topics which
chiefly occupied John's mind. He took them up each
evening much as he had left them the night before, and
they went sluggishly round in his head, ending, when
supper was ready, pretty much where they began. The
first of these was how he should lay out the purchase
money of the fields he had sold to the best advantage
of the farm: that he was already laying it out as fast
as his capacity for swallowing spirits would permit, if
not for his own advantage, for his own solace, was not a

point that need be considered. According to his reckoning all he had spent of it was just the matter of ten pounds for the insurance of the house for the coming year against fire: so there were a hundred and forty pounds left of it. After the disaster to his ewes and lambs in the spring, he was not disposed to increase the livestock, and with the sale of the two pasture fields there would not be more than enough grazing for such stock as he had of sheep and cows. But he had often considered building a couple more rooms on to the house, with the view of getting another lodger during the summer. Lodgers were safer bread-winners than sheep or indeed corn, after the ruin of this year's harvest, especially if he could secure such large payers and such paltry trenchermen as the girlie, for he scarcely ate more than his piping bullfinch. A pound a week, when he came to reckon up, had covered the cost of his keep; that meant a clear profit of three pounds a week instead of the two pounds he had calcu-lated on, and Willis had been here for twenty-two weeks before he left at the end of October, and intended to come back again next summer. There was a golden goose indeed; all that the little fellow wanted was to go quacking all day, and dress himself up, like the girlie he was, and draw pictures of Dennis, and lay these golden eggs as regular as Mollie's fowls. Then there was all the money he gave Dennis for sitting to him, five shillings an hour he paid the boy for cocking himself up to be looked at, and that had saved John money, too, for it was only in reason that he should cut Dennis's wages down by half, not but what he did as much work as any other labourer working full time. Well indeed he might, since he was employed on the property that would one day be his. So there was

a sum to be done to see what Willis had been worth
to him all this summer: three pounds a week, and
Dennis's wages reduced by a half. It would be a fine
thing to get another such boarder; and there was plenty
of room to build a second lodging, studio and bedroom,
beyond the end of the house, and the money he laid
out on it would earn a pretty dividend.

Arithmetic would have become difficult by now, and
his mind slid off on to the second of its standing topics
for fireside meditation, which was Dennis himself, and
John took a good gulp from his glass to help him to
steady his attention. The damned dog: whatever he
himself spent, whether on building or on livestock,
would all go to fill Dennis's pockets some day. There
was no getting out of that: all that he could do was
to spend the price of those fields in drink, for Dennis
couldn't get hold of it then. Already he had a hundred
and fifty pounds lying in the bank, without reckoning
up what Willis had been giving him all these weeks
for lounging round in his studio in an attitude. Every
evening as John's mind, regular as clockwork, turned
on him, a blacker hatred and envy of the boy for his
youth and his strength and his contemptuous indifference to himself rose in him like some bitter bile of the
brain. Time and again all this year, starting from
mere acts of defiance and disobedience, then proceeding
to tigerish bodily violence, and from that to his own
even more humiliating defeat in that bad business of
the purchase money, Dennis had proved his effortless
mastery. Right across John's face now, a reminder to
him, whenever he shaved himself, ran the mark of the
healed scar which the young devil had slashed there,
and there was another on the thumb of the hand that
carried his glass to his mouth; and Dennis was flush

with the money he had forced his grandfather to pay him, and every night he pillowed his head on the bosom of the prettiest lass for twenty miles round. . . .

And yet, what could he do to get upsides with him? That had always been running in his head ever since his mauling in the spring: round and round it went, a series of vivid pictures. In some of these he saw himself throttling the life out of him, with hands gripped tight round his throat, but that could never be realised: he had tried it before and got a bashing for his pains. To shoot him was the best way: he had often thought of that. He could get a good opportunity for it, for now and then he went out with his gun, hiding quiet in the cover of the hedge by the field where the circle stood, to kill a pigeon or two that came to feed on the ruined corn, and Dennis often passed up the path there on his way back from work. John imagined himself standing screened there, and when Dennis passed, he would just whistle so that Dennis turned his head, and saw what was coming, and then perhaps he would say, " Ah, you dog, I've got you now," and pull the trigger. It would be pretty easy to account for the accident: Dennis had come into line at the very moment that he loosed off at a pigeon. But he might have to wait long for the right opportunity, for there must be nobody about. . . . Again, there was a fine strong stuff called vitriol: you used it, very dilute, on the warts that the cattle got sometimes, one part to ten of water, and the crust came crumbling away. But a splash of it pure, on a man's face, would eat the flesh off his bones, and cause his eyeballs to smoke away in their sockets, like guttering candles whose light was spent. Perhaps one day, Dennis and he would be using it. . . .

Then there would come a movement, or a mumbled

counting of stitches from the chair beside him, where
Mollie sat knitting, and his mind skidded off on to the
third topic that filled these silent hours.   All that fierce
energy which for years had lain bubbling in her had
been absorbed by the passion with which she looked
forward to the bearing of her expected child, for whom
she was for ever knitting and sewing.   Already there
was made for him—she knew it would be a boy—a
cap of pink wool that would come down over his ears
against the March winds, and a jersey with long sleeves,
and a pair of teeny woollen gloves with one stall for
the thumb and another for the bits of fingers to keep
warm in together, and a pair of woollen breeches reaching down to his ankles to be tucked into his socks.
They'd keep him warm, the pet, in case he was like his
mammy and felt the cold as she did.   The first thing
she would do with him would be to have him rubbed
over with fish-oil, and then Sally Austell should take
him to be dipped in the spring that bubbled up in the
heart of Penrith copse, for that was a rare spell to make
a baby's blood run brisk.   She would drop a word or
two about such things to John, as they sat together by
the fire, but then catch herself up, for to speak of them
might bring ill-luck.   Every night when she went up
to bed she took her knitting to her room, and put it
handy on her table, so that if she lay awake in the
night she could light her candle and get to work again.
    Sometimes as the two sat together Mollie's certainty
that she was waxing with child would convince John
she was right: a woman surely knew the symptoms, and
besides, he thought she was beginning to grow a bit
big.   But at other times he could not bring himself
to imagine it possible that her hands and limbs growing
ever thinner and more emaciated could be the harbour-

age for new life, and she was yellowing like an autumn leaf, when the sap has drained out of it; whereas Nell was like a bud in spring-time, and radiant with blooming vitality. Mollie was ill; one night she had had spasms of sharp pain, and he had got her consent to let Dr. Symes have a look at her. But in the morning she was better again, and no persuasion would induce her to see him. She crawled very slowly about the house now, stopping two or three times to get her breath if she must go upstairs, often not leaving her bed till near on noonday, but coming down eager to count the eggs which Nell brought in from the hen-yard. Sometimes she would go out to have a look at the new run, or go forth into the garden at dusk, saying she would be the better for a saunter, but for the most part she sat over the fire, bunched up and stooping low over her work.

December slipped away and January: on those short days the sun scarcely cleared the trees beyond the garden, and had sunk before it could look into the kitchen window to the west. Harry Giles had gone back to London many weeks before, so now Nancy was never in a hurry to get supper done. She had heard from him two days ago, and he had asked her to come up to London and live with him as his housekeeper. It required but little thought to make her decision, and she intended to write to him to-morrow, to say she would come. She had had enough of the farmhouse and its dark ways: twenty years she'd spent there, in cooking and housework, and it was time she had a bit of life of her own, before the greyness of age came on her. It was enough to give anyone the creeps to look at those two sitting by the fire all evening, and never a bit of joy came to her now that Harry had gone.

On this Sunday evening late in January she and Nell were washing-up, and when that was done Nell came and sat with Dennis in the window-seat to wait for John to have had enough drink to be ready for his prayings. There was a new moon that night, and Dennis pointed to it.

" Just a sliver of a moon," he said. " 'Tis new."

Mollie turned round quickly in her chair by the fire.

" What's that? " she asked.

" Naught, Granny," said he. " Just the young moon."

She got up, putting her hands over her eyes.

" Just the young moon, say you? " she cried. " As if that's naught indeed! I mustn't see a glint of it through glass. Here, one of you, lead me out into the yard, so's I may see it fair."

" Eh, I'll go with you," said Nancy, " and I hope a breath of air'll do you good, Mrs. Pentreath, for you've taken neither bite nor sup to-night."

" That's a kind woman," said Mollie. " Now lead me careful, for I'll go blindfold till I'm out."

Nancy led her far out into the yard, from where she could get a view of the slim crescent uncrossed by tree branches, and, as bidden, left her there, casting a rather fearful glance behind her, as she closed the kitchen door again.

" Lor', Mrs. Pentreath fair frightens me sometimes," she said. " Such mutterings and curtseyings you never saw. It's as if there was someone nigh to her to talk to. Well, I hope they may do her good, pore old lady."

Soon Mollie came back, stepping more briskly. At the moment Dennis said something to the girl that made her laugh, and Mollie snapped her fingers and joined in with a high cackle.

" Eh, that's right, Nell," she cried. " 'Tis proper
for us as'll soon be mothers to laugh for the joy of
our hearts. And 'tis a fine pure maid of a moon, up
on high, and kind she looked on me. She'll be a good
friend to us whose time is nigh, and I feel easier nor
I've felt all day. And if it ain't a trouble, you might
get me a bit o' that cold beef you had for supper, for
I must see that I'm well nourished. Eh, you buxom
wench, 'tis good for such as us to laugh loud and eat
solid."

She sat down by the fire again, and took a mouthful
of the meat which Nell brought her, sucked it with
mumbling movements of her mouth, and swallowed it
with an effort.

" Yes, 'tis good," she said, " but I don't know as I
relish more of it now. And it's time for you, John, to
get to your prayings, for we can't go wrong with having
friends on all sides, maybe, as are looking after us. Eh,
I'd best not have swallowed that meat, but it's gone
now. But do you have your prayers, and put up a
word about me, and we'll see what comes of it all."

She sat smiling to herself as the others gathered round
the table. John had drunk handsomely that night, and
when Mollie called to him to begin prayers he was
in drunken meditation on one of his standard topics,
that of Dennis. It was no wonder then that he led off
with a marrowy passage about the sins and offences of
youth, about the stiff-necked and adulterous generation
that honoured not their fathers nor yet their fathers'
fathers. A fine bawling piece it was, with phrases
culled from the savager psalms of King David, but it
was familiar now, and Dennis and Nell, kneeling opposite along the kitchen table, sent a smile and a nod
of recognition to each other.

Then following on to his next topic of meditation,
John closed his eyes and raised his voice in more urgent
appeal.

"And for us, Lord, who fear Thy holy ways, and
bow to Thy judgments, and walk in Thy paths with
Thy rod and Thy staff to comfort us, grant the fulfilment of our just desires. Bless, O Lord, the union of
marriage ordained and sanctified by Thee. May the
wife be as the fruitful vine on the walls of my house,
and her children like the olive branches——"

Suddenly Mollie bent herself together, clutching the
arms of her chair, and screamed aloud for the pain
that stabbed her.

"Eh, 'tis enough, 'tis enough," she cried, "for sure
my time's come. The fruitful vine, aye, the fruitful
vine's what did it. But come and hold me tight, John,
for it's more'n I can bear."

She slid forward from her chair, collapsed on to the
floor, and lay there writhing.

"Run like hell, Dennis, for the doctor chap," cried
his grandfather, shuffling to his feet. "Bring him
with you if you have to take him up and carry him.
'Tis her seventh month, by her reckoning, and maybe
she's right, and the pains are on her. There, Mollie,
just hold yourself together, and think what's coming
to you, why, the desire of your heart, and Nancy and
I will get you up to your bed as easy as easy. Nay, I
can carry you myself: run on, Nancy, and get her bed
ready for her—do you bring along the lamp, Nell."

It was scarcely a quarter of an hour before Dennis
was back again with Dr. Symes, carrying his case of
instruments. Nell was waiting at the garden door to
show them a light: she told them that Nancy was upstairs with Mrs. Pentreath, while loud bawling suppli-

cations from the kitchen indicated that John had resumed his praying.

"What's that row?" asked the doctor, as Dennis,
carrying the light, preceded him upstairs.

"Grandfather at his Sunday prayers," said he.

"Drunk, I suppose?"

"Drunk as a lord," said Dennis, "and full o' prayers
as any passon. He stopped a bit when Granny was
took bad, but I reckon he's off again now. That's her
door."

"Give me my case then, and go downstairs and stop
your grandfather making that unholy noise, if you call
yourselves a Christian household."

"Sure I never did that," said Dennis.

John ceased his supplications when Dennis entered.

"And you brought the doctor for the old woman?"
he asked. "You've been quick."

"Yes: he's gone up to her."

"Good, and she'll soon be out o' her pain now, I
reckon, for great's the power I've put into my praying
to-night. I fair wrestled with the Lord, I did, same
as Jacob. And there's a sign for you, if ever there
was, for 'twas just when I prayed as she might be like
the fruitful vine that the pangs took her. Astonishing
it was, even to me as knows the strength of the arm
of the Lord! But a fine fright it gave me, and I want
a bit of steadying. I'll thank you to get another jugful
of water, for Dr. Symes will surely want a drink when
he's through with his job. Eh, to think that a son'll be
born to me this very night!"

He settled himself in his chair again, and went
maundering on, with hiccups for punctuation.

"There were times when I misdoubted whether she

was with child. 'Twas a lack of faith, was that. But now I reckon I'll have a son to be a bit o' comfort to me in my old age, though all others turn their faces from me. Your mother and Nell and you, you're not a friendly household for a God-fearing man, a man's foes you may say 'stead of friends. Nancy behaved kind to me, I'll say that for her, when you'd bitten me like a mad dog, and she'd come in her shift to my bedside when I lay tossing and fevered with your teeth, but then came a hitch: things turned out different from what I thought. And talking o' teeth, just look round about the oven and see if your Granny's not spilt hers there. I thought as much! None gives a thought o' kindness to her but me. Put them in a mug of water, and I'll take them to her soon. Let's see, I was talking of Nancy."

He chuckled to himself.

" She'd other fish to fry," he said, " and I hope she did them brown. But there! You're the son of her, and it's little you'd honour your mother if I told you, though, maybe, you've guessed. But don't you ask me."

" Don't be feared o' me: I'll not ask you," said Dennis.

" Well, I'm sure that's mighty kind o' you. You may take a drink for that handsome speech, and by God, everyone in this house'll take a drink when the news comes that there's an uncle born to you. That's queer, that is, to think that you're nigh to being a father yourself before your uncle's born: a comical thing indeed! . . . I wonder how they're getting on up above. There was groanings and screamings a while back, when you was gone for the doctor, and that put me on my knees again, thinking o' your granny, whom I've brought to bed after all these years."

" I heard you at it," said Dennis, " as soon as ever
I got inside the door."

John looked round for his whisky bottle, though his
hand was closed on the neck of it.

" And where's my drink gone? " he said. " Who's
been meddling with my bottle? Eh, there's another
comical thing, for my hand was on it all the time.
'Tis like we shall have to sit here and wait, for I'm
not going to sleep while Mollie's got the pains on her,
and I'll have a nip to pass the time. So you heard
me at my prayers when you came in. As you came
across the garden was there no sound of me? "

" Not to my ears," said Dennis, yawning, but keeping an eye on him, in case he got up to some trick.

" Faith, and I'll tell you the reason o' that," said
John with drunken solemnity. " 'Twas like this: there
are enemies of the Lord out in the garden, owls tu-
whooing and what-not other crittures o' the night, and
they dulled the sound of my praying, lest it should
be a protection from all evil things abroad. They fear
the voice of a godly man calling on the Lord, and, by
God, well they may! I'm a match for them, and they
know it. 'Twas like that."

" Yes, maybe 'twas like that," said Dennis.

" Maybe, d'you say? I tell 'ee that was how it was.
Who should know better nor I? The whole black brood
o' them wamble with fear o' John Pentreath when the
spirit of prayer's on him, and with good reason, too.
There's not one o' them as is not afraid of old John
when he calls on the Lord. You've been powerful 'feared
of me, too, sonny, when I tied your hands up and licked
the skin off your back with yon whip, so you know how
the evil spirits feel. Maybe, I'll give you another bashing yet, for I stand no nonsense in my house."

" Aye, you're a terrible fearsome man, for sure," said
Dennis.

The old man was nodding and mumbling now: another touch of the drink and he'd be snoring. But there
were a few more religious speculations first.

" Yes, terrible I can be," he said, " and always seeking
to map my ways to the path of godliness. Perhaps I
should 'a' been a bit stricter yet. Happen I ought to
have put Nell to sleep in your granny's room, and put
a bed for you in mine, and then there wouldn't 'a' been
all this trouble about a brace o' babies coming, and one
conceived in sin. Eh, there's a peck o' pain and trouble
in the world, and I wonder God Almighty ain't scared
sometimes, when He looks down on us all, and beholds
what He did when He set the world going. But that
can't be mended now, and here's the whole bilin' of
us miserable worms messing about and hating and loving. God, how I hate you, and there's Nell loving
you, and Nancy bedizening herself, the whoresome
slut, and the old woman upstairs with her withered
bosom and her fruitful womb, and me just praying the
Lord to soften your sinful hearts. The fruitful vine!
Why, the words were on my lips——"

" Aye, we've talked o' that," said Dennis.

John gave a great yawn.

" I'll take a snooze," he said, " while we're waiting
for that doctor chap. A queer thing that the barren
woman's to become a joyful mother o' children at her
time o' life, for barren she was but for the little dead
puppy years ago. Eh, if it had only been t'other way
about, and I'd had my son sitting here, 'stead of you."

He dropped back in the chair and fell asleep: Dennis
was wondering whether he couldn't leave him, and go
up to Nell, who had slipped away to bed, when he heard

a step coming down the stairs.   Slight though the sound was, it roused his grandfather, as if someone had shaken him awake.

" There's news on the way," he said in a voice quite steady and sober, and he jumped up.   " Hush, it comes down step by step, as if 'twas a Jacob's ladder."

There was a hand on the latch, and Dr. Symes came in.

" So you've come to tell me, doctor," he said. " Out with it, and we'll drink a health."

Dr. Symes had expected to see a tipsy fellow, who had best be sent to bed, and told in the morning when he was fit to understand.   But his suspense seemed completely to have sobered John, and here he was erect and steady and master of himself.

" Is it a boy, man? " he asked.

" No, there's no boy."

" A girl, then?   Well, there's no harm in a girl. . . . You don't mean to tell me it's another little dead thing like what she had before? "

" Sit down, Pentreath," said the doctor.   " I've got news for you, and it's bad news."

" Mollie's not died? "

" No.   But there's neither boy nor girl, nor ever will be.   She's not with child at all."

" But she was growing great," said John.   " 'Twas there to see."

" Yes, I've seen it.   But she's got no child that's making her great.   It's a tumour; the wonder is that it hasn't killed her already."

" Tumour?   Is that what they call the lump hereabouts? "

" Yes."

John stared at him a moment, his teeth raking his lip.

" God!   Them as should have holpen her have tricked

17

her fine! " he said. " She danced in the circle, she did, on Midsummer Eve, and she's been busy with her spells and what-not, ever courtin' them, and 'tis this they've sent her. Often I 'monished her to turn to the Lord, but she wouldn't hear, and now here's the end of it all. I'll pray constant for her night and day. . . . Doctor, hasn't it broken Mollie's heart to know it? "

" She doesn't know it, and we've got to keep her from knowing it. The woman can't have many weeks to live, and I've told her that she's with child all right, and that she'll be delivered when her time comes. She's in her seventh month now, she thinks."

" And can't you cut the lump from her?" asked John.

" Quite impossible. All that can be done is to save her pain; perhaps she won't have much, for sometimes it happens so. Now I've given her a drug that will keep her drowsy, and I'll be up here again in the morning."

" And how do you reckon the lump came? " asked John.

" Maybe some injury started it. Can you remember her having a fall or bruising herself low down on her stomach? There's a mark of such."

John Pentreath had stood steady enough during this, but now he felt his knees weaken, and he gripped the table hard to stiffen himself.

" 'Twas that as might have started it? " he asked, feeling the cold sweat stand on his forehead as on a pitcher of water.

" Pretty certain."

John passed the back of his hand over his forehead.

" Nay, I can't remember any such a thing," he said, " and 'twouldn't be likely that I'd forget it."

His eye fell on Dennis, and his hatred flared.

" By God, yes, I mind me now," he said. " There was a day last spring when she riled that boy, and he went for her hot-blooded, and gave her a crool clout. 'Twas that: sure 'twas that."

Dennis shrugged his shoulders.

" 'Tis just his thunderin' lies," he said to the doctor.

" Nay, it's not my lies, don't you heed the boy," cried John. " I mind it well. 'Twas one night. . . . Eh, it's gone from me again. But strike her he did, that's sure."

Dr. Symes nodded at Dennis, taking no notice of the other.

" Nay, but you don't believe me," cried John. " He's a ruffian, that fellow, and if his granny dies 'twill be next door to murder, same as he tried on me. Sure it was that that did it. And if he says it's lies, there stands the liar for you. I shouldn't wonder if he said it was me next. Come on, say 'twas me."

" An' so it was," said Dennis. " My mother told me, Doctor Symes, for she saw the clout given. And she bade me keep it to myself, but when it comes to him saying 'twas I, it's time to speak."

" And what have you got to say to that, Pentreath? " asked the doctor.

John looked first at one, then at the other, and back again. Neither believed him: a pretty state of things in his own house. Then some muddled notion came into his head that if he told the truth God might be better pleased with him: besides, he had had every excuse for that blow.

" Well, maybe I did give her a push," he said, " for she angered me sore with a trick she played me, and before God my fist had gone out at her before I knew it. There's not a man in the world who wouldn't have struck a woman for what she did. A whoreish trick, if ever there was one for a wife to play. I'll tell you how it was——"

"You'll do nothing of the sort," said the doctor sharply.

John took a staggering step towards him, with a trembling hand held out in front of him. "Don't tell me it was that push I gave her which started it," he said.

"And just now you said it must have been, when you were putting it on Dennis."

"I spoke hasty then. Just a push it was: sure it can't have been that, doctor."

Dr. Symes had an impulse of pity for this sodden wreck of a man with his lies and his pieties streaming indifferently from his mouth.

"No, I don't say it must have been that," he said; "and whether or no, there's no good in thinking on it. I'll be going now and be back in the morning. And look you here, Pentreath, I've warned you once, and I warn you once more, that you're killing yourself with your soaking. You won't last long unless you take yourself in hand now. Last time I saw you, you were in a fair way to break yourself of your boozing, but to-day you're not the man you were then, and you're going to bits as quick as a man can."

John put the cork in his bottle with an air of great determination. It was something of a feat to find the opening.

"I've done with it!" he said magnificently.

Dr. Symes turned to Dennis.

"Come out and see me across the garden, lad," he said, "for it's black as pitch under the trees, and your young eyes can see where mine can't. Get you to bed,

Pentreath, and let me find you sober in the morning."

He took Dennis's arm to guide him as they stepped out into the darkness.

"Now you've got to be wise and cautious, young fellow," he said. "Your grandfather's as bitter an enemy of yours as you need, and in a way I don't wonder, for you bashed him pretty savagely not long ago."

"Lord, yes, he hates me like poison," said Dennis.

"Bear it in mind, then. He's half-crazy with drink already, and perhaps the sooner he gets through with it the better. Now there's another thing. Your grandmother thinks she's with child, and you've all got to make her go on thinking so. And tell me this: has she been queer lately?"

"She's always been what you'd call queer," said Dennis, "dwelling in her secrets and her spells."

"She went on devilish queerly when I was with her," he said, "saying she must get up and go to Kenrith copse. Something about dancing there and the blood of a cat. Was that just raving, or was there something in it, do you know?"

"'Twasn't raving," said Dennis, "'twas all true enough that she acted so, for I saw her at it."

"You're a pretty household! And how's your Nell?"

"Coming on fine, an' happy as a queen. Sorry she is, too, for her Aunt Mollie, for she always guessed that she wasn't with child."

"Well, good night: I can see my way here. I'll be up in the morning."

Once more the household adjusted itself to a new routine. Nancy undertook the nursing of the sick

woman, and moved into John's room next door to
hers; a girl from the village came to help Nell in the
housework. For several days Mollie lay in a half-
stupor, with occasional fierce spasms of pain for which
now Nancy had the morphia needle handy, but the
progress of her disease seemed temporarily to be stayed:
these bouts became rarer and less violent, and in a
week's time she was sitting up in bed, busy with her
knitting again, for the conviction that she was far
advanced in pregnancy remained unshaken, and the
family all spoke of it to her as a sure thing. She took
an interest in the affairs of the farm; Nell brought the
daily yield of eggs into her room that she might count
them, and when she had gone over them she would
bid the girl stop and chat.

" I shouldn't wonder, Nell," she'd say, " if my day
didn't come before yours, though you're great, too.
Eh, there's my knitting dropped. Pick it up for me,
dear. 'Tis a little woollen jersey I'm at for him to wear
when t'other's in the wash. Pretty colour, ain't it? "

" Rare pretty, indeed, it is, Aunt Mollie," said Nell.
" He'll come into the world with a wardrobe fit for
a young king."

" Yes, and all o' his mother's making: not a bit of
shop stuff will he wear. You'll be going down to St.
Columb's, I reckon, with my eggs, so just pick a posy
if there's aught in flower yet, and put it on top
o' one of the tall stones in the circle, and say naught
about it."

Another afternoon Nancy would come in, and Mollie
spoke sometimes of that collapse of hers at the prayers
on Sunday evening.

" Mortal afraid I was," she said, " when I came round
after that sleepy stuff the doctor gave me, that I'd

had a miscarriage, for that would have fair broken
me up."

"Not much call to worry about that, Mrs. Pentreath," said Nancy, cheerfully. "Anyone as looks at
you could see you'd not had a disappointment. And
here's your cup of tea with a good dollop of thick cream
in it, for that's strengthening for you."

"What, is it time for my tea already? Seems a
short while ago since morning."

"Yes, you've been having a nice long sleep, but it's
struck four. The days are lengthening out now with
the coming of the spring. But it's a cloudy evening
to-day, and dark's drawing on."

"Aye, that it is," said Mollie, peering out into the
gathering dusk, "and it's ever the gloaming that's the
best hour o' the day with me. Seems friendly like. . . .
There, you may take the tea away, for I don't seem to
fancy it. You'll be going down to St. Columb's maybe
to-night, if your man ain't tired of you yet."

"Lor', he's been gone this long time," said Nancy,
"and as for his being tired of me, Mrs. Pentreath, he
wants me to go and keep house for him in London.
That doesn't look as if he's tired of me, does it? And
I wrote to tell him I'd come, but naturally, said I,
that'll have to be put off a bit, till I've seen you through
your trouble. I'm not a one to run away like that, I
hope. But after that I'll be packing. Lor'! how I
shall like to see the gas-lamps and the crowds of a night
when the folk are coming out of the play-houses."

Mollie's hard drawn face softened.

"Well, that's right good o' you, Nancy," she said.
"You're a kind woman, and kind you were to John,
too, when that boy o' yours mashed him up. We've
had a year of it, indeed, what with that, and then with

John coming back to me again, and the dancing on
Midsummer Eve. I reckon I'll be dancing again when
next it comes round."

"Why, to be sure you will! " said Nancy. " You'll
have a regular family soon."

Mollie gave a little shrill laugh, laughing with the
mouth and eyes only, and rigid in breast and stomach,
as if she had been cased in iron.

"I shouldn't wonder," she said, " for there's a life
in me now, and why not again? But get you gone, for
I'll be having a snooze. And set the window open
first, for I'm warm in bed, and I like to have the
gloaming creep in about me."

So Nancy betook herself to her room next door, and
lit her candle and had a read at her book. The wall
between the two rooms was but thin, and to-night,
not for the first time, she heard the sound of a voice
from where her patient lay.

" She's just having a jabber in her sleep," she said
to herself, and went on with her reading, till it should
be time to go down to the kitchen, and get supper.
Dearly would she have liked to cut free, and go straight
up to London, but that was impossible while the poor
old body next door was wanting her. " Mean-like it
would be," she thought to herself, " and Mr. Giles'll
just have to wait, though I reckon he won't have to
wait long, neither. Once I've been to the funeral,
decent and proper, then I'll pack my boxes quick
enough, for I shan't be needed here any more. Lor'!
what a comic letter he wrote me, telling me of the old
moke as does for him now, giving him soup that's fitter
to swim in than to nourish you, and a chop roasted
to a cinder. I'll make things more comfortable for
him, and he for me, and it's more than his dinner that

he wants of me. But there! No decent woman could think of leaving that pore stricken old thing, till she's out of her worries, and that'll be only one way. I'll give myself a good smearing of my perfume when I go in to make her tidy for the night, for there's a smell of corruption that fair turns my stomach, in spite of her open window. . . . How she goes on gabbling! Perhaps I'd better see if she wants anything."

Nancy got up, and took her candle in her hand, and quietly opened the door. There was Mollie, lying fast asleep to all appearances, and dreamlessly slumbering. But on the sill of the open window was perched one of those great brown owls which were for ever flitting round the house when dusk fell. It hissed angrily at her, and, startled out of her wits, she dropped her tin candle-stick on the floor, with a clatter fit to wake the dead. But the candle burned still, and when she picked it up the bird had slid off into the night. That metallic crash had not disturbed Mollie: she lay quiet and sleeping.

Another visitor to the sickroom, not so frequent as Nancy, but as regular, was John Pentreath: he brought up his glass after the midday dinner, and smoked a pipe by her bedside. Drowsier she grew every day, and sometimes she would lie there dozing for ten minutes before she became aware of him, with her hands still holding her knitting. But then her eyes opened, and her arms, no more than a couple of bones in a loose bag of skin, reached out to him, and her fingers closed on his.

"Aye, old woman, sure, 'tis I," he said, and he glanced at her face, and away again, for it was now just the face of a brown, withered mummy long dead, and it was the hand of a skeleton that grasped his thick-veined fingers. But in that dead face were set two jewels of life, and in her eyes was gathered all the vitality that the tumour had not sucked from her. Those eyes still burned with unquenched desire, and now and then their circle of vitality spread to her mouth and set it smiling. When only Nancy was there or Nell, it shone like light through a window with the blind down, but when John was with her it poured out unobscured: even then it was stale and wan, as if it were some phosphorescence from decayed wood. Often she would ask him to pack the pillows behind her, so that she could be more upright in bed, and then she sat with her hand over his.

" My time's drawing near now," she mumbled, " and he'll be a bonny fellow. Back to me ye came after all these years, and we were sappy yet. Look, John, a second little pair o' breeches for him, soft wool they are as'll keep his pink little behind warm."

She stroked his hand.

" There's a fist, indeed," she said, " and once I felt the weight of it. But I never laid that up against ye, for back ye'd come to me then."

The voice died away, an echo of a voice it seemed, coming from very far. But as often as he looked up, replying, there were her eyes fixed and unwinking. Then her eagerness wearied her, and she would drop into a doze again. There were no Sunday evening prayers any more, for once, soon after she had taken to her bed, as his voice rose over some drunken denunciation, there came a thumping on the ceiling from Mollie's room above, and Nancy got up from her knees and hurried upstairs.

" I'll go and see what ails her," she said. " Lor',
she's screaming now."

Mollie was sitting up in bed, in some frenzy that
gave her strength, thumping on the floor with the chair
that stood by.

" Stop it, stop it," she cried. " 'Twas just that as
brought on the false pains that nigh killed me, and
they're coming back again now, and it's like a sword
slashing in me."

Nancy fetched the morphia needle.

" There, there: I'll make you easy again in a jiffy,
Mrs. Pentreath," she said, " and don't go on so, fit to
deafen me. He stopped the moment he heard your
thumpings. Lor'! but there's power in you to make
such a banging: you fair made the room shake."

" I won't have it: I won't have it," yelled Mollie.
" He's cursing them as are helping me. I'll call 'em
in——"

Nancy gave a terrified glance at the window, not
knowing what she feared, but utterly on edge with the
hideous energy of that screaming.

" Now you're injuring yourself if you behave like
that," she said, " and doing a mischief to your babby.
Mr. Pentreath's stopped his praying, so just lie down,
and hold yourself together, and in a minute now you'll
be soothed and sleepy."

So now there was no sound of praying when supper
was cleared away on Sunday, but John Pentreath sat
silent, smoking and drinking by the fire. Now and
then, perhaps, he slid to his knees, and his mouth moved
in silent supplications, for he dreaded what wrathful
judgment of God might fall on him if he neglected
those atrocious devotions, but soon he would shuffle to
his feet again with terror from another quarter that

some mysterious knowledge of his employment might penetrate to the room upstairs and cause some equally fearful dispensation. There he sat, sipping and biting his nails, threatened on both sides, and over his mind again, black as the swift approach of night, there drove up the one thought that now obsessed him, so that his hatred of Dennis was smothered in it. He it was, he felt convinced, who, by dealing Mollie that blow in his fit of passion, had brought her to this. It was no use for Dr. Symes to say that it might not have been that: John Pentreath knew better, and that conviction was to him as certain as the monstrous tumour itself. Mollie did not know that: she thought that he had put life within her, and what he had dealt her was death. But when her fierce spirit had shuffled itself free of its tortured habitation it would know the truth, and in what concentration of wrath and revenge would it not return for his undoing? He made no question that those whom men called the dead lived on, if their deeds had been evil, in everlasting punishment, for his black religion had taught him that, while his superstitions, equally engrained in him, had taught him that such spirits could return from the flames that died not any more than they, with terrors and vengeance for those who had injured them. For every look of yearning and unfounded joy that she gave him now, as he sat by her bed, for every touch of her withered hand, she would visit him with the potency of disembodied hate. Already, with his conviction of guilt, she was terrible to him even in her ignorance, but what would she be when she knew? He feared her dead infinitely more than he had ever feared her living, and if he could have chosen he would have had her live on just as she was rather than that she should die and be quit of her pains.

Then there was a loneliness gathering round him that scared him, for the others seemed to shun him, seldom speaking to him, except when there was need. He would have thought a year ago that nothing could have mattered less to John Pentreath than how Nancy and Dennis regarded him, so long as one cooked the dinner and the other did his work. But this withdrawal of all human contacts made his terrors the more insupportable: he was not the strong, self-sufficient man he had been, and he longed for a word or a look behind which he could detect a kindly impulse. It was strange, indeed, he thought, that John Pentreath should want such flimsy nonsense, when drink and stubborn health and the fear of God had sufficed him so long.

CHAPTER XIII

MOLLIE PASSES

On a warm, windless evening a month later Nancy was sitting by the bedside in Mollie's room, waiting for old Sally Austell to relieve her, and take on the watching through the night, for the sick woman required constant attention now, though for the most part she lay in open-eyed stupor. How she still held to life was a wonder: nothing but her conviction that she would soon be delivered of her child could have kept her.

Nancy was longing to be gone, and to rinse, not body alone, but her soul also, so to say, with a sight of Nell and her week-old son. That would be a cleansing and a healthiness after being shut up all day in the poisoned room, which so soon now must be the death-chamber. Like most simple-minded folk Nancy had not an atom of horror at death in itself, for that was natural, but to-day Mollie had been restless, and Nancy had been through hours fit to turn pity sour, hours of incessant muttered talk, of hideous gestures and cacklings and sawing breath.

Sally was in the house, for Nancy had seen her black bonnet bobbing along through the garden ten minutes ago, but she was having a bit of an argument with John Pentreath, demanding her week's pay for her ministries in advance, and he had muttered and mowed at her, saying he would give it to her when she had earned it. From above, as Nancy waited for her relief, she could hear the wordless murmur and clack of their voices in the kitchen.

"Nay, I'll take my money now," said Sally, "or not a foot of mine will I set in that pleasant chamber upstairs. 'Tis a most reasonable sum I ask ye for, too, for could ye get anyone but me, as has always been a friend of hers, to pass the night there?"

John drained his glass.

"Get away home then," he said, "and good night to you."

"I wish ye the same, John Pentreath," she said, "and I'll be off. And a quiet night may ye have, though happen it'll be a bit disturbed. She's lasted out the day, but she'll never get through another night, if 'tis like the last."

"Nay, she'll not die to-night, nor for many a moon yet," said he.

Sally picked up her great black bonnet, which she had taken off and laid on the table.

"Then 'tis my error," she said, "for John Pentreath's always in the right, so a peaceful night I wish him and all in this house, when Mollie goes forth on her journey all alone. A good God-fearing soul like she will be sure to have a peaceful passing, and mind ye to make the sign of the cross over her, and then quiet and content she'll lie when that rattle of her breath ceases, and she'll trouble you no more. Eh, I've learned a lot about ye all, for she was gabbling half last night, and I'll go have a gossip in the ale-house instead of watching."

John looked round, peering into the dark corners of the kitchen, and fumbled in his pockets. There was a fresh menace here, and it was unwise, anyhow, to cross Sally Austell.

"Eh, dear me, I'll pay you for this coming week," he said to her, "though 'tis a cruel sight of shillings you charge me for just sitting there with your old friend."

She laughed.

"Well then, ye'd best take my place this night," suggested Sally, "an' spare your pretty shillings, John Pentreath, and I'll be getting home——"

He pushed them across the table to her.

"Nay, gladly I give ye them," he said, "for sure I won't grudge Mollie any bit o' comfort she can have. 'Tis weeks she's lingered, when doctor thought there was but days for her, and who can tell she won't bide with us many more yet?   And mind this, Sally Austell, you keep her breath in her body, and don't let her pass. Mollie's been a good wife to me, all these years, and I should be broken without her."

Once more he cast a terrified glance round the room.

"Where's that lamp," he said, "as ought to have been lit ere now?   But look 'ee here, Sally.   Ain't there no word o' yours as'll keep Mollie from passing?   Can't you rivet her to the living, so's she can't 'scape?"

Sally counted over the silver, found the tale correct, and dropped it jingling in her pocket.

"Thank ye, John," she said.   "I'll do my best with her, but she's in awesome plight, a bag of bones she is, and the lump such as I've never seen it yet.   Eh, 'twould be a litter she was bearing you, if 'twas that as ailed her.   But I'll hold her to life for all I can.   Sure she clings to it, for all she's suffered, till she's borne her child, and that wouldn't be this side a dozen Midsummer dancings.   Well, I'll be getting to my job, for I'm late with this talking."

She went briskly upstairs, making the banisters creak,

for she was a weighty woman. Nancy heard her coming, and opened the door to her.

"I'm glad you've come, Mrs. Austell," she said, "for 'tis fit to choke you to-night, and I'll be off to get a wash and a breath of air. But there! you seem to thrive wherever you be. Give me Mrs. Austell's constitution, I often says, and I ask nothing no more. I'll lay your supper outside the door, as per usual."

Sally was used to politeness, and was always polite herself to the pleasant-spoken.

"Thank ye kindly; there was something stewing in the oven as smelt rare and tasty," she said, taking up a candle. "I'll just have a look at her ere you go."

She bent over the bed, and looked into the wide eyes that met hers with recognition.

"She's far gone," she said to Nancy, "and I warrant I'll have to summon you this night if ye want to be there at the passing. 'Tis wonderful she's living yet."

She replaced the candle.

"Tap on the door when my supper's ready," she said. "An' the doctor feller said he'd be up before long, and I'll clean her up a bit before he comes. The butcher or the baker would be pretty nigh as much use as he."

These hours of horror had not quenched Nancy's innate compassion, though glad she was to be gone. "Poor old body," she said to herself, "she's got a peck to bear and no mistake. It's croolest of all for her, though, maybe, she knows little of it all." She went to her room, next door, and stripping herself of every stitch she had on, soaped and bathed herself and scrubbed again. There was some dreadful odour of corruption that still clung to her, and before she went to see Nell and her baby she strolled out in the garden to get the clean air into her. The month had been as mild and warm as it was just a year ago, and the beds were gay with the blossomings of full spring.   After her day in the sick chamber these aromas of the earth's awakening were an ecstasy, and for the sheer joy of handling the juicy stalks of daffo-dils, and searching among green leaves for the fragrance of violets, she made a handful of these blossoming things for a nosegay to take to Nell.   There was health and life in them, and she stroked their cool petals as she plucked them, and chewed a primrose stalk.   After this awful day of watching and listening to the babble from the bed, and of sponging away the dross of the body that lay there, and of the perpetual sight of those burning eyes and that dim discoloured face over which the skin was stretched like mouldy parchment, it was just the evidence that sweet things were still growing and that breezes could be pure that she desired, and the garden was more to her mind than Piccadilly and the crowds and the gas-lamps reflected on the wet pavements.   So she drifted about in the dusk and the dewy fragrance of the soft falling night: soon, when she felt clean again, she would go to see Nell, who now occupied the bedroom above the studio, which was a bit removed from the horrors of the rest of the house, and have a look at her and Dennis-the-less.   Nell had been through her delivery without any sleepy stuff, and never was there a lustier pair than she and her baby.   She had been up and sitting out to-day: to-morrow she in-tended to begin taking a hand in the housework again.

Nancy had turned at the garden gate, and was now about to go indoors and have a look at Nell, when there came a step on the gravel of the path, and there was Dr. Symes.

"Lor'! I'm glad you've come," said Nancy. "It's been a terrible day with her, for ever talking and babbling on, and between whiles her breathing like the sawing of wood. 'Twas enough to make a body stop her ears. Why, you can hear it now."

"Has she been conscious all day?" asked the doctor after a pause.

"Bits at a time: she's often called to me by name to go and tend her, and then she's asked for the breeches she's knitting, and then it'll be just gibberish again for all I could make out of it, though Mrs. Austell had a talk with her last night. And then often she's been expecting the pains to take her again. It's just the thought of her babby coming that keeps her alive, I'm thinking, else surely she'd 'a' gone before now."

"And the other two, Nell and her boy?" asked he.

"Ah, there's a bit of all right. It makes me proud to be a granny. Nell's been out in the garden already. Eh, what's that. Lord save us all!"

From the room above came the sound of thin screaming, shrill as a whistle, and he nodded to her and hurried indoors.

Nancy could not face entering the house till that was still, for to-day had tried her nerves beyond all bearing, and she took another turn up to the garden gate, hasting to get away from the sound of it. Just then Dennis came up from the fields beyond where he had been ploughing, for with his grandfather sitting all day now by the fire he was seldom in till supper-time. But there was a bit of wholesome stuff to cling to, for he smelt of soil and sweat.

He put his arm round her waist.

"You look terrible overgone, Mother," he said. "Been a bad day?"

" Eh, something shocking," she said.   " Hold me
tight, dear; give me a chunk of wholesome flesh to cling
to.   I was going in to Nell, but the old woman started
screaming, and I couldn't face the house."

Dennis listened.

" Nay, then, she's stopped now, for 'tis all quiet
again."

" Thank the Lord.   I'll go in and see Nell: there's
summat to think on, as should keep me steady.   Why,
here's Mrs. Austell coming out.   She'll be wanting
her supper, maybe; so I'll make it ready.   Well, Mrs.
Austell? "

" Poor Mollie can't last many minutes now, thinks
Dr. Symes," she said.   " So 'tis time for her kin to
gather round and speed her, and be quick.   I'll go tell
John Pentreath."

Dennis had a rinse at the sink in the scullery, and
he and his mother went upstairs together.   Dr. Symes
had thrown the window wide, and lit some aromatic
pastilles; a lamp burned steadily on the table by the
dying woman, and John was sitting near the bedside.
His eyes, red and terrified, looked this way and that,
but shrank from the sight of his wife: now they glared
at Dennis, now they were lifted in wild appeal to the
doctor, now they peered out into the dusk where a
fading primrose light lingered in the west.   And indeed none but Sally Austell looked long at that fallen
face on the pillow, but she smiled and nodded and whispered as if well pleased with her patient.

" I doubt she's going fast," she said, " for 'tis low
tide at sunset, but she'll come back and look on us all
once more afore she passes.   There'll be a pretty moment."

Suddenly Mollie's rattling breath, the sound of which filled the room, grew lighter: her skeleton hands which had been picking at the bedclothes began to make firmer and more definite movements, one fumbled at her breasts, feeling for them, the other curved itself as if supporting something, and her mouth twitched with unformed inaudible speech. Then these twitchings shaped themselves into clear coherent talk.

" Aye, my little one," she said, " here's your mammie's breast, full and firm for ye. 'Tis the spring-time, and now ye've come to gladden me, and my labour's past, though sore it was and long. Such pangs ye gave me, and here's a kiss and a cuddle for each o' them."

" Eh, 'tis a wonder to see," whispered Sally. " She'll be herself afore she passes, and sure there'll be no babby at all, poor soul."

Nancy broke into sobs.

" Lor'! it's more than a woman should be asked to bear," she cried, " for she'll break her heart at the last. Can't we give her just one happy minute, the pore old woman, as'll comfort her for what she's been through? Can't none of us help her? Eh, I've an idea."

She turned to Dennis, laying her hand on his arm.

" Dennis, lad, it's you as can help her," she said. " Just go and fetch your little one, for a moment, cradle and all, and let her see it laying there. She shan't touch it, I promise you that, and it can't hurt your babby just to be set where her eyes can fall on it, and I warrant she'll pass happy then, for she'll think it's her own. Do 'ee, my dear. Why, I'm sure if I thought she'd be deceived, I'd put my own head down against her breast for her to cuddle."

He hesitated, then got up.

" Aye, I'll fetch him," he said, " if doctor gives me

his word she shan't touch him, for that mustn't be."

"She shan't, she shan't," sobbed Nancy. "Bless you, darling, and be quick, for she won't tarry long now."

John slid on to his knees by the bed.

"That's a good thought," he said, "she'll get better when she thinks she's her babby there. We'll pull her round yet, and she'll be up and about again one of these days. The Lord be praised for all His mercies. Praised be the Lord!"

Dennis was back again at once, carrying his burden. The child, who had been asleep, stirred and woke and cried, and at that sound Mollie's eyes lifted, and she saw the baby in his wicker cradle by her side. She laughed aloud.

"Eh, my chick!" she cried. "Come to me, then."

She tried to raise herself in bed, but her head fell sideways across the pillow. One sigh she gave, and all was over.

Nancy dried her eyes.

"I'll bless you for that, Dennis, till my dying day," she said, kissing him. "Now take the boy away back to Nell."

John tried to clutch the cradle.

"You just leave the child there," he whispered. "She's gone asleep, but she'll be waking when she's rested herself, and she'll pick up fine when she sees it. Eh, we'll soon have her better!"

"La, Mr. Pentreath," said Nancy, "where's the use of talking like that? She's passed quiet and happy, pore thing, and you can praise the Lord for that, for there indeed is a mercy to be thankful for."

He rose to his feet, and peered at the dead face.

"Mollie!" he said. "Mollie. . . . What? She's not gone?"

"Yes, indeed," said Sally, "and you'd better be gwine, too, John Pentreath. I'll take a bit o' supper in your kitchen now, and then I'll get to my job, if so be you want me to do the laying out."

The funeral took place as soon as could be, for there was good reason for having no delay. Despite John's awful forebodings of what might befall when Mollie had gone, the intervening hours passed peacefully enough, and at Sunday supper on the evening of the funeral he found fresh causes for confidence. There were just the three of them there, John, Dennis and Nancy, for Nell, though about the house again, had had her supper earlier, and gone back to her baby. At the end of the table opposite John stood Mollie's chair, the rocking-chair in which she was used to sit by the fire all afternoon, and which she dragged up to the board at supper-time.

"Mollie'd have been rare pleased at all we've done this day for the poor vessel o' her body," he said, "and maybe she's 'ware of it, who knows? A fine set-out it was, indeed; eh, Nancy?"

"Yes, 'twas very handsome," said Nancy.

"Handsome? Sure, that was my orders, or I'd 'a' known the reason why. There's not been a burying to match it in St. Columb's since I can remember. I'll take a portion more o' that pie. One o' Mollie's chickens, I reckon, and juicier nor some I've wrastled with."

As he took his replenished plate back his eye fell on the empty chair opposite him.

"Nay, I'll take back that word," he said. "Mollie

was always fine and liberal with her fowls and her
eggs, and I'll have no talk against her now she's gone,
and I'll have none o' your dark looks on me, Dennis."

Dennis had not glanced at his grandfather as he passed
his plate back to him.

" I gave ye no look, dark nor light," he said.

" Happen you did or you didn't, 'tis no odds. A fine
show it was, I was saying, and I don't grudge a penny
of it.   A black varnished coffin and silver-plated
handles to it, and a pair o' black horses, with brave
plumes on their heads, a-nodding in woe with every
step they took.   Glass sides to the bier, too, and black
hat-bands and gloves for the bearers.   A queen couldn't
have had more done for her."

He paused as he poured himself out a fresh drink,
as if listening, and then fell to his pie.

" No, 'twas nothing," he said.   " I thought I heard
a step on the stairs, but all's quiet. Just draw the
curtains over the window, Nancy: who wants the night
looking in? . . .   Yes, a fine burying it was, as was meet
for her that's gone."

Nancy had gone round the end of the table to draw
the curtains, and as she went back to her place her
sleeve caught in the arm of the rocking-chair and set
it on the move.   John's knife and fork clattered on
his plate and he sprang up.

" God, there's Mollie's chair rocking," he said.
" What's that about? "

" Lor', Mr. Pentreath, don't give me such a turn
and yourself, too," said Nancy.   " I brushed by it and
set it bobbing."

He sat down again.

" Aye, that was the way of it, no doubt," he said.
" I'm glad you mentioned that.   The burying now, as

I was speaking of. All of us with our mourning bands, and such a sight of folk there too, for they wouldn't miss such a funeral: no fisher-boat, I'll be bound, put out till they'd paid their respects to her. A bit of a tiff I had with the undertaker chap, as wanted to put a cross on her coffin. 'No,' says I, 'silver-plated handles and all as handsome as you can furnish, but naught else.' And cards I'll send out to all as knew her with a thick black line round them. 'In loving memory,' they'll say, 'of Mollie Robson, well-beloved wife of John Pentreath,' and then a bit of a motto. 'Rest in peace,' and the date. God, she ought to be well content, and mind you, I pay for every penny of it. No bargaining about me: why, I've paid Sally Austell a'ready for a whole week's night-nursing, and 'twas only one night out o' the seven she watched, and that but for an hour, and all the laying out extra. Mollie sure'll rest quiet if so be she knows all I've done. I'll be taking a drop more o' my drink, for 'twas thirsty work to-day. Fetch me a fresh bottle, Nancy, out of the cupboard. 'Tis but a filling of water they put into it these days, with a bit of saffron, belike, for colouring."

He gave another glance at the rocking-chair as he rose to go to his usual seat.

" Eh, there was some comforting things said at the burying," he hiccupped. ' 'Tis sown corruptible,' said Passon, and right he was there, ' and 'tis rais'd incorruptible.' Then there was about being delivered from the pains and miseries of this sinful world. Mollie should be thankful for that. Lord, how the old house creaks to-night, though there's not a breath of wind stirring. Happen the spirit of it's walking about, wondering what's come to its old mistress. There's an owl

tu-whooing again. It's been scouting round this last
hour."

"Aye, and it got among the poultry this evening,
afore I penned them, and killed two chicks," said
Nancy, " and it's been hovering round the yard ever
since. You'd better lie up at dusk to-morrow, Dennis,
and see if you can't shoot it."

" Nay, nothing of the sort," cried John. " Yet they're
Mollie's chickens. I wonder what she'd have counselled! "

He brooded in silence over this, while Nancy finished
clearing away. Supper had been late, and by the time
she had washed up the tall clock whirred for the hour
of ten.

"It's late," she said, " so if we're to have prayers,
Mr. Pentreath, let's have them now, and then I'll be
off to bed."

" Prayers? " he said. " I wonder now——"

" Well, then, leave 'em out," she said. " I but
thought you'd find a bit of comfort in 'em, but, lor',
it's no odds to me."

" Happen I might make a prayer or two, low and
quiet," he said, " but there was a terrible to-do, ye'll
not forget, when last I lifted up my voice of a Sunday
evening."

" Then I'll be off to bed," said she, " if you don't
feel prayerful, for I'm tired out with the day we've
had."

He fidgeted in his chair with the pipe which he had
forgotten to fill stuck in his mouth. Sure enough,
there could be no screaming and thumping on the floor
overhead to-night, but the old house had been creaking
oddly, and that might be some warning. And what
should he say if he prayed, that would please the Lord,

and not bring risk of giving offence to those who walked in other ways? Perhaps in a week's time if all went on peacefully he might get more confidence, and bellow away again. There was a queer sinking feeling creeping upon him to-night; an hour ago at supper he had been full of pluck, thinking of all the honour he'd done to Mollie, but that had vanished, and a trembling and a fearfulness was come over him.

"Nay, there'll be no prayers to-night," he said in a loud voice so that anyone could hear. "The spirit o' prayer seems to have gone from me, and then there's you and Dennis, and no petition o' mine would be a guidance and a strength to you: 'tis like casting pearls before swine. But it's full early yet, and the nights are long still, and I don't fancy lying in my room with the empty chamber next door, now that old Sally's not keeping an eye on the dead. But if you want to get to bed, Nancy, there's Dennis who'll keep me company awhile. 'Tis a thousand pities, Dennis, that you've never learned to take your liquor yet, as a Pentreath should, or I'd let you take your will o' my bottle, and we could sit and quaff all night."

He got up, shaking and holding on to the table.

"Eh, I can't lie in that room," he said, "till we see whether Mollie's bed in the churchyard's to her fancy. I won't sleep there, I tell ye. I'm scared to think on it."

Dennis looked at him with a certain contemptuous compassion, scarcely sorry for the man himself, but rather for such an abjectness.

"You can sleep in my room then," he said, "if you're so scared o' your own, for Nell's still bedded above the studio."

"Well, thank ye kindly, I'm sure, for telling your

grandfather where he may sleep," he cried in a sudden flame of anger against Dennis.

Dennis got up with a shrug of his shoulders.

" Sure, 'tis for you to sleep where you like," he said. " I'm off to bed."

" Nay, but don't you both leave me," stammered John. " 'Tis company I want, 'tis being alone that's beyond me. And there've been no prayers. God forgive me. I'll put up a petition or two now, just silently, if ye'll bide a minute yet."

He went down on his knees, and covered his face.

" He's fair gibbering to-night," said Nancy to Dennis in a low voice, " and, lor', whatever are we to do with him? I doubt he's got the horrors coming on."

" No, 'tisn't the drink, 'tis fear," said Dennis. " Here, Grandfather, get you up, and you can put your mattress and pillow on the floor in my room. And I'll take th' old dog whip with me, so mind you don't come within reach o' my bed. Now up we go."

CHAPTER XIV

SUNDAY BY THE SEA

IT was a Sunday morning in mid-May and Dennis was walking along the footpath that led through the fields south-eastwards from the farm to the sea. It passed from field to field through gateless stiles which were floored with three stone blocks set lengthways across them, with a dug-out space of a couple of feet between them. This simple device was sufficient to prevent the straying of the grazing sheep, for it never entered their silly heads to step steady from block to block till they were over. You'd see a young ewe going careful with a foreleg, and then a hind-leg would slip into the drop between the stones, and that was no go. It would turn about in a bungle and leap to the field it came from: it learned its lesson after a few such experiments, and tried no more. Dennis thought of his grandfather when in his cups, trying to negotiate such a passage: he'd step firm on to one block, and then, as like as not, trip between the next two and bark a shin. But then nowadays he'd never think of going abroad after dusk had come on; he'd be back in the kitchen before the gloaming, and be drinking himself blotty. He had broken up Mollie's rocking-chair one evening when Dennis, with a sly foot, had set it bobbing, just for mischief. A rare turn that had given him, but he was courageous that night, and had gone for it with the wood-axe, and stuffed the bits of it into the fire, so there would be no more rocking.

They had had a bad time with him after the evening of Mollie's funeral. Nancy, good soul, had stopped at the farm for a couple of weeks after that, though she had intended to go up to London as soon as the burying was over, till she saw them more settled. But she had been of little use, for she was all of a twitter herself, after the strain of that gruesome nursing, and Nell was getting upset, too, which would never do, while her child was yet unweaned. Dennis had said something of this botheration to his Willie; he hardly liked to be out all day, leaving the two women with the tipsy old dodderer, and good God, wasn't Willie a brick! He just gave a grunt or two, but no more, and an hour afterwards there was he at the kitchen door with a bag of his clothes in his hand, come to do housework, if 'twas needed, and be there, anyhow, day and night to help them along. There was no jaw about it: he just said he was out of a job, and he'd work on the farm, while Dennis stopped at home, or he'd bide there while Dennis was out at work, and they'd both be there for nights. And what a head of teak he had! John was ever so pleased to have a young fellow who'd keep him company and drink with him, when the milk-and-water folk had yawned themselves to bed, and an hour later Willie would hoist the old tipsy-cake up the stairs, and see him stowed in his room, and then get to snoring sound himself in the chamber next door, where Mollie had died. There'd been a noisome stink there at first, but soon it got purified, and one night as he was undressing a great brown owl had perched on the sill of the open window. Willie had just taken off his belt, and he whipped it fine with the buckle of it, across its hissing mouth, and off it went, for sure it was welcome in that room no longer. Happen it was the same bird, thought Dennis, as had raided the hens on the afternoon of his grand- mother's funeral. He had tried once and again to get a shot at it, but it was a wary bird as well as bold, and was away before he could loose off. Willie's advent had set Nancy free, and now she was up in England keeping house for Mr. Giles in London.

Dennis had a towel over his shoulder, for he would have a swim on this warm morning, and he carried a basket of victuals in his hand. Nell was to follow him presently, bringing the boy with her, and they meant to spend the day on a little sandy beach tucked away below a bit of a hamlet down there, while Willie, the handy fellow, cooked dinner for himself and John Pen- treath; and after that he would leave the old man for his Sunday Bible-reading, and be back for supper. There was the sound of bells, distant and blurred, in the air, and John had already gone off to church at St. Columb's in his napless top-hat, which had its thick new mourning band around it, clothing its nakedness.

A rare day it was, the sun as hot as midsummer, while spring and all its jubilant freshness still lingered. Once more the meadows were tall with the growing hay, and there was a promise of just such a bumper crop as last year. A strip of downland to the edge of the low cliffs succeeded the fields, and a band of gorse fringed its upper edges, grown so thick that Dennis must sidle through it. All winter long it had been in flower, and now under this hot sun the pods were popping with minute explosions and scattering their seed. The honeyed scent of it lay on the air like streaks of oil on water, and Dennis paused once and again to pluck a blossom and suck the sweetness from the heart of it.

Then came a steepish descent, where lichened blocks of granite stuck out of the soil with ferns growing in the cool crevices between, and the scent of wood-smoke from the cottages below where dinner was cooking drifted up the hillside. On the strip of level where the road wound round from St. Columb's were orchards of full-blossomed apple-trees with circles of lime daubed round their trunks to keep the crawling creatures off them, and Dennis struck the road here and followed it through the hamlet. The stream from Kenrith copse ran channelled at the edge of it, and the thatched cottages stood behind, with fuchsia-trees and japonica covering their walls, and bee-skeps in their bits of garden. He turned off down a short lane that led direct to the shore, and passed through a grove of silver poplars that winked and twinkled in the breeze that came up from the sea. Thickets of blackthorn starred with flowers lay about them, and the hawthorn buds were opening. Then came a further small cluster of thatched roofs, and perched on a hewn platform the red-brick Methodist church. There was singing going on within, and Dennis puckered his lips and joined his whistle to a familiar tune.

The lane came to an end just above the beach, where tawny fishing-nets lay drying. Outside the last of the cottages was a grey collie-dog, dozing in the sun, who looked sleepily up as Dennis passed, sniffed to see if he could be trusted, and put his head down again on his outstretched paws. A bank of boulders lay along the top edge of the beach, and a short curving pier, tall and strong enough to resist the inpouring of waves from the south-west when the sea ran high, jutted out from the right-hand side of this small bay, and at its base lay a couple of fishing-boats moored to rings there, not now afloat, but lying tilted sideways on the sand uncovered by the ebbed tide.

Dennis gave this beach the go-by, and went on along the short turf above it for another hundred yards, where was the rendezvous he had appointed with Nell. There was a scrambling descent among some rocks, and at the bottom a small sequestered stretch of sand lying between two reefs running out into the water. A cave among these rocks would serve as a dressing-place for her, if so be she was firm in her resolve to have a dip, and there was this sun-warmed sand for the baby to roll on. But she would not be down for a while yet, and Dennis stripped and walked out along the reef to take his plunge into deeper water, cursing at the sharpness of the limpets and barnacles that made their horny homes there. Tepid rock-pools lay along it, with delicate forests of green seaweed waving in them, which housed pulpy sea-anemones, red as droppings of currant jam. Tiny fish whisked away from his foot, as he splashed into one of these, taking cover in the weeds, and a small crab, defiant with gaping pincers, scuttled from the edge of the pool. "There's a spunky little warrior, indeed," thought Dennis, and he squatted down with the sun warm on his shoulders and must needs rout it out from its hiding-place among the pebbles in a high state of indignation, and make it fight his fingers, till the wash of a ripple from without bore it away upside down with its legs clutching wildly at the water. Then he stood up, taut and erect, pulling a long breath into his lungs before he threw himself with arms stretched out above his yellow head into the shining of the sea. He swam out till he had passed the end of the pier and could look across the small enclosed harbourage and up the hillside down

19

which he had come. He whistled to the drowsy dog, who stared blankly about and vented a couple of tentative barks by way of answer, and then he spied Nell coming down the lane above. He shouted to her, and her sharp eyes saw his head and waving arm, for she stopped and danced the baby up and down, as a signal of reply. Then he turned and swam seawards again, arm over arm with a frill of water standing up round his neck, and lay floating there awhile.

" God, it's good to be in the water again," he thought. " I yearned for it this morning, and to get away with Nell for a day in the open."

Presently he heard his name called, and there she was at the top of the scramble down the rocks, distrustful of her stepping with the boy in her arms.

" Bide there," he shouted, " and I'll come and take him from you."

He foamed back to land and ran across the sandy beach.

" Eh, Dennis, you're a disgrace," she called. " Pray and hitch a towel round you, for all the folk are coming out o' chapel, and 'tis in full sight o' them if you climb up here."

He picked up the towel from where his clothes lay, and went up to her.

" Give me the boy," he said, " for I'm barefoot and can't slip, and I'll carry him down and then come back to give you a hand."

" Nay, I can manage easy for myself," she said, following him. " 'Twas only that I wanted an arm to spare to steady myself. Look at him: he's eager to come to you, the ingrate he is. We'll soon have his duds off him, and give him a taste o' the sun."

Dennis tucked the baby into the crook of his arm,

and depositing him on the beach began fumbling with the abstruse strings of his clothes.

"Here, Nell, I'm making a silly job o' these fastenings," he said. "'Tis more in your line."

The baby chuckled and crowed with delight when, as Nell slipped his socks and swathings from him, he felt the sun warm on his dimpled limbs and rolled over on the sand.

"Eh, put a towel round him, Nell," said Dennis. "'Twould be a scandal if the folk from chapel saw a great feller like him without a rag on. It's a fair disgrace you allow your boy to be."

She answered him only with a smile, for she was watching the antics of the child as he turned himself over in the sand and kicked at the air. Then from him her eyes went back to Dennis. His shoulder, close to her, still glistened with the wet, and he smelt of the sea out of which he had just come. There was a wisp of weed like a strip of plaster clinging to it, and she peeled it off.

"The pair of you!" she said, "and to think that some day he'll be bigger than his daddy, maybe, and looking out for a wife. Sit him on your shoulder again, for that's a thing to make him crow."

Dennis reached out a hand and caught the little naked body up and perched him there, while the aimless hands caught at his hair and buffeted his face.

"What'll he be thinking of, I wonder?" said she. "He can't tell as you're his daddy, but just something warm and wet and comfortable to sit upon. I must get me into the sea, too, for I brought my dress down."

"Aye, there's the cave," said Dennis. "Get you ready quick, and we'll go for a swim together."

Dennis waded out after her when she came forth
again with the child still on his shoulder.

" May I be dipping him, Nell? " he called.   " A taste
of the salt makes them hard and strong, don't it? "

" Aye, dip him just once, but put your wet hand
on his head first to see if the water's to his mind. Lord,
the lamb! Don't he like it! So put him in quick and
gentle just up to his shoulders, and see the water don't
get in his eyes."

A gurgle and a gasp followed, and marvellous
mutterings.

" 'Tis enough," she said.   " Give him a rub in your
towel, and set him on the beach again."

Nell had launched herself, and he swam out after
her. She had been used to the sea since her childhood,
and, at ease in the water, moved along as unconsciously
as she walked, in her tunic and knickerbockers, with
arms and legs bare to the shoulder and knee, and an
eye ever watchful of the bundle on the beach. Then
presently she had had enough for the first dip of the
year, and got back to land to dress the baby, and let
the water dry off her. She was scarcely less dumb
than her child to express the sense of renewal and
cleansing that this morning of sun and sea brought to
her, and it was just a wordless ecstasy of sweetness to
be here with two wholesome creatures that were the
world to her. They had all cut free from the dark
house, and the shadow that brooded over it, and from
the more definite presence of John Pentreath, with his
unquiet eyes that seemed always to be on the lookout
for something they feared to see, and the grim mouth
that seldom spoke. Often, when he was half tipsy in
the evening, he would sit looking at Dennis, busy hating
him, and sometimes that gave Nell an uneasy moment,

but it was an empty fear, surely: what more occupied him was something he himself dreaded, and, as like as not, that was an empty fear, too. It was something to do with her Aunt Mollie, she felt sure, but the poor soul had laid quiet in her grave now for two months and more, and all that she had left behind her, the bees and the poultry, prospered wonderfully. Only a few days back Nell had taken an early swarm herself, independent of veil or gloves, as Aunt Mollie had bade her, but just crooning the bee-song to them, as she dropped them by the handful into the new hive. This looked as if Aunt Mollie, poor soul, was kindly to the farm, if so be she was Aunt Mollie still, and not a mere lump of earthworms. Yet fear sat ever in John Pentreath's eyes, and what else could he be fearing? A dismal wreck he had become by now, sallow and shaking and dirty. Going fast downhill, said Dr. Symes, and perhaps the sooner he came to the bottom of it the better. . . . But just now all thoughts of such things were scoured off her by the sea and the sun: mind and body alike were cleansed from these dark tarnishings.

She had dressed herself by the time Dennis came back from his swim, but he would have naught to do with his clothes yet, and ate his food with but the towel to gird him. His thoughts apparently had been running on the same lines as hers.

" 'Tis a bit better here than being stewed in the kitchen at home," he said. " Sunday and all, which is the worst of the week with Grandfather. Lord, Nell, it's little more'n a year ago that you and I would sit there mum all afternoon, with those damned stories of Romans and Christians to read, and 'twas the Romans I fancied best of the two. And now we're free as the gulls."

" Aye, and who is it as sets us free? " she asked.
" 'Tis your Willie, you know. Lord, how the lad
loves you, Dennis! Neither girl nor woman, nor boy
neither, in St. Columb's, would have come to bide at
the farm, for the sake of me, as he does for you. An'
sleeping next your grandfather and all, in Aunt Mollie's
room. I'd be proud to have a friend like that."

" And it's proud I am," said Dennis.

" Can't you thank him? " asked Nell. " Can't you
tell him we know what he's doing for us? "

" God, no," said Dennis. " He'd think me mazed.
Willie and I don't manage like that. He knows and I
know; that's sufficient. Don't you try to understand,
Nell, for sure I couldn't explain, except by just telling
you it's like that between us. So it's always been and
will be."

" Well, some folks talk by keeping mum," said Nell.
" And what does your mother say from London? " she
asked, after a pause. " You got a letter from her,
didn't you, this morning, just before you set out? "

" Bothered if I didn't put it in my pocket and forget
about it," he said, reaching out for his coat.

He opened the letter, sniffing at the voluminous
sheets as he unfolded them.

" 'Tisn't that old musk scent any more," he said.
" Mother's got hold o' something new. Wallflower-
like."

He knitted his forehead into wrinkles over Nancy's
sprawling scrawl.

" Lord above! " he exclaimed. " Why, that's a bit
o' news, sure enough, and to think that it lay in my
pocket waiting for me to read it. Ye'll never guess."

" She's been and married," said Nell, as certain as a
lord-judge passing sentence.

" Eh, you've been reading over my shoulder," said Dennis, " and spelling it out quicker nor me. Else how could you know? "

" 'Twas easy enough: I reckoned she wasn't dead, or she could never 'a' written to you, and what else could it be as made you cry out like that? Is it to the painter feller? "

" Well, o' course, and there's her signing at the end Nancy Giles."

" But what does she say? " cried Nell, bursting with curiosity to hear it all. " Why don't ye read it out, ye unclad image, 'stead of enjoying it all to yourself? "

" Well, here 'tis then," said he, " and leggo my hair. . . ." He read.

" ' *If I ain't got a bit of news for you this morning, Dennis darling, for I was married yesterday* '—'tisn't me talking, Nell, but my mother—' *I was married yesterday, and you'll never guess to whom.* ' "

" Of course ye did, for ye looked at the end," said Nell.

" Don't interrupt, woman," said Dennis. " 'Tis task enough to read her fist without your clacking. Sure she got in a fine mix-up with the inkpot, and it's as if a spider was hitched on to her pen. Where was I at? "

" Never guess to whom," prompted Nell.

" Aye.

" ' *Never guess to whom, and I declare I had no idea of his thinking of that till one night, it might have been Thursday last week, he says to me,* " *There's not a woman I've seen this many years what suits me as you do, Nancy, and never shall I see one neither.* " " *Lor', Harry,* " *said I, for I was bringing him in his dinner, and it was a dinner that nourished him proper,*

*instead of such the old moke used to serve him with,
always sniffing, with a bit of burned skin and bone as
she called a chicken, or red and raw, and a morsel of
soup, and a drop of cold jam in a mess of hard-boiled
egg for an omelet, with the bills three times the price
as I did better for him on . . .' "*

Dennis broke off.

" Where the hell 've we got to? " he asked.

" Just get along," said Nell. " It's a bit zig-zag, as
was always your mother's way, but it'll all straighten
out in the end."

" Let's hope that," said Dennis, picking up the last
words.

" '. . . *as I did better for him on, and little to show
but a stomach-ache in the morning, and I had to put
down the dish I was bringing in, for you might have
knocked me down with one of my own cheese-straws,
light as they were. Well, then he said that if I was
half as willing as he, we'd get married and have done
with it, and married we were at a registry office yesterday. And he's taken the house he had last year at the
entry of Kenrith Lane, where we met first, you may
say, and we'll be down there before June's out for a
couple of months, and lor', what a change! But you
mustn't think, dearie, that I'll be stuck up with you,
nor Nell either, for you're of my blood, and a good
boy you've been to me, and me and Harry will always
treat you as one of the family . . .' "*

Dennis slapped the page.

" Well, there's a piece of impertinence, to talk of the
Pentreaths like that! " he cried.

" Never you mind that," said Nell, " she's not
gwainter be stuck up with you, the condescendin'
woman. Go on! "

Dennis continued.

"'And your grandfather, too, he'll always be welcome to come and have a cup of tea in my parlour, and would you believe it, there's the picture Harry made of me last summer in the Royal Academy, and he told me nothing about it when he took me to what they call the private view of it, which only the tiptops of society come to, and such a fuss they made of it, and me standing close by it for half an hour, I should say, to listen to all the remarks they passed on it. They admired the figure of me terrible. I blushed all over, dear, though I wouldn't have missed what they said for anything, and to make it stranger yet, there was the picture the girlie did of you, though not in the grand room where I was, only I wish you'd brushed your hair a bit and put on something better than that soiled shirt. So when I'd heard them talk about me I went and listened to what they said about you, and they considered you a handsome boy indeed, and that you are, so you and me is famous now.

"'Here's a long letter, and so me and Harry will be down before long, travelling first class, and glad I'll be to see the old place again, and if there's a bit of money you and Nell want for the little one, and money's scarce as I warrant it is, why, you know where to come for it, for there's one as will pour out her purse for you, dearie, and that's your loving mother, Nancy Giles.

"'Send me a bit of news, Dennis, and tell me how's the old man.'"

There was a pause.

"'Tis a warm, foolish heart," said Nell.

"Aye, kind and silly she always was. But, God, the airs of her, and her pride as she ain't proud! 'Twould

be as good as a play to see her giving Grandfather a cup
of tea in her parlour, but I warrant there won't be
much tea served in her parlour for him. And he'll
'stonish her, he will, wi' some pretty compliments if
she sets up to be over-kind to'm."

Dennis thrust the letter into his coat pocket, and lay
back on the sand.

" 'Tis mellowing to lie here," he said. " The sun
gets through my skin, and goes purring in my blood.
It's as good as a running at night, but of another sort.
And about my mother's letter now, when she asks how
th' old man is. Much as ever, I suppose I'll be saying."

" Do 'ee think that? " said Nell. " For my part I
don't. I've watched him often, though I've not spoke
of it to you. He's changing, Dennis; there's a fear and
a horror gaining on him, and I doubt it'll drive him
crazy ere long. His drink used to make him fierce, or
maybe it made him gay, but now there's fear in his
glass."

" Aye: I've noticed that, too," he said.

" I reckon we both know it well enough, so let's
out with it. I reckon it's Aunt Mollie he's afraid of,
lest she'd come back and visit him. Why else did he
spend twenty pounds, as might have ben more'n a hundred bottles of his mucky spirits. in plumes and black
horses for her funeral, but for that? 'Twas to make her
kind. 'Tis fear of her as makes him curtain the windows, so's night can't look in, and when your Willie's
hoisted him up to bed, sometimes he'll go pacing about
his chamber by the hour, for Willie had a savage tooth
t'other night, and heard him walkin' and walkin', till
he bawled to him to stop it, else he'd leave Aunt Mollie's
room and bed with you. Grandfather thinks she's got
a down on him, though whatever can that be for? "

" God, I reckon you've hit it," said Dennis, remembering Nancy's disclosure to him; " but 'tis not to be spoken of. Dr. Symes, he knows, too."

" Well, I'll not ask then," said Nell; " but that's the way of it. And that's why there's no prayers o' Sunday night, for fear they'd rile her."

She broke off suddenly.

" Them's dark things, and we'll speak of them no more," she said. " And bless me, with all this talking, 'tis time I put the boy cool and comfortable in the shade, where he'll have his sleep, and I shouldn't wonder if I snoozed too. I'll give him his bottle first, and a chew at a morsel of raw meat in a bit of muslin for him to suck the goodness out of it. What'll you be doing? "

" Just a turn in the sea," said Dennis, sitting up.

" Nay, don't go and bathe again, for your stomach's a jumble o' victuals, and you'll get the cramp in it, and sink like a stone," said Nell.

" There's twiddling talk! " said he. " Why, my victuals have nourished me fine, and they're safe stowed in my blood by now. Or shall I come and sleep with you in the shade? "

She got up laughing.

" That you won't," she said. " Go and have your dip then."

The sun had wheeled westwards, and the sandy beach was half-covered with the flood tide, when Dennis carried the child up the steep scramble of rock above. Here he dusted and dried his feet, and put on his shoes, and with the child on his arm, while Nell carried the empty basket, they strolled slowly up the darkling hillside. Instead of the brisk sea breeze of the morning there now streamed down the combe the warmer tide

of the land breeze. The air had hovered motionless over
fields and gardens and gorse for the still sunny hours of
the afternoon, and now the scents of blossom and of
green things had soaked thick into it, and it blew laden
with fertility, with here a streak of cool moisture
gathered from the stream, and here a warm breath of
gorse-flower, and here a flavour of wood-smoke.   In
the hamlet the gossips were about their doors, and the
women must have a peep at the baby and make cautious
inquiries about Dennis's grandfather, and how things
prospered at the farm.   There was just a hint of something unspoken below these politenesses, for one hoped
that John Pentreath had not been " troubled," and
another said that he looked but middling as he came
down to church at St. Columb's that day, and there
were glances and noddings of heads as they passed on.

Dusk was falling softly, layer on silent layer, as they
crossed the fields at the top of the hill where the daisies
were already folded for the night, and when they came
to the garden at the farm Nell stopped, looking round
puzzled and frowning.

" Why, whatever's happened? " she said.   " There's
scarce a flower left in the beds.   Someone's been plucking the lot o' them."

Even as she spoke John Pentreath appeared at the
door into the house.

" Come you in: come you in," he said, " and let's
have all snug and shut up.   I'll have no dallyin' out
there in the dusk, and entering after night.   'Tis
wholesomer for all within."

Nell carried her baby upstairs.   The child was sleepy
after his day in the air, and after she had made him
comfortable and stowed him in his high-sided crib,
she came down into the kitchen.   Dennis was laying the

table for supper, with Willie to help him, and she made up the fire to heat the broth. John seemed more confident to-night, for the window still stood open, though night was falling.

"I've been fine and busy since church-time this afternoon," he said, "and I've got a relish for my supper, so hurry it on a bit. I've plucked all those gauds o' flowers from the beds, and it's a barrowful I've laid on Mollie's grave. Three times up and down did I go, with my basket full o' them: you can't see the mound beneath for the blossoms I've put there. A gay and sweet-smelling garden, indeed."

"So that's what's come to them," said Nell. "I saw there was scarce a bloom left."

"Aye, and what better could come to them?" he asked. "And they're mine, ain't they, to do with as I will? They'll please her, I can fancy her lingering there all night looking at them and smelling o' them."

Nell poured the hot soup into the plates and they sat down.

"I heard from my mother to-day, Grandfather," said Dennis. "Fine news from her, too, for she's married."

John thumped the table and laughed.

"Well done, Nancy," he cried. "So she's trapped him, has she? I reckon we won't see her in these parts again. A disgrace to the house she was, trapesing about, with her paint on her face, inviting all and sundry, enough to call the wrath o' God on us all. It's to that painter chap, I reckon, him as she was baiting last spring."

"Yes, that's he. But you'll see her again before long, for Mr. Giles's taken the house he had before. She says you'll always be welcome to take a drink o' tea with her."

"Why, there's a bit of graciousness," said John.

He looked round.

"And ain't I to have no drop o' drink to-night?" he said, "me that's been going thirsty all day to the glory of the Lord, and mindful of the dead? . . . Why, if the bottle isn't standing at my elbow all the time, and me not noticing it."

He did not trouble the water-jug for his first draught, but drank four fingers of the raw spirits in sips, gargling it round his mouth before he swallowed it.

"Ah, that's rare!" he said, "and I feel mettlesome to-night, and happy as ever I've done for a long while back, at the thought of the show o' flowers I've made for Mollie. Take a whack, Will, and another when you've finished that."

He wolfed his cold beef and a lump of cheese, and pushed back his chair.

"And mark you this," he said. "We'll have our prayers to-night same as we used, for 'tis a long while since we've had a godly Sunday evening, such as the Lord looks for from His servant. But, to tell the truth——"

Suddenly his eye fell on the open window.

"Eh, there's a careless business," he cried. "Shut it, Dennis, you lout, and pull the curtains across. To think that we've been sitting here this while with the night looking in. What mayn't 'a' got in, while we've been talking?"

He sat huddled in his chair till this was done, then opened the door a chink and stood there listening.

"All's still in the house," he said, "and I reckon we'll have a prayer, for 'tis a fine flower garden I made for Mollie and that'll pleasure her all night long. I'll take a drop more first, and then I'll speak low and quiet to vex nobody."

But hardly had he got to his knees when he scrambled up again.

" There's summat hoverin' round," he whispered. " I went on my knees, I tell 'ee, just to look for my pipe as I'd dropped. Iss sure 'twas for naught else, and that's for all to hear."

CHAPTER XV

THE PURGING BY FIRE

NANCY had been a bit disappointed about the effect of her resplendent return to St. Columb's: nobody seemed to think more highly of Mrs. Harry Giles than of Nancy Pentreath. She went up to the farm the day after she arrived, but found no one at home, and so left her card and her husband's on the kitchen table, hers turned down at the top right-hand corner to show she had been there in person, for that was the London mode. On her second visit she was more fortunate, for Dennis was hoeing in the garden, and presently, after a talk to him, she went indoors, where Nell was doing her ironing in the kitchen. But she was just through with it, and Nell took her upstairs to have a peep at her baby in his crib, who was having his afternoon sleep, and they came back to the kitchen again for a cup of tea. Very smart indeed was Nancy in her London clothes: she rustled richly as she walked, by reason of the silk lining of her skirt, and she was lofty in her manner, as was only proper for Mrs. Henry Giles.

" I'm sure me and Harry hoped to see Mr. Pentreath down at our little place after I'd left our cards here," she said; " but there! I'm glad enough to have no formalities, though I must say I thought he'd have popped down just to be introduced to Mr. Giles, their not having met before, neither the one nor the other. I dessay he never saw the cards."

As a matter of fact, he had done so, for he had

picked Nancy's up and read the inscription with a bellow of irony. "Mrs. Henry Giles!" he roared. "And hasn't the Queen of England come, too? How's that? Mrs. Henry Giles, the Lord help and deliver us," and he chucked both of the cards into the grate.

Nell did not think it necessary to speak of this.

"It must have slipped his memory," she said. "And then, you see, Mr. Pentreath isn't much of a hand at visiting. I doubt if he's been through the door of another house save his own for a year and more."

Nancy was really longing to get on homely terms again, but a bit of swagger first was irresistible.

"Well, it does seem strange to live like that," she said, "when I think of life in London, where there's scarce a night when Mr. Giles and me aren't either bidden somewhere or it's a playhouse or a music-hall instead. But I'm not one to be dignified, and you may tell Mr. Pentreath that we'll both be very pleased to see him. Lor', it's queer to be in this little kitchen again, and think of the change that's come since I was cooking and slaving here last, like you, Nell. And there's not a day now but what we don't go out pleasuring when Mr. Giles is through with his morning's work, for he's regular at his paints, and often he says to me, ' I'm a working man, and don't forget that, girlie.' It was a drive to St. Orde's yesterday, and tea at the hotel, for Harry's hired a victoria and a coachman in livery on the box, and a pair of tall black horses. Such steppers you never saw, and piff! why, we're at the top of a hill before you'd think you'd commenced the ascent. And then going down that steep hill into Penzance terrible fast, there was Mr. Giles, I thought, having forty winks, so I said to the coachman, ' Don't go so fast, Charles,' I said, ' for Mr. Giles doesn't like taking

20

the corners so sharp,' for I was frightened myself, see? And would you believe it, he wasn't asleep at all, for he calls out, still with his eyes shut, ' Get on a bit quicker, Charles, for Mrs. Giles hates going like a snail.' So I was fair had over that. We did have a laugh, to be sure."

" Well, that was a rare bit o' fun! " said Nell.

" That it was. And some day, I promise you, I'll take you and your baby out for a drive, and call for you right here at the kitchen door, and say, ' Is Mrs. Pentreath at home? ' "

" Eh, 'twill be too grand for me," said Nell.

" Not a bit of it, for if I've had the luck to marry into the gentry, why shouldn't my own son's wife take a slice? And as I told Dennis in my letter, if there's anything you want out of the ordinary for your baby, as is my grandson, you know where to go for it. Lor', here's Midsummer's Eve's come round again, and there's you and Dennis married, and me married, too, and poor old Mrs. Pentreath in the churchyard. There were dark days, to be sure, before she got her congy."

" There were happenings then, as I know little of," said Nell. " Dennis and me don't tell of them."

" And right you are," said Nancy. " But to think that on this very night a year gone there the poor old lady was kicking and capering in the ring, and believing a child was coming. As I came up to-day I saw them finishing the bonfire for the leaping."

" Yes, Dennis and Willie and I all helped in the piling of it, one time or another this morning," said Nell.

" And I warrant you and Dennis'll be down there to-night and have a dance in the circle, a-thinking of the next one to come," said Nancy.

" Happen you and Mr. Giles'll be having a dance

yourselves," suggested Nell.

Nancy pursed her lips.

" No, there's no thought o' that," she said, " though I dessay we shall look on awhile, after we've had our dinner, me in my evening gown, as I put on regular, company or none."

" Sure, you're fine enough, just as ye stand now, to dine with all the Lord Mayors and dukes of London," said Nell politely.

" Lor', 'tis nothing but a costoom for the day," said Nancy, " and hat to match, as Madame Elise of Bond Street made for me, though I'm sure she charged enough for it, and I should have been real scared to bring the bill to Mr. Giles, but that he'd told me to get something a bit out of the common. It's the fashionable shade of red just now, a bit bright maybe, but cheerful. What was we saying? Yes, about the bonfire and the dancing. I reckon Mr. Pentreath won't come down to view it, for it'll remind him of how he and your Aunt Mollie was there last year, and he won't want to recall that."

" No, he won't be there," said Nell, " for he's never out o' the house now after the dusk's drawing on. And, maybe, you'll be so kind as not to mention to him that it's Midsummer Eve, if he comes in before you go, which I hope'll be a long while, for we think he don't know it's the day. You see, Willie and us were thinking of coming down soon after supper's over, when Mr. Pentreath's settled to his drink, saying we were off to bed, and then sure he'll sit quiet over his bottle till we're back. But if he knew we were leaving him alone in the house, happen he'd have the horrors."

" To be sure I'll say nothing of it," said Nancy, " for I reckon he's getting a handful to manage. He was

queer enough before I went, and Dennis says there's not
much to boast of since.   Lor', when I sit in the studio
down at our place so cheerful and comfortable and Mr.
Giles sometimes making a sketch of me like old times,
it's often I think o' the dark evenings in the kitchen
here, with the two old folk, and me with my book, and
the sound o' the rain hishing outside, and the scullery
door ajar, and the clock there whizzing for the hour.
Why, bless me, it points to five minutes to twelve,
and what's the cause o' that? "

"Mr. Pentreath he muddled it up a month since,"
said Nell, "when he made to wind it, and there came
a sizzle from its innards, and never a tick has it gone
since.   But he won't have it looked to, for he says 'twas
the Lord's hand as stayed it, though 'twas his own
awkwardness, sure enough."

"But I'm thinking what'll you do with your baby,
when you all go to the dancing to-night? " said Nancy.
"You'll never leave him all alone in his crib with the
old man boozing away down in the kitchen? "

Nell laughed.

"Nay, I shouldn't go to do that," she said.   "That
would be a queer thing indeed.   I'm going to step
down with him presently to Willie's mother, who'll see
to him while we're at the dancing, and I'll fetch him
away after it's done.   There's to be no spread of buns
up here to-night, with Mr. Pentreath the way he is.
You can't tell what he'd be doing or saying."

Nancy consulted the little gold watch she wore on
a chain.

"Eh, how the time's flown," she said.   "Let's walk
down together, then, for I've made a long visit already, and we're going for a bit of a saunter, Mr. Giles
and me, in the cool of the day."

Even as she spoke there came a fumble at the kitchen door; then it was flung open, and John Pentreath stood in the doorway.   Haggard and yellow he was, and three days unshaven, and his clothes hung round him as if he were but a peg for them.   Nell and Dennis, accustomed to seeing him every day, did not realise how ruinous his deterioration was, but to Nancy, beholding him now for the first time after a lapse of so many weeks, his appearance was a shocking thing. He stood a moment on the threshold, seeming to listen for any sound in the house.   Then he banged the door behind him, and his eye fell on Nancy in her bright red dress.

"Lord, there's a fire been lit in the midst o' the kitchen," he said, "and fine it's flaring.   God bless me, I see it's a lady now, and I'm sure I beg your pardon, ma'am, whoever you be, for thinking you was a pile of blazing faggots."

Nancy pulled herself together.

"Well, I declare if Mr. Pentreath doesn't see who I am," she said.   "Out o' sight, out o' mind, they say."

He gave a cackle of a laugh.

"Why, 'twas just my fun," he said.   "Sure I know it's Nancy, or Mrs. Henry Giles, I should say, as left such a handsome piece o' pasteboard on me.   Proud indeed I am to welcome you, and I'll thank you to get me my bottle, and we'll drink your health together."

"And here's a bit of old times, Mr. Pentreath," said she, "to hear you talk like that.   Now, where's your bottle kept, for I declare it's gone out o' my head."

Nell fetched it for him, and mixed his glass, which he drank straight off.

"Now have a go, Nancy, won't 'ee?" he said.

"Never for me," she said; "I never touch the stuff."

" Well, if you won't, I know someone else who will,"
he said.

He sat himself down: often now he would pass the
day without a word crossing his lips, but the sight
of Nancy seemed to have unloosed his tongue.

" And so you've come back to us again after this
long while," he said, " and glad I am, for you'll be a
light to lighten our darkness, and there's too much
darkness these days.   The nights are long, Nancy,
longer nor I've ever known them in summer-time, and
sunset's upon us almost as soon as it's day, like the door
as has just been opened slammed to again.   God save us
all when they grow longer yet, for there's the terror
by night o' which King David tells.   It comes creepin'
up in the darkness, it does, moving slow, for the grave
clothes are about its feet, and the hill from St. Columb's
churchyard is steep to climb, and it must be back again
afore dawn, but I reckon it gets as far as the garden-
gate even now, and where'll it get to when the winter's
on us?   But now you've come back to us, maybe 'twill
keep away.   ' Why, 'tis Nancy,' it'll think to itself,
' 'tis Mrs. Henry Giles from London town, and she
looked after me kindly in the day of my trouble.' "

Nell was watching him ill at ease: this manner of talk
was something new, and she wished Dennis and Willie
would come in.   She gave a touch to Nancy, to encourage her to keep on with him, for the fit of mad
babbling would pass, she thought, and he would get
fuddled and quiet again.

" Well, I'm real glad you're so pleased to see me, Mr.
Pentreath," said Nancy.   " And, lor', what's there to
worry about in the night, for the night's the time for
us all to get to sleep, and be fresh and bright come
morning.   There's good times in store for us all, I'll

be bound. That's what I always say when Mr. Giles
has a bit o' the hump, and he plucks up amazing."

"But you'll bide here, Nancy?" he asked. "You'll
sup and sleep here, surely? You'll read your book again
in your chair, and then give a yawn and say you're
a sleepy-head?"

He gave a hiccupping giggle at the fresh topics
which this suggested.

"Well I mind those times," he said, "and strange
things came o' them, the judgments of the Lord. Some
day, when I've a bit o' leisure, I'll make a clear tale of it
all, for the thoughts come crowding into my head
faster nor I can sort them out. God, I was taken with
you, Nancy, and then Mollie made her conjuring trick,
and that angered me."

"Oh, pray-a be done with all that, Mr. Pentreath,"
cried Nancy. "Give it the go-by, and it'll trouble you
no more."

Dennis came in, and Nancy hastened to be gone.

"Well, I'll be stepping," said she. "Nell was taking
me on my way. Good night to you, Mr. Pentreath.
Always pleased to see you if you pop in down at our
place, and I'll be looking in on you all again, never
fear."

Nell went upstairs to fetch her baby, and the two
women set off together. As soon as the door was shut
John pointed with his thumb over his shoulder, and
giggled again.

"Do you know who's that?" he said. "'Tis the
scarlet woman o' Babylon out of Revelation. And saying she was Nancy! I saw through her, though I
humoured her. A handsome jade, too."

Dennis found no reply to this, and his silence pro-

duced a sudden explosion of wrath from his grandfather.

"God, I'll teach you to heed me one o' these days,"
he shouted.

Dennis looked at him, just bracing his hand on the
arm of his chair, in order to rise swiftly if need be.
But the old man began sipping again, and made no
movement. Presently he dozed off: he was breaking up
fast, surely. Then Willie came in, and the two young
men played a game of cards together till Nell returned.

It was a silent supper: the three young folk spoke
but little, and as for John not a word, black or white,
came from him, while the thoughts he had not time to
sort out went buzzing in his head, like bees about to
swarm. They were all centred on one thing now, and
that was to make an end of Dennis. He forebore even to
look at him, lest the sight of the boy should lash him
into some outburst, which would put him and the others
on their guard. He had no fears about Mollie just
now: that had sunk out of sight below the more
pressing business, and he even wanted to be alone, un-
distracted by other presences, in order to concentrate
on this: he wished they'd go off to bed and leave him.
He had soon finished with his eating, and took to his
arm-chair again with his pipe and his glass, and presently
the table was cleared. It was growing dark, and Nell
lit the couple of lamps which were always kindled now
at nightfall, for one alone gave too little illumination
for him, and set one of them on the supper board, and
another on a small table by his side. Dennis and
Willie were doing the clearing and washing-up to-night,
and she heard them talking low in the scullery as she
drew the curtains across the windows, and locked the
kitchen door into the farmyard. Perhaps they'd made

a plan together, for soon Willie strolled off without
a word to any.

The other two got out the cards again and played
awhile.   Then Nell gave a nod to Dennis and got up.

"I'll be off to bed," she said.

"I'll be coming, too, Nell," said Dennis.   "Good
night, Grandfather."

They went out, crossed the hall, and through the
door into the garden, which Dennis closed quietly.

"Willie's gone down," he said.   "Grandfather might
'a' scented something, if we all went off together."

"That's right: he's taken no notice," said she. "Lord,
he's in a queer way to-night.   How he babbled on to
your mother, before you came in, and then just locked
his mouth at supper.   She was shocked to see him and
no mistake: he's breaking up fast, she says.   And
what's he thinking on to-night?   He's thinking steady
about summat, with none of those scared glances
around."

"Pleasant thoughts, for sure," said Dennis, putting
his arm about her.   "But I reckon I'll get Dr. Symes
to have a look at him to-morrow, for I doubt his mind's
going.   Eh, Nell, I long to hold you in the midst of
them stones, twisting about in the fruitful dance."

Already the sky ahead to the east was bright with the
flames from the bonfire that cast a ruddy glare on the
wheat of the nearer field and the hedgerows, but here,
just under the trees by the garden gate, it was dark.
Then Nell gave a startled cry: there on the gatepost
sat a big brown owl.   It hissed at them, and slid noiselessly away over the garden, its wings red in the glare
from the bonfire.   They saw it perch on the ash-tree
close to the house.

" Lord, that gave me a turn," said Nell. " 'Tis lucky I drew the curtains in the kitchen, for Mr. Pentreath 'ud go crazy if he saw it. . . . Eh, Dennis, but there's a queer thing, for he was talking in his wild way o' the terror by night as came up from St. Columb's yard as far as the garden-gate, and there was the night bird sitting on the post."

" Well, if the terror by night'll come and sit there again to-morrow eve, when I've got my gun handy," said Dennis, " it'll be sorry it came so far. 'Twas strange, though, for they're shy, wary things, and it let us come within an arm's length of it. I warrant it's the same bird as raided the hens, and sat on Willie's sill one night till he fetched it across the face with his belt."

There was a crowd to leeward of the bonfire, waiting for the flames to die down, so that the leaping might begin, and Willie joined them.

" There'll be naught doing yet awhile," said Dennis. " Let's go up to the circle, Nell, and have a dance. Why, good Lord, there's no one footing it. How's that? "

" Somehow they're not fancying it to-night," said Willie.

Dennis laid a hand on his shoulder.

" Ye've heard some talk, I warrant, Willie," he said. " Let's have it, lad. What's it all about? "

" 'Tis like this," said he. " The fellers remember what happened a year gone, how the old mistress up to the farm was kicking and skipping higher nor any; and what came of that, they say. Looks as if there was a mischief there. Don't 'ee dance, you and Nell."

" A pack o' rubbish, Will," said Dennis. " That

wasn't where the mischief came from. Are you fear'd, Nell?"

"For sure I'm not with your arm about me," she said. "And the fewer the folk, I reckon there'll be more o' the power for us. Come away, and I'll dance with you till morning, and never tire."

Meantime John Pentreath sat quiet in the kitchen of the empty house, drinking pretty steadily, and unusually free from the terror the night brought with it, for his mind had settled on something else, and clung tight to it. More than a year ago it was now since Dennis had handled him so savagely, and not many days had passed after that on which John had not pictured himself bashing the life out of him, or blinding him with that fine acid stuff that quenched the light of the eyes and stripped the flesh from the bones like a hungry dog. Yet all the time he had done nothing; he could devise no safe plan of finishing him; always there were risks and possible mischances. But there must be no further delay about settling this long score: it should be wiped off with a balance in his favour, before another day dawned.

His eye fell on his gun that stood in a corner of the kitchen. He had often had an idea of hiding behind a bush to shoot the pigeons that came to feed on the ruined corn last year, and killing Dennis as he came back from his work. Vividly he had pictured it, but never had he come near doing it, and to-night any business with the gun would be impossible. Dennis would be sleeping with Nell in the room that had once been portioned into two, but was now thrown into one again, and there'd be the child with them. Half crazy as he was, he couldn't see himself shooting a

woman who lay asleep, for if he killed Dennis, sure the
other must go too. . . . It was no use thinking of
his gun.

He shuffled across the room to fetch himself a fresh
bottle from the cupboard. There was a pile of cases
there, full of straw, but empty of all else, and he had
to rummage among these till he found one that con-
tained a bottle, and that seemed to be the last. On
his way back to his chair he noticed that the hands of
the clock pointed to a few minutes short of twelve,
and forgetting that it had stopped for the last month,
only thought that the night was getting on, and
there was nothing settled yet. Perhaps another drink
would give him a notion.

He sat down again, stroking the three days' bristles
on his chin, but never a fruitful thought came near
him. Presently, all on fire with drink and maddened
by this impotence of invention, he pushed back his chair
and got up. As he did so, he upset the small table at
his elbow on which burned one of the two lamps. It
crashed to the ground, the chimney and the glass re-
ceptacle for the paraffin were smashed, and the wick,
still alight, set fire to the spilt oil. There were but a
few spoonfuls of it, for Nell had forgotten to fill it up,
the flame flared high and smoky for a minute or two,
then died down again, leaving a charred place on the
boards of the floor. Instantly the idea for which he
had sought so long flashed upon him. He would set
fire to the house while all slept sound upstairs, and
then go running down to St. Columb's, spite of the
dark, to get help. A rare notion: his crazy brain
exulted at the thought of it.

Thoughts came fast now: they were sorting themselves out finely. There were Dennis and Nell and the

baby in that room with the narrow slits of windows out of which they'd never creep. Willie must still be out; he had gone off alone, he remembered, soon after supper, and he'd have been sure to have sat and had a drink if he'd come home. He must lock the door on the passage upstairs, leading to the studio and the bedroom above, and take the key, so that Dennis and Nell couldn't get out that way. He would do that at once, and he crept upstairs in his slippered feet, pausing to listen if there was any sound from their room; then he peeped into Willie's room, but that was empty, and so back to the kitchen again. He would pile a lot of stuff here, and set light to it, and he'd pile a lot more on the stairs, and he'd drench them both with paraffin, so that there would be no getting down the stairs at all, and even if they could leap it, they could never win to the kitchen door, for the blaze would be roaring there. The garden door he would leave for himself to escape by, when he'd seen that the flames mounted high, and lock it after him.

He went swiftly about his preparations. He fetched a couple of tins of paraffin from the store-hole beyond the scullery and sticks and faggots for firing. He brought out the empty cases of whisky from the cupboard, strewed the stairs with the straw from them, and set the cases on the steps. Then going back to the kitchen, he made a pile there and ranged straw and faggots about them, and laid two wicker chairs on top. He poured one tin of paraffin over the stairs and the fuel he had placed there, and the other over the pile in the kitchen. " 'Tis a burnt offering to the Lord," he muttered to himself, " 'tis a pillar of fire by night, 'tis a fire as'll never be quenched till the whole is consumed. And, by God, if I didn't insure the house against fire. There's a providential thing! "

All was ready now, and he set light to the pile in
the kitchen. Up it flared, pouring out volumes of black
smoke. Then plucking a flaming brand from it he
ran with it to the foot of the stairs and thrust it
into the straw. High leaped the flame, mounting
swiftly from step to step, roaring as it rose.

He stood there just for a moment, exulting in his
deed. Never had he imagined that there'd be so brave
a blaze, such clouds of black smoke with the flames
piercing through them. Why, if those who were sleeping above came out into the passage they'd be suffo-
cated, and never could any plunge through that raging
furnace. They'd have to wait for their leaping till
John Pentreath's bonfire died down.

Suddenly the big fanlight above the garden door
close beside him crashed down in splinters of shat-
tered glass, and there sailed in a great brown owl. It
circled round him, menacing him with claws and beak,
and as often as he tried to get near the door into the
garden, it beat its heavy wings in his face. Panic
seized him, for there was come in that terror by night,
which had been creeping up from the churchyard at
St. Columb's. Mollie had come back knowing all.

He screamed aloud, and rushed back into the kitchen,
slamming the door behind him, to keep that dread visit-
ant out, meaning to escape by the kitchen-door into
the farmyard. The room was choked with smoke, from
which long tongues of flame darted like swords. But
though he had banged the door, it had failed to latch
itself, and there, now shrouded in smoke, now with
eyes gleaming in the fierce light, was the bird circling
round him again. He shuffled across the floor, groping
along the wall, to get to the door, but he had missed

his bearings, and as he clutched, so he thought, at the corner of the doorway, it rocked in his hand, and the tall clock went headlong to the ground with a jingle of striking and a crash of glass. He stumbled against it and fell prone on the ground, his head so close to the flame that he heard his hair singe. Once more he managed to get to his feet, and wings flapped in his face.

Dennis and Nell had danced till they could dance no more, and now, panting for breath, they were lying in the shadow of one of the stones, alone under the night, for none had come to the circle. A hundred yards away there was noise of shouting and laughing, for the bonfire had died down, and the leaping had begun.

Suddenly Dennis sat up.

" 'Tis strange," he said, " but I smell burning, and there's smoke in the air. The wind sets opposite, so it's not from the bonfire. Lord, what's that? "

He pointed in the direction of the farm. The trees that stood between them and it were black against a red glow behind them.

" 'Tis the house afire," he cried. " Speed down quick to the folk, and bid them fetch the engine. I'll go up there."

He ran through the wheat already growing high, and leaped the garden fence, and trampled across the beds. The garden-door was unlocked, as he and Nell had left it, but so fierce a blast of heat poured out from the burning stairs that there was no getting in that way. He bolted round to the farmyard to see if there was access by the kitchen, but flames blazed from the windows, and even as he looked the door fell in and showed the furnace within. Back he went to the garden side, and saw that the windows in the upper story were still dark, not lit from the blaze on the ground-floor, and he fetched a ladder, propping it against the wall below his grandfather's room.

" Just the bare chance that he's gone tipsy to bed, and hasn't awakened," he thought, as he climbed up. The window was unlatched, and he threw it open and stepped in. The room was thick with smoke, but not alight yet, and he felt his way across to the bed, and ran his hands over it, but there was no one there. He tried Willie's room next door, but that was empty, and when he opened the door into the passage, so fierce was the heat of the fire on the stairs, and so dense the smoke, that there was no facing it.

By the time he had got down the ladder again the crowd was streaming up from the field, and soon there arrived the small fire engine, hand-worked, which was all that St. Columb's could supply. But the fire had now taken such hold that nothing could have been of any avail. The roof fell in, and the flames soared higher yet, but the stout-built walls of stone still stood, and they alone were left when the blaze burned itself out.

The short midsummer night brightened into day: the sun swung up over the hills to the east, and larks mounted and sang in the sparkle of the morning.